Mytica

LIMEROS

THE IRON COAST

THE GRANITE COAST

Ravencrest

The Temple of Valoria

Castle Damora

THE IMPERIAL ROAD

BLACK HARBOR

PAELSIA

Basilius's Compound

FORBIDDEN MOUNTAINS

TRADER'S HARBOR

THE

SILVER

THE WILDLANDS

KING'S HARBOR

The Temple of Cleiona

AURANOS

Castle Bellos/ City of Gold

SEA

Hawk's Brow

Elder's Pitch

THE RADIANT COAST

REBEL SPRING

REBEL SPRING

BOOK 2 IN THE
FALLING KINGDOMS
SERIES

MORGAN RHODES

razor
bill

An Imprint of Penguin Group (USA)

razOr
bill

A division of Penguin Young Readers Group
Published by the Penguin Group
Penguin Group (USA), 345 Hudson Street
New York, New York 10014, U.S.A.

USA / Canada / UK / Ireland / Australia / New Zealand / India / South Africa / China

Penguin.com

A Penguin Random House Company

Copyright © 2013 Penguin Group (USA) LLC

Library of Congress Cataloging-in-Publication Data

Rhodes, Morgan.
Rebel Spring: A Falling Kingdoms Novel / Morgan Rhodes.
pages cm
Summary: When the evil King Gaius announces that a road is to be built into the Forbidden Mountains, formally linking all of Mytica together, he sets off a chain of events that will forever change the face of this land, forcing Cleo the dethroned princess, Magnus the reluctant heir, Lucia the haunted sorceress, and Jonas the desperate rebel to take steps they never could have imagined.
ISBN 978-1-59514-592-5 (paperback)
[1. Fantasy. 2. Princesses—Fiction.] I. Title.
PZ7.R347637Re 2013
[Fic]—dc23
2013029554

Printed in the United States of America

1 3 5 7 9 10 8 6 4 2

CAST OF CHARACTERS

Limeros: The Conquerors

GAIUS DAMORA	The king
ALTHEA DAMORA	The queen
MAGNUS LUKAS DAMORA	Prince and heir to the throne
LUCIA EVA DAMORA	Adopted princess; prophesied sorceress
CRONUS	Captain of the guard
HELENA	Attendant
DORA	Attendant
FRANCO ROSSATAS	Assistant engineer on the Imperial Road
EUGENEIA ROSSATAS	Franco's daughter
LORD GARETH	A friend of the king

Auranos: The Defeated

CLEIONA (CLEO)	Imprisoned princess
ARON LAGARIS	Cleo's betrothed
NICOLO (NIC) CASSIAN	Cleo's best friend
MIRA CASSIAN	Nic's sister
LORENZO TAVERA	Dressmaker from Hawk's Brow
DOMITIA	Accused witch

Paelsia: The Rebels

JONAS AGALLON	Rebel leader
BRION RADENOS	Jonas's second-in-command
LYSANDRA BARBAS	Rebel
GREGOR BARBAS	Lysandra's brother
TARUS	Young rebel
NERISSA	Rebel
ONORIA	Rebel
IVAN	Rebel
TALIA	Old woman
VARA	Friend of Lysandra's

The Watchers

ALEXIUS	Watcher
PHAEDRA	Watcher
TIMOTHEUS	Council member
DANAUS	Council member
MELENIA	Council member
STEPHANOS	Dying Watcher
XANTHUS	Exiled Watcher

Visitors

ASHUR CORTAS	Prince from the Kraeshian Empire

PROLOGUE

Death cast a long shadow across the barren miles of Paelsia. The news of Chief Basilius's murder spread swiftly, and villages throughout the land fell into a deep mourning. They grieved a great man—a sorcerer who could touch magic and whom many in this land with no official religion thought of as a living god.

"What will we do without him?" was a constant cry in the days and weeks that followed. "We are lost!"

"Honestly," Lysandra grumbled to her older brother, Gregor, as they snuck out of their family's cottage at twilight. "He never showed any true magic. It was all just talk! It's like they forget he taxed us all to death. The chief was a liar and a thief who lived high and mighty at his compound, sucking down wine and food while the rest of us starved!"

"Hush," Gregor warned, but he was laughing. "You speak your mind far too much, little Lys."

"I'm sure you have a point."

"It'll get you in trouble some day."

"I can handle trouble." Lysandra aimed her arrow at the target on a tree twenty paces away and let go. She hit the very center. Pride warmed her on this cool evening and she glanced at her brother for his reaction.

"Nice shot." His grin widened and he nudged her aside to take his turn. "However, this will be nicer."

Easily, he split her arrow in two. She couldn't help but be impressed. They'd been practicing like this for months in secret. She'd had to beg her brother to share his knowledge of archery, but he finally relented. It was unusual for a girl to be taught how to use weapons. Most believed girls were meant to cook and clean and look after the men.

Which was ridiculous. Especially since Lysandra was a natural at this.

"Do you think they'll be back?" she asked Gregor quietly, scanning the small village nearby, the thatched roofs, the mud and stone exteriors. Smoke wafted from the chimneys of many of the small homes.

His jaw tensed. "I don't know."

A week ago, important-looking representatives of the conqueror, King Gaius, visited their village, asking for volunteers to go east and begin work on a road the king wanted quickly built, one that would snake not only through Paelsia, but through the neighboring lands of Auranos and Limeros as well.

Gregor and their father had been chosen to greet the men, and the pair had stood up to the bright smiles and smooth words without allowing themselves to be intimidated or swayed. The village had declined the offer.

The King of Blood thought he now ruled them. But he was

sorely mistaken. They might be poor, but they were proud. No one had the right to tell them what to do.

King Gaius's men had left without argument.

"Idiot Basilius," Lysandra mumbled. "He may have trusted the king, but we're smart enough not to. Basilius deserved to be skewered. It was only a matter of time. Makes me sick to my stomach that he'd be such a fool." Her next arrow flew off course. She needed to work harder on her concentration. "Tell me more about the rebels who plan to stand up against the king."

"Why do you want to know? Do you want to be the one of the few girls to join their ranks?"

"Maybe I do."

"Come, little Lys." Gregor laughed and grabbed her wrist. "There have to be a few rabbits we can find to practice your aim on next. Why waste arrows on trees and breath on silly words? Don't worry about the rebels. If anyone will soon be joining them in their fight against the king, it'll be me."

"Not silly," she mumbled.

But he did have a point—at least when it came to their target practice. The trees were scarce here anyway. Most of the area was brown and dry with a few small greener areas in which her mother and other women tended vegetable gardens that, each year, yielded fewer and fewer vegetables, but many tears. Her mother had not stopped crying since she'd heard of Basilius's death.

It wrenched Lysandra's heart to see her mother so upset, so inconsolable, but she tried to reason with her. "I believe we make our own destinies, every last one of us," she'd told her mother last night. "Who leads us makes no difference."

This was met with a sad, weary look of patience. "You're so naive, daughter. I pray it won't lead you astray."

And now her mother prayed to the dead chief about her rule-breaking daughter. This wasn't unexpected. Lysandra had always caused her mother grief by not being an acceptable daughter who did acceptable things. Lysandra was accustomed to not fitting in with her friends, who couldn't understand her fascination with making arrows until she got blisters on her fingers or staying outside until her nose burned so red it practically glowed in the dark.

Gregor put his arm out to halt Lysandra's steps.

"What?" she asked.

"Look."

They were less than a mile from the village. Before them was a small clearing, barren of any vegetation at all. It was surrounded by dry bushes and leafless trees. An old woman, one Lysandra recognized as Talia, the eldest in their village, stood in the middle of the clearing. The carcass of a red fox lay in front of her. The woman had drained the blood from the animal into a wooden cup. With this blood, she drew symbols on the parched, cracked earth with the tip of her finger.

Lysandra had never seen anything like it in her life. "What's Talia doing? What's she drawing?"

"Four symbols," Gregor said, his voice hushed. "Do you know what they are?"

"No, what?"

"The symbols are of the elements: fire, air, water, and earth." He pointed to each in turn, a triangle, a spiral, two stacked wavy lines, and a circle within a circle. His throat worked as he swallowed hard. "I had no idea. Our village elder . . . she's a witch. An Oldling."

"Wait. You're saying that old, simple-minded Talia's a . . . *witch*?"

She waited for him to start grinning and tell her he was just joking. But he was serious—deadly serious.

Gregor's brows drew together. "I had my suspicions, but this is the proof. She's kept her secret well over all the years. You know what can happen to witches."

In the neighboring kingdom of Limeros, they were burned. Hanged. Beheaded. Witches were considered evil, even here in Paelsia. Bad luck. A curse upon this land making it wither away and die. In Limeros, many believed that witches were what had cursed that land to turn to ice.

Lysandra remembered Talia's unusual reaction when she'd learned the chief had been murdered by King Gaius. She'd nodded once, grimly, brushed off her dusty skirts, and said four words:

"And so it begins."

Everyone thought the old woman was mad so they paid no attention to her ramblings, but for some reason those words had resonated with Lysandra and sent a chill down her spine.

"So what begins?" She'd caught the old woman's arm. "What do you mean?"

Talia had turned her pale, watery eyes on Lysandra. "The end, my dear girl. The end begins."

It took a moment for Lysandra to speak again to Gregor, her heart pounding loud in her ears. "What do you mean by Old-ling?"

"It's one who worships the elements. It's an old religion—older than anything except *elementia* itself. And by the looks of this" —he nodded toward the clearing—"Talia is working blood magic tonight."

A shiver went down Lysandra's spine. *Blood magic.*

She'd heard of such things before but had never seen any proof until now. Gregor had always been more of a believer than she in that which was unseen and rarely spoken about—magic, witches, legends. Lysandra barely listened to the storytellers, interested more in tangible facts than whimsical tales. Now, she wished she'd paid more attention

"For what purpose?" she asked.

Just then, Talia's eyes shot directly at the two of them, hawk-like, picking them out in the dying light of dusk.

"It's too late," she said, loud enough for them to hear her. "I can't summon enough magic to protect us, only to see the shadows of what is to come. I'm powerless to stop them."

"Talia!" Lysandra's voice was uncertain as she called out to the woman. "What are you doing? Come away from there, it's not right."

"You must do something for me, Lysandra Barbas."

Lysandra glanced at Gregor, puzzled, before looking back at Talia. "What do you want me to do?"

Talia held her blood-covered hands out to either side of her, her eyes growing wider and wider as if she saw something horrifying all around her. Something truly evil. "Run!"

At that moment, a huge flaming arrow arched through the air and hit Talia directly in the center of her chest. She staggered backward and fell to the ground, her clothes catching fire quicker than Lysandra could comprehend.

Lysandra gripped Gregor's arm. "She's dead!"

He craned his head urgently to look back in the direction the arrow had come from, then yanked Lysandra to the side to avoid another arrow aimed directly at them that instead sliced into a tree trunk. "I was afraid of this."

"Afraid of what?" Lysandra spotted a figure fifty paces away, armed with a crossbow. "He killed her! Gregor—he killed her! Who is he?"

The figure had spotted them and had begun to give chase. Gregor swore loudly and took hold of her wrist. "Come on, we need to hurry!"

She didn't argue. Clutching each other's hands, they ran back to the village as fast as they could.

It was on fire.

Chaos had swiftly descended upon the village. Horrified screams of fear and pain pierced the air—screams of the dying. Scores of men in red uniforms astride horses galloped through the streets, holding torches that they used ruthlessly to set each cottage ablaze. Townspeople ran from their burning homes, trying to escape a fiery death. The sharp swords in other guards' hands fell upon many, slicing through flesh and bone.

"Gregor!" Lysandra cried as they came to a wrenching halt, hidden from the soldiers behind a stone cottage. "King Gaius—this is his doing! He's killing everyone!"

"We told him no. He didn't like that answer." He turned and took her by her arms, staring fiercely into her eyes. "Lysandra. Little sister. You need to go. You need to run far away from here."

The fire heated the air, turning dusk to nightmarish daylight all around her. "What are you talking about? I can't go!"

"Lys—"

"I need to find Mother!" She shoved away from Gregor and raced through the village, dodging any obstacle in her path. She staggered to a halt outside their cottage, now engulfed in flame.

Her mother's body lay halfway across the threshold. Her father's body was only ten paces away, lying in a pool of blood.

Before she could fully register the horror, Gregor caught up.

He grabbed her and threw her over his shoulder, running beyond the village limits before dropping her clumsily to the ground. He tossed her bow and a handful of arrows at her.

"They're dead," she whispered. Her heart felt like a stone that had dropped into her stomach.

"I was watching and listening as I ran. The king's guards are gathering any survivors up and they will make them work the road." His voice broke. "I must go back to help the others. Go— find the rebels. Do what you can to stop this from happening anywhere else, Lys. Do you understand me?"

She shook her head, her eyes burning from the smoke and from hateful tears. "No, I won't leave you! You're all I have left!"

Gregor took her chin sharply in his hand. "Follow me," he growled, "and I'll put an arrow through your heart myself to save you from whatever fate now lies before our friends and neighbors."

It was the last he said before he turned and ran back to the village.

And all she could do was watch him go.

CHAPTER 1

JONAS

AURANOS

When the King of Blood wanted to make a point, he made it as sharp as possible.

It was midday. With bone-chilling thuds, the executioner's ax fell upon the necks of three accused rebels, severing their heads from their bodies. The blood dripped through the stocks and spread across the smooth stone ground before a swelling crowd a thousand deep. And all Jonas could do was watch in horror as the heads were then mounted upon tall spikes in the palace square for all to see.

Three boys who'd barely reached manhood, now dead for being menaces and troublemakers. The severed heads stared at the crowd with blank eyes and slack expressions. Crimson blood trickled down the wooden spikes while the bodies were taken away to be burned.

The king who had quickly and brutally conquered this land did not give second chances—especially not to anyone who openly opposed him. Rebellion would be dealt with swiftly and remorselessly—and publicly.

With each deadly fall of the blade, a growing uneasiness slithered through the masses like a heavy mist they could no longer ignore. Auranos had once been free and prosperous and at peace—but now someone with a taste for blood was seated upon the throne.

The crowd stood shoulder to shoulder in the large square. Close by, Jonas could see young nobles, well dressed with tense jaws and wary expressions. Two fat, drunk men clinking their wine-filled goblets together as if toasting to a day filled with possibility. An old, gray-haired woman with a deeply lined face and a fine silk dress, her gaze darting around suspiciously. All were clambering for the best spot to see the king when he entered onto the marble balcony high above. The air was scented with smoke from both chimneys and cigarillos and with the aromas of baking bread, roasting meat, and the fragrant oils and cloyingly floral perfumes liberally used by many in lieu of bathing regularly. And the noise—a cacophony of voices, both conspiratorial whispers and deep-throated shouts—made it impossible to think clearly.

The Auranian palace glittered before them like a massive golden crown, its spires rising high up into the cloudless blue sky. It was set in the direct center of the City of Gold, a walled city two miles wide and deep. The walls themselves were heavily veined in gold, which caught the sunlight and reflected it like a pile of gold coins in the center of acres of green. Inside, cobbled roads led to villas, businesses, taverns, and shops. Only the privileged and important were able to make this city their home. But today, the gates had opened to all who wished to hear the king's speech.

"This place is impressive." Brion's voice was hard to hear above the incessant chatter of the throng.

"You think?" Jonas shifted his grim attention from the impaled heads. His friend's dark blue eyes were fixed upon the glittering palace as if it were something he could steal and sell for profit.

"I could get used to living here. A roof over my head—golden tiles at my pampered feet. All the food and drink I can swallow. Sign me up." He looked up at the executed rebels and grimaced. "You know, providing I keep my head attached."

The rebels who'd been executed today had been Auranian and not a part of Jonas and Brion's group—a gathering of young, like-minded boys who wished to rise up against King Gaius in the name of Paelsia. For three weeks now, ever since the siege upon the castle, they'd made their home in the thick of the forest that separated Auranos from their much poorer homeland. The Wildlands, as this forest was called, had a fearsome reputation of being filled with dangerous criminals and wild beasts. Some superstitious fools also believed dark and evil demons and spirits found home in the shadows of the thick, tall trees that blocked out all but a sliver of daylight.

Jonas could deal with criminals and beasts. And he, unlike the overwhelming majority of his countrymen, thought such legends were created only to incite fear and paranoia.

When news reached him of the executions scheduled for today, Jonas had wanted to see them for himself. He'd been certain they would strengthen his resolve, his certainty, to do anything, risk anything, to see the stolen kingdoms slip like sand from the hands of the tyrant who now ruled them.

Instead, they had filled him with dread. Each boy's face turned into that of his dead brother Tomas's as the ax fell and their blood flowed.

Three boys with their lives and futures spread before them—now silenced forever for speaking differently than what was permitted.

Such deaths would be considered by most to be destiny. To be fate. Paelsians, especially, believed that their futures were set and that they had to accept what they were given—be it good or bad. It only served to create a kingdom of victims afraid to stand up against opposition. A kingdom easily taken by someone happy to steal what no one would fight to keep.

No one, it would seem, except for Jonas. He didn't believe in fate or destiny or magical answers. Destiny was not set. And if he had enough help from those who might be willing to fight at his side, he knew he could change the future.

The crowd hushed for the briefest of moments before the swelling murmur rose again. King Gaius had emerged onto the balcony—a tall and handsome man with piercing, dark eyes that scanned the crowd as if memorizing each and every face.

The sudden need to hide gripped Jonas, as if he might be picked out from the multitude, but he forced himself to remain calm. While he had once met the king face-to-face, he would not be discovered here today. His gray cloak hid his identity well enough; it was a cloak similar to the one worn by half the men here, including Brion.

Next upon the balcony strode Magnus, crown prince to King Gaius's throne. Magnus was a near mirror image of his father, but younger, of course, and with a scar that sliced across his cheek, visible even from a distance.

Jonas had briefly crossed paths with the Limerian prince on the battlefield; he did not forget that Magnus had stopped a blade from finding his heart. But now they were no longer fighting for the same side. They were enemies.

The regal-looking Queen Althea joined her son to the left of the king, her dark hair streaked with silver. It was the first time

Jonas had seen the woman, but he knew who she was. She cast a haughty gaze down at the crowd.

Brion grabbed hold of Jonas's arm and Jonas glanced at his friend with mild amusement. "Did you want to hold hands? I don't think that's—"

"Just remain calm," Brion told him, not cracking a smile. "If you lose your head you might, uh, lose your head. Got it?"

The next moment Jonas understood why. Lord Aron Lagaris and Princess Cleiona Bellos, the youngest daughter of the former king, joined the others on the balcony. The crowd cheered at the sight of them.

Princess Cleo's long, pale, golden hair caught the sunlight. Once, Jonas had hated that hair and had fantasies of ripping it out by its roots. To him, it had symbolized the richness of Auranos, only an arm's reach away from the desperate poverty of Paelsia.

Now he knew nothing had ever been as simple as he'd thought.

"She's their prisoner," Jonas breathed.

"Doesn't look like a prisoner to me," Brion said. "But, sure, if you say so."

"The Damoras killed her father, stole her throne. She hates them—how can she not?"

"And now she's standing dutifully next to her betrothed."

Her betrothed. Jonas's gaze slid to Aron and narrowed.

His brother's murderer now stood above them all in a place of honor next to his future bride and the conquering king.

"You all right?" Brion asked warily.

Jonas couldn't answer. He was busy envisioning himself scaling the wall, jumping onto the balcony, and tearing Aron apart with his bare hands. He'd once imagined many different methods to exact death on this preening waste of life, but he'd thought he'd set aside his desire for vengeance in favor of the loftier goals of a rebel.

He'd been wrong.

"I want him dead," Jonas gritted out.

"I know." Brion had been there when Jonas grieved for Tomas, when he'd raged about getting his revenge. "And you will see that day. But it's not going to be today."

Slowly, very slowly, Jonas reined in his mindless rage. His muscles relaxed and Brion finally loosened his hold on him.

"Better?" Brion asked.

Jonas hadn't torn his gaze from the hateful, arrogant-looking boy on the balcony. "I won't be better until I can watch him bleed."

"It's a goal," Brion allowed. "A worthy one. But like I said, it won't be today. Calm down."

Jonas let out a breath. "Issuing orders now, are we?"

"As second in command of our little band of merry rebels, if my captain suddenly goes crazy, I'll take over. It kind of comes with the job."

"Good to know you're taking this seriously."

"First time for everything."

On the balcony, Aron drew closer to Cleo, reaching down to take her hand in his. She turned her beautiful face to look up at him, but no smile touched her lips.

"She could do better than that jackass," Jonas mumbled.

"What?"

"Never mind."

The crowd had grown even more massive in minutes, and the sweltering heat of the day beat down on them. Sweat dripped down Jonas's brow and he wiped his forehead with the sleeve of his cloak.

Finally, King Gaius stepped forward and raised his hand. Silence fell.

"It is my great honor," the king said, his voice strong enough to carry easily over the crowd, "to stand here before you as the king not only of Limeros, but now of Paelsia and Auranos as well. There was once a time when the three kingdoms of Mytica were united as one—strong, prosperous, and at peace. And now, at long last, we shall have that again."

Those in the crowd mumbled quietly to each other, the majority of faces set with lines of distrust, of fear, despite the king's smooth words. The King of Blood's reputation preceded him. From whispered conversations in the crowd before and after the executions, Jonas heard many say that their opinions could be swayed today to believe the king was a friend or a foe. Many doubted that the dead rebels had been right in whatever anarchy they'd attempted; perhaps such rebels only made conditions worse for everyone by angering the king.

Such ignorance—such readiness to take the easy path, to bow before their conqueror by believing whatever words left his mouth. It sickened Jonas to his very core.

But even he had to admit the king was a master speechmaker, every word seemingly coated in gold, giving hope to the hopeless.

"I have chosen to live here with my family in this beautiful palace for a time, at least until the transition is complete. While it is much different from our beloved home in Limeros, we want to get to know you all much better, and we feel that it is our welcome duty to help guide all our citizens into this new era."

"Also helps that Limeros is frozen over like a witch's heart,"

Brion sneered, despite some surrounding murmurs of approval from others. "He makes it sound like a hardship to live somewhere that's not crusted with snow and ice."

"Today I have an important announcement to make that will benefit one and all," the king said. "On my command, construction has already begun on a great road that will unite our three lands as one."

Jonas frowned. A road?

"The Imperial Road will commence at the Temple of Cleiona, a few hours' ride from this very city, cutting through the Wildlands to enter Paelsia, where it will travel east into the Forbidden Mountains and then north across the border to Limeros, to end at the Temple of Valoria. Several teams are already in place, working night and day to ensure the road is completed as quickly as possible."

"*Into* the Forbidden Mountains?" Jonas whispered. "What good is a road that leads where no one wants to go?"

What was the king up to?

A flash of gold in the sky caught his attention and he looked up to see two hawks circling high above the crowd.

Even the Watchers are interested.

Such ridiculous thoughts he'd hold on to rather than share with Brion. The stories of immortals who entered the mortal realm in the form of hawks were just that: stories told to children before bedtime. His own mother told him such tales.

The king's lips stretched back from his teeth in a smile that would look warm and genuine to all who did not know the darkness behind it. "I hope you are as pleased as I am about this road. I know it's been a difficult time for everyone and I take no pleasure in the blood spilled in the process."

There was a swelling of displeased and uneasy murmurs in the crowd, but not nearly as many as there should have been.

It's working, Jonas thought. *He's fooling those who wish to be fooled.*

"Yeah, right," Brion said. "He loved it. He would have bathed in all that blood if he'd had half a chance."

Jonas couldn't agree more.

King Gaius continued, "As you all can see here today, your Princess Cleiona is very well. She was not exiled or imprisoned as the daughter of my enemy. Why would she be? After all the pain and grief she's bravely endured, I have welcomed her into my new home with open arms."

He made it sound as if he'd given her a choice, but Jonas didn't believe it.

"My next announcement today concerns your princess." King Gaius stretched out his hand. "Come here, my dear."

Cleo cast a wary glance at Aron before turning toward the king. She hesitated only briefly before crossing the balcony to stand at the king's side. Her face was unreadable, her lips tight but her head held high. A sapphire necklace sparkled at her throat and jewels also dotted her hair to match her dark blue gown. Her skin glowed radiantly under the sunshine. Excited murmurs now rose through the crowd about the daughter of their former king.

"Princess Cleiona has suffered great personal loss and heartbreak. She is truly one of the bravest girls I've ever met and I see why those in Auranos love her as much as they do." The king's voice and expression both seemed to hold affection as he gazed at the princess. "It is well known to all that she is betrothed to Lord Aron Lagaris, a fine young man who defended the princess in Paelsia against a savage boy who meant her great harm."

Brion grabbed Jonas's arm again and dug in tightly with his

fingertips. Jonas hadn't realized he'd taken a step forward, his fists clenched at his sides, prompted by the lies about his brother.

"Stay calm," Brion growled.

"I'm trying."

"Try harder."

The king drew Cleo even closer to his side. "This is how Lord Aron proved his worth to the late King Corvin and was given the princess's hand and the promise of a wedding I know Auranians have been greatly anticipating."

A smile played at Aron's lips and a look of triumph lit his eyes.

It suddenly dawned on Jonas what this was leading to. The king was about to announce Aron and Cleo's wedding date.

King Gaius nodded in the boy's direction. "There is no question in my mind that Lord Aron would make a fine match for the princess."

Jonas silently seethed that this bastard got to preen and glow in the light of his wrongdoings—to be rewarded for them. Jonas's hatred was a palpable thing, an ugly monster that threatened to renew his obsession with vengeance and blind him to everything else.

The king continued, "Yesterday I came to an important decision."

The crowd went completely silent, leaning forward collectively in anticipation of what he would say next. Jonas couldn't look away from Lord Aron and his bright and cheerfully vile expression.

"I hereby end the betrothal between Lord Aron and Princess Cleiona," King Gaius said.

A gasp went through the crowd and Aron's gleeful expression froze.

"Princess Cleiona represents golden Auranos in all ways," the king said. "She is the daughter of you all and I know she is in your hearts. I see this as an opportunity to unite Mytica even more than it already is. Therefore, today I am pleased to announce the betrothal and upcoming marriage forty days from today between my son, Prince Magnus Lukas Damora, and Auranos's beloved Princess Cleiona Aurora Bellos."

King Gaius took Cleo's hand and Magnus's hand and joined them. "Immediately following the wedding, there will be a wedding tour—Magnus and Cleiona will travel across Mytica as a symbol of unity and the bright future we all share together."

There was a moment of silence before the majority of the crowd began to cheer with approval—some nervously, some with full appreciation of such a proposed union and tour.

"Huh," Brion said. "I wasn't expecting that at all."

Jonas stared up at the balcony for several stunned moments. "I've heard enough. We need to get out of here. Now."

"Lead the way."

Jonas turned from his view of blank-faced Cleo and began threading his way through the madness. It was the news of the Imperial Road he was most concerned with—what did it mean? What were the king's true intentions? The fate of a princess now engaged to her mortal enemy should be the very least of his concerns.

Still, Cleo's new betrothal bothered him deeply.

CHAPTER 2

CLEO

AURANOS

"Today I am pleased to announce the betrothal and upcoming marriage forty days from today between my son, Prince Magnus Lukas Damora, and Auranos's beloved Princess Cleiona Aurora Bellos."

Cleo's breath left her in a rush.

The world blurred before her eyes and there was a ringing in her ears. She felt a tug as the king pulled her closer, and the next moment something warm and dry grasped her hand. She looked up to see Magnus next to her, his face as impassive and unreadable as always. His black hair hung low over his forehead, framing his dark brown eyes as he focused on the crowd—a crowd that cheered and yelled as if this stomach-churning horror was wonderful news.

Finally, after what felt like an eternity, Magnus dropped her hand and turned toward his mother, who had taken hold of his arm.

Aron grabbed her wrist and drew her back into the castle past the others on the balcony. His breath, as always, smelled like wine and acrid cigarillo smoke.

"What just happened out there?" he hissed.

"I—I'm not sure."

Aron's face was as red as a beet. "Did you know this would happen? That he planned to break our engagement?"

"No, of course not! I had no idea until . . . until—" Oh goddess, what just happened? It couldn't be true!

"He can't change what is meant to be." Aron was so livid he was literally spitting. "We're supposed to be together, no one else! It was decided!"

"Of course we are," she managed to say, much more demurely than she felt. She had no deep affection for handsome but vapid Lord Aron, but she would rather spend a thousand years in his constant company than an hour alone with Magnus.

The dark prince had killed the first boy she'd ever loved— stabbed him through the back with a sword while Theon had been trying to protect her. The memory of Theon's death made a fresh swell of grief rise within her, hot and thick enough to choke on.

Imprisoned for weeks at the palace after her capture, Cleo had experienced the very depths of despair and grief—for Theon, for her father, for her sister, Emilia. All ripped away from her. Such sorrow had carved a cold, bottomless hole in her chest that could never be filled. She could lose herself in such darkness if she wasn't careful.

"I can fix this." The scent of wine on Aron's breath was even greater than normal today. His gaze moved toward the king as he exited the balcony. "Your majesty, it's imperative that I speak with you immediately!"

The king wore a bright smile on his face to match the golden, ruby-encrusted crown Cleo's fingers itched to tear from his head. That crown and everything it represented belonged to her father.

It belonged to *her.*

"Of course I'd be happy to speak with you on any matter, Lord Aron."

"In private, your majesty."

King Gaius raised an eyebrow, dark humor lighting his face as he gazed at the sputtering young lord before him. "If you insist."

The two departed without delay, leaving Cleo standing there alone, supporting herself against the cool, smooth wall as she tried to gather her breath and her thoughts—both racing.

Magnus was next to leave the balcony. He glanced at her, his face like stone. "Seems that my father had a little surprise in store for us today, didn't he?"

The prince was both coldly handsome, like his snake of a father, and imposingly tall. Cleo had seen many girls look at him in the last three weeks, their eyes sparkling with interest. The only thing that marred his good looks was a vicious scar on his right cheek, an arc that went from the top of his ear to the corner of his mouth.

The taste of bile rose in her throat at the sight of him. "Don't try to make me believe you knew nothing about this."

"I'm not trying to make you believe anything, princess. Frankly, I don't particularly care what you believe about me or anyone else."

"It won't happen." Her voice was quiet but strong. "I will never marry you."

He lifted a shoulder in a lazy shrug. "Explain that to my father."

"I'm explaining it to you."

"My father makes the decisions and he likes them followed

without argument. You're more than welcome to fight him on this."

Her outrage had quickly dissipated and she was left only with disbelief. "This has to be a dream. No, not a dream. A nightmare—a horrible nightmare."

Magnus's lips thinned. "For us both, princess. Make no mistake about that."

Queen Althea approached and clasped Cleo's hands. Hers were dry and warm, just like her son's. It seemed as if she were attempting a smile, but the expression looked as false on her finely lined face as feathers on a goat.

"My dear, it's my honor to welcome you into our family. One day I'm sure you'll make an extraordinary queen."

Cleo bit her tongue nearly hard enough to draw blood in order to keep from blurting out that she already *was* queen. Only the King of Blood stood in the way of her rightful title.

"We will have a great deal to do to plan a wedding befitting my son," the queen continued, as if she hadn't noticed Cleo's lack of reply. "And we'll need to do it quickly given the swiftness of the wedding date. I have heard of an exemplary dressmaker in Hawk's Brow who will be perfect to create your gown. We'll make a trip there soon. It will be good for the people to see their beloved golden princess walking among them once again. It will raise spirits throughout the entire kingdom."

Cleo couldn't find enough words to speak, so she didn't even try. She nodded and looked down, eyes lowered to conceal her rage. Through her lashes she saw Queen Althea glance at Magnus, as if delivering some sort of message through her pale blue eyes, before she nodded at them both and moved away down the hall.

"My mother knows a great deal about fashion and beauty,"

Magnus said flippantly. "It's her passion, one she always wished my sister shared."

His sister—Princess Lucia. For three weeks now the Limerian princess lay comatose after being injured in the explosion that tore open the entrance to the palace and allowed King Gaius and his army their violent victory.

Cleo had noticed that the mention of his ailing sister was the only thing that ever seemed to bring a flicker of emotion to Magnus's steely gaze. Many healers had come to see Lucia, some of the greatest and most accomplished in the land. No one could determine what was wrong with her or find any wound she'd sustained to explain her condition.

Cleo had suggested that her own dear friend, her sister's former lady-in-waiting, Mira Cassian, be assigned as Lucia's attendant in hopes that the king would find Mira too useful to demote to scullery maid. Thankfully, it had worked. Mira told Cleo the princess would rise up from her slumber as if in a trance, enough to consume food specially blended smooth to ensure her ongoing survival, but was never truly conscious. It was a true mystery what had befallen the princess of Limeros.

"Let me make this very clear, Prince Magnus," Cleo said evenly, fighting to keep the tremor from her voice. "I will never be forced to marry someone I hate. And I hate you."

He regarded her for a moment, as if she was something he could easily crush beneath the sole of his boot if he chose to. "Be very careful how you speak to me, Princess Cleiona."

She raised her chin. "Or what will you do? Will you run a sword through me when I turn my back on you as you did with Theon, you spineless coward?"

In an instant, he grabbed hold of her arm tight enough to

make her shriek and pushed her up against the stone wall. Anger flashed through his gaze, and something unexpected—something like pain.

"Never, ever call me a coward again if you value your life, princess. Fair warning."

His current fiery expression was so different from his usual look of ice that it confused her. Was he furious or wounded by her words? Could he be both?

"Release me," she hissed.

His eyes—cold, like black diamonds, soulless, evil—pinned her for another moment before he let go of her so abruptly that she slumped down against the wall.

A guard wearing the all-too-familiar red Limerian uniform approached. "Prince Magnus, your father summons both you and the princess to his throne room immediately."

Magnus finally tore his gaze from hers to cast a dark look toward the guard. "Very well."

Cleo's stomach tied itself into knots. Could Aron have been successful in his argument against this new betrothal?

In the throne room, King Gaius had draped himself upon her father's golden chair. Sprawled on the floor at his feet were two of his horrible dogs—large, slobbering wolfhounds that growled whenever she came even a step too close. They always seemed more like demons from the darklands to Cleo than dogs.

A sudden memory from her childhood flashed before her eyes—her father seated upon this very throne, his arms stretched out to her when she'd successfully slipped away from her strict nursemaid to run directly toward him and crawl up on his lap.

She prayed that her eyes didn't reveal how very much she wanted to avenge her father's death. On the surface, she was just a girl not yet out of her teens, small in stature and slight in figure, born and bred into a spoiled life of excess and luxury. At first glance, no one would ever perceive her as a threat.

But she knew that she was. Her heart now beat for one reason, the only thing that helped stanch the flow of incapacitating grief.

Vengeance.

Cleo knew she continued to live and breathe because King Gaius saw value in keeping the Auranian princess alive and well. She was required to represent what remained of the royal Bellos family line in all matters when it came to the king's agenda and his power over the Auranian people. She was a sparrow in a gilded cage, taken out to show others how pretty and how well-behaved she was when needed.

So she would be pretty and well-behaved. For now.

But not forever.

"My dear girl," the king said as she and Magnus approached. "You grow lovelier with each day that passes. It's quite remarkable."

And you grow more hateful and disgusting.

"Thank you, your majesty," she said as sweetly as she could. The king was a snake in the skin of a man and she would never underestimate the strength of his bite.

"Were you pleased by my surprise announcement today?" he asked.

She fought to keep her controlled expression from slipping. "I'm very grateful that you've allowed me such an honorable place in your kingdom."

His smile stretched, but it was one that never met his dark brown eyes—the exact same shade as Magnus's. "And you, my son.

I'm sure you were caught unawares as well. It was a last-minute decision, to tell you the truth. I thought it would please the people, and I was right. It did."

"As always," Magnus replied, "I defer to your judgment."

The sound of the prince's voice, low and even and so much like his father's, set Cleo's nerves on edge more than they already were.

"Lord Aron wanted to speak with me in private," the king said.

Private? A half dozen guards stood around the edges of the room, with two on the outer side of the archway leading into the throne room. Next to the king on a smaller throne sat Queen Althea, her gaze straight forward, her lips set into a measured expression that betrayed no emotion at all. She might as well have been sleeping with her eyes wide open.

Aron stood to the right, his arms crossed over his chest.

"Yes," he spoke up, his tone arrogant, "I explained to the king that this is an unacceptable change. That the people were looking very much forward to our wedding. Mother has already taken great strides in planning our ceremony. I wanted to talk to the king and have him reconsider his decision today. There are plenty of beautiful, titled girls in Auranos who would be much better suited to Prince Magnus."

King Gaius cocked his head, regarding Aron with barely restrained amusement, as if he were a trained monkey. "Quite. And how do you feel about this abrupt change, Princess Cleiona?"

Her mouth had gone dry after hearing Aron's little rant, which sounded like a child stomping his foot when his toys were taken from him at bedtime. Aron was so accustomed to getting his way that it had completely disrupted his common sense. However, she couldn't entirely blame him for trying to salvage what little power he had in the palace. But if he were smart—and she already knew brains were never Aron's greatest asset—he would see that Cleo no longer wielded any power here, had no influence apart from being a figurehead meant to keep the Auranian people in line and gain their trust.

She forced a smile. "Of course, I certainly bow to whatever decision the wise king makes on my behalf." The falseness of the words twisted in her throat. "It's just . . . Aron might have some weight to his argument. The kingdom was rather smitten by the thought of us together after Aron's very . . . well, *fierce* protection of me that day in the Paelsian market."

She inwardly shuddered at the memory of Tomas Agallon's murder, an act that had nothing to do with protection and more to do with Aron overreacting to a personal insult.

"I assure you, I did consider this." The king's stolen crown caught the torchlight and glinted. "Lord Aron is wholly embraced by the Auranian people, without question. It's one of the reasons I've just informed him of my decision to bestow the title of kingsliege upon him."

Aron bowed deeply. "And I am very pleased by this honor, your majesty."

"*Kingsliege*," Magnus mused from beside her, loud enough for only Cleo to hear. "Such a lofty title for one who's never even been in battle. How deeply pathetic."

King Gaius studied Cleo closely. "Do you wish to remain engaged to Lord Aron?"

She wanted to answer immediately and in the affirmative— Aron, despite his shortcomings, was a more palatable prospect than Magnus—but found herself pausing to think it through. She wasn't simple-minded enough to believe such "wishes" would be granted. After announcing the wedding date to the citizens out-side, there was absolutely no chance the king would renege on his proclamation. All agreeing with Aron would do was make her look like a fool—an ungrateful and disrespectful fool.

Cleo lowered her head and studied the dogs by the king's feet as if too shy to meet his gaze directly. "Your majesty, I wish only to please you."

He gave her a shallow nod, as if it was the correct response. "Then I appreciate your allowing me to make this choice on your behalf."

Aron let out a grunt of disgust. "Oh, come on, Cleo!"

She gave him a wary look, silently cautioning him to be care-ful what he said. "Aron, you must see that the king knows what is right."

"But we were meant to be together," he whined.

"You will find another bride, Aron. But I'm afraid it can't be me."

Anger lit his gaze and he spun to face Prince Magnus. "It's very important for a bride to be pure on her wedding night. Is this not so?"

Cleo's cheeks began to flame. "Aron!"

He gestured wildly at her. "Cleo already gave her chastity to me. We've shared flesh. She is not pure!"

A deadly silence fell.

Cleo grappled to hold on to her self-control but felt it slipping from her grasp. Here it was, her horrible secret kept hidden from the world—tossed out like a landed fish, flopping and slimy for all to see.

Foggy memories of a party, too much wine, a spoiled princess who enjoyed forgetting herself and having fun—and then Aron, a handsome and popular lord all her friends desired, who wanted to be with her more than anyone else. Once she sobered, she realized it was a horrific mistake to sacrifice her virginity to such a vain and shallow boy.

To be viewed now as a fallen princess in a land that valued purity as a bride's most important virtue could be her ultimate downfall. She would lose what little power she had left in the palace.

Only one choice could help her salvage this situation.

"Oh, Aron," she said as drily as she could manage. "I almost feel sorry for you that you must lie to such extremes today. Can't you simply accept defeat gracefully?"

His eyes widened so much that she could see the whites all around his irises. "Lie? It's not a lie! You wanted me as I wanted you! You must admit that this is the truth and be grateful that I even still want you!"

King Gaius leaned back in the throne and regarded them, his fingers templed. "Seems that we have a disagreement here. The truth is very important to me, the most important thing of all. Lies are intolerable. Princess, are you saying that this boy would lie about something so important?"

"Yes," she said without hesitation. She gazed at the king, clear-eyed. "He lies."

"Cleo!" Aron sputtered, outraged.

"Then," the king said, "I have no choice but to believe you." He flicked a glance at Magnus. "Tell me, my son, what do we usually do in Limeros with those who would lie to a king?"

Magnus's face was unreadable as always, his arms crossed over his chest. "The penalty for lying is to have one's tongue cut out."

The king nodded, then gestured toward the guards.

Two guards stepped forward and took hold of Aron's arms tightly. He gasped, his face wild with fear.

"Your majesty, you can't do this! I'm not lying! I would never lie to you—I obey your command in all ways. You are my king now! Please, you must believe me!"

The king said nothing, but nodded at another guard who approached, drawing a dagger from the sheath at his waist.

Aron was forced to his knees. A fourth guard took hold of his jaw, grabbed a handful of his hair, and wrenched open Aron's mouth. The guard used a metal clamp to pull his tongue out from between his lips and Aron let out a strangled cry of horror.

Cleo watched all of this unfold in cold shock.

She hated Aron. She hated that she'd allowed herself to share flesh with him—taking solace only in the fact that she'd been too drunk to remember much about the act itself. She hated that he'd killed Tomas Agallon without a moment's remorse. She hated that her father had betrothed her to him. She hated that Aron was so thoughtless that he didn't understand why any of this was so vile to her.

He deserved to be punished in so many ways. He *did*.

But not for this.

He'd told the king the truth.

However . . . to admit *she* was the one who'd lied . . .

Oh, Goddess Cleiona . . . Cleo hardly ever prayed to her namesake, the Auranian deity, but she'd certainly make an exception today. *Please, please help me.*

She could let this happen without protest. It could be her secret until the day she died. No one would ever believe Aron after this punishment.

Her fists were clenched so tight her fingernails bit painfully into her palms as she watched the dagger move toward Aron's mouth. He let out a terror-filled screech.

"Stop!" Cleo shouted, the word escaping her before she even realized it. She trembled from head to foot, her heart pounding so hard that it rocked her entire frame. "Don't do this! Please, don't! He didn't lie. He—he was telling the truth! We were together one single time. I did give my chastity to him knowingly and without reservation!"

The guard holding the dagger froze, the edge of the blade pressed to Aron's pink, squirming tongue.

"Well, now," King Gaius said softly, but Cleo had never heard more menace in anyone's voice. "That certainly changes things, doesn't it?"

CHAPTER 3

MAGNUS

AURANOS

Princess Cleo's face was pale, her body literally shaking with fear in the face of King Gaius's wrath.

And to think Magnus had assumed this golden kingdom would have no worthy entertainment.

His mother sat silently next to the king, her face impassive through all this drama, as if she had no opinion on either severed tongues or lost virginity. Somewhere behind that flat expression of hers, he knew she most certainly had an opinion on what her husband chose to do and to whom he did it.

But the queen had long since learned not to speak such thoughts aloud.

King Gaius leaned forward to peer more closely at the tarnished princess. "Did your father know of your shameful loss of innocence before his death?"

"No, your majesty," she choked out.

This was truly torture for her. For a royal princess, even one from a fallen kingdom, to openly admit that she'd been defiled before her wedding night . . .

Well, it simply wasn't something that happened. Or, at least, it wasn't something anyone ever admitted to as publicly as this.

The king shook his head slowly. "Whatever are we to do with you now?"

Magnus noticed that Cleo's fists were clenched at her sides. Through all this, her eyes had stayed dry, her expression haughty despite her obvious fear. She did not cry, nor did she fall to her knees and beg forgiveness.

King Gaius loved it when people begged him for mercy. It rarely helped their cause, but he did enjoy it.

That pride of yours will be your undoing, princess.

"Magnus," the king said, "what do you suppose we should do now that this information has seen the light of day? It seems I have betrothed you to a whore."

Magnus couldn't help the snort of laughter that escaped him. Cleo cast a glare toward him, one made of sharp, broken glass, but he hadn't meant the laugh to be at her expense.

"A *whore*?" he repeated. Well, his father *had* specifically asked for his opinion, which was a rare opportunity indeed. Why waste it? "The girl admits to being with Lord Aron one time, a boy she planned to wed. Perhaps they have since realized they acted impulsively by giving in to their . . . passions. Quite honestly, I don't see this as quite as much of a crime as you do. In case you're unaware, I have not retained my chastity, either."

Speaking so plainly could have several different outcomes— negative or positive. Magnus ignored his churning gut and kept his expression as neutral as possible as he waited to find out which it would be.

The king leaned back, regarding him coolly. "And what of her admittance to lying to me?"

"If I were in her position I have no doubt I would've done the same in an attempt to gather my scattered reputation."

"You believe I should forgive her this indiscretion?"

"That, of course, is for you to decide." From the corner of his eye, he could see Cleo staring at him as if she was stunned he would say anything in her defense.

This wasn't defense. This was an excellent chance to test the borders of the king's patience with his son and heir now that he'd reached the age of eighteen. Magnus was a man now, so he would no longer act like a boy and cower away from his father's potential rages.

"No," the king said. "I wish for you to tell me. Tell me what you think I should do, Magnus. I'm fascinated to hear it."

There was caution in the king's tone, one unmistakably like the rattle of a snake moments before it struck.

Magnus ignored it.

After the unexpected announcement on the balcony, he felt reckless and unconcerned about consequences. At the time, Magnus had cast a stunned look in his father's direction and had been met with one of steel. One that told him in no uncertain terms that if he argued this decision he would be very, very sorry.

Magnus would never underestimate his father. The scar that marked his face was a constant reminder of what happened when he did. The king had no problem hurting those he claimed to love the most—even seven-year-old boys.

His father insisted on playing games, but Magnus was no pawn; he was the future king of Limeros—now of all of Mytica. He too could play games if there was a chance of winning.

"I think you should forgive the princess this one time. And you should apologize to Lord Aron for scaring him. The poor boy looks rather distressed."

The shivering Lord Aron was now covered in enough sweat that he looked as if he'd just gone for a swim in the lake.

The king stared at Magnus incredulously for several very long and very heavy moments. Then he began to laugh, a deep, rolling sound from the back of his throat. "My son wants me to forgive and forget—and *apologize*." He said the last word as if it was unfamiliar to him. Probably because it was. "What do you think, Lord Aron? Should I apologize to you?"

Aron continued to kneel on the floor as if he did not have the energy to stand without help. Magnus noticed the damp patch on the crotch of his trousers from where he'd wet himself.

"No—no, of course not, your majesty." Aron managed to use the tongue he'd come very close to losing. "It is I who should apologize for attempting to dissuade you from any plans you would make. Of course, you are right in all things."

Now, that's what my father likes to hear, Magnus thought.

"My decision," said the king. "Yes, my decision to unite my son and the young Cleiona. But this was before I learned the truth about her. Magnus, tell me, what should happen now? Do you wish to sully yourself by a betrothal to a girl like this?"

Ah, so now he'd come to the inevitable fork in the road. How appropriate, since roads were so much on his father's mind today.

One word from him could break this ludicrous engagement and free him from any ties to the princess, who made no attempt to hide her bottomless hatred for him. Reflected in her eyes was the brutal moment that had changed Magnus forever.

It wasn't so much that Theon Ranus had been Magnus's first

kill. The young guard had to die, for he would have killed Magnus without question in order to defend the princess he loved. It was the fact that Magnus had slain the boy by stabbing him through his back that would forever haunt him. That had been the act of a coward, not a prince.

"Well, my son?" the king prompted. "Do you wish to end this betrothal? The decision is yours."

Up until today, his father had valued Cleo as a symbol of his new and tenuous hold on Auranos. Despite his well-known reputation as a harsh king who doled out punishment without mercy, King Gaius wished to be respected and admired by his new subjects rather than feared, wooing them with pretty speeches and lofty promises of a bright future. Such citizens would be much easier to control—especially with a Limerian army now spread thin across three kingdoms—and the king believed this would quell any anarchy, beyond a few scattered but troublesome rebels.

Despite what had been revealed about the princess, Magnus believed Cleo would continue to be a valuable asset during this tenuous time of transition. A piece of golden power to light the dark path ahead.

Power mattered to his father. And it mattered to Magnus as well.

Whatever power he could gain for himself was not something to be cast aside without forethought. And while he wished he could go home to Limeros as fast as a ship could take him, he knew it was impossible. His father wanted to stay in this gilded palace.

While here, Magnus would have to make choices that best served him now and in the future.

"It's a difficult decision, Father," Magnus finally said. "Princess Cleiona is most certainly a complicated girl." More so than he ever thought possible. Perhaps he was not the only one who felt the need to wear masks every day. "She has admitted to sacrificing her chastity to this boy. Have there been others, princess?"

Cleo's cheeks flushed, but by the look in her fierce gaze, it was more from fury than embarrassment. Still, he felt it was a valid question. She had claimed to love the dead guard—a claim she'd never put forth about Lord Aron. Just how many had warmed the Auranian princess's bed?

"There has been no one else." Each word was a snarl. And thanks to the steady, unflinching look in her aquamarine eyes, he believed her.

He didn't speak for a moment, instead letting the seconds stretch to an uncomfortable length. "If that's so, then I don't see any logical reason why this engagement should be broken."

"You accept her?" the king asked.

"Yes. But let's hope there aren't any more surprises when it comes to my future bride."

Cleo's mouth had dropped open in shock. Perhaps she didn't realize that this distasteful match was all about *Magnus's* power and nothing else.

"Unless you require anything further of me, Father," Magus said evenly, "I would like to visit my sister's bedside."

"Yes, of course." The king watched Magnus with a narrowed, appraising gaze, as if he too had been surprised his son hadn't taken the opportunity to end the unexpected betrothal. Magnus turned and walked briskly out of the throne room, hoping that he hadn't just made a very costly mistake.

The attendant jumped as Magnus pushed through the wooden doors to Lucia's chambers. Her gaze dropped to the floor and she twisted a finger nervously through her long, dark red hair.

"Apologies, Prince Magnus. You startled me."

Ignoring her, he moved into the room, his attention solely focused on the girl in the canopied bed. So unlike their more austere Limerian living quarters, these had marble floors and thick fur rugs. Colorful tapestries depicting beautiful meadows and fantastical animals—one appeared to be a rabbit crossed with a lion—adorned the walls. Bright sunshine fell in soft rays from the glass doors leading out to the balcony. Fireplaces were not constantly being attended to keep the cold from seeping into the palace, for here in Auranos the climate was warm and temperate compared to Limeros's ice and frost. The sheets upon this bed were made from luxurious, pale silk, which only made Lucia's raven-colored hair seem that much darker, her lips that much more red.

His sister's beauty always caught him by surprise.

His sister. It was how he'd always viewed Lucia. Only recently had he come to learn that she was adopted, stolen from her cradle in Paelsia and brought to his father's castle to be raised as the Limerian princess—all because of a prophecy. One that said Lucia would become a sorceress able to channel all four parts of *elementia*: air, fire, water, and earth magic.

The confusion of learning she was not his sister by blood, the relief that his unnatural desire for her was not truly one of the dark sins, and her look of disgust when he'd been unable to hold back his need to kiss her—all flowed through his mind now.

Bright hope had been forever tainted by dark pain.

Lucia loved him, but it was the love of a sister for her older brother; that was all. But it wasn't enough. It would never be enough.

And now, the thought that she'd sacrificed herself to help their father and might never wake up again . . .

She *had* to wake up.

His gaze flicked to the attendant, the Auranian girl whom Princess Cleo had insisted would be perfect for this placement.

"What's your name?" he asked.

She was plump, but not unpleasantly so. Her soft curves showed that she was not a girl who'd experienced many hardships, despite now wearing the plain gray dress of a servant. "Mira Cassian, your grace."

He narrowed his eyes. "Your brother is Nicolo Cassian."

"He is, your grace."

"In Paelsia, he threw a rock at my head and then rendered me unconscious with the hilt of a sword. He could have killed me."

A tremor went through her. "I'm very grateful my brother did you no lasting harm, your grace." She blinked, her eyes meeting his. "I haven't seen him in weeks. Does—does my brother still live?"

"He certainly deserved to die for what he did, don't you think?"

He had not shared this story with many. Nicolo Cassian had attacked Magnus to get him to unhand Cleo after he'd killed Theon. It had been Magnus's duty to bring the princess back to Limeros so the king could use her as a bargaining chip against her father. He'd failed and instead woken up alone, surrounded by corpses and bitter defeat.

Nic now toiled in the stables, knee deep in the filth of horses and not allowed to enter the castle. The boy should be eternally thankful that Magnus had not demanded his life.

He turned his back on Mira and focused instead on Lucia. He didn't hear the door open, but it wasn't long before the shadow of his father fell upon him.

"You're angry with me for my announcement today," the king said. It was not a question.

Magnus gritted his teeth and measured his reply before speaking. "I was . . . surprised. The girl hates me and I feel only apathy for her in return."

"There is no need for love or even affection to play any part in a marriage. This is a union of necessity only, of political strategy."

"I know this."

"We will find you a mistress able to give you every pleasure lacking in your marriage. A courtesan, perhaps."

"Perhaps," Magnus allowed.

"Or perhaps you'd prefer a pretty little servant to attend to your every need." The king flicked a look toward Mira, who smartly stayed to the back of the room and out of earshot. "Speaking of pretty little servants, do you remember the kitchen maid who caused us some difficulties back home? The one with the tendency for spying. What was her name? Amia?"

Amia had been a casual dalliance of Magnus's, as well as a pair of ears eager to listen for palace gossip. She would have done anything for the prince. Such loyalty had gotten her tortured and whipped, but even then she hadn't revealed her ties to him. But why would his father have bothered remembering her name?

"I seem to recall. What about her?"

"She ran away from the castle. Probably thought I wouldn't notice, but I did."

She'd run away because Magnus had sent her away with enough coin to start a new life somewhere else. "Is that so?"

The king leaned over to brush the dark hair back from Lucia's face. "I sent some men after her. The news has reached me that they found her easily with a bag of gold she'd stolen from us. Of course, they executed her immediately." His attention then shifted to Magnus, a small smile playing at his lips. "I thought you'd want to know."

Magnus ignored the sharp and sudden twinge of pain in his chest. He measured his words before he spoke. "It was . . . the end such a thief deserved."

"I'm glad we agree."

Amia had been innocent and foolish—a girl who lacked the steel in her heart to survive the harshness of the Limerian palace. But she hadn't deserved to die. Magnus waited to feel grief but felt only coldness slide over his skin. Part of him had been expecting this since the moment Amia's carriage had departed the castle, but he'd hoped for the best. He should have known better. His father would never allow one to escape who might possess secrets that could be used against him.

The girl's fate had been set from the moment her path had crossed that of the Damoras. This was only confirmation of it. Still, it incensed Magnus that his father said such things casually when Amia's death was anything but. The king was testing him—checking for weaknesses in his heir.

The king was always testing him.

They were silent for a while, Lucia the focal point between them.

"I need her to wake," the king said, his jaw tense.

"Hasn't she done enough for you already?"

"Her magic is the key to finding the Kindred."

"Who told you that?" His growing impatience with his father's decisions today made his words sharper than usual. "Some random witch with a need for silver? Or perhaps a hawk perched upon your shoulder and whispered—"

The sting of his father's hand across his scarred cheek caught him entirely by surprise. He pressed his palm to his face and stared at the king.

"Never mock me, Magnus," the king growled. "And never again try to make me look like a fool in front of others as you did today. Do you hear me?"

"I hear you," he gritted out.

His father hadn't struck him recently, but it had been a common practice in his youth. Much like the cobra, the official sigil of Limeros, King Gaius struck out violently and venomously when angered or challenged.

Magnus wrestled against the urge to leave the room since he knew it would make him look weak.

"I learned this new information from my latest royal advisor," the king said finally. He moved to the opposite side of Lucia's bed, his attention fixed again upon her peaceful face.

"Who is it?"

"That's none of your concern."

"Let me guess. Did this mysterious advisor also suggest building your road into the Forbidden Mountains?"

This earned Magnus a look that had regained some respect. He'd asked the right question. "She did."

So his father's new advisor was a woman. This didn't come as a complete surprise to Magnus. The king's last trusted advisor had been his longtime mistress, a beautiful if treacherous witch by the name of Sabina.

"You really believe the Kindred are real."

"I believe."

The Kindred were a legend—Magnus had never thought them anything more than that—four crystals, containing the very essence of *elementia*, that had been lost a thousand years ago. To possess them would give their bearer omnipotent power—the power of a god.

Magnus was tempted to think his father had gone insane, but there was no madness in his steady gaze right now. His sight was clear and focused, if obsessed. The king truly believed in the Kindred and he believed in the existence of Watchers. Until recently, Magnus had not shared this belief. But the proof of magic, of *elementia*, lay in this very bed. He'd seen it with his own eyes. And if a prophesied sorceress could be real, so too could the Kindred.

"I will leave you to watch over your sister. Inform me immediately if she awakens." The king then departed from Lucia's chambers, leaving Magnus alone with the sleeping princess and his own troubled thoughts.

Her magic is the key.

He was silent for a long time, his gaze focused on the balcony and the bright sunshine this afternoon. Potted olive trees waved gracefully in the warm breeze. He could hear the chirping of birds and could smell the sweet scent of flowers.

Magnus hated it here.

He much preferred the snow and the ice, which was what Limeros was best known for. He liked the cold. It was simple. It was perfect and pristine.

But this golden land was where his father believed he could begin his search for the very essence of elemental magic, not in Limeros. And if this beautiful girl who lay sleeping before him was the key to finding it, Magnus couldn't ignore such knowledge.

With the Kindred in hand, he and Lucia would truly be equals in every way. He didn't dare let himself hope further—that perhaps possessing the Kindred would cause Lucia to look at him differently. Instead, he reflected that if he managed to find this lost treasure, he would prove his full worth to the king and earn his father's complete respect once and for all.

"Wake up, Lucia," he urged. "We'll find the Kindred together—you and me."

His gaze flicked, startled, to Mira, who'd drawn close enough to fill a water goblet. She met his eyes and seemed jolted by the icy glare she received.

"Your highness?"

"Be very careful," he warned in a low voice. "Ears that are too eager to listen to secrets run the risk of being sliced off."

Her face flushed a deep crimson and she turned away from him to scurry back to the far side of the room. A servant had no say in the shaping of her own destiny. But the son of a king—well, that was another matter entirely.

The king wanted the Kindred so he could possess their eternal, omnipotent power. This could prove to be the ultimate test for his son and heir.

For if they truly existed, Magnus decided, gripping Lucia's velvety blankets in his fist, *he* would be the one to find them.

CHAPTER 4

LUCIA

THE SANCTUARY

Lucia remembered the explosion—the screams, the cries. The bodies lying bloody and broken all around her. Dead eyes staring out from heads lying in scarlet puddles. Then darkness fell for so long she thought she was dead and hadn't gone to the peaceful everafter, but to the darklands, the place evil people went when they died—a place of endless torment and despair.

There were times she felt that she had woken, only to be pushed back down into the bottomless depths of sleep again, her mind foggy and uncertain.

She'd desperately prayed to the Goddess Valoria to forgive her . . . to save her . . . but her prayers to the Limerian deity had gone unanswered.

But then, finally, there was a dawning. Rays of sunshine warmed her skin with the heat of a summer's day. And slowly, slowly, she opened her eyes, blinking to clear her vision. The colors were so vivid and bright that she had to shield her eyes until she became used to the unexpected intensity.

Lucia found she wore flowing white silk, a beautiful gown with gold embroidery at the edges of the bodice, as fine as anything the most accomplished dressmaker could create.

A lush meadow spread out for miles all around her. Above stretched a glorious cerulean sky. The scent of wildflowers filled the warm air. A cluster of fragrant trees laden with fruit and blossoms stood to her right. Soft grass and moss pressed against her palms as she pushed herself up enough to take in her surroundings with growing shock.

At first glance, the meadow appeared to be like any other, but it was not. Several of the trees that looked similar to willows shimmered as if made from crystal, the branches sweeping to the ground like delicate glass feathers. Other trees appeared to bear golden fruit from branches adorned with jewel-like leaves. The grass was not only emerald green, but was swirled together with silver and gold as if each blade had been dipped in precious metal.

To her distant left were rolling green hills—beyond which was a city that appeared to be built entirely from crystal and light. Closer to the meadow were two beautifully carved white stone wheels set into the earth facing each other, each the height of three grown men, sparkling in the daylight as if coated in diamonds.

It was all so strange and beautiful that for a long, breathless moment she couldn't look away.

"Where am I?" she whispered.

"Welcome to the Sanctuary, princess."

Her head whipped back in the direction of the trees to see that a young man now approached. She fought to rise to her feet as quickly as possible, scrambling back from him a few steps.

"Stay back!" He'd surprised her, and her heart now beat like a wild thing trapped in her chest. "Don't come any closer."

"I mean you no harm."

Why would she believe him? She clenched her fist and summoned fire magic. Her hand burst into flame.

"I don't know you. Stop right where you are or I swear I will defend myself!"

He did as she asked, now only five paces from her. He cocked his head and studied her hand as if fascinated. "Fire magic is the most unpredictable piece of *elementia*. You should be careful how you choose to wield it."

"And you should be careful whom you approach unannounced if you don't want to get burned."

She tried to sound calm, but he had taken her by surprise. Now all she could do was stare at the single most beautiful boy she'd seen in her entire life. Tall and lean, with golden skin, his hair burnished bronze, his eyes the color of dark silver. He wore a loose white shirt and white pants and he stood barefoot upon the soft, shimmering grass.

"I witnessed what you did to the witch when your powers fully awakened," he said casually, as if they were having a regular conversation. "The king's mistress tried to force you to use your *elementia* in her presence. You reduced her to ash."

She felt a wave of nausea at the mention of Sabina's horrific death. The stench of burning flesh still haunted her. "How is it possible you witnessed such a thing?"

"You'd be surprised what I know about you, princess." His voice was liquid gold, and it caused a shiver to race through her. "My name is Alexius. I am one of those known to mortals as Watchers. I've . . . *watched* over you since you were an infant."

"Watcher." The word caught in her throat and her gaze snapped to his. "You're a *Watcher*?"

"Yes."

She shook her head. "I don't believe in such stories."

"They're not stories." He frowned. "Well, I suppose they *are* stories, but that doesn't mean they're not true. Believe me, princess, I'm very real. Every bit as real as you are."

Impossible. He was far too *unreal*, just as this meadow was. She'd never seen anything like him before in her life.

She kept her fist clenched and burning. "And this place? You said it's the Sanctuary?"

He glanced around before his gaze again locked with hers. "This is only a copy of what my home looks like. I'm visiting you in your dreams. I needed to see you, to introduce myself, and to tell you that I can be of assistance to you. I have wanted to do this for so long, but I'm very happy to finally meet you face-to-face."

Then he smiled—such a genuine, open, beautiful smile—and Lucia's heart skipped a beat.

No. She couldn't let herself be distracted by such things. Her head swam with what he'd said so far, and his very presence had her off-balance.

In Limeros, only books that held facts, that held solid truths, were permitted by the king in the palace to educate his children. But Lucia had been born with a desire for knowledge of all kinds, beyond that which was allowed. She'd managed to get her hands on forbidden childhood storybooks, in which she'd learned the legends of Watchers and the Sanctuary. She'd read the stories about their ability to enter the dreams of mortals. But that was all they were—only stories.

This couldn't be real. Could it?

"If you've watched over me for as long as you say—" It seemed utterly impossible that he had. He couldn't be much older than she was. "Then why have you only introduced yourself now?"

"It wasn't the right time before." His lips quirked. "Although, believe me, of those of my kind, I am *not* the most patient. It's been difficult to wait, but I'm introducing myself now. I can help you, princess—and you can help me."

He spoke nonsense. If he really was a Watcher, an immortal being who lived in a world apart from that of mortals, why would he need the help of a sixteen-year-old girl?

Then again, she realized, she was no regular sixteen-year-old girl, as she'd readily proven by setting her fist ablaze with a mere thought.

"I don't believe anything you say to me." She put as much conviction into her words as she could muster, even though she had a sudden desire to learn as much as she could about Alexius. "Watchers—they're only legend, and this . . . *this* is just a silly dream. I'm dreaming you, that's all. You're nothing but a figment of my imagination."

She'd never realized her imagination was this incredible.

Alexius crossed his arms, studying her with both interest and an edge of frustration, but didn't attempt to get any closer. He looked again at her clenched fist, which continued to burn like a torch. It caused her no discomfort, only a slight warm sensation. "I thought this would be easier."

She laughed at that, the sound raw in her throat. "There's nothing easy about this, Alexius. I want to wake up. I want out of this dream."

But how could it be a dream when it felt so real? She could smell the flowers, she felt the ground beneath beneath her bare feet, the damp sponginess of the moss, the ticklish spears of grass. No dream had ever been this vivid. And what was that crystal city just over the hill? There was nothing like it in the mortal world—or like this strange and magical meadow. She would have heard of something so astonishing. Even in the books describing the legends about Watchers, she'd never seen an illustration or description of such a city.

He followed her line of sight. "That is where we live."

Lucia's gaze snapped back to his and her breath caught. "Then why aren't I there? Why am I here in this meadow?"

Alexius briefly scanned the area. "This is where I fell asleep so I could find you in my dreams. It's private here and quiet. Very few know I like to come here."

She began to pace in short, quick lines, her white skirts swishing, so long that they nearly tripped her up. She focused all her attention on Alexius, half expecting him to lunge forward and attack her at any moment. For him to peel back his handsome face and reveal something horrific and ugly beneath. Perhaps he was a demon keeping her asleep and trapped in nightmares—she'd once read of such a thing, although, again, it was in a child's book of stories she'd read quickly before tucking it away beneath her bed so no one would see it.

Fine. If she was stuck here, she needed to talk. She needed answers to questions that bubbled up in her throat—about the strange and alluring Alexius, about everything.

"How old are you?"

His brows rose, as if he hadn't expected this question. "Old."

"You don't look old."

"None of us do." His amused expression had begun to enrage her. There was nothing amusing about this. "You can put out the fire, princess. I mean you no harm today, I assure you."

Her hand continued to burn. With a focused thought, she made the flames higher and brighter. She would take orders from no one, especially not some imaginary boy from her dreams.

It only made Alexius's smile grow. "Very well, have it your way. Perhaps if you see for yourself—even in the confines of this dream—what I am, you might begin to believe it. This is only our first meeting. There will be others."

An unbidden shiver of anticipation slid up her spine. "Not if I have anything to say about it. I will wake soon and you'll be gone."

"Perhaps. But mortals need to sleep every day, don't they? You won't be able to escape me quite that easily, princess."

Lucia glared at him but had to admit it was a point well made.

"Watch me." He stepped backward and raised his hands to his sides. There was a swirling around him, blurring his image for a moment, the air shifting, shimmering, turning.

The next moment, his arms were wings, his skin sporting golden feathers that shone beneath the sunlight. With a flap of these wings, he took flight.

He was a hawk, one who soared high into the clear blue sky. Amazed, Lucia shielded her eyes from the bright light, unable to look away—and noticed her fire had extinguished without her even realizing it.

Finally, he came to perch in a nearby tree, laden with golden apples. Both hesitant and fascinated, she drew closer and studied him, surprised that his eyes had remained the exact same shade of dark silver.

"This proves nothing," she told the hawk, but her heart pounded hard and fast. "Anything can happen in a dream. It doesn't make it real."

He let go of the branch with his sharp talons, but before he touched the ground he had shifted back into the form of a young man. He looked down at himself.

"Usually when we shift form, we don't retain our clothing—feathers become flesh, flesh becomes feathers. It's the only difference you would note in the waking world."

Heat touched her cheeks at the suggestion that he would currently be completely nude if she was awake. "Then I suppose I should be thankful this is only a dream."

"You know this is real because you know who you are, what you are. Your destiny is tied to the Sanctuary, princess. It's tied to the Watchers, to the Kindred." He boldly drew closer, his gaze intensifying. "Your destiny is tied to *me*, and it always has been."

His nearness disturbed her and, for a moment, made it impossible to concentrate or speak.

She realized there was substance and truth to what he said. Her body might be lying unconscious in a bed, but her mind, her spirit . . . they were here.

"You've watched me because of the prophecy," she said.

A frown creased his brow as he studied her, as if memorizing her features. "Yes. You are the sorceress I've been waiting a millennium for."

"That *you've* been waiting for?"

Alexius nodded. "Many didn't believe, but I did. And I waited until you came into your magic before I could talk to you. To guide you. To help you." He was silent until she, again, looked up to meet his silver eyes directly. "Your magic is far too powerful for you right now and it's only growing stronger by the day. You don't even realize it yet."

"Oh, believe me," she said quietly, "I'm very aware of how powerful it is."

Her father, King Gaius, had her use her newfound magic to break down the protective warding on the entrance to the Auranian castle after a bloody battle outside the City of Gold's walls. It rose up like a fiery dragon before her, and the combination of the warding's magic and her own *elementia* had caused the explosion that killed so many people.

"Will I ever wake?" she whispered. "Or will I die in my sleep as punishment for what I've done?"

"You were not meant to die in your sleep. This much I know for sure."

Relief rose within her at his words. "How do you know?"

"Because we need you. Your magic will make the difference to us, to the Sanctuary."

"How?"

Alexius tore his gaze from hers to scan the meadow, his expression growing strained. "The elemental magic that exists here, that has been trapped within my world like sand in an hourglass, has been slipping away ever since the Kindred were stolen from us and lost. Ever since the last sorceress ceased to exist—the sorceress who had the exact same magic as you have. Her name was Eva and she was also an immortal Watcher."

"Eva is my middle name," Lucia said, surprised.

"Yes, it is. And it was Eva who gave the prophecy with her last breath before she died—that the next sorceress would be born in a thousand years—a mortal girl who would wield *elementia* as she could. It is you. King Gaius knew of this prophecy all this time. He knew what you were to become. That is why he raised you as his own daughter."

Lucia's mind tripped over itself in an effort to keep up with him. "What happened to Eva? How could an immortal Watcher die?"

"She made a mistake that cost her life."

"What?"

A sad smile tugged at the corner of his mouth. "She fell in love with the wrong boy—a mortal hunter who led her astray and away from her home and those who protected her. He destroyed her."

Lucia realized that she'd drawn even closer to Alexius without realizing it, so close that when he turned to face her again his sleeve brushed her arm. Despite this being a dream, she swore she felt the heat of his skin against hers.

She took a shaky step back from him.

Lucia had always been one to soak up books and information, her mind hungry for more than her tutors wanted to teach her. And no one seemed to know much about *elementia*, since magic was mostly considered legend, apart from some accused witches. Even Sabina, who proclaimed herself to be a witch, had shown no true sign of magic to Lucia—at least, not enough to defend herself when Lucia had protected herself and Magnus from that evil woman.

You didn't have to kill her, a little voice said inside of her. The same voice that had tortured her ever since it happened. The memory of Sabina's lifeless, charred body dropping to the floor flooded through her mind yet again.

"Tell me more, Alexius," Lucia whispered. "Tell me everything."

He raked a hand through his bronze hair, his expression growing uncertain. "It was a long time ago that Eva lived. Memories of her grow unclear, even for me."

"But it was a thousand years ago that she gave the prophecy with her last breath. Didn't you say that?"

"Yes. The same time the Kindred were lost to us."

Her breath caught. "You have unclear memories of a sorceress who lived and breathed a thousand years ago. How old are you?"

"I already told you, princess. Old."

"Yes, but exactly *how* old?"

He hesitated, but only briefly. "Two thousand years."

She stared at him in shock. "You're not old. You're an ancient relic."

He raised an eyebrow, a smile tugging again at his lips. "And you are sixteen mortal years. A mere child."

"I'm not a child!"

"You are."

Lucia groaned with frustration. Such arguments were getting her nowhere, as were thoughts of how it was possible a two-thousand-year-old Watcher could appear so young and attractive—more so than any other boy she'd ever known. She had to focus on gaining more knowledge, more information that could help her. She pointed toward the city. "I want to go there. I want to talk to someone, someone whose memories aren't unclear about what exactly happened with the last sorceress, who she was, what she did . . . anything!"

"That's impossible, princess. This is a dream, and like I said, this is only a copy of what is real. And even if it wasn't, mortals do not enter the Sanctuary, just as Watchers do not leave it, unless in the form of a hawk."

This might be a real conversation, but it was still within the confines of a dream. What she saw before her had no more weight in reality than a painting or sketch. She thought of Alexius's hawk form and how he used it to travel to the mortal world to spy on her. It was an unsettling thought that he'd been watching her since she was only a baby.

"It is such a gift to take the form of something that can fly," she finally said.

"A gift," he said softly, and something sharp and pained in his voice tugged at her heart. "Or a curse. I suppose it depends entirely on how you look at it."

She frowned, uncertain about his shift in tone. "You drew me into this dream because you say you can help me. How? Or is that unclear for you too?"

She did not mean to sound petulant, but she couldn't help it. He hadn't told her anything helpful, only tantalizing bits of information that had no solid use. Alexius's face turned to the left, his brow creasing deeply. "Someone is here."

She looked around. They were alone. "Who?"

Finally, his expression relaxed. "It's my friend, Phaedra. She means us no harm. She probably wonders where I disappeared to."

"Another Watcher?"

"Yes, of course. She's helping with the search for information, part of what we have to—"

The next moment he vanished. One moment he was there, the following he was gone.

Lucia turned around in a circle, alarmed. "Alexius?"

And then the meadow, the Sanctuary, were gone, disappearing like broken glass falling away and leaving only darkness behind.

CHAPTER 5

JONAS

AURANOS

Hawk's Brow, the largest city in Auranos, was an excellent place to witness the true effect of having the King of Blood on the throne.

It was also a great spot for two rebels to seed some revolution before heading back to their camp in the rough forests of the Wildlands.

"Look at them," Jonas said to Brion as they moved down the side of the road in the heart of the vibrant business district—shiny taverns, luxurious inns, and shops selling all sorts of wares, from flowers to jewelry to clothing. "Going about business as usual."

"Auranians are certainly . . ." Brion paused to find the right word. "Adaptable?"

"Gullible's more like it. It's sickening." A boy about their age strode past them and Jonas called out to him. "Do you live here?"

The young man had blond hair. He was dressed in the finest silk, a tunic the color of emeralds and decorated with gold-threaded details.

"I do," the boy said, frowning as he swept his gaze over the pair's torn and dusty cloaks. "You're . . . not from around here, are you?"

Jonas crossed his arms. "We've come to Hawk's Brow in search of information about how the people of this fine city are dealing with the new king."

The boy's gaze darted to others passing them by without second glances, and then to the far right where there were two of the king's uniformed soldiers patrolling the next crossroads.

"Do you work for King Gaius?" he asked.

"Consider us independent researchers," Brion replied.

The boy shifted his feet nervously. "I can only speak for myself, but I am more than happy to welcome a new ruler to Auranos. I have heard of his speech last week and all the wonderful promises he made—about the construction of the road and the betrothal of his son to Princess Cleiona. We're all very excited about the royal wedding next month."

"Do you believe it's a good match?" Jonas asked.

His expression grew thoughtful. "I do. And, if you ask me, the princess should be thanking the goddess for such a lofty betrothal. It shows that King Gaius is willing to put aside hard feelings for a smooth transition to his rule. He puts his new citizens first. And, really, not much has changed despite the"—again, his gaze moved toward the soldiers in red—"increased presence of his men."

Not much has changed. Perhaps not for someone who spent his pampered life with his head stuck up his own arse. Jonas and Brion had talked to many in this city since they arrived yesterday and most had had the same response as this fool. Life had been easy before, and they believed if they did as King Gaius instructed and didn't cause problems, life would continue on that way indefinitely.

"Are you aware of a growing rebel presence in Auranos?" Brion asked.

The boy's brows drew together. "Rebels? We don't want any problems like that."

"I didn't ask if you wanted problems, but if you'd heard of them."

"I have heard of a few scattered rebel groups—both Auranian and Paelsian—causing difficulties. Destroying property, inciting riots."

Inciting riots? Brion and Jonas exchanged a curious glance.

Such rumors sounded as if the rebels were aimless in their goals. They were not. Everything Jonas chose to do—be it property destruction, poaching for food, or stealing a ready supply of weapons for practice and protection—was to create a stronger group of rebels who would be ready to rise up fully against the king when the time was right. He also focused much of his attention on recruiting new rebels to enter his ranks.

Jonas's main reason to journey to Hawk's Brow was to source new recruits. As the largest city in Auranos, less than a half day's journey from the City of Gold, it was a key area where Jonas knew he needed rebel support. Just that morning, Jonas had convinced a young and pretty Hawk's Brow maiden to join their cause, and to await his future instructions. The riots this boy spoke of, though, must be the work of other factions—perhaps even Auranians. It was a good indication that they weren't all as useless as this one.

The boy continued, "I've also heard that any rebels who are captured are put to death. What sane person would ever want to join their ranks?" His gaze then shifted with growing alarm between the two boys, as if realization had finally dawned on him with whom he spoke. "I, uh, really must be on my way. I hope you enjoy the rest of your day."

"Oh, we will," Jonas called after him as he scurried away without another word. "We certainly will."

"Definitely *not* rebel material," Brion murmured.

"Perhaps one day, but not today. He hasn't seen nearly enough hardship."

"He actually smelled like jasmine and citrus. Who smells like jasmine and citrus?"

"Certainly not you," Jonas said, laughing. "When was the last time you . . ." His words trailed off as he saw a fresco on the side of a building of King Gaius's handsome face. The words STRENGTH, FAITH, and WISDOM—the Limerian credo—were in the mosaic below, along with the larger word TOGETHER.

"He's doing it," Jonas grumbled. "That bastard is fooling them into submission with his shiny speeches and pretty promises. They don't realize that he'd happily destroy them at his whim."

"Hey, where are you going?" Brion called after him as Jonas marched across the road toward the mural. The artist must have just finished, for the plaster was still wet. Jonas began to tear at it, smearing what could be smeared and crumbling the dry parts away in his hands.

"Jonas, we should go," Brion cautioned him.

"I won't let him win. We need to show everyone what a liar he is." His fingers had quickly begun to bleed from the effort.

"We will. I mean, we *are*. We're going to make a difference." Brion looked nervously over his shoulder at the people that were gathering to see the vandalism of the king's mural. "Remember those Auranian rebels who lost their heads last week?"

Jonas's hands stilled. He'd managed to destroy the king's face completely. It was very satisfying to wipe away the smug expression. He longed to do it in real life. "Yes."

"Let's not join them, all right? And on that note, let's start running."

Jonas's gaze whipped to the right to see that several guards were drawing closer, their swords in hand.

"Stop!" one shouted at them. "In the name of the king!"

Running was definitely a good suggestion.

"Your new king lies to you all!" Jonas yelled at the crowd as he and Brion darted past them. A girl with long dark hair and light-brown eyes studied him curiously and he directed his next words at her. "The King of Blood will pay for his crimes against Paelsia! Do you stand next to a deceitful tyrant or do you stand with me and my rebels?"

If he could change just one mind today, then it would be worth it.

The guards stayed on Jonas and Brion's tail as they tore down cobblestone streets, along narrow alleyways, barely avoiding the carriages and horses of wealthy Hawk's Brow residents. With each sharp turn, Jonas thought they might have lost their pursuers, but the guards were not so easily evaded.

"This way," Brion urged, grabbing Jonas's arm and pulling him down a side street next to a small tavern.

But there was no exit. The two came to a staggering halt at the stone wall blocking their path and turned to face the three armed guards. A hawk on the tavern's roof took off in flight.

"Couple of troublemakers," a guard growled. "Now we get to make an example out of the two of you."

"You're arresting us?" Brion asked hopefully.

"And give you a chance to escape? No. Only your heads will be making the journey back to the palace with us. The rest of you can stay right here and rot." He smiled, showing off a broken tooth. His compatriots chuckled.

"Wait," Brion began, "we can figure something—"

"Kill them," the lead guard instructed, stepping back.

Jonas grappled for the jeweled dagger he kept at his waist—the very same dagger Lord Aron had used to take Jonas's brother's life—but it would be little use against three sharp swords. Still, if he would die today, he would take at least one of these brutes with him. He gripped the dagger tightly. Brion clutched another blade in his hand as the two guards approached, their hulking forms blocking the sunlight.

Then both guards staggered forward, their expressions registering pain and confusion. They fell forward, hitting the ground hard. Sticking out of each of their backs was a deeply embedded arrow. The third guard spun around, his sword raised. There was a sickening sound and he, too, fell to the ground, an arrow protruding from his throat.

A girl stood at the entrance to the alleyway. As she lowered her bow, Jonas realized it was the same girl he had seen in the crowd earlier, but now he noticed that she wore the tunic and trousers of a boy. Her dark hair hung in a thick braid down her back.

"You said you're rebels. Is this true?"

Jonas just stared at her, dumbfounded. "Who are you?"

"Answer my question first and I might tell you."

He exchanged a look with Brion, whose eyes were wide as saucers. "Yes. We're rebels."

"And you mentioned Paelsia. You're Paelsian?" She swept her gaze over them. "Well, that should be obvious by how you're dressed. Not nearly enough tailored silk between you to pass for Auranians. Tell me, though . . . do you nearly get yourselves killed every day?"

"Not *every* day," Brion said.

The girl checked over her shoulder. "We should move. There are plenty of guards in this city, and they will soon wonder what happened to their friends, especially when they hear of the fate of the King of Blood's mural." She looked at Jonas. "Nice work there. Messy, but effective."

"I'm glad you approve. Now, who are you?"

She shoved her bow into the holder strapped to her back and pulled her cloak to cover it and her boy's attire. "My name is Lysandra Barbas and I, too, am Paelsian. I've traveled across Paelsia and Auranos looking for rebels. Looks like I've finally found a couple."

"Do you need our help?" Jonas asked.

She looked at him as if he might be stupid. "Clearly, you need *my* help. I'm joining your group. Now come on, we can't stay here."

Lysandra turned and began walking swiftly away from the alley, leaving the bodies of the three guards behind without another glance.

Before Jonas realized what he was doing, he was following her, Brion jogging alongside him to keep up to their fast pace.

"Lysandra," Jonas said. "Are you sure you know what you're saying? The life of a rebel is dangerous and uncertain. You're very good with a bow and arrow"—*amazing, actually*—"but where we make camp in the Wildlands, it's not safe or secure. They're a dangerous place, even for us."

She turned on him, her eyes flashing. "Is this about me being a girl? Don't you have any female rebels?"

"A few," Jonas admitted.

"I'll fit in just fine, then."

"Don't get me wrong, we're thankful for your interference back there—"

"Interference?" She cut him off before he'd managed to get an entire sentence out. "I saved your lives."

She wasn't exaggerating. Those guards would have executed both him and Brion on the spot if she hadn't interfered. He had come to Hawk's Brow seeking new recruits and Lysandra appeared to be full of potential. Still, there was something about her that made him hesitate.

That fire in both her eyes and her words—it wasn't something shared by every Paelsian. Jonas's own sister Felicia was a fighter, a warrior when necessary, but Lysandra's passion and willingness to fight was as rare as diamonds.

Still, his gut told him—rather loudly, in fact—that Lysandra Barbas would be trouble.

"How old are you?" he asked.

"Seventeen."

Same as both Jonas and Brion. "And where is your family? Do they know you're off seeking a life of danger?"

"My family is dead."

The words were delivered flatly and without emotion, but they still made Jonas wince.

"King Gaius's men came to my village to recruit everyone to work on a road he's started to build," she explained. "When we said no, they came back and burned my village to the ground. They butchered almost everyone who tried to run away. Those who lived were enslaved and carted off to one of the road camps. For all I know, I was the only one who managed to escape."

King Gaius's road—the one he'd announced during his speech a week ago. "When was this?"

"Two weeks ago. I've barely slept since. I've tried to keep moving, keep searching. Most in Paelsia are so accepting of fate—of destiny. It sickens me. Those here in Auranos are delusional, thinking King Gaius isn't as bad as his reputation. They're wrong—all of them. Now that I've found you, I can join your numbers and help to free our countrymen."

Jonas swallowed hard, his chest tight. His feet pounded against the ground as they continued to put distance between them and the dead guards. "I'm sorry for your loss."

"Don't be sorry. I'm here and I'm ready to fight against the King of Blood. I want to see him suffer. I want to see him lose his precious crown and have his world burn to the ground as he dies screaming. That's what I want."

"That's what we all want. My rebels are ready to make a difference and we're—"

"*Your* rebels," Lysandra said sharply. "Are you saying you're the leader?"

"Of our group, yes."

"What's your name?"

"Jonas Agallon."

Her eyes widened. "I've heard of you. Everyone in Paelsia knows your name."

Yes, the murder of his brother Tomas—the inciting incident that brought about King Gaius's bid for war against the Auranians with naive Paelsians fighting at his side—had made both their names well known throughout the land. His fingers brushed against the jeweled dagger he held on to only so he could one day use it to end Lord Aron's life.

Lysandra flicked a glance at Brion. "And who are you?"

He smiled eagerly. "Brion Radenos."

She frowned. "I've never heard of you."

Brion's expression fell. "Well, not yet. I will be famous one day too."

"I have no doubt." Her attention returned to Jonas. "What have your rebels been focused on?"

He eyed the alleyway they swiftly moved past, but there were no guards lying in wait for them. "We're recruiting all over Pael-sia and Auranos—there are nearly fifty of us now. We're causing trouble where we can, so the king knows we're here and that we're a growing threat. And while we are in Auranos we're spreading the word to the citizens that the king is a liar and they shouldn't so easily buy in to his promises."

"Your group hasn't made a move on the king himself?"

"Not yet." The memory of the three rebels' heads mounted on spikes haunted him, a tight, hard knot in his gut. He wanted to do whatever it took to defeat the king, but to lose anyone—to have them suffer and die at his command . . .

It would be like seeing Tomas's murder again and again, and being personally responsible for it this time.

"Destroying murals and recruiting potential rebels isn't going to defeat King Gaius." Her steps finally slowed and she chewed her bottom lip, as if deep in thought. "He's enslaving our people to build his road. Our Paelsian brothers and sisters throughout our land are being forced to work for him against their will—or they're being murdered for trying to resist."

"I had not heard of this." The thought of such an atrocity made him see red. "The king spoke of the Imperial Road in his speech as if it would unite all of Mytica as one people, and Auranians are lapping it up like cream offered to a housecat."

"Auranians are idiots." She cast a glance around them. They now stood on the side of a busy street, away from the swell of the crowd. A busy fruit market was fifty paces away. "They deserve a king like this forced upon them, but Paelsians do not. What else did he say in this speech?" She looked at Brion for this information.

"He announced the betrothal between Prince Magnus and Princess Cleiona," Brion told her.

Her eyes widened. "So, the golden princess is cozying up to the enemy rather than risking a single day of her pampered lifestyle, is she?"

"She's not," Jonas said under his breath.

"Not what?"

"The princess is not cozying up to the enemy. The betrothal wasn't—couldn't have been her idea. The Damora family destroyed her life, killed her father, and stole her throne."

"And now she's been welcomed into that family, with a gilded roof over her head and attendants to serve her breakfast in bed and see to her every need."

"I disagree."

"You can disagree, but it doesn't change anything. I don't care a fig for Princess Cleiona. What I care about is my people—my brother, those from my village, and every other Paelsian who's been enslaved. We must mount an attack on the road immediately! If you want to show the king that we're a threat, as you said, that we're a force to be reckoned with, this is how to do it. We free the slaves and destroy any progress that's been made."

"We?" Jonas repeated.

Her cheeks were flushed from her vehemence. "Yes, we."

"Would you be so kind, Lysandra, as to give me a moment to discuss matters with Brion?" He nodded toward the nearby line of fruit-selling stalls. "We'll meet you over there shortly."

"You will take me to your rebel camp?" she persisted.

He didn't speak for a moment, just studied this wildcat who'd saved his life and shown her remarkable skill as an archer. He wanted to tell her to go away and not cause him any additional problems—since it was clear to him that she would be difficult to deal with. But he couldn't. He needed passionate rebels, no matter who they were.

"Yes, I will."

She finally smiled, a bright and attractive expression that lit up her entire face. "Glad to hear it. We're going to make a difference. Just you wait and see."

Without further comment, Lysandra turned and walked swiftly to the market. When she was out of earshot, Jonas turned to Brion.

Brion met his gaze. "That girl . . ."

"I know. She's a handful."

His friend flashed him a big grin. "I think I'm in love!"

Jonas couldn't help but laugh. "Oh, no. Don't do it, Brion. Don't fall for her. She's only going to be trouble."

"I hope so. I like trouble when it looks like that." Brion sobered. "What about her plan to attack the road?"

Jonas shook his head, thinking of the dead rebels' blood trickling down the wooden stakes in the palace square. "Too dangerous right now. I can't risk losing any of us until we know we have a fighting chance. What she's proposing would mean death to too many."

Brion's jaw tensed. "You're right."

"But I do need more information—about the road, about the king's plans. The more we know, the more we can do to stop him. And when we find that weakness, we'll exploit it." A fresh fire had lit under his skin at the thought of enslaved Paelsians. "I swear I'll take him down, Brion. But right now, we're completely deaf and blind to his agenda unless he announces everything in a speech. I need eyes and ears in that palace."

"A few spies would be essential. Agreed. But what's to keep them from being discovered and getting their heads mounted on spikes?"

"A good spy would have to be undetectable. A guard, or someone posing as a Limerian guard."

Brion shook his head. "Again, head on spike. It would be a suicide mission so soon after King Gaius's victory. Sorry."

Jonas worked it over in his mind. An idea that had been gestating since the day after Auranos fell took firmer hold. "Then it would have to be someone already in the palace. Someone close to the king and the prince . . ."

CHAPTER 6

CLEO

AURANOS

As the date of her dreaded wedding drew closer, Cleo's anxiety grew. She dreamed of escape—of growing wings like a bird and flying away from the palace, never to return.

But, alas, she was a bird still locked tightly in her cage. So, instead of dwelling on what awaited her in the weeks to come, she focused on what she could control. Knowledge. Studies. Praying she could find the answers she sought before it was too late. She found herself moving toward the palace library for the second time that day, but this time she encountered Mira sobbing in the hall outside the library's tall doors.

"Mira!" Cleo rushed to her and pulled the girl into her arms. "What's wrong?"

It took a moment, but Cleo's friend finally managed to form words. "I still can't find my brother anywhere! They've killed him, Cleo. I know it!"

Cleo drew her further away from the Limerian guards that

seemed to lurk in every shadow, instructed, she knew, to keep a close eye on the princess lest she stray from the castle.

"Nic's not dead," Cleo assured her, tugging Mira's hands away from her tear-streaked face.

"How do you know?"

"Because if he was, Magnus would have been certain to rub it in. For me to know that Nic had been executed for what he did in Paelsia . . ." Even the very thought of it was like a hot poker shoved through her heart. "He knows it would destroy me. And he wouldn't hesitate to use it against me. I know we haven't been able to find Nic yet, but he's alive, Mira." *He's got to be,* she thought.

Her words were sinking in. Slowly, Mira regained control and stopped crying. She rubbed her eyes wearily, a trace of anger now lighting within them. "You're right. The prince would celebrate your pain. I hate him, Cleo. I hate it every time he comes to see Princess Lucia. He's a beast."

Cleo had barely seen the prince over the week since he'd chosen to continue this horrible betrothal. It seemed that he wished to have very little to do with Cleo, which was more than fine by her. "I couldn't agree more. Just try to stay out of his way, all right? How did you slip away from Lucia's bedside? I feel as if I haven't seen you in ages."

"The queen is visiting her daughter right now. She told me to leave and return later. Of course, I didn't argue. I'd hoped to find a friendly face in this nest of vipers. Yours is the first I've seen today."

Cleo repressed a smile. Nest of vipers, indeed. "Well, I'm glad for the chance to see you. It's the only good thing that's happened all day."

She stood with her friend at the edge of the hallway, sweeping her gaze over the large portraits of each member of the Bellos family, which lined the hall outside the library doors. She couldn't look away from the painted eyes of her father. Her last memory of him was of his death in her arms from a wound inflicted during the attack on the castle. In his final moments, he'd given her a ring passed down from generation to generation in her family, a ring said to somehow help lead the way to the Kindred. He hoped, with that magic in her possession, she would be able to crush King Gaius and reclaim the throne. But he'd died before he could tell her anything else.

Cleo believed it to be the very same ring rumored to have belonged to the sorceress Eva, the ring that allowed her to touch the Kindred without being corrupted by the endless elemental power of the lost crystals. Cleo had hidden the ring in her chambers behind a loose stone in her wall, and she'd come here to the library every day since, searching for more information to help her figure out her next move. Her father had believed in her so much, far more than she believed in herself. She couldn't let him down now.

Mira touched her arm, her eyes now dry. "You're trying to be so strong, but I *know*, Cleo. I know how much you miss him. How much you miss Emilia. I miss them too. It's all right to let yourself cry. I'm here for you."

Cleo swallowed hard, her heart swelling to know that she had a friend who understood her pain. "I try not to look upon their faces for too long when I come by here. When I see them, I . . ." She exhaled shakily. "It so strange. Sometimes I can't see anything past the darkness of my grief. Other times I'm angry, *so* angry that they left me to deal with all this on my own. And I know how selfish that sounds, but I can't help how I feel. So, don't you see? I can't let myself cry. If I cry again I might not ever be able to stop."

"You should know, princess . . ." Aron's voice cut between them as effectively as the edge of a blade. "The king has instructed that these portraits—apart from the one of you, of course—are to be taken down and replaced with those of the Damoras."

Cleo spun to face yet another lurker in the shadows. That was what Aron did now that their engagement was called off. *Lurk.*

She had hoped he would go away, back to his parents' villa elsewhere in the City of Gold, but it appeared that he had moved into the palace permanently.

"And will you do it yourself?" she asked, her words twisting. "I know, as the king's new lap dog, you will do anything he asks of you for the mere promise of a treat."

He gave her a tight smile. "No, why should I? Since I am fully capable of giving orders of my own. And why wait?" He gestured toward the two red-uniformed guards who'd accompanied him. They immediately went to the wall and began to remove the portraits. Mira clutched Cleo's arm as if to prevent her from lurching forward. Fury rose within her like a tidal wave.

She glared at him. "How can you do this, Aron?"

"*Lord* Aron, Cleo. As kingsliege, and since we are no longer betrothed, it will show more respect if you begin to use my proper title."

Of course. *Kingsliege.* The king had gone ahead with his promise to bestow the lofty—but, in Cleo's opinion, meaningless—title on Aron. He was still a "lord," only now it was a title Aron felt he'd earned, rather than inherited through his family line. Everyone of importance in the palace had been required to gather in the throne room for the ceremony yesterday. Now Aron wore his new status like a suit of armor, shiny protection against anything that might attempt to hurt him.

It sickened her. He acted as if he'd been born with Limerian blood running through his veins. Once, Cleo might have dismissed this as merely a necessary survival tactic against the enemy now in power. But Aron did everything asked of him with a smile on his face, as if he relished being one of the King of Blood's trained dogs.

"He finds you an amusement, you know." She couldn't stop herself from speaking her thoughts. "Pray to the goddess that you make yourself invaluable to him before this amusement wears thin."

"I could say the same for you, princess," Aron said evenly.

"What are you going to do with the paintings, *Lord* Aron?" Mira asked with the barest edge of sarcasm detectable in her tone. "Hang them in your chambers?"

There was once a time when Mira had had warm feelings for the handsome lord, but no more. She too saw him for what he truly was. An opportunist who would sell his own mother's soul to a demon from the darklands if it meant he might gain the king's favor.

"They'll be burned," he said simply, and Cleo's heart wrenched. He gave her a smirk. "On the king's orders."

Somehow, the horrible thought that her family's portraits would be destroyed brought a coolness to her, a calm that held power. Her hatred now burned with ice, not fire.

"I'll remember this, Aron."

"*Lord* Aron." As the guards finally yanked Emilia's portrait down from the wall, Aron nodded at them. "Good. Take them outside and leave them by the stables for now. They may as well become coated with filth, just like that idiot friend of yours now is."

"Idiot friend?" Cleo asked quietly. Cautiously.

"That he yet breathes is a constant surprise to me. But knee deep in horse dung is a fair punishment for—"

But she was already walking away down the long hall, pulling Mira with her.

"Cleo?" Mira asked, uncertain. "Where are we going?"

"I think I know where Nic is."

Mira's eyes widened. "Then we must move quickly!"

Ignoring both the shadowy guards and Aron, who now followed them, Cleo and Mira moved swiftly through the castle. She may be little more than a glorified prisoner within these walls, but this was Cleo's home and she knew the labyrinthine hallways better than anyone. As a child, she and Emilia had played hide and seek with their nursemaids—although the nursemaids had never found much amusement in the impromptu games.

They emerged outside into the courtyard, a walled, open-air space in the center of the palace filled with herb gardens, apple and peach trees, and lilac bushes in full bloom that scented the warm evening air with their perfume. The moon was full and bright, lighting their way along the winding cobblestone path.

No one tried to stop Cleo as she pushed open the gate leading out of the courtyard, went down a long hallway, and exited the east side of the castle toward the stables, Mira following close behind. Beyond the stables was the rest of the walled city, home to many thousand Auranian citizens. Here she was as close to freedom as she'd been since King Gaius had destroyed her world and taken her father's throne. She had no doubt that if she attempted to breach the outer palace walls she would be stopped and dragged back inside.

But escape was not her goal tonight.

As they neared the stables, the stench of manure hung heavy in the air. And there she saw him.

"Cleo . . ." Mira whispered, then louder: "Cleo! You're right—he's here!"

Heart in throat, Cleo hurried her pace as the girls rushed toward Nic. A few other stablehands looked on with interest. Nic watched their approach with wide eyes, then dropped the two buckets he carried. They sloshed against the ground. However, before Cleo or Mira could get any closer, the guards closed in and grabbed each of the girls' arms to stop them.

"Unhand me!" Cleo struggled against her captor. "Nic . . . Nic! Are you all right?"

Nic nodded with one firm shake of his head. "I'm fine. You don't know how glad I am to see you two."

"Let me go!" Mira snarled, fighting against the guard who held her in place.

Aron had followed them leisurely and now he approached, his arms crossed over his chest, a lit cigarillo protruding from the fingers of one hand. "Well, seems that I have revealed a little secret, haven't I? Doesn't matter, I suppose. It won't change anything."

"You don't think so?" Cleo retorted. "Now that I know where Nic is I'll make sure he's released from these lowly labors!"

"You confuse yourself with someone who still has great power here, princess."

"And you confuse yourself with someone who has *any*."

"Working knee deep in horse shit is his punishment. Although, if you ask me, he should be dead for what he did to Prince Magnus."

The memory tore through her mind before she could try to stop it. Theon's broken body, his eyes staring upward, unseeing. Magnus with blood on his face from where she'd clawed him as he tried to wrench her to her feet. Nic, throwing a rock to stop him, which met its mark. Cleo had taken a heavy sword and very nearly plunged it into the prince's chest while he was disoriented, but Nic feared the ultimate repercussions of such an act and stopped her. He'd knocked Magnus out cold so he couldn't follow them.

I'm so sorry, Theon. I'm so . . . so sorry. I led you to your death, and then couldn't avenge you.

Her eyes burned, but she didn't cry. She needed Theon's memory, the recollection of his strength, his confident belief in her, to aid her now. Tears wouldn't help. Commands wouldn't help. Aron was right, she had no power here anymore. No influence.

However . . .

She turned toward Aron—this time with a smile.

"Come on, Aron," she almost purred. "You were once our friend—our *good* friend. Can't you find that within yourself again? Not everything has changed, has it? Mira thought her brother was dead. Don't keep them apart. Please."

Aron might have expected rage from her but clearly didn't know what to do with cordiality. He hesitated for a moment, nonplussed, before he finally nodded at the guard who held Mira. The guard released her and Mira ran directly into Nic's arms.

"We couldn't find you anywhere," she said, choked. "I was so worried about you!"

"Oh, Mira." Nic gripped his sister tightly, snorting softly into her long hair. "Honestly? I was worried about me too."

She pulled back from him a little and scrunched her nose. "You stink!"

He laughed out loud at that and ran a hand through his messy and matted red hair. "Glad to see you too, dear sister."

This time, the smile Cleo gave Aron was sincere. "Thank you."

He watched the siblings with a sour look. "Remember this favor, Cleo. You owe me one."

She fought to hold on to her pleasant expression. "Of course, *Lord* Aron."

Aron smiled, pleased, at this.

It was good to know she could easily handle this fool when necessary.

The guards accompanied Cleo back to her chambers and closed the door behind her. She knew one would remain stationed outside until morning in case she even thought of escaping. There had been times she'd scaled the ivy outside her sister's balcony to leave the castle, but in her own chambers, it was a sheer drop from her window to the ground thirty feet below.

The king might acknowledge her as a "guest of honor" publicly, but at this very moment she felt every bit a prisoner of war. She supposed she should consider herself lucky her own chambers had been returned to her. For days after the battle, they had been given to Lucia until other accommodations for the ailing Limerian princess had been found.

Seeing Nic and Mira reunited, though, had given Cleo a twinge of hope that things could change. She held tight to the knowledge that she'd been right, that Nic still lived. He could use a very long bath, but he was alive.

If she allowed herself to admit it, it *did* surprise her that Magnus had not demanded his head. Did he really think toiling in the stables was the best punishment?

"He's still horrible," she whispered. "But Nic still breathes. I must be grateful for that much."

Her chambers were dark. Her attention slid over to the stone wall by her vanity table, to the very location where she'd hidden the amethyst ring. Her hands itched to take it out and put it on her finger. To feel the coolness of the gold against her skin, the weight of the stone. To have something tangible that might be able to help her. Something tied to her family. To history. To *elementia* itself.

She would return to her search for information tomorrow. There had to be something in the library that would tell her about the ring, help her learn how to properly use it. Emilia had always spent hours upon hours in the library, reading both for pleasure and for knowledge. And Cleo had always avoided such things. Until now. She had hope that somewhere in one of the thousands upon thousands of books that lined the library's shelves lay the answers she sought.

She wrapped her arms around herself and moved to the window to look down on the moonlit courtyard far below. A warm breeze brushed against her skin.

It was then that she sensed the presence of someone else in her room.

Cleo spun around, searching the shadows. "Who's there? Show yourself!"

"Did you have a nice evening, your highness?" His deep voice slid across the room, wrapping itself around her and holding her prone with instant, remembered fear.

She ran for the door, but he caught her before she got there, grabbing hold of her arms and pressing her up against the wall.

"I'll scream," she warned him.

"Screaming would be the wrong move." He pressed one hand against her mouth and with his other hand trapped both her wrists so she couldn't move.

Jonas Agallon smelled like the forest itself, of evergreen needles and warm earth.

She attempted to drive her knee up between his legs, but he avoided this attack effortlessly.

"Come now, princess. It doesn't have to be like this. I only came here for a chat . . . unless you cause me problems." The surface of his words was friendly, but the malevolence behind them was unmistakable. "I'm going to remove my hand now. If you speak in a voice louder than a whisper I promise you'll regret it. Understand?"

She nodded once, willing herself to remain calm.

He pulled his hand away but otherwise didn't loosen his hold on her.

"What do you want?" She kept her voice low and controlled. For now.

"I just stopped by to see how you're doing."

She couldn't help but laugh drily at this. "Really."

Jonas's face was in shadows, his eyes dark as he scanned the length of her. "Last time I saw you, you were cloaked and armed with a dagger."

"Yes, and that was right before you alerted Prince Magnus to my presence in the crowd."

He raised an eyebrow. "I did no such thing."

"And I should believe you? You worked with him before. With the king himself! You kidnapped me, leaving me with no food or water for a week, waiting to hand me over to my enemy."

"It was three days, princess. And you were given food and water. Anyway, my dealings with the King of Blood and his ilk came to an end when he deceived my people."

"Anyone with half a brain could have seen he was deceptive from the very beginning."

He glared at her. "Easy to say that now."

She'd touched a nerve. Perhaps he did feel like a fool for helping King Gaius. "Let go of me."

"I don't trust you. You'll try to scamper off and alert the guards."

Fueled by her success earlier with manipulating Aron, she decided to try the same with Jonas. Anger or demands wouldn't work, that much was certain. She looked up into his dark eyes and worked some pain into her own. "You're hurting me."

Jonas laughed, low and throaty. "Speaking of deceptive . . . trust me, princess, I don't underestimate you either."

Her gaze frantically skimmed her familiar room, searching for anything that might help her. "What am I to think with you here? There was a time you wanted to kill me."

"Believe me, if I were here to end your life, you'd already be dead. I wanted to see for myself how much you've been taken in by them now that you're betrothed to the prince. I witnessed the announcement. Despite the rough beginning, it looks like you've been accepted into the king's family with open arms. How nice for you."

Nausea coursed through her gut that he'd think this; that *anyone* would think this. "You think I'd welcome the inclusion to such an evil family?"

"I don't know." He studied her carefully. "Maybe."

He believed her allied with the vipers themselves. The thought was so foreign that she couldn't wrap her head around it. Venom coated her next words. "I shouldn't have to defend myself to someone like you. What do I care what you think?"

Jonas pressed her harder up against the wall, making her gasp. "I know you think I'm nothing more than a Paelsian savage."

She refused to look away from him. "Are you denying it?"

"I'm no savage, your highness. I'm a rebel." He said it as if he was proud of it. Like it should impress her.

"If that's true, then it's only a matter of time before your head finds its way onto a spike, just like those of your rebel friends."

He flinched at the mention of the executions. "Perhaps. But at least I'm attempting to change things."

"By sneaking into my chambers and trying to bully me? I think I have my share of bullies in this palace to deal with already. I'll say it one more time: let go of me."

Finally, he did as she asked and stepped back. He watched her warily, as if he expected she'd immediately flee to the door and call for the guard. Part of her was tempted to do just that.

Instead, she watched him back just as warily. She couldn't deny that in looks alone, Jonas Agallon was very attractive. Black hair, dark eyes, deeply tanned skin from working outdoors like most Paelsians. A tall, muscular body with broad shoulders and narrow hips. Beneath the dark gray cloak he wore, his clothes were dusty, torn, and simple, but he held himself like no peasant she'd ever seen before.

There was an arrogance to this boy that was similar to that of Prince Magnus—despite their vastly different upbringings. Jonas's eyes weren't as cold and serpentine as the prince's, but they were still sharp and dangerous. They looked as if they could pierce right through her and pin her to the wall as easily as he'd done with his body.

There was a time not so long ago that he'd looked at her as if she was a hateful, spoiled creature who needed to die. Now there was a great deal of suspicion in his gaze, but also an edge of interest, as if he was curious about her plans now that she was betrothed to the son of her greatest enemy.

"Are you aligned with King Gaius?" Jonas asked again, his words harsh.

He was the rudest person she'd ever met. Ruder, possibly, than Prince Magnus himself. "How dare you enter my private chambers and demand answers like this? I'll tell you nothing."

His hands fisted at his sides and his glare intensified. "Princess, you could make this easier for me."

"Oh, yes, that's exactly what I want to do. Because you've always been such a good friend to me."

Her sardonic tone coaxed the barest edge of a smile to his lips. "I *could* be a good friend."

She went completely silent for a moment. "How?"

"That depends entirely on you, your highness."

Jonas used the title as an insult, with no respect implied whatsoever, just as he had when he'd taken her captive in Paelsia. This much had not changed. "Talk quickly, or soon you'll be trapped in the palace with no chance for escape. The guards will begin patrolling the courtyard very soon now that night has fallen."

Jonas swept his gaze through the small room, coming to rest on the canopied bed. "Then I would have to stay here for the night, wouldn't I? Would you help to hide me away under your covers?"

She ignored the heat that touched her cheeks at the suggestion. "Continue speaking nonsense and your time continues to drain away. Talk. *Now.*"

"Always issuing orders. Is that what a princess who's lost her kingdom still does—or the future bride of Prince Magnus? Does it make you feel powerful to boss me around?"

"Enough of this." She turned toward the door and opened her mouth as if to shout.

Jonas was behind her in an instant, his hand coming over her mouth, his arm across her chest to pull her tightly back against his body. "Summon the guards and I'll tell them I'm your secret lover. What would Prince Magnus think about that? Would he be jealous?"

She bit his hand hard enough to taste blood. He pulled away from her, his eyes wide with pain even as a grin curled up the corner of his mouth.

Cleo wiped her mouth with the back of her hand. "You need to know one thing. I don't care *what* Prince Magnus thinks, nor will I ever. I hate him and I hate his father. No matter what happens to me, that much will never change."

"You want to destroy them."

It wasn't a question. Cleo just stared at him, unblinking. Unspeaking. Admitting anything at all to this boy felt far too dangerous.

But he didn't seem to need any confirmation. He nodded once. "I told you that day in the crowd to be ready. It's time, princess. I need your help."

The thought was absurd. "You need *my* help?"

"The rebels need information about the Damoras. Their plans, their schemes. And this road—the one the king announced during his speech. Did you know he's butchering entire villages and enslaving Paelsians to help him build it as quickly as possible? It means something to him, this road. Something important. Something beyond what anyone else believes it to mean."

Butchering villages? She felt the blood drain from her face. "What?"

"That's what I want you to find out. I want you to be my spy."

For a moment, she couldn't seem to form words. "What you're asking could get me killed."

"The very act of *breathing* could get you killed. Same for anyone else. You might be trapped here, but you've been given great privilege. The king underestimates how deep your hatred for him flows. He doesn't know what you're capable of."

Cleo did fully mean to destroy the king and everyone who had aligned with him in order to reclaim her throne. She would not stand by and see her people—or *any* people from any land, for that matter—abused and enslaved by this man.

But could she be a spy for Jonas? Could she net him the information he was looking for to help the rebel cause?

Perhaps she could.

She would have to give this more thought. And she could not think with the rebel here in her presence.

"I need to consider my options," she said quietly. Not that she had many to consider.

Jonas cocked his head as if he hadn't heard her correctly. "Princess, you need to—"

"I need to do nothing, not when it's something that involves *you*. You thought to barge into my chambers, wait for me in the dark, and expect me to be drooling at the very idea of working together to defeat the king? You may underestimate me, but you vastly overestimate yourself." She didn't want to say no to him, but she couldn't say yes, either. Not yet. "I don't trust you. I will *never* trust you, Jonas Agallon."

His mouth dropped open. "Are you denying me?"

His reaction was nearly comical. "I will assume this is not something you normally deal with when you ask a favor from a girl."

He frowned. "Actually . . . it's not."

She heard a rustle outside her door. Any moment it could swing inward and a guard might enter and capture Jonas. "You must leave."

Her breath caught as he grasped her chin and drew her closer. "You will help me when you realize it's the only way you will ever have a chance to be queen."

"I will be queen, no matter what I must do to achieve it. I am betrothed to a prince, remember? One who will one day take the throne."

He actually laughed at this, a sound that held no humor. "You can't honestly believe King Gaius will ever let that happen. Open your eyes, princess. Your wedding is only another distraction to try to keep his new citizens satisfied and looking in directions other than where the king's true greed lies; and so no one realizes how thin his army is now spread policing all of Mytica. Beyond that, you're a liability to the crown, to the king's power and the prince's claim to the throne. You have great value to them, perhaps, but it will be short-lived, as you too will be if you choose to remain here."

She'd already thought of this herself, but it was shocking to hear it put into cold, hard words. Once she'd become worthless to the king as a figurehead to the Auranian people, there was no doubt in her mind that he'd quietly have her killed and disposed of. She remained silent.

"I'll be in touch again, soon, your highness, once you've had more time to consider what I've said."

Jonas released her and turned to her window. The warmth of his touch lingered for the briefest of moments as she watched him slide out the window and scale the wall as if he were a cliff-dwelling creature like those rumored to live in the Forbidden Mountains. He effortlessly dropped the last ten feet to the ground and within moments disappeared into the shadows.

CHAPTER 7

MAGNUS

AURANOS

Another day. Another speech.

Magnus attempted to ignore the incessant heat in this green and sunny kingdom that coaxed a trickle of perspiration to slide down his spine beneath his dark clothing. A glance at the line of palace guards showed varying levels of discomfort on every face. Their thick red uniforms were meant for cold Limerian days. Even the queen's brow shone under the bright glare of the hot day.

"Today we officially break ground here at the starting point of the Imperial Road." King Gaius addressed the crowd of a few hundred who'd gathered at the Temple of Cleiona, a three-hour carriage ride from the palace. "It's my pleasure to share this moment with you all."

The king nodded toward Magnus, who took his cue and bit into the ground with the sharp edge of the shovel handed to him. The crowd cheered, and he swept his gaze over those closest to the front.

Not all were cheering. Some watched with narrowed eyes and suspicious expressions. Many were well aware that the road was already under construction at several points across Mytica. Today was just for show.

"Well done, your grace," Aron said.

Magnus grimaced at the sound of his reedy voice. It really would have been much easier if the boy had been relieved of his tongue after all. Then he wouldn't always be trying to make friendly conversation with Magnus as if they were equals.

"You think?"

"You broke ground with confidence and certainty, befitting your position."

"I'm so glad you think so." He glanced directly at the chattering weasel. "Why are you here again?"

Aron looked momentarily offended but recovered quickly. "At the king's wishes. He has been very kind and generous to me, and, of course, I will avail myself to him in any way he wants."

"Right. Well, you should go right ahead and avail yourself," Magnus said, nodding toward the king, surrounded by important nobles and other dignitaries who'd come out for the event. "Over there."

"Yes, of course. I will. But first I wanted to—"

A drunken voice from the crowd shouted out, loud enough to be heard over everyone else.

"Fools! Every last one of you! You would believe the King of Blood's empty promises and accept his gifts without question? You think he means to unite us as one happy kingdom? Lies! He's driven only by greed and a lust for power! He must be stopped, or we're all doomed!"

Silence fell.

Magnus's gaze shot toward the king to see if he'd heard.

He had. With a flick of the king's hand, four guards marched toward the crowd, located the man, and wrenched him forward so forcefully that he fell to his knees just left of where Magnus had dug into the soft, grassy earth. When he tried to rise, a guard pushed him back down. The empty bottle he clutched in his right hand fell to the ground.

King Gaius approached, beckoning for both Magnus and Aron to come to his side.

The man wore what looked like finely tailored clothes that had slowly tattered to near rags. A jeweled ring, crusted in grime, encircled his left index finger. His face held a few weeks' worth of dark beard and he smelled as if he hadn't had bathed in the same amount of time. His eyes were glazed with however much wine he'd consumed but otherwise fiercely fixed on those who now faced him.

The king swept his gaze over the man. "What is your name?"

He answered defiantly. "Darius Larides, lord of this land, formerly betrothed to Emilia, late crown princess of Auranos. I chose to fight in the battle against you. And now my family is dead for having opposed you, my home destroyed. My future holds nothing but pain—but I assure you, yours holds the very same! The people here will not always believe your lies. They will not allow you to rule unchallenged. More rebel forces gather even as we speak. Auranians are not as stupid and self-involved as you think we are."

The king's expression was unreadable. He raised his voice loud enough to be heard by those gathered nearby. "Lord Darius thinks I believe you all to be stupid and self-involved. I do not. You are the wisest of all your fellow countrymen for coming here to celebrate with me today. This lord is full of drink and foolish bravery.

Perhaps another day he would not be so bold to insult a king who only wishes the best for his kingdom."

There was a tense pause.

"I'm sure we can find a good place for him in the dungeon," Magnus said, looking away as if bored. "He may yet have worth. It sounds as if he comes from an important family if he was betrothed to the eldest Bellos girl."

"Do you agree, Lord Aron," the king asked, "with what my son suggests?"

Aron's brow creased, as if he was grappling for the correct response. "I don't know, your grace."

Magnus glared at the useless boy. Why did his father care to even ask his opinion?

"It's difficult," the king said, nodding. "But such moments as these require a decisive statement. Stand up, Lord Darius."

With rough prompting from the guards, the lord got to his feet. He moved his hateful glare over the three that stood facing him, his arms held tight behind him.

"Would you take back your words?" the king asked smoothly. "And issue a public apology for what you've said here, spoiling my ceremony with your lies and insults?"

Magnus's gaze moved to the knife in the king's hand, which caught a glimmer of sunshine.

Lord Darius saw this too. He swallowed hard, but he did not lower his gaze. "Take me to your stinking dungeon. Put me on trial for treason. I don't care."

King Gaius smiled slowly. "Of course you don't. But kindly remember one thing, Lord Darius, if you could . . ."

"What?"

"A king does not take orders from a worm."

The knife moved so quickly that all Magnus saw was a flash of glinting metal. The next moment, blood sprayed from the drunken lord's throat and he fell to the ground.

The king raised the weapon above his head to show the crowd. "A fitting blood sacrifice for my road, for you all to witness for yourselves. Lord Darius was an enemy to you all, as much as any common rebel. I truly wish to be a benevolent king to all citizens of the newly united Mytica, but I will not tolerate those who would stand against me."

Magnus watched the blood seep from the gaping wound on the lord's throat, soaking into the ground. Lord Darius's gaze was on Magnus himself, filled with hatred even as the last bit of life faded from his eyes.

"Well done, your majesty," Aron murmured. "Of course, you were right. He deserved no pity."

Of course, you were right. Words that the prince himself should be saying, but he found they did not arrive readily on his tongue. Despite the heat of the day, the death of the lord had sent a violent chill through him. It felt wrong. Unnecessary. Indulgent. But of course he would never admit this aloud.

The crowd remained quiet, looking on at this turn of events with confusion, fear, or revulsion in their eyes. Many—more than Magnus might expect—looked on with respect at the actions of their new king. Then they turned to each other with alarm as a tremor rumbled beneath their feet. Magnus felt the vibrations pulsing through the shovel he still held. Lord Darius's empty wine bottle rolled until it hit a tree, hard enough to break the glass.

"Goddess, what is that?" the queen whispered, her face paling. She'd drawn close enough to grip Magnus's sleeve.

It was over as quickly as it began.

The king swept his gaze across the crowd, his brow furrowed as if he was concentrating very hard. "Is this what she meant, I wonder?" he murmured.

"What did you say, Gaius?" the queen asked, her voice shaky.

"Nothing of interest." He handed the bloody knife off to a guard and wiped the bit of blood that had sprayed onto his face with a cloth offered by another guard. "Come with me. We will tour the interior of the temple. I've decided this is where the wedding will take place."

"Here?" Magnus finally tore his gaze completely from the dead lord, whose eyes sightlessly glared at Magnus with reproach. "In the temple dedicated to the arch enemy of the Goddess Valoria?"

"I had no idea you were so devoted to our goddess that you would be offended."

He wasn't, of course. Most Limerians were very devout in their faith, dedicating two days a week to silence and prayer, but Magnus had found it difficult to believe in anything with true passion in his life. Still, this venue struck him as an unusual choice.

The more he considered it, however, the more he realized it was strategic. Where else would the princess be wed but in the place her people, even those who'd recently strayed from strong adherence to their collective faith, would find most sacred? Limerians were already under the king's thumb. Paelsians were too poor and downtrodden to be considered a true threat to the crown, especially now that they were being rounded up to construct the road. But Auranians—they were still the wild card as they began to emerge from their collective, hedonistic slumber.

Thirty chiseled white marble steps led into the massive temple. The entire building seemed to be carved out of the material, which also seemed to be everywhere in the palace. It reminded Magnus of the ice that stretched out before the Limerian castle. Pale, cold, pristine.

Massive marble pillars stretched up to the roof, lining the interior. The main sanctuary had a twenty-foot-tall statue of the goddess Cleiona at its entrance, her arms stretched to her sides. Carved into her palms was the triangular symbol for fire and the spiral symbol for air, the elements she embodied. Her hair was long and wavy, her expression haughty but strangely captivating. For a moment, the goddess reminded Magnus of the one named for her, the princess herself.

The heady scent of incense and fragrant candles wafted through the air. At the altar, a fire burned, representing Cleiona's eternal fire magic. There was nothing like this in Limeros. The Temple of Valoria was dark and utilitarian and always filled to overflowing with worshippers.

This place, though . . . it felt like magic.

Aron caught Magnus's eye. There was now a sour look on the lord's face.

"I'm so pleased for you," Aron said, his voice tight. "May you and Princess Cleo have many wonderful years together."

"I can only pray I will be able to make her as happy as you would have," Magnus replied wryly.

"Of course." There was a catch to Aron's voice as if he wished to say much more than this. Wisely, he didn't.

The king approached. "Well, well. I'm so glad to see the two of you are becoming good friends."

"How could we not?" Magnus said. "We have so much in common."

"Go find Cronus," the king said to Aron, referring to the captain of the palace guard, "and tell him to ready the carriages to bring us back to the city."

"Yes, your majesty." Aron bowed, then turned to hurry out of the temple.

Magnus couldn't help but ask. "Why do you tolerate him?"

"He amuses me."

"Certainly worth an appointment to kingsliege. Amusement."

"He does whatever I ask. Perhaps you could learn much from him." It was delivered lightly but felt more like a lead weight than a feather.

"I don't have much of a taste for licking boots."

"Or for unexpected public displays of death, it would seem. You didn't approve of what I did outside, did you?"

Magnus measured his next words. "He spoke out against you publicly. Of course he deserved to die."

"I'm glad we agree. I do think it was meant to be. A splash of blood on the starting point of my road is symbolic—a fitting sacrifice for a chance to find the ultimate treasure."

Finally, a topic worth discussing further. "Have you had any luck in your search?"

"Not yet. We've only begun, my son. Patience will do us both good in many areas."

Patience? Not exactly something his father had ever possessed in spades.

"Of course," Magnus said instead, moving toward the smooth white wall and absently tracing the etching of the symbol for fire, a repeating motif throughout the temple, with the tip of his finger. "You're speaking of my impatience with Lucia's recovery, too, aren't you?"

"I am."

"The attendant said that Lucia had stirred in her sleep yester-day, and she believed she would awaken. But then she didn't, of course. Mother, did you know this?"

Queen Althea drew closer. "Yes, I was there. It's happened be-fore. Every few days she stirs, she murmurs as if she's dreaming. And then she goes silent again."

"You visit her bedside regularly," the king said. It wasn't posed as a question since he already knew the answer. The king knew everything that happened within the palace walls.

"Daily." She nodded. "I read to her. She looks so peaceful I can sometimes fool myself that she's only sleeping. I still have faith she'll return to us soon, that she's not lost to us forever."

The king scoffed. "You try to make it sound as if you haven't resented her existence since the day she was brought to Limeros."

"I haven't resented her." The queen patted her graying hair, as if it might have come loose from the tight twist that drew her skin taut at her temples. "I love our daughter as if she was of my own womb."

King Gaius gazed to the left at a fresco mural of a large sun shining down over the City of Gold and its inhabitants. "How interesting that it's taken this tragedy to finally bring out your maternal instincts. For sixteen years you've ignored Lucia or treated her like a rag doll you can dress up and show off. I thank the goddess that she was a natural beauty; otherwise I imagine you'd have demoted her to servant girl a long time ago."

Magnus saw his mother's subtle flinch, which told him the king's words cut deeply. But he couldn't totally disagree with them.

"When she wakes I'll be different with her," the queen said softly. "I've seen the error of my ways and wish to make amends.

I do care for Lucia—truly, I do. And I swear to the goddess I shall prove it."

"That's the spirit," the king said, although his words were cold. "I have a new healer arriving tomorrow to take a look at her. I want her at the wedding if possible."

"If it's not, I'll stay by her bedside."

The king was silent for a moment. "No. You will attend the wedding either way."

The queen fiddled with the sleeve of her dark green cloak. She frowned so deeply that deep lines appeared between her brows. "I don't trust the Bellos girl, Gaius. There's something in the girl's eyes—something dark and sharp. I fear what she means to do to us. What she might do to Lucia or Magnus."

This coaxed a laugh from Magnus. "Mother, don't worry about me. I can handle the princess, even if there is a shadow of vengeance within her. She's only a girl."

"She hates us."

"Of course she does," the king said gently. "I took her throne, her father's throne, her sister's throne. I took it with force and blood. And I apologize for nothing."

"Find Magnus another bride," the queen urged. "I can think of several who'd be much better suited for him. Whom he might fall in love with in time."

"Love? If Magnus wants love he can find it in a mistress, as I did. Not in a shrew of a wife."

The queen blanched at this. "I only speak from my heart."

"Mark my words, Althea . . ." A coldness entered the king's tone. "Everything that will happen from this day forward, be it good or bad, shall happen because it is my choice. Because it serves me. And I warn you, do not cross me or—"

"Or what?" She raised her chin and looked directly into his eyes. "Will you take a blade to my throat as well? Is that how you silence every voice that opposes you?"

Fury flashed through the king's gaze and he took a menacing step toward her, fists clenched at his sides.

Magnus stepped between them and he forced a smile to his face. "Tempers are rising with the heat of the day. Perhaps it's time we leave."

The king's fiery glare fixed on him instead and slowly cooled. There was still a smudge of blood on his cheek from before, just under his left eye. "Yes. It's time. Meet me outside when you're ready."

He turned his back on them and, a guard at each side, moved out of the cavernous temple and back into the bright light of day.

"We must go." The queen's voice caught as she turned in the same direction.

Magnus placed a hand on her shoulder before she'd taken more than a few steps. He turned her to face him and raised her chin so her tear-filled eyes met his. The pain he saw there reached into his chest to squeeze his heart. "I don't remember the last time I saw you cry."

She pushed his hand away. "And you shouldn't be seeing it now."

"He doesn't take well to argument. You know this already."

"He deals with argument as he always has. With an iron fist and a heart carved from ice." She searched his face. "You don't want this marriage, do you, my son?"

"What I want is irrelevant, Mother."

It always is.

She was quiet for a moment. "You know I love you, don't you?"

Magnus willed himself to remain impassive in the face of this unexpected sentimentality. The woman before him had been cold and distant for so long he'd forgotten she could be the opposite. "What has triggered this, Mother? Are you really that distraught over my being placed into a loveless marriage to strengthen my father's grip on this slippery kingdom? Or is this due to something else? Lucia's condition perhaps?"

The queen's expression shuttered as she drew in a long, shaky breath. "It's been a difficult year for us all. So much loss. So much death."

"Yes, I know you were quite heartbroken over the king's mistress being incinerated."

A muscle in her cheek twitched. "I don't mourn Sabina's passing, nor do I spend much time distressed over the manner of her death. All I care about in this world is you and Lucia—you're all that matters to me."

Her unfamiliar words of devotion confused him. "I don't know what you want me to say, Mother. My father wishes me to wed the Bellos girl, and if it truly comes to that, I will do so without argument. It will strengthen my place in the kingdom." And it would keep him fully in his father's confidence when it came to the road and the secret search for the Kindred.

Queen Althea searched Magnus's face. "Is that what you've come to crave, my son? Power?"

"It's what I've always craved."

Her lips thinned. "Liar."

The word felt like a slap. "I'm the crown prince, Mother, in case you forgot. The heir to the throne of Limeros—now the throne of all of Mytica. Why would I not want that, and more?"

"Your father is a cruel man who searches for a treasure that doesn't even exist. His obsession borders madness."

"He's driven and focused on what he desires most. And I would caution you not to call the king mad. He wouldn't take well to such statements."

Now that the king had left their presence, she didn't look concerned. She looked more confident about her words with each one she spoke. "Will you tell him?"

His jaw tensed. "No. But when you insult the king, you insult me as well. Father and I—we're very much the same. We'll do whatever it takes to get what we want, and we'll hurt whoever gets in our way, no matter who they are. Without conscience or remorse."

This bold statement finally brought a glimmer of a smile to her face, which immediately helped ten years vanish from her age as if by magic.

Magnus watched her warily. "Did I say something to amuse you?"

Her gaze was soft, as soft as he'd seen from her in recent years. "In looks, yes, you're just as handsome as Gaius, without any doubt. But that's where the comparison ends. Oh, Magnus, my son, you're nothing like him. And you never will be."

He flinched as if she'd struck him. "You're wrong."

"You think I mean this as an insult? I don't."

"I've killed, Mother. Many men. I've watched them suffer and bleed and die before me on the battlefield in order to secure the Auranian palace. I've even slain one who didn't deserve my blade, one who acted out of courage and bravery. I cut him down with the fear of a coward." The words felt like broken glass in his throat. "I stood by while Father had an innocent young girl tortured and I didn't say a word to save her. She's dead now and it's my fault." He looked away, shielding his weakness. "My heart is carved from ice, just as you say the king's is."

The queen drew closer and raised her hand to the right side of his face, the side with the scar. She caressed it like she had when he was a little boy, and his chest began to ache. "You are *not* like Gaius. He is a monster with a cold heart and a black soul. You've made mistakes, yes. And I have no doubt, just as anyone who lives and breathes, that you will make many more in your life. But it doesn't change who you are deep down inside. You have a kind heart, Magnus. And there's nothing you can do to change that."

His eyes burned as he pushed her hand away. "We must join Father outside. This conversation is over."

CHAPTER 8

LYSANDRA

PAELSIA

L ysandra left the rebel camp at dusk, grabbing a torch from the pile of supplies in order to keep the shadows of the Wildlands from tightening around her like a noose. Over the weeks since her village was attacked, since the last time she saw her parents alive or spoke to Gregor, she'd tried to harden herself in both mind and spirit. And it had worked. Even in this thick forest that filled all but those with the darkest souls with dread, she was bold and fearless.

She startled when the howl of some nearby fanged beast cut through her. A shiver went down her spine and she tightened her grip on the torch.

Yes, so very bold and fearless.

Or so she tried to tell herself.

She walked past a small clearing where a crackling fire lit the area, which had grown darker with the dying of the day. A trio of boys dragged the carcass of a freshly killed deer into view.

The camp consisted of ramshackle shelters and hammocks built into the trees like birds would build nests. Many boys, and a few driven girls, now called this their home. A refuge away from King Gaius's iron fist. By day, the rebels would head out in small groups—hunting, scouting, thieving—to benefit the rest of them, but by night they stuck together. There was safety in numbers when one chose such a dangerous and wild place as their home. And they trained here in hand to hand combat, as well as with sword, dagger, bow and arrow, so they could go out and cause havoc across Auranos, attempting to spread the word of the king's lies and sway all who crossed their path to the rebel side.

Alas, there had been few victories.

And worse, Jonas refused to mount an attack with his rebels on the road camps, fearing defeat and loss. Lysandra had grown weary of asking. But not as weary as she was of missing her brother, so viciously that it hurt. Was Gregor still alive?

If no one would help her to do what was right, she had to take matters into her own hands.

However, it wasn't long before she realized that two very specific rebels had followed her out of camp.

Brion was panting by the time he caught up to her. "You walk fast."

"Not fast enough, apparently," she mumbled.

"Where are you going?"

"Away."

"Are you leaving us?"

"Yes."

His expression fell. "Lys, don't go. I need—uh, I mean, *we* need you here."

She sighed. The boy was like a friendly dog, always eager for any kind word she might offer up. If he had a tail, she had no doubt it would wag if she even looked in his direction. She didn't want to, but she couldn't help but like Brion Radenos.

But then there was the *other* one.

"Running away?" Jonas's familiar deep voice made her grimace. "Without even a farewell?"

For a week she'd lived with the rebels, eaten with them by the campfire, hunted with them, trained with them. He'd barely spoken directly to her if he could help it, since she usually wanted to talk of her plans and ideas for what the rebels should be focusing their attention on.

"Farewell," she said, giving the rebel leader a tight and insincere smile over her shoulder.

She returned her attention to the path ahead. It would be a long and treacherous hike through the Wildlands before she got to her destination. The moment she arrived at the first village in Paelsia, she decided, she would find a horse.

"You're going to scout the road camp by yourself?"

She kept walking. "Yes, Jonas, that's exactly where I'm going since you refuse to do anything to help our people."

He might refuse to mount an attack at this time, but he had at least succeeded in gaining more information about the precise locations of the road camps currently under construction in Paelsia. Many who might not wish to join the rebels completely were sometimes willing to whisper secrets if there was no chance of being caught.

Lysandra planned to investigate the camp located by Chief Basilius's deserted compound, for it was the closest location to her destroyed village. It was here she expected to find people she knew—those who had survived. If she could free any of them, help any of them, she needed to try. And perhaps Gregor would be there. But the painful hope squeezed her chest too tightly, so she put the thought out of her mind.

"Don't go, Lysandra," Jonas said. "We need you back at camp."

This made her stop walking and look at him suspiciously, pushing aside the branch of a tree to see him properly through the gathering darkness. "You *need* me, Jonas?"

"You've proven your worth as a rebel—and your skill with a bow and arrow. We can't lose you."

His words surprised her, since she had the impression he couldn't care less about her. "I will return." She hadn't been certain she would, but his unexpected praise coaxed the words from her lips. "But I need to see for myself what's become of the people from my village. It can't wait another day."

"I won't be able to protect you if you run off and do your own thing."

"I don't need your protection." She tried to keep her tone even and controlled, but the suggestion that she was a weak girl who needed a strong boy to protect her was infuriating. "Don't worry about me, Agallon. Spend your precious time worrying about Princess Cleo. Perhaps she'll jump aboard the next scheme you come up with that doesn't dare put anyone at risk of spilling even one drop of blood."

She twisted the words as if they were a weapon and succeeded in making Jonas wince. His decisions were ludicrous to her. After all, each and every rebel had known the potential for danger when they'd signed up for the job!

Jonas shot Brion a withering look. Lysandra had learned quickly that a few kind words, a mere touch of his arm, or a smile would have Brion eating out of her hand and telling her secrets. Such as

Jonas's clandestine visit to the princess, which resulted only in failure.

"We should go with her," Brion said firmly, ignoring Jonas's glare. "We need to see for ourselves the proof of how the king is treating our people."

Lysandra's heart swelled. "Thank you, Brion."

His eyes locked with hers and he offered her the edge of a smile. "Anything for you, Lys."

Jonas was quiet, his expression hard, as he looked at both of them in turn.

"Fine," he finally said. "You and Brion wait here for me while I go back to camp and put Ivan in charge while we're away. We'll go together and we'll return together."

Lysandra wasn't sure why the stubborn rebel leader's decision felt like a major victory for her. But it did.

During their two days' journey, the trio encountered an enormous black bear who'd appeared to them like a demon, barricading their path. Brion had barely managed to escape the swipe of its razor-sharp claws, and Lysandra had felt the heat of its breath on her neck as she snatched him out of its way just in time. Later, they also found a small camp of outlaws who, when offered the chance to join the rebel ranks, unsheathed their daggers and threatened to cut the three into tiny, bloody pieces and eat them for dinner.

They took that as a firm no.

Finally they emerged from the forest and moved east into Paelsia—the tips of the jagged Forbidden Mountains visible at the horizon, stretching tall and ominous into the gray clouds above.

Chief Basilius's compound was a walled area with clay and

stone huts and cottages. Everyone who'd made it their home had scattered after the chief's murder, leaving it deserted. It had been transformed into a temporary city of tents for the guards and soldiers who surveyed the area.

Here, the ground still held some vegetation, the trees some leaves. To the south, the edge of the Wildlands was a half day's journey. To the west and toward the Silver Sea lay small villages, including the remains of Lysandra's.

Swarming with Paelsian workers, the king's road cut into the ground like a fresh wound. It was incredible to Lysandra how quickly it was being constructed, as if the king had slid his finger across the dusty Paelsian landscape and the road's path had magically appeared wherever he touched.

But there was no magic here. Only sweat. Only pain and blood.

The three looked on grimly at the sight before them from where they crouched unseen in a forest thick with evergreens near the compound and camp.

A meager river wound through the dusty land parallel to the road, the only fresh water this area had to offer. Beyond it, literally thousands of Paelsians lined up along a two-mile section to toil. All ages—from young to old. Two Paelsian boys worked feverishly thirty paces away from the hidden rebels, sawing a thick tree trunk. Others carried heavy stones that had been painstakingly chiseled flat to the front of the road, which was out of sight from where Lysandra pressed up against a tree, the bark's sap leaving its sticky trace on her skin. Whenever anyone slowed their pace, the crack of the guards' whips sounded out, slicing brutally across bare backs.

"You see?" Lysandra whispered. "I wasn't lying. This is what it's like here. This is how our people are being treated."

"Why are they being abused like this?" Brion's voice was hoarse. "No one could work at this pace without rest."

"These are not people to these guards. They're animals who serve one purpose." Lysandra scanned the area until her eyes were strained, searching for familiar faces—searching for Gregor. Her gaze finally moved to Jonas's tense expression. He stared at the sight before them with disgust. His hand had dropped to the jeweled dagger at his waist as if he itched to use it.

"We need information," Jonas finally said. "But how do we get close enough to talk to anyone without the guards seeing us?"

"They keep the slaves in line by intimidation and threat." Brion's brow furrowed. "But there are no chains, no walls."

Lysandra had stopped listening. She'd spotted someone she recognized from her village and her heart began pumping hard and fast. She waited until a guard on horseback had turned his back so he wouldn't see her approach, and then she slipped away from the shield of trees and into the midst of the Paelsian laborers.

"Vara!" Lysandra thundered up to the girl, who looked at her with wild, scared eyes. "You're alive!"

"What are you doing here?" Vara whispered.

The area was as crowded as a small city and buzzing with activity. Everywhere Lysandra looked there were piles of wood and rock as tall as cottages. Dotted along the edges of the road were large tents where the Limerian guards could take breaks and step out of the harsh sunlight.

Lysandra pulled Vara behind one of these tents to shield them from a nearby guard. "Where's Gregor?" When the girl didn't reply, she shook her. "Where is he?"

"I—I don't know. I haven't seen him."

Lysandra's heart twisted. "When did you see him last?"

"In the village—when they descended upon us." Her voice broke and her eyes welled with tears. "Lysandra, so many are dead!"

It was only confirmation of what she already knew was true. "How many still live?"

"I don't know. You shouldn't be here! They might capture you too!" She bit her bottom lip, frowning. "But . . . but you're a good fighter—I know this. You can help us."

"Help you? With what?"

"Our escape." Vara nodded firmly, but Lysandra noticed there was a strange, unhinged look in her eyes. "It was already supposed to happen. I'm only waiting for the sign. You're the sign. You *must* be. It's time for us to free ourselves."

"What are you talking about? Is there really a plan for escape?" It lightened Lysandra's heart to think that her people would be planning a revolt here, even against so much armed opposition. Jonas had been right about one thing—attacking a place with so many guards would lead to many, many deaths of rebels and slaves alike. And certainly no guarantee of victory.

Most Paelsians accepted life as it was handed to them, believing that fate and destiny were unchangeable. Jonas was one of the few she'd met who had something inside him—something that defied this belief. This certainty shone through his very skin, and she knew it was what had singled him out as a leader. Jonas *was* a leader. He believed that destiny wasn't to be accepted with head bowed; it was to be challenged at every turn.

That Vara, too, wanted to break free was a sign that there was a chance for others to do the same.

"I dreamed it would be me," Vara whispered. "That I would kill them all."

She turned and Lysandra winced to see the red lash wounds on the girl's back. What remained of her dress was in tatters.

Still, there was something very wrong about the way Vara spoke. "Of course you will. They will die for what they've done, I promise you that."

Vara glanced over her shoulder and gave Lysandra a big grin that sent a shiver down her spine. "Watch me."

"Watch—watch what? Vara, what are you talking about?"

Picking up a mid-weight, jagged rock from the ground, Vara began walking directly toward a guard. Lysandra's heart began pounding wildly. What was she doing?

"Sir . . ." Vara said.

"What is it?" The guard looked at her.

Without hesitation, she smashed the rock into the guard's face. He let out a pained roar as his nose and teeth were crushed by the force of it. She crouched over him when he fell to the ground and continued to beat him with the stone, over and over until there was little left of his face but red pulp.

Lysandra looked on from the edge of the tent, horrified, as other guards shouted out an alarm. They rushed toward the assault, pushing past other workers, swords drawn.

There was no hesitation as one guard thrust his sword through Vara's side, straight through to the other side, and she let out a piercing scream, losing her grip on the bloody rock as she fell to her side on the ground. Dead within moments.

Lysandra clamped her hand down over her mouth to keep from making a sound, but a strangled cry escaped her throat. Other slaves were not so quiet. Many began to wail and scream at the sight of the blood, the dead guard, the dead girl.

An older man with thick muscles and a heavy beard roared out in fury. Lysandra took only an instant to recognize him as Vara's father. He ran toward the guards and took hold of a guard's sword, wrenching it from his grip. He struck quickly and brutally, severing the guard's head where he stood.

In mere moments, three dozen Paelsians joined the fight in an attempt to kill as many guards as they could—with rocks, with chisels, with their bare hands and teeth. Other slaves stood back, looking on with fear and shock etched into their faces.

A swarm of new guards approached at a run. One raised his arm to bring his whip down upon a young boy, but then the guard staggered backward. With wide eyes, the guard looked down at the arrow that had sunk into his chest, just below his shoulder. His gaze shot to Lysandra.

When he opened his mouth to yell, to point her out to the other guards as a target, another arrow impaled his right eye socket. He fell to the ground without uttering a sound.

The first arrow had been from Lysandra's bow. Her already callused fingers felt raw from the speed with which she'd nocked an arrow and let it fly.

But the second . . .

Brion and Jonas swiftly moved toward her. Jonas let free another arrow aimed toward an approaching guard, catching him in the throat.

"Get her," Jonas barked.

Brion didn't argue. He grabbed Lysandra and threw her over his shoulder. She was shaking violently and couldn't think straight. Couldn't see straight.

She fought him, digging her fingernails into his back. "Let me go! I need to help!"

"And let you get yourself killed?" Brion snarled. "Not a chance."

Vara had walked right into that without thinking twice. There had been no organized plan of revolt. The girl was mad. The death she'd seen in the village, and whatever nameless abuses she'd suffered here . . . they had driven her insane.

Jonas led the way, making use of his jeweled dagger, slashing his way past any guard who stepped into their path so the three could make it back to the tree line. Once cloaked by the branches, Brion finally put Lysandra back down on the ground.

She stared back at the camp with horror. She couldn't count the bodies that now lay bleeding and broken and surrounded by masses of chaotic, rioting slaves and the guards attempting to restore order. Thirty, forty . . . maybe more had been slaughtered in mere moments. Both Paelsian and Limerian, their blood now soaked into the parched ground.

It was a massacre.

"Are you all right?" Brion was shouting at her, but his voice sounded a million miles away. "Lys, listen to me! *Are you all right?*"

Finally she looked at him, into his blue eyes, which held deep concern for her. "I was trying to help," she said faintly.

Relief flashed through his gaze, followed by anger. "You had me worried. Do *not* do that to me again, you hear me?"

A breeze brushed against her face when before the air had been still. Brion felt it too, and looked up. A roaring noise approached, growing louder by the second.

"What is that?" he asked.

Something strange and unexpected now moved across the land, pulling up dust and debris, wood and rock, as it gathered strength. Something that had formed out of nothing so suddenly that no one had noticed until it fully hit.

A tornado. A swirling cylindrical mass that twisted its way

toward the road camp. The winds picked up, blowing Lysandra's hair back from her face, making it impossible to speak. The noise was so loud now that they wouldn't be able to hear each other anyway. Dark storm clouds quickly gathered, blocking out the sunlight within seconds.

Slaves and guards alike ran to escape its path, but some were swept up into it, disappearing for moments before being thrown free, like broken dolls as they hit the ground.

"It's coming!" Jonas shouted. Brion grabbed her hand and they started running but didn't get far before the force of the approaching wind blew them off their feet. Evergreens were pulled up out of the ground by their roots and hurled through the air like arrows.

The roar of the tornado was like thunder—only more deafening. More terrifying. Lysandra couldn't catch her breath, couldn't think. Something whipped past her face, cutting her cheek, and she felt the warmth of her blood. She found she now clutched on to both Brion and Jonas for fear of being picked up and carried away by the cyclone. For a moment, she was certain that would happen.

Nearby, a thirty-foot-tall tree rose up from the earth and crashed down to the forest floor, missing them by only a few paces. She stared at the tree over Brion's shoulder, knowing it could have crushed them to death.

It felt as if it had gone on forever, but finally the tornado grew smaller and smaller until it disappeared completely just before it fully reached them. The thunderous noise faded to nothing. A few more moments of eerie stillness stretched out before the birds resumed chirping and the insects began to buzz. Cries could be heard from the camp a hundred paces away as all present reeled from the disaster.

A pair of guards had spotted them through the felled trees and had broken away from the rest of the pandemonium. They stormed into the forest line, swords drawn.

"We need to move," Jonas growled. "Now."

Clutching tightly to her bow, Lysandra shakily got to her feet and tore after Brion and Jonas through the forest, her boots sinking into the loose earth and tangled roots.

"Halt in the name of the king!" one guard shouted.

A branch whipped Lysandra in the face, and she tasted the coppery tang of her own blood as she shoved it away. They couldn't slow. After what had happened at the road, these guards would cut their throats immediately, assuming them to be slaves who'd escaped during the disaster.

The shouts of the guards faded, but the three continued to run for as long as they could before finally slowing.

"What happened?" Brion said, his expression strained. "What just happened back there?"

Lysandra found she was shaking. "What part?"

"All of it. That tornado . . ."

"A coincidence," Jonas said. He was winded but kept striding quickly.

"Too strange to be a coincidence." Brion scratched the back of his head. "Buckets of blood spilled results in something like that? Out of nowhere? My grandmother used to tell me stories . . . about witches, about blood magic . . ."

Lysandra looked at him, her eyes widening. "I saw a witch like that just before my village was attacked. She was using blood magic to try to see the future, I think. My brother called her an Oldling, one who worshipped the elements. She—she's dead now. Like so many of the others."

"I don't believe in magic," Jonas said firmly. "Belief in magic is what has kept our people down for centuries, what keeps them from fighting back like they should. What I believe in is what I can see with my eyes. Paelsian weather has never been predictable. That's all that was. But as far as the camp—I've now seen what the king has done. You were right, Lysandra."

After what she'd experienced, Jonas's confirmation was small comfort. "As long as the king lives, the road continues to be built and our people will die every day."

"We need something to use against the king." Jonas's brow furrowed. "Something that holds value for him that can help shift some power to our rebels. Something that will give us a chance to hurt him, to slow him down so we'll have the chance to stop him completely." He was quiet for a moment, but then his brown eyes met hers. "I know just the thing."

She stared at him for a moment. "What?"

"Not what. Who. Princess Cleiona."

"Her again? What about her this time?"

"No, listen. I don't think she'll always be an asset to the king, but she is now, particularly when it comes to his new grasp on Auranos. If she wasn't worth something to him, something very important, she'd already be dead. That makes her valuable to us." His lips thinned. "After what I've seen here today, I'm willing to do whatever it takes to free our people from his tyranny."

"You mean to assassinate the princess to send a message to the king," Lysandra said, her voice breathless.

"Jonas . . ." Brion looked uneasy at the suggestion. "Are you sure you want to do something like that?"

"I'm not planning to assassinate her." Jonas met each of their gazes in turn. "I'm planning to kidnap her."

CHAPTER 9

KING GAIUS

THE SANCTUARY

The king sensed her presence before she came into view in the stark, windowless room, which had now become familiar territory to him. "You've kept me waiting far too long."

He didn't try to keep the edge of impatience from his voice.

"Apologies, your majesty," she soothed. "Please tell me I was worth the wait."

He swiveled on his heels to let his gaze sweep over her. She wore a gown that seemed spun from pure gold. Perfect skin, long golden hair, eyes like flawless sapphires. She was the most stunning woman he'd ever seen, without exception.

His last mistress had been a mortal witch. This one was an immortal goddess. Or as close to it as he'd ever known.

"Beautiful Melenia," he said. "I could wait an eternity to be blessed with just one more dream about you."

It felt unseemly to lie to a near-goddess, but women always responded to such silvery words.

"But this is more than just a dream. So much more." A smile played on her lush mouth and his gaze lingered there for a moment. Tonight, however, his need for information trumped anything else he might desire from this ethereal creature.

"I know you're real. That what you say to me is real. If I didn't, I wouldn't consider doing what you've asked of me."

"Of course not." Melenia slowly slid her hand up his arm, then across his chest. "And you've done so well with my road, my king. But . . . there's a problem."

"Problem?"

"Time grows short. You must move more quickly to complete it."

A rope of frustration tightened within him, but he didn't let it show on his face. "The road is being built with mortal hands, as many as I can gather. It's being constructed as quickly as possible."

Something flashed in her blue eyes, something unpleasant, but then it disappeared and a smile flickered on her lips again. "Of course it is. I have received some progress reports from Xanthus as well. But the man rarely sleeps, so it is sometimes difficult to connect with him. It's a good thing that I trust him implicitly."

Xanthus. The engineer responsible for mapping out the road and for leading the construction. He was essential to the process, skilled, smart, and dedicated.

Dedicated to Melenia.

Xanthus was an exiled Watcher whom this beautiful immortal had at her command. The earth magic he still possessed after two decades of living in the mortal world was integral to the Imperial Road in ways that Melenia had yet to share.

"Apologies for my impatience," Melenia said softly, "but I've already waited so long. And now that everything is beginning to align and I see the proof of our actions, I know there is only a small window of opportunity for us to get what we want."

"Proof. What proof do you have?"

"Signs, my king. Incredible signs that all is aligning as it needs to. Pieces clicking into place exactly as they should. Words spoken at just the right time; connections made; whispers overheard by eager ears." Her smile grew to compensate for her cryptic words. "What might seem like a series of coincidences is but perfect timing to an immortal. A sign that all is as it should be."

Her beautiful smile didn't begin to temper his frustration. "I need more, Melenia. Tell me more."

She brushed past him. "I'll do better than tell you. I will show you, my king, what you need to see to give you incentive to hasten progress."

He turned to see a round table appear on the black marble floor in the center of the large room. He moved to it to look at the map of Mytica on its surface. It was a familiar sight, since he had a map just like this in the Limerian palace.

Melenia slid her slender index finger sensually along the western coastline as if she were caressing a lover. "It's all yours. Every mile. Every mortal. Mytica belongs to you now, even without more magic than you already have at your disposal."

The mention of magic drew his attention back to her flawless face. "When will she wake?"

He had used Lucia's magic to defeat King Corvin before Melenia had shown herself to him. Before she'd drawn him into a dream like this and explained who she was and what she wanted from him. She needed a powerful mortal's assistance, and out of everyone in the world, she'd chosen him.

"The young sorceress will wake when it's time," Melenia replied.

Gaius smashed his fist down against the map. "Not good enough. I need her to be awake now. A promise of future magic is no good to me when I have magic already in my possession but currently useless."

Many would cower in the face of his rage—those who possessed intelligence and self-preservation, that was.

Melenia was different. She feared nothing. "Do you think I will bow down before you and beg for your forgiveness, your majesty?" She continued to smile, as if he amused her. It both infuriated and intrigued him that she should show such disrespect. Not even Sabina had been so bold. "I bow before no one."

"Those who don't bow before me die."

"I'm immortal—the first of my kind. I've lived for more than four thousand years. I've seen this world change and evolve and grow from its very infancy. I've seen the birth of mortal kings and their inevitable deaths so many times it's become tedious. That is, until you. Shall I tell you a secret—the reason why I first came to you with my plans? It was not only a lovely coincidence, my king."

"You said this road would lead to the Kindred; that its location would be revealed to me in the Forbidden Mountains and that Xanthus would keep me informed on everything." Frustration welled within him, swirling like lava. "But I've received no word of anything found in the mountains so far. No clues, no signs. Where do we look? I need more proof that what you're telling me is true, Melenia."

"And I need you to trust me."

"I trust no one."

"No one? Not even your son, who you believe is so much like you?"

"He's still young. He has much more to prove to me before he fully earns my trust."

"And yet you told him about me."

"I told him only that I had a new advisor. He's not ready to believe anything more. Not yet. But if there is one I would tell about you, about everything, it would be him."

This beautiful immortal could have spies listening in on his private conversations. Her kind could take the form of hawks to watch over mortals. But not Melenia herself. She was trapped in the Sanctuary, as all the eldest Watchers were. There was no escape for her, no contact with the mortal world, except in dreams like this.

"Your adopted daughter will wake, but not yet. She is integral to my plan, to your future. To your . . . prophecy."

He stilled. "*My* prophecy?"

Melenia nodded, sliding her cool, light touch over the line of his jaw. "Yes. It is one I saw for myself, so I know it is true."

"What prophecy?"

When she replied with only a mischievous smile, he took hold of her arms tight enough to make any normal woman flinch.

"Tell me," he growled.

"Let go of me and I shall, my king."

The desire to hurt her, to cause her pain and force her to speak truths, was strong, but he knew it wouldn't help. She looked so delicate in stature, as if her bones might snap like twigs with the merest amount of pressure. But she wasn't delicate—just the opposite. He had to remember that. If he mistreated her, in insult or action, she might never give him audience again.

He wasn't willing to risk that. Not yet.

He released her.

"The prophecy is that there would one day be a mortal king who would rule over this kingdom." She brushed her hand against the map of Mytica again. "One who would discover a great magic that would turn him into an immortal god. That he would rule his kingdom with a goddess as his queen. And that they would in turn rule everything, this world and all that lies beyond, and everyone, be they mortal or immortal, would bow before them. It is you, my king. And I shall be your queen."

The glowing lines of the map of Mytica had spread, sliding down the table and running along the black marble floor like lines of fire, lighting the edges of other lands, other kingdoms and empires far across the sea and beyond. Gaius followed its path until it disappeared from view in the darkness surrounding them.

"All of it," he breathed.

"You are destined to be an immortal god. No one has ever had more power than what you will have. The universe itself will cower in fear before you."

He nodded slowly. Her words were honey, so sweet and so true. They fed something deep inside him that had hungered for far too long. "I knew this. I knew I was destined for greatness."

"Yes. So now you see, you must increase the speed of the road so we can find that magic. The blood spilled in Auranos, in Paelsia, the effect it had upon the elements . . . it's the first sign I've been waiting for."

"Of what?"

"That it's working." Her eyes practically glowed, just like the endless map that surrounded them in its sea of black. "We're finding them, together."

"The Kindred." He found his mouth had gone dry. Could he really be so close? "You know where the crystals are hidden."

"Their location has been shielded all this time from others of my kind. But it's time. Here, now. And I am certain that you are the one who will bring it all into being."

His breathing had increased; his heart pounded harder than it had in recent memory. This was what he wanted more than anything. "I'm ready to do whatever it takes."

She nodded. "Blood is essential to all of this. It must continue to spill. Many will die; many *must* die for us to succeed."

"Then many *will* die . . . my queen. As many as it takes."

"I hope you mean that."

"I do."

Melenia had told him everything he needed to know, everything he'd already known on some level. He was born for a greatness beyond that which he'd already achieved. He was born to be an immortal god, the most powerful king the universe had ever known. Everything and everyone would bow before him.

Eternally.

CHAPTER 10

CLEO

AURANOS

Cleo clutched the gold and amethyst ring in her fist so tightly she was sure it would leave a permanent imprint on her skin. Squeezing her eyes shut, she tried to sense something from it. *Anything.*

Finally, she opened her hand to look at the small piece of jewelry. *"It belonged to your mother,"* her father had told her moments before his death. *"She always believed it had the power to help find the Kindred. If you can find it, you'll be powerful enough to take back this kingdom from those who seek to destroy us all."*

"I'm trying, Father," she whispered, tears of frustration and grief stinging her eyes. "But I don't know how. I wish you were here. I miss you and Emilia so much."

The weeks of searching in the palace library had yielded nothing. *Maybe he was wrong.*

There was a hard knock on her door and she quickly scrambled to hide the ring behind the loose stone in her wall. A moment later, the door opened and two young attendants entered, one fair, one dark. Both Limerian. Cleo wasn't allowed to have servants from her own kingdom anymore.

"We've been sent to help you get ready for your trip," the fair-haired one, Helena, said.

"Trip?" Cleo repeated. "Where am I going?"

"To Hawk's Brow," the other, Dora, said, bottomless envy shining in her dark eyes. "The queen herself is taking you there. You have an appointment with Lorenzo today."

It was a name Cleo knew well from a simpler time. A famous man known throughout Auranos for his flawless taste and exemplary style, a man who had dressed Cleo and her sister since they reached adolescence.

The reality of the situation dawned. Queen Althea was accompanying Cleo to the fitting of her wedding gown.

Her stomach sank. The sensation of being cornered, of being ordered to do what she didn't want to, settled over her. But then she realized this would be the first time she left the palace since the day after she had been captured.

There was a chance Lorenzo might secretly assist her, and her thoughts went again to the ring. Hawk's Brow was the home of many scholars and artists—citizens who were well versed in history and legend. If she could speak with the dressmaker alone and enlist him to her cause . . .

"Fine," she said, raising her chin. "Then let's not keep the queen waiting."

"I hear you're going to Hawk's Brow today, Cleo."

The slithering words slowed her steps as she moved down the hallway after dismissing Helena and Dora once they'd dressed her in traveling robes.

"Lord Aron . . ." Cleo turned to see him loitering nearby.

The last time she'd been in Hawk's Brow had been nearly a year ago, she remembered. It was a gathering of friends who'd spent a few days in the large Auranian city, nestled along the coastline, without a single care on their minds apart from having fun. Aron had been there as well. At the time, she'd thought herself infatuated with him.

How times had changed.

"I know you're still angry with me for revealing your secret." His eyes glittered from the torchlight set into the smooth stone wall beside him.

She forced a gracious smile. It took effort. "Such unpleasantries are in the past now. Let's leave them there."

He took hold of her arms as she tried to slip past him. "You really think I've given up so easily?"

The wine was heavy on his breath. He only drank Paelsian wine, which caused deep inebriation with no chance of illness afterward. This, of course, made it difficult to know when best to stop.

"Easily? What part of this has been easy?"

"Despite everything, I still want you."

She wrenched away from him, shoving him backward. "Don't be so pathetic, Aron. You never wanted me. You wanted the position marrying me would put you in. You would be very wise to let it go now. You've lost."

We all have . . . for the moment.

Aron narrowed his eyes. "If that's so, then maybe I'll set my sights on your little friend, Mira. She wouldn't deny me—not if she knew what was good for her. Would it make you jealous if I took her as a lover?"

She willed herself to remain calm. "Leave Mira alone, you drunken ass."

"Or what?"

"Or, trust me, I'll cut off more than your tongue."

She had no time for this nonsense, disturbing though it was. Cleo turned and began walking away from him, but his footsteps followed her. She swiftly moved past the library, avoiding looking directly at the portraits of the Damoras that now hung in the place of her family's.

Eyes focused on her path, she nearly ran right into Magnus as he emerged from the library, books in his arms. He glanced at her uninterestedly, then looked over her shoulder. At the sight of Magnus, Aron's steps faltered. He nodded to the prince and continued on past them, slowly, to disappear around the next corner.

"Seems you're being pursued, princess. My father's new kings-liege doesn't give up on true love easily, does he?"

True love. Such a notion was laughable. "He will. Eventually."

She eyed the books the prince held. It surprised her to see they all had to do with magic and legend—books she'd already skimmed only to find they held no useful answers.

He noticed that his selections had drawn her attention. "Just a little light reading to pass the boring days."

She chanced a look into his dark brown eyes. "You believe in magic?"

"Of course not. Only a fool would believe in such nonsense." He gave her an unpleasant smirk. "You care what I might believe in?"

"I thought you only cared about power and position at any cost. What more should I know?"

"Nothing at all." His smirk held, but his eyes were cold. "Seems your other admirer also lingers nearby. So many boys seem to be enamored of you, I'd need a ledger to keep track of them all."

"Princess," Nic's voice called out from her left, "I was sent to find you."

She tore her attention from the loathsome prince. Nic approached her swiftly, but his wary gaze was focused on Magnus.

The sight of Nic was always a relief and lightened her mood—even in the presence of an enemy. But today, her expression soured to see his clothes. Not clothes. *Uniform.*

Red. Familiar. Hateful. But necessary.

After finding Nic toiling in the stables, and the morning after her shocking and unwelcome visit from Jonas Agallon in the darkness of her chambers, Cleo had gone directly to the king himself. She made no mention of the rebel but asked—or, rather, begged—for Nic to be reassigned to another part of the palace. Magnus had been present during this and had argued for Nic to remain indefinitely exactly where he was.

"You sent the former king's squire to work in the stables and didn't tell me?" the king asked, perplexed. "Such a boy would have more value than that to me elsewhere."

Cleo had been surprised to learn Magnus hadn't shared anything with his father about what Nic had done to gain him such a punishment. Nor did the prince choose to reveal such details presently. Perhaps he was ashamed and embarrassed by what had happened in Paelsia the day he'd killed Theon.

He should be.

"There are reasons for everything I do," was all Magnus would say. "Nicolo Cassian deserves to remain in the horse filth indefinitely."

"Unless you can give me a solid reason why, I will have to disagree with you."

Magnus kept his mouth closed but cast a dark look at Cleo, who inwardly glowed from this small victory.

Cleo had won this round. However, instead of shoveling muck and horse filth, Nic had been assigned to the palace guard and was now forced to wear the uniform of their enemy. Nic's jaw was tight and his focus didn't leave Magnus. "Princess, is everything all right?"

"Of course," she said quietly. "As well as can be expected."

Magnus actually snorted at this. "Don't worry. I haven't heaped any indignities upon your fair princess today. Then again, it is quite early."

Nic's gaze burned with hatred. "If you should ever think to harm her, you will answer to me."

"And you should be very careful how you speak to your superiors. That sounded very near a threat."

"Make no mistake, Prince Magnus, no matter how low you try to push me, I won't let anything unpleasant happen to Cleo ever again."

Magnus's expression remained amused. "You entertain me, Cassian. Perhaps I'm glad I didn't ask for your head."

"Why didn't you?" Cleo asked curiously. "And why didn't you tell the king what happened that day?"

Magnus's mouth tightened. "I felt it . . . unnecessary. Now, if you'll excuse me, I must visit my sister. May you have a fruitful journey to Hawk's Brow with my mother, princess."

Cleo studied the prince as he walked away. The boy was a complete and utter enigma to her.

She preferred to keep it that way.

"I hate him," Nic said through clenched teeth.

"Really?" Cleo turned to him, angry now. "You hide it so well."

"You expect me to—"

"You must not say such things to him no matter how you feel! Say them to me in confidence, but *not* to him. He could still order your execution for the slightest insult and you know it!"

Nic grimaced, eyes now lowered to the ground. "You're right. Apologies, Cleo."

"No apologies necessary. I only ask that you be more careful." She took a deep breath and let it out slowly. "I refuse to lose you. *Ever.* Understand?"

"The feeling's entirely mutual." He was smiling now.

"What is it?" she asked, confused. She saw no humor at all in this conversation.

"You're different than you used to be. More opinionated. More . . . forceful." His smile faded. "However, such strength has been forged through pain and loss. I wish I could take it all away so you wouldn't have to suffer anymore."

Cleo felt an urge to tell him about her ring, but she held her tongue for fear of endangering him with such information. The ring would remain her secret . . . at least until she learned all of *its* secrets.

"Let's go," she said instead. "Off to Hawk's Brow. I shall insist that you're to be my personal bodyguard who will stay by my side every moment we're gone."

This summoned a grin once again. "Do you need such protection for a simple dress fitting?"

"I think so," she said, finally finding her own smile. "Don't forget, I will be forced to spend the entire day in the company of the queen."

"I haven't seen very much of Auranos in my life," the queen said a few hours later, sitting across from Cleo in the enclosed carriage. They had a half dozen guards on horseback riding in front and behind them. Nic sat up front with the driver, leaving Cleo to her fate within.

"Oh?" She forced herself to respond. To say the ride had been awkward, with the two stuck making small talk about the warm spring weather and the sweeping green landscape stretched out before them, would be putting it mildly.

"Of course, Gaius and I included Auranos in our tour of Mytica after our wedding. Gaius's father felt it was an excellent idea to strengthen relations between the lands. Alas, it didn't last long. Apart from our short-lived trip back here ten years ago to meet your family, I've remained in Limeros ever since."

And I can't wait to send you back there with great force, Cleo thought.

"How did you meet King Gaius?" she asked, feeling as if she was required to keep up her side of this strained conversation, as if she cared to learn more about Queen Althea or her horrible family.

"I was chosen to be his bride. My father was a friend to King Davidus, Gaius's father. My father was rich. I was . . . beautiful. It seemed the perfect match." The queen folded her hands on her lap, her expression serene. "Arranged marriages are a necessity of royalty, my dear."

"I know that." After all, it had been drummed into her head since she was a child.

"You should also know that I love my son very much. I want him to be happy, no matter whom he marries. That Gaius has decided it is to be you, I must admit, gives me some reservation."

"Really?" That made two of them, but that the queen chose to admit this aloud was very interesting.

"There have been moments of . . . *strain* . . . in my marriage." The queen's pallid cheeks tightened. "But I have always done what is right to uphold my position as a dutiful wife. For nearly twenty years I have stood by my husband's side in times both dark and light. Even when I've disagreed with his decisions, his actions, I have not publicly said a thing against him. This is how a proper queen must conduct herself."

"Of course it is," Cleo said, the words sticking in her throat. That was not how *she* would conduct herself, if and when she retrieved her kingdom.

"I'm not blind, princess. I see how difficult it's been for you, and believe me, I do empathize with all you've lost due to my husband's lust for power. But I need you to know one very important thing . . . and I mean this with all my heart and soul, speaking as one woman forced into an arranged marriage to another."

Her soft, almost kind words came as a great surprise. "What is it?"

Queen Althea leaned forward and grasped Cleo's hands. "If you cause my son any pain, I will see you dead. Do you understand me, my dear?"

The woman said all this quietly, but there was no mistaking the weight of such a warning. A shiver ran down Cleo's spine. "I understand, your highness."

"Good." The queen nodded and released her grip on Cleo's hands. She glanced out the window. "Ah, very good. We've arrived in Hawk's Brow."

Heart pounding from the unexpected threat, Cleo peered out the small window to see the city she remembered so well, the home to forty thousand Auranians.

Cleo had always loved it here so much. The color. The spectacle. The flamboyant citizens and the music in the air no matter where one went. The carriage wound its way along streets made from polished, interlocking brick that sparkled under the bright sun. The shops and taverns lining the street gleamed silver and bronze, with bright copper roofs. Large trees heavy with the pink and purple blossoms of the season leaned over the roadways, creating natural arches of colorful and fragrant beauty.

With King Gaius on the throne, she'd expected it to be different now. Perhaps the music would be silenced. The colors would be muted. She'd expected to see shutters closed as the carriage rolled past small homes and larger villas.

But there was nothing like that. The city seemed much the same as the last time she'd been here, with one major difference. Red uniformed guards spotted the cityscape like drops of blood, mixing with Auranians as if this was a normal sight.

The king wished to rule over her people, to fool them into believing he was a good king with an unfortunately harsh reputation. It was easier to control gullible citizens fearful of losing their status or lifestyle than those who were downtrodden and abused and motivated to rise up and oppose him. So, except for some increased security, Hawk's Brow appeared just as it had the last time she was here.

She should be glad for this, that her people were not suffering as horribly as she'd expected with a greedy king perched upon Auranos's throne.

Instead, cold dread slithered into her gut.

This will not last.

How long would it be before everything changed and the people here, unsuspecting and soft from generations of luxurious living, would feel the pain caused by the King of Blood ruling over them? Or before those who did not so readily accept their new king caused enough unrest to unleash his wrath upon the innocent, rather than only upon accused rebels? It was a disturbing thought.

The carriage came to a halt in front of the dress shop Cleo remembered so well. There was a crowd of about a hundred citizens gathered here, a burst of welcome color and friendly greeting.

"Princess Cleo!" a group of young girls called out to her. "We love you!"

Their collective voices caused a lump in her throat. She waved from the window in their direction and tried to smile brightly.

Nic jumped down off the top of the carriage to open the door and help the queen out and then Cleo herself. "And here we are," he said, a half grin on his face.

"Here we are."

He lowered his voice so the queen would not hear. "Are you ready for this?"

"I suppose I must act as if I am."

"A warning. Do not look to your left if you wish to keep ahold of your breakfast."

Of course, with a warning like that, she had to look to her left. There, two artists were toiling feverishly on a mural on the side of a popular tavern: a plaster fresco that looked a great deal like a portrait of her and Magnus. She shuddered.

"How can they accept all this so easily?" she whispered. "Are they really so naive?"

"Not everyone," Nic replied, his jaw tight. "But I think most are too afraid to see the truth."

A familiar man moved out of the store before them and rushed enthusiastically toward Cleo and the queen. The tunic he wore was the most vivid shade of purple Cleo had ever seen. It reminded her of squashed grapes on the brightest summer day. He was completely bald, and his large ears gleamed with gold hoop earrings.

He bowed so deeply it looked painful. "Queen Althea, your gracious majesty. I am Lorenzo Tavera. I am deeply honored to welcome you to my humble store."

The store he referred to could never honestly be described as humble. It was roughly the size of Aron's family's large villa in the palace city, three stories tall and encased in sparkling stained glass windows trimmed with silver and gold.

"I am pleased to be here," she replied. "I was told you are the best dressmaker in this or any other land."

"If I might be so bold to say, you were told correctly, your highness."

The queen extended her hand and Lorenzo kissed her ring with a loud smacking sound.

"And Princess Cleiona, I'm very pleased to see you again." Lorenzo squeezed her hands. Despite the joviality in his tone, his searching gaze held a momentary glimpse of both grief and sympathy.

She swallowed hard. "And I you, Lorenzo."

"It's my true privilege to create your wedding gown."

"As it will be my true privilege to wear it."

He nodded once, shallowly, then tore his gaze from hers to look at the queen, flashing her a big smile. "Let us go inside, your majesty. I have something very special to show you."

The queen raised an eyebrow, intrigued. "To show *me*? Really?"

"Yes. Please, follow me."

Inside the store waited a dozen attendants and seamstresses, lined up six on each side, their heads lowered obediently. The expansive store was lined with bolts of silk, satin, jacquard, and lace for as far as the eye could see.

"I have been working very hard on a dress befitting a queen of your high esteem." Lorenzo moved toward a mannequin that had been draped in a magnificent indigo gown. It was embroidered with gold thread and beaded with sparkling stones. "I believe I've succeeded. What do you think of this, your majesty?"

"It's divine," the queen said, her normally expressionless face tinged with the tiniest pink, her words hushed. "Beautiful. This is my absolute favorite color. Did you know that?"

Lorenzo smiled. "Perhaps."

This vibrant shade was the queen's favorite? Cleo had never seen her in anything that wasn't black, gray, or a muted shade of steely green. Since Magnus and his father also wore nothing but black, she'd assumed it was a strange Limerian custom at odds with the red-as-blood uniforms.

The queen's eyes narrowed with suspicion. "Who have you been speaking to about me that would give you such personal information?"

Caution shone now in Lorenzo's gaze. "It was in my previous correspondence with the king. I asked. He responded."

"How strange," she murmured. "I had no idea Gaius even knew my favorite color." She turned her attention to the gown again. "I would like to try it on."

"Of course, your majesty. I will attend to you myself." There was a fine sheen of perspiration on Lorenzo's brow now at having come very close to offending such a powerful woman. "Princess, if you please, you can go with my seamstress into the fitting room. I will be with you as soon as I can."

A pretty young girl approached, curtseying before her.

"I am Nerissa," she said. "Please, your grace, follow me."

Cleo glanced toward the queen, but the woman's attention was fully fixed on the beautiful gown and nothing but. Nic stayed by her side as Cleo began to follow the attendant.

"I'm coming with you," he said when she looked at him curiously. "You did want me to be your bodyguard today, remember?"

"This is a dress fitting," Cleo said. "Therefore, I will be undressing."

"A hardship for me to endure, I agree." Again, that welcome

grin of his flickered on his lips. "But I will try to keep my focus."

She stifled a laugh. "You will wait outside this door for me to finish."

"But, princess—"

"Nic, please. Do as I ask. Don't make a fuss."

He stopped walking and bowed his head. "As you command, your highness."

Cleo needed as few people in this room as possible. When Lorenzo entered, she would send the attendant away so she could speak with him privately about secretly helping her.

Nerissa led the way into the large fitting room, closing the door between them and Nic. Inside there were messy swaths of cloth and half-made gowns. On one mannequin in the center of the room was Cleo's wedding gown. It was made of silk and lace with shades of gold and ivory. It had tiny pearls, sapphires, and diamonds stitched into patterns of swirling flowers on the bodice. The translucent, flowing sleeves appeared to be as light as air.

The gown was so beautiful that it took her breath away. "Nerissa . . . Lorenzo completely outdid himself."

There was no reply.

She turned. "Nerissa?"

The girl was gone. Only then did Cleo notice how dark it was. Sunlight from the window shone upon the area of the dress, but not into the corners of the cavernous room.

"Swayed by pretty frocks, your highness?" a voice said from the shadows. "Why am I not surprised?"

Her heart began to pound hard. "You."

"I did say you'd be seeing me again soon."

Jonas Agallon stood in the shadows at the edge of the room, where he must have been since she entered. She hadn't noticed him. Which surprised her, since now she couldn't see anything else *but* him. He wore tan leather trousers, black leather boots, and a simple brown tunic that bore a slight rip in the sleeve. As he drew alarmingly close to her, he smelled not of dirt and sweat, which she might have expected, but the clean scent of the forest, just as he had when he'd snuck into her chambers.

Her gaze scanned the room again as quickly as she could. "What did you do to Nerissa?"

"Nerissa is a help to me and my rebels. One of those girls you mentioned before who says yes to what I ask of them instead of giving me a difficult time. You might learn much from her."

"I'm surprised at you for endangering her. There are more than a dozen guards in the very next room who are on alert for any rebel activity."

It was an exaggeration, but there was no reason he had to know this. The king did not take the threat of outside attack lightly, yet he'd sent so very few guards along on this trip.

Jonas didn't seem alarmed at the threat of guards. He touched the sleeve of the wedding gown, sliding the sheer material between his fingers. "Have you given any more thought to my proposition?"

Her eyes narrowed. "Is that what this is about? Another attempt to woo me to the rebel cause?"

"Believe me, princess, I would never attempt to woo you. Far too much work for very little reward." A smile tugged at his lips. "So here you are, ready to be fitted in the gown you will wear to wed Prince Magnus. Very soon you'll truly be one of them."

"A gown does not make a bride, just as a few empty threats do not make a rebel."

His grin fell away. "The tongue of a snake. Yes, I think you'll fit in well with the Damoras."

"What do you want, once and for all? Speak quickly and leave. I have no patience for useless games."

"I'm asking you again. Will you help me destroy the king?"

Without realizing it, she'd drawn closer to the rebel—far closer than was comfortable. She couldn't shout, couldn't raise her voice louder than a harsh whisper. They were now very nearly touching. She forced herself not to take a shaky step back and show him that his proximity disturbed her.

She'd given this much thought since she'd last seen him. Perhaps this *was* an opportunity that could serve her well. She had put far too much hope into the idea of her ring leading her to answers that might never come.

Her stomach fluttered nervously. "If I help you, how do I know it will benefit me?"

Jonas's brows drew together. "If you help me, I believe we'll have a better chance of defeating the king currently seated upon your throne. Sounds beneficial to me."

She wrung her hands. "I don't know."

"This is not an answer helpful to either of us."

"What are the rebels' plans to overthrow King Gaius?"

"I can't tell you that."

There was a knock on the door, then a rattle of the handle. The door was locked.

"Princess?" It was Nic. "Is everything all right in there?"

Jonas swore under his breath. "I suppose I can tell you part of my plan—my immediate plan. Had you been more agreeable the last time we spoke, it might not have come to this."

She tore her gaze from the wooden door. "What? Speak quickly. They'll be coming in here in moments."

"Concerned for my safety?"

"No, for mine. If I'm found alone in a room with a rebel—"

"It would put a damper on your betrothal to the prince, wouldn't it?"

"And cost both of us our lives. You must leave while there's time."

"You're coming with me."

He must be mad. "I'm doing no such thing."

Jonas shook his head. "Apologies, your highness, but you really should have said yes the last time we spoke. It might have helped avoid the necessity of this."

Alarm grew in her chest at the dark look that had come over his expression. She turned to the door and opened her mouth to yell for help. Nic now banged on the door, attempting to break it open.

Jonas was behind her, crushing her back against his chest. His hand covered her mouth—it held a cloth that smelled strange. Of strong herbs.

"You won't believe me," he said into her ear, "but I mean you no harm."

She'd smelled the same thing once—a healer had used it to induce sleep when she'd broken her ankle as a child. To avoid further pain, and for him to have the opportunity to reset the broken bone, he'd administered this powerful medicine.

She tried to scream but found she had no voice. Darkness fell all around her.

CHAPTER 11

MAGNUS

AURANOS

The palace had been in an uproar for hours, ever since the carriage returned from Hawk's Brow without Princess Cleiona. She'd been taken from a private room in the dressmaker's shop and a note had been left behind, addressed to the king himself, tucked into the folds of the wedding gown she'd been there to see.

I have the princess. If you wish her returned unharmed, you will immediately cease construction on your road and free all those you've enslaved to work on it.

"Will you do as the rebel demands?" Magnus now asked the king. He and his father were in Lucia's chambers, standing on either side of her bed, the sleeping princess between them.

"No. I need my road finished, and soon. It will stop for nothing, especially not the demands of a rebel."

Magnus's gaze snapped to the king. "Then he'll kill her."

A nod. "Most likely."

Even for the king, this utter lack of emotion was surprising, at least until Magnus realized that this played well into his father's plans. Such an end for Cleo would gain him great sympathy from the Auranian citizens. And it would paint the rebels as abhorrent villains who would harm an innocent young girl loved by thousands of her subjects.

Still, it troubled him.

"There was no need for her to travel to another location for such a trivial thing," he said. "The fitting could have happened here."

"Yes, it could have."

Magnus frowned. "Did you know this would happen?"

The king's expression grew thoughtful. "I thought it a possibility that the rebels might act."

"So you put her in danger with the knowledge that there might be an attack?" Rage, still controlled, boiled beneath his skin at the very thought of it. "Mother was also on that journey!"

"And your mother is fine, only shaken. Magnus, you think me so cold that I would put my wife and the princess in harm's way without a single care about their safety?"

Magnus managed to hold his tongue. "So now what? We wait for the next letter to arrive listing further demands you won't meet?"

"No. I've already sent out a search team. There are rumors a Paelsian rebel group has set up camp in the Wildlands not many hours' journey from here. If they find her, your upcoming marriage can be a grand event to continue to distract the masses. But if they don't . . ." He leaned over to absently stroke a lock of dark hair off Lucia's pale forehead. "Then it's fate. The rebels will be seen as the murderers of Auranos's golden princess. They will be outcasts, hated by every person in this kingdom and beyond. Either way, we win. They lose."

Magnus flicked a glance at the attendant, Mira, on the far side of the room. She cleaned the balcony railing, running a rag along it. Her plain gray dress, the innocuous outfit of a servant, allowed her to move about dim rooms without notice, hiding in the shadows, available when needed but otherwise unnoticeable.

But Magnus couldn't help but notice that the girl's face held both worry and outrage. She knew of Cleo's kidnapping. Her brother, Magnus remembered, had gone along with the carriage as additional protection.

Some protection. Magnus personally would have taken the opportunity to have Nic punished for such a failure if the boy hadn't looked absolutely destroyed when he'd returned with the rest of the guards.

"Kill me now," Nic had spat at him, his voice breaking. "I deserve it for letting this happen."

"And interrupt your misery?" Magnus had studied his tortured expression for a moment before turning away. "Not today."

Magnus would not admit it to anyone, but the idea of the rebels capturing the princess disturbed him greatly. He didn't want to care what horrors she might be experiencing at this very moment. Besides, the princess's death would put an end to this ridiculous betrothal his father had insisted upon. It would be for the best.

But, still . . . it bothered him.

Irrelevant.

There was only one beautiful girl he gave a damn about and she was the one that lay in this bed.

"Do you know someone named Alexius?" the king asked after silence fell between them for a time.

"No. Who is that?"

"I visited Lucia yesterday for a few moments after your mother left her side. She murmured the name in her sleep."

Magnus's shoulders stiffened. Lucia had spoken in her sleep? "Did she say anything else?"

"No, only the name."

He wracked his mind but came up blank. "I don't know anyone named Alexius."

"Perhaps it's a boy she was enamored of back in Limeros."

"Perhaps." His mouth was suddenly dry. He reached for the nearly empty pitcher of water on the bedside table and poured himself what was left. He'd never heard of an Alexius before. And now this boy resided in Lucia's dreams? A ribbon of jealousy twisted within him.

"She'll wake soon," said the king.

"How can you sound so certain?"

"Because it's her destiny to help me reach *my* destiny."

There was something in the way the king said this, an absolute confidence that resonated like an echo in a canyon. "Who told you this?"

The king's dark gaze flicked to Magnus, sweeping the length of him as if assessing his son's worth. "Her name is Melenia."

"Let me guess. Your mysterious new advisor."

"That's right."

"Tell me, Father, will I ever meet this Melenia?"

"Perhaps one day. For now, it's impossible."

"Why?"

The king again hesitated before replying. "Because I see her only in my dreams."

Magnus blinked. Surely he had misheard. "I don't understand."

"Melenia is a Watcher, one with great knowledge about the

Kindred and how to go about finding them. She is over four thousand years old but blessed with eternal youth and incredible beauty."

"Your new advisor is a beautiful four-thousand-year-old Watcher who visits you in your dreams." The words were heavy in his mouth.

"Yes." The king smiled at this, as if recognizing the absurdity of what he claimed. "Melenia has confirmed for me that Lucia is the key to finding the Kindred and harnessing its power. That before this, before she existed, it was simply not possible to find it. That's why no one has ever succeeded in such a quest."

This was one of those moments that Magnus had come to recognize. A test. The king was giving him a test. How he responded to something so fantastical would set the tone for the immediate future.

Would he assume his father mad for making such statements? Believing such things? Would he be unable to hold himself back from laughing?

Once he would have, earning the king's wrath and perhaps another scar.

No more.

His entire life, he'd denied the existence of such a thing as magic, but Lucia had proved to him it was true. It was real. *Elementia*, according the books he'd recently read here in the Auranian palace library, tied back to the immortal Watchers. And Watchers, so legend told, could sometimes visit mortals in their dreams.

Magnus knew his father was dangerous, vengeful, and remorseless. However, there was one thing the king was not.

He was not stupid enough to believe in imaginary things that served no true purpose.

If his father said this, if he admitted such a thing aloud, then it had to be true. And Magnus needed to know more.

"How is Lucia the key?" he asked evenly.

"This I don't yet know." The king's brows drew together slightly. "All I know for certain is she *will* wake."

"Then I believe you."

The king's eyes lit with approval and he reached across the bed to pat Magnus's scarred cheek. "Very good, my son. Very good. Together we will find the Kindred."

"With Lucia."

"Yes." He nodded. "With Lucia."

Four crystals holding the essence of *elementia*. Magnus saw their worth, just as his father did. Such incredible and endless power and strength. If he possessed them, even one of them, he would feel equal to Lucia in more ways than he did now. He would be more than just a prince, more than just a brother. They would have magic in common and she would see and appreciate this. Appreciate *him*. And such strength would show the king that Magnus was not a boy any longer; he was a man who went after what he desired most, no matter the cost.

It was everything he'd ever wanted.

Mira had approached to refill the water jug, making eye contact with neither Magnus nor the king. She moved quietly as if hoping to remain unnoticed.

"What is your name again?" the king asked her, his voice soft.

Her shoulders went rigid as she straightened, and her gaze moved from the ground next to the bed to meet the king's directly. "Mira, your majesty."

"You haven't, by chance, been listening to anything my son and I have been discussing, have you, Mira?"

"No, your majesty," she said immediately. Her brows drew together, as if surprised by the question. "I focus on the room, cleaning, and tidying, and taking care of the princess. That's all. I don't listen."

The king nodded. "I'm very glad to hear that. With the rebels so active now, we must be very conscious of what we say and to whom we say it. Spies could be anywhere, couldn't they?"

"Of course, I completely understand." Her shoulders relaxed ever so slightly. "Was there anything else, your majesty?"

The king scratched his chin, as if considering. "I'm curious to know if my son believes you."

Magnus tensed.

His father easily wore the mask of indifference that Magnus currently struggled with. "I know you're familiar with servants who develop unhealthy habits of overhearing information by accident," the king continued, "so I'd like your opinion on the matter."

Magnus remembered the icy walls of the tower where Amia had been restrained, beaten, and questioned about her crime of eavesdropping—which she'd done on his orders. He'd sent the girl away so she'd have the chance at a better life—at *any* life—but his father had her hunted down and killed anyway. Magnus chose his next words very carefully.

"We were speaking quietly and this girl was on the other side of the room. I believe she heard nothing that would cause any problems. Besides, even if she did hear something, she would take it no further if she knew what was good for her. Am I right, Mira?"

The girl glanced at him, distrust in her gaze that he might say anything to defend her. "Yes, your grace."

The king let out a long sigh. "Of course you're right. Listen to me. I've become an old man convinced that enemies are hiding in every shadow." He laughed as he moved around to the other side of the bed so he could pat her cheek affectionately, just as he'd done before to Magnus. "Mira, my dear girl, please accept my sincere apologies for alarming you."

The hint of a smile appeared on her pretty face. "No apology is necessary, your majesty."

The king regarded her a moment longer. "However, I do believe in taking certain precautions."

With unexpected speed, he took hold of her head with both hands and twisted sharply. The girl's neck broke with a loud crack. She crumpled to the ground, her wide eyes now blank and glazed and absent of life.

It had all happened in an instant.

Magnus stared at his father, unable to conceal his horrified shock. "You didn't have to do that!"

The king wiped his hands off on the front of his black surcoat. "Meaningless servants can be replaced. She was nothing special. I'll find another to attend your sister."

Nothing special. Only a friend to Princess Cleo. Only a sister to Nicolo Cassian. Only another whose life had been snuffed out by the king while Magnus stood idly by.

He wanted so desperately not to care about this—not to care about *anything* but finding the Kindred for himself and for Lucia— to be as cold and ruthless as his father found it so easy to be.

If only that were possible.

After the king left Lucia's chambers, Cronus entered. Wordlessly, the large, brutish guard swept Mira's lifeless body up into his arms and departed the room.

A beam of sunlight shone in through the balcony window,

illuminating a small patch on the floor. Otherwise, the room was in shadows. A collection of candles next to the bed lent their flickering light to the princess's tranquil face.

Magnus held on to the edge of the silk sheets, squeezing hard and trying to concentrate on nothing but the smooth feel of the fabric. His heart still thundered from what had happened. The girl hadn't meant any harm, he was sure of it.

Yet now she was dead.

His legs weakened and he sank down to his knees next to Lucia's side. He squeezed his eyes shut and pressed his forehead against the edge of the bed.

Then he heard something. A quiet moan. Then a deep intake of breath.

He opened his eyes. Lucia's eyelids fluttered, as if she was having another dream—perhaps one about Alexius. Whoever he was.

Then he caught a glimpse of her bright blue eyes beneath thick black lashes. Slowly, she turned her head to face him.

"Magnus?" she whispered, her voice hoarse.

His breath caught. Surely, he had to be the one who was dreaming now. "Lucia . . . is this true? Are you really awake?"

She squinted at him as if the meager amount of light in this room was too much for her to bear. "How long have I been asleep?"

"Far too long," he managed to reply.

A frown creased her brow. "What about Hana? Is Hana all right?"

It took him a moment to understand what she meant. Hana was Lucia's pet rabbit, a gift from Magnus that he'd brought back to her at the Limerian castle after a hunt. "Hana is fine. In fact, Mother brought her along for you when she journeyed here to be with us. She arrived a few days after we took over this palace."

The worry that had been in her eyes lessened. "Good."

"This is incredible." He pushed himself up to his feet, wanting to pinch himself to prove he wasn't asleep. "I didn't think you'd ever open your eyes again, but you're here. You're back!"

Lucia tried to raise her head off the pillow but failed. Her gaze slid around the room as if she was searching for something. For *someone.*

"You didn't answer me before," she said. "How long was I gone?"

"Forever. Or it seemed like it to me. It's been almost a month and a half since the siege upon this castle." The joy this moment should summon was dampened as Magnus remembered the girl who'd just lost her life and how she had dutifully attended Lucia for much of the time she was comatose. Lucia would never meet her, could never thank her.

Lucia's eyes widened. "That long?"

"Father insists on staying here in Auranos as a physical reminder to everyone of his claim upon this kingdom and throne. All of Mytica is now his after . . . after his alliance with the Paelsian chief fell through." Actually, the king had murdered Chief Basilius during a celebratory dinner. All part of King Gaius's master plan.

Magnus sat down on the edge of the bed and gazed into Lucia's eyes. He wanted to pull her into his arms and hold her tight, but resisted the urge. Given the strain between them from when he'd kissed her before, he knew that wouldn't be wise.

He didn't believe his heart would recover from her rejection, but here he was, and his pulse pounded hard and fast now that she had finally returned to him. Another chance to prove himself to her. He would not act so impulsively again.

"You're awake now and all is well," he said. "How do you feel?"

"Weak. And . . . horrible." She drew in a shaky breath. "I killed people with my magic, Magnus."

More than two hundred had died in or because of the explosion, but he chose not to share such distressing numbers with her. "No one blames you for anything that happened. It had to be done. And had it not, we wouldn't have won. We would be the ones who died. It's not your fault."

"That's what he told me too—that it wasn't my fault."

He looked at her sharply. "Who told you?"

She pressed her lips together and looked away. "No one."

"Who is Alexius, Lucia?"

Her eyes, now wide, returned to lock with his. "Where did you hear that name?"

"I'm told that you whispered it in your sleep." Something dark and endlessly unpleasant stirred within him.

"Alexius, he's . . ." Lucia shook her head. "No one. Just a dream. Nothing more than that."

Before Magnus could ask another question, the door creaked open and the queen entered, alone.

She greeted Magnus with a smile. "I wanted to check on Lucia, to see if she's—" She gasped and closed the distance to the bed in only a few steps. "Lucia! My darling! You've come back to us. Praise the goddess!"

Lucia's distressed expression froze away. "My, my. What a greeting. I must truly have been close to death to elicit such devotion from you."

The queen flinched. "I suppose I deserve that."

Lucia's face paled. "Apologies, Mother. I—I didn't mean such poisonous words. I'm sorry. It's as though I couldn't hold them back."

"Nor should you, my darling. You must always give voice to how you feel. Don't hold it inside." The queen quickly composed herself and sat down on the edge of the bed. "Do you remember the last time you rose from your slumber? This has happened before."

Magnus's gaze shot to her. "It has?"

She nodded. "Twice before when I was here. Alas, it never lasts more than a few minutes and then she falls asleep again."

He fisted his hands at his sides. "Why didn't you tell me this?"

His mother turned her head at his sharp and angry tone, her expression patient. "Because I knew you would only be disappointed. I know how deeply you love your sister."

There was something in the way she said it. Did the queen know Magnus's dark secret as Lucia did?

He wished that they might wipe the slate clean. To return to how it was when everything was simpler between them. To start again.

Impossible.

"I don't remember waking before," Lucia said, confused, as she pushed herself up to a sitting position.

"You still should have told me, Mother," Magnus growled. "And told Father, too."

"And risk one of his rages when she slipped away yet again? No, my son. I certainly shouldn't have. We will see how this goes, if she stays with us this time, before we say a single word about it to him."

"I *will* stay awake," Lucia insisted.

"Go now," the queen said, standing up and squeezing Magnus's hands in her own. "I'll attend to my daughter."

"But, Mother—"

"Go," she said, her tone firm. "And say nothing to the king until I tell you otherwise."

The anger that had risen inside him at the thought that his mother would keep such secrets from him hadn't yet lessened, but he did understand why she'd chosen to do so. After all, he would have done exactly the same to protect Lucia.

"Fine." The word was uttered through clenched teeth. "But I will come back."

"Of course you will. You've never been able to stay away from her for long. She's the only one you've ever truly cared about, isn't she?"

A muscle in his scarred cheek twitched. "Wrong, Mother. I cared about you. And I could again, if you let me."

His words had succeeded in bringing a glistening to the queen's eyes, but her only reply was a shallow nod. He shifted his gaze to Lucia. "I'll return soon. I promise. Please . . . don't fall asleep again."

Then he left them alone just as the queen commanded.

CHAPTER 12

LUCIA

AURANOS

The majesty of the room around her took Lucia's breath away. Compared to her more austere chambers in the Limerian palace, this was the very definition of luxury. The floors and walls shone as if set with precious metals. The breeze from the open balcony window was warm, not frigid. The canopied bed was soft, covered in imported fabrics that were colorful and silky, with fur throws that were pure white and as soft and warm as Hana's fur.

So very strange—it was as if she was still dreaming.

Dreaming.

Alexius . . .

At first, she thought it had been him sitting vigil at her bedside as she woke. But Alexius's hair was bronze, not black. His eyes golden and full of joy, not dark brown and pained. She hoped Magnus had not seen the disappointment in her own eyes that it was he she saw, not the boy from her dreams.

The queen sat back down on the edge of the bed and pressed her cool hand to Lucia's forehead. "How are you feeling, my darling? Thirsty?"

Lucia nodded. "I don't remember waking before. But you say I did?"

"Yes. Twice. But it was only for a moment."

"Only a moment . . . not like this?"

"No." The queen smiled. "Not like this. Then you drifted off again."

Her gaze moved to the balcony, to the sliver of blue sky she could see beyond it. "I want to see Father."

"Of course. Very soon."

The queen moved off to the side to pour her some water and brought it back, holding the silver goblet to Lucia's lips. The water was blissfully cool as it slid down her throat.

"Thank you," she whispered.

"I've heard what you did. How you used your *elementia* to help Gaius take this palace. Take this kingdom." The queen sat again beside Lucia. "Many people died that day, but your father got the victory he desired."

Lucia swallowed hard. "How many died?"

"Countless innocent lives were lost. I arrived as quickly as I could. I wanted to be here with my family, no matter what the outcome of the war. Gaius didn't know I'd be traveling so soon. In fact, he was angry with me that I'd arrived unannounced. But I'm here. And I've watched over you every day since."

Countless innocent lives.

She couldn't blame herself for this, she told herself frantically. Her father and Magnus had been in danger—all of Limeros had been in danger. She did what she had to for her family, for her kingdom. Magnus had nearly died in front of her from injuries he'd sustained in the battle. Only her earth magic had healed him in time. Without it, he'd be gone.

And she'd do it again—every bit of it—if necessary to save those she loved.

Wouldn't she?

Her eyes were so heavy. She was weary after only being awake a short time. It worried her that she might fall asleep again as her mother said she had before.

"Your *elementia* is destructive, Lucia," the queen said softly. "You've proven that—both with Sabina's murder and the horror of what you did here."

Lucia's stomach twisted. "I didn't mean to kill all those people. And—Sabina . . ." The memory of the flames, of her father's mistress burning, screaming, sent a shudder through her. "She had a blade to Magnus's throat. I . . . didn't think. I didn't intend to kill her, only stop her."

The queen gently stroked the long, dark hair back from Lucia's face. "I know, my darling. Which makes it even worse. Gaius celebrates everything you can do, but there's a heavy price that must be paid for such dark power. He's not the one who will be forced to pay it, though. You are. And you don't even realize it yet."

Her mother's words confused her. "You call it dark power? *Elementia* is natural magic . . . from the elements that created the universe itself. It's not dark."

"It is when it's used to destroy. To kill. And that is what Gaius wants you for—it's *all* he wants you for." Her expression soured. "His endless quest for ultimate power. But at what cost?"

"He's king. A king wants power." Lucia moistened her dry lips with the tip of her tongue. "You don't have to be afraid of me,

Mother. Despite our past differences, I swear to the goddess I would never harm you."

The queen smiled humorlessly at this as she lifted the goblet to Lucia's lips so she could swallow another mouthful of the cool, soothing water. "There will soon come a time when you don't realize whom you're harming with your magic, Lucia. When you have no control over it anymore. When its evil completely takes you over."

"I'm *not* evil!" While she'd rarely received anything but sharp words from this woman in her sixteen years of life, rarely had she been as wounded from them as she was right now.

The queen placed the empty goblet on the carved ebony bedside table and turned to grasp Lucia's hands in hers. "I've sought answers to questions no one has asked. You don't know what's ahead—what to expect. You have so much *elementia* inside you that now it's awakened it can only grow larger—like a volcano simmering, ready to erupt. And when that eruption happens . . ."

Lucia tried to harness her racing thoughts. "What? What will happen?"

There were dark circles under the queen's eyes that hinted that she hadn't slept well for some time. "I won't let him destroy you for his own gain."

"Mother, please . . ."

Her jaw tensed and she pulled away from Lucia's grip. "He thinks I'm weak, that I stand by and watch him work his darkness without opinion or judgment. That I am only a dutiful wife who is of no consequence. But he's wrong. I see my purpose now, Lucia. It's to stop him any way I can. He doesn't realize what it is he hopes to unleash upon the world. He thinks he can control that which is uncontrollable."

Lucia found she was now trembling.

"I need to get up." Alarmed, but still weary, she struggled to swing herself out of the bed, but the queen pressed down on her shoulder to keep her prone.

"I must kill you," the queen whispered. "To save you from what I fear is ahead. To end this as it's only beginning. But I can't—not yet. When I look at you, I see the tiny, beautiful baby that was brought to me sixteen years ago. I hated you then—and I loved you."

Lucia stared at the queen, horrified by her words.

"Now," the queen continued, "only love remains. Love is the only thing that matters in the end. What I've done has been out of love, Lucia."

A wave of dizziness washed over her and Lucia's gaze shot to the silver goblet. "The water . . ."

"It's a very powerful potion." The queen touched the drinking vessel, sliding her finger around the sparkling edge. "Undetectable to anyone through taste. Sleep, my darling. Such darkness will not touch you in your dreams. Sleep in peace. And when I finally find the strength to end your life, I promise I will be gentle."

A potion—a sleeping potion . . .

"Sleep now, my dear girl," the queen's voice soothed.

Lucia's gaze slid to the balcony to see the golden edge of a hawk's wing.

"Alexius," she whispered as the luxurious chambers around her faded away.

CHAPTER 13

ALEXIUS

THE SANCTUARY

Phaedra summoned him to the crystal palace and Alexius had no choice but to go to her immediately. He found her there, her beautiful face etched with worry.

"It's Stephanos," she said.

The name of Phaedra's beloved mentor drew him closer. After Phaedra's own brother was exiled from the Sanctuary twenty years ago, she had turned to both Stephanos and Alexius as her closest friends in this realm. "What's wrong with him?"

"He's dying." The long, flowing cloak she wore today was a shade of platinum, nearly an exact match to her hair.

"Dying?" The word was so foreign that it felt false on his tongue.

Dying was for mortals, not for those who lived in the Sanctuary.

She grabbed hold of his shirt to pull him closer. "They don't want many to know, but I needed you here so you could see for yourself. There's not much time left."

She was frantic, and Alexius knew nothing he could say to her right now would ease her pain.

"What can be done?" he asked.

She just shook her head. "Nothing. There's no way he can be saved."

His heart sank. "Take me there."

Phaedra led him to the uppermost level of the palace and into a large room surrounded by a circular glass wall. Otherwise, it was open to the sky—always blue and always day, never night. The room was bare apart from a raised golden platform in the center. On this platform lay Stephanos. He was surrounded by the Three—those that made up the council of elders that governed this world. They were the oldest and most powerful of the immortals.

"Why is *he* here?" the elder named Danaus asked, his voice as unwelcoming as the question itself. He was the member of the Three that Alexius trusted the least—one he would never tell about his shared dreams with Princess Lucia, nor his discovery that she was the prophesied sorceress. Danaus was always prying into his business and trying to learn more about what Alexius did during his journeys to the princess's world and the never-ending search for the Kindred.

The elder was jealous of Alexius's ability to take hawk form and enter the mortal world. Since the Kindred had been lost, the three elders could no longer take hawk form. For all their power and influence among the immortals, they were trapped here and had been for a millennium.

"I wanted him here," Phaedra said, her chin raised high. She wasn't intimidated by any of the elders and never had been.

Then again, Phaedra didn't know some of the secrets that

Alexius did. Perhaps if she did, her bravery would waver.

"This is a private matter," Danaus growled. "And it must remain so."

"It's all right," Stephanos said, his voice as frail as his appearance. "I don't mind another witness. You are welcome to stay, Alexius."

"Thank you, Stephanos."

Stephanos's chest moved rapidly with labored breathing. Since the last time Alexius had seen him, his previously dark hair had turned white and brittle, his perfect golden skin now pallid and deeply lined like that of an old man.

A face that had never looked older than twenty-five mortal years now looked four times that.

The sight of such sudden and unexpected decay soured Alexius's stomach, and both pity and revulsion swirled within him.

Timotheus, a more welcome sight to Alexius, nodded in his direction. He was Alexius's own mentor. In looks alone, he could be Alexius's older brother, even though Timotheus was twice his age. The thought of losing such a wise friend, as Phaedra was about to lose her own, pained him deeply. But Timotheus looked as young and strong as ever. The only place the elder showed his age was in his golden eyes, now heavy with worry and grief.

Timotheus nodded in his direction and offered him the edge of a grim smile to show that he did not share Danaus's unwelcoming attitude when it came to Alexius's presence.

And then there was the third member of the council.

Alexius felt the weight of her gaze before he chanced a glance in her direction.

Melenia's beauty, even among the beautiful immortals, was legendary. The elder seemed chiseled from gold, her pale hair falling to her knees in soft waves, a vision of perfection in every way—physically, the most glorious immortal ever to exist. While she appeared to be as young as the others on the council, Melenia was the oldest of their kind—her age countless. Eternal.

"Yes, you are welcome to stay," she said smoothly. "Unless you would rather not, Alexius."

Phaedra's grip tightened on his hand. She wanted him here, to support her in this difficult time. If she didn't, she wouldn't have wasted her magic in summoning him.

"Why is this happening?" Alexius asked, his throat tight.

Melenia arched her brow. "It is tragic but very simple what is happening. Our magic is fading enough that it cannot sustain every one of our kind. This is the result."

"The tornado in Paelsia was magic—*air* magic," Phaedra said. "I saw it myself—I was there in hawk form. It drained power from the Sanctuary, and that—I'm sure that's what triggered Stephanos's condition. But how? How does what happens in the mortal world affect us? I didn't think we were connected at all. Do you think it has something to do with the road the mortal king builds through his land?"

All eyes went to Phaedra.

"You're mistaken," Melenia said. "What is happening to Stephanos is the result of a slow draining away of our magic that has happened over time. A natural disaster that occurred in the mortal world has nothing to do with this."

Phaedra shook her head. "Perhaps King Gaius is being guided by one who knows about us—about how to access our magic for his own gain."

"Nonsense," Danaus said, looking down his nose at her. "No mortal has any effect on us, no matter who he is."

"Are you certain of that?" Timotheus asked.

Danaus's expression tensed. "I am."

Timotheus smiled, an expression that did not extend to his eyes. "Must be nice to always be so certain of everything."

"Don't be so sure of what you speak, Danaus," Melenia said. "Perhaps there is some validity to what Phaedra suspects. She has always been very clever. We must keep a close watch over King Gaius and his future actions. He could be a threat."

"A threat?" Danaus scoffed. "If so, he'd be the first mortal to ever threaten us."

"And yet, here we are." Melenia cast a glance toward Stephanos, who'd squeezed his wrinkled eyes shut as if experiencing deep, unfathomable pain.

"All this means," Danaus said sourly, "is that our scouts must find the Kindred to restore our magic completely so we don't all wither away and die."

"We're trying," Alexius growled. Although, in truth, he had ceased searching for the crystals when a princess with sky-blue eyes and jet-black hair had captured his full attention.

"Doesn't seem to me that you've tried very hard."

"We have. The search has never stopped, not even long after it should have. The Kindred cannot be found."

"You've given up? With so much at stake? Who will next be affected after Stephanos? Perhaps it will be you!"

"Silence, Danaus." A muscle in Timotheus's cheek twitched. "Squabbling amongst ourselves solves nothing."

Alexius knew that Timotheus didn't favor either council member; in fact, he barely tolerated both of them. The Sanctuary was a small enclave, with a few hundred immortals forced to live together indefinitely. For all its beauty, it was a prison, escapable only by forfeiting both magic and immortality. And the inmates didn't all get along.

"If nothing else," Timotheus began, "this is absolute proof that our world is slowly descending into darkness like a sun in the mortal world slipping beneath the horizon. Even if the Kindred were returned here tomorrow, it could be too late to stop this."

"Always the pessimist," Melenia said drily.

"Realist," Timotheus corrected.

Stephanos cried out in pain.

"It is time," Melenia whispered. She walked back toward Stephanos, gazing down at his face. "I wish there was something I could do to save you, my dear friend."

Despite her kind words, he didn't look up at her with affection. In fact, it was as if he was seeing her today for the first time. His eyes narrowed. "You think your secrets will die with me, Melenia?"

But before he could say another word, he cried out again and arched upward, his frail body shuddering violently. And then bright white light exploded from him. Alexius staggered backward and shielded his eyes to keep from being blinded. The scream of a hawk pierced the air and the glass wall all around them shattered into a million crystal shards.

Everything before him went stark white as the scream continued. It felt as if they could never survive such a violent onslaught of both sight and sound.

Fear ripped into Alexius and he fell bruisingly hard to his knees, clamping his hands down over his ears, a scream building in his own chest.

But then all went silent. The light faded, the sound vanished. The golden platform was now empty. Stephanos's body was gone.

It had returned to the essence of pure magic it began from, the magic that sustained their world.

Phaedra staggered toward Alexius as he pushed up to his feet. He held his arms out to her and she collapsed against him, shaking.

"I thought we'd have more time!" she cried.

"It is done," Danaus said to Melenia.

"Yes," she replied solemnly. "He will be missed."

Timotheus eyed the beautiful immortal curiously. "What did he mean, Melenia? What secrets did he speak of?"

She offered him a weary smile. "His mind was decaying faster than his body. So sad to witness such an end to one of the brightest and best of us all."

"Who is to be next?" Danaus's expression was tense. "Who of us will die next?"

"The Kindred still exists," Melenia said evenly. "If we exist, then it exists. And it can be found before all is lost."

"You're certain about that?"

"I've never been more certain about anything." She moved toward Alexius and Phaedra, clasping both of their hands in hers. "The loss of Stephanos has bound us together. We will go forth stronger, in trust and friendship. Yes?"

"Of course," Alexius agreed. Phaedra remained silent.

"Go now. And speak of this to no one."

They didn't need to be told twice. Alexius and Phaedra departed without another word. They didn't talk again until they'd left the palace, left the city, and journeyed as far as Alexius's favorite meadow. He expected his troubled friend to collapse with grief. Instead, when he turned to face her, she shoved him very hard. He staggered backward, rubbing his chest and staring at her with confusion.

"What was that for?"

"For lapping up every lie that spills from her lips."

"Who?"

"Melenia, of course. Who else? The pretty spider in her silvery web, spinning tales to wind around us all. You heard him at the end! Stephanos wanted to expose her lies."

"He was dying. He didn't know what he was saying."

"Are you that blinded by her beauty that you can't see the truth? She's evil, Alexius!"

"You should be careful what you say about Melenia."

She raised her chin. "I'm not afraid of her."

"Phaedra—"

"Does she know about your little sorceress? Do any of them other than me?"

Alexius froze. "What?"

"The one you visit in your dreams." A tense smile now played on her lips. "You think I don't know what you do out here all alone? You talk in your sleep—Lucia . . . *Lucia*. A terrible habit for someone with secrets to keep. Are you falling in love with a mortal, Alexius? Others have walked such a path only to find themselves lost and unable to find their way back home."

He *knew* Phaedra had been watching him. Such questions, such accusations made him feel exposed, cornered. "You will tell no one of this."

She shook her head with disgust. "I need to go. I have places to be, mortals to watch. Dreams to visit. You're not the only one keeping watch over specific mortals, Alexius."

"Phaedra, no. We need to talk about this."

Phaedra's eyes sparkled. "I'm done talking. All I can tell you is one thing—watch out for Melenia. I've never trusted her, but lately . . . I know she's up to something—and I think I know what it is. And trust me, if you aren't smart, she will destroy you."

Without another word she turned and began to run. Her form shimmered and shifted, taking the shape of a golden hawk that flew up high into the clear blue sky.

CHAPTER 14

JONAS

THE WILDLANDS

When Princess Cleo awoke, she found herself in the back of a rickety horse-drawn cart speeding across the countryside, her wrists bound.

Jonas had thought it best to restrain her. He knew she wasn't going to be very happy with him. This was, perhaps, an understatement.

"Welcome back," Jonas greeted her as she opened her aquamarine eyes.

She regarded him sleepily as the rest of the sleeping drug wore off.

Then clarity entered her gaze.

"You beast!" she snarled, lunging for him even while secured. "I hate you!"

He gently pushed her back down to a seated position. "Save your breath, your highness. You'll strain yourself."

Her gaze moved frantically around. "Where are you taking me?"

"Home sweet home."

"Why have you done this?"

"Desperate times, princess."

"You overestimate my worth to Prince Magnus and his father. Whatever you've asked for will be denied!"

"I asked him to stop construction on his road."

Her brows shot up. "That was a stupid request! There are a million more important things for a rebel to demand from a king. You're not very good at this, are you?"

Jonas leveled a dark look at her. Sometimes he forgot just how sharp her tongue could be. "Do you even know what that road is doing? How much Paelsian blood has soaked the ground at the construction camps? How many have died in the last month?"

Her mouth fell open. "No. If such horrors are true . . . I'm so sorry."

It was not the first she'd ever heard of such atrocities—he'd mentioned it before, though not in detail, when he'd visited her chambers. But she would not have seen any proof. Despite her lofty betrothal to the prince, Jonas still believed her to be very much a prisoner of war told little of what happened outside the palace walls.

"The King of Blood does not have a gentle hand in dealing with slave labor. He may have lulled the majority of your Auranians into a false sense of security, but I assure you, the same cannot be said for my people. I saw for myself what his guards have full permission to do without penalty or opposition. And it must be stopped at any cost."

The high color in her cheeks drained away. "Of course it must be stopped."

Her words were unexpected and full of sincerity. It took him a moment to find his voice. "Looks like we do agree on a few things after all. How shocking."

"You want to paint me with the same brush you paint the Damoras.

I'm not like them. But if you wanted to kidnap someone with influence in that family, it shouldn't have been me. My death at the hands of a rebel would ultimately be a gift to the king, not a hardship."

In the dress shop, he'd told her he'd meant her no harm, but he couldn't blame her for thinking the worst. This was the second time he'd kidnapped her. He must seem truly beastly to this girl. Jonas leaned toward her, ignoring her automatic flinch, and began to untie her bindings so her hands would be free.

"I guess we'll have to wait and see about that, won't we, princess?"

Once they reached the edge of the Wildlands, thirty miles from Hawk's Brow, Jonas thanked the driver of the cart—an Auranian sympathetic to the rebel cause he'd met during his previous visit to the city, at the same time he recruited Nerissa as a helper—and guided Cleo into the darkness of the thick forest.

She didn't run from him or fight. It took very little pressure on her arm to keep her at his side as they moved across the tangled terrain.

"Murderous thieves make their home here." She failed to keep the tremble from her voice.

"Absolutely," Jonas replied.

"Dangerous animals, too."

"Without a doubt."

She slanted a look toward him. "Perfect place for you."

He repressed a snort. "Oh, such compliments, your highness. You're going to make me blush."

"If you took that as a compliment, you're even more stupid than I thought you were."

This time he couldn't hold back his grin. "I've been called worse than stupid."

A royal like her would never normally have journeyed past the tree line to see how dark the forest could get, especially this close to dusk. The thick leaves on the tall, imposing trees blocked out any sunlight, casting a soulless darkness all around them, as if this were the middle of the night. Cleo stumbled on the twisting roots of the trees, nearly falling. Jonas gripped her arm tighter. "No time to stop, princess. Not much farther now."

Even he didn't like to tarry long in such a place without the protection of a larger group.

She yanked at her skirts to keep them out of the muck and weeds and gave him a dirty look.

Finally, they arrived at a slight clearing. A bonfire crackled, lending light to the gathering darkness. The strong scent of cooked venison told Jonas that the hunt had gone well today. The rebels wouldn't go hungry tonight.

The princess's steps faltered again as shadows approached. At least three dozen rebels with ragged clothes and unfriendly expressions drew closer. Some began to climb the trees. Cleo looked up, her eyes widening at the sight of the makeshift shelters strung together with rope, sticks, and thin pieces of wood twenty feet up into the thick branches.

"This is where you live," she said with surprise.

"For now."

Cleo crossed her arms and swept a glance through the camp. Only a few rebels looked directly at her—some with curiosity, but most with distrust or contempt. Not the friendliest place in the world for a royal princess, that was for sure.

Tarus raced out in front of them, flashing Jonas a grin as he pursued a rabbit. At fourteen, he was one of the youngest of the rebels and endlessly enthusiastic, if currently unskilled in combat. Jonas had taken him along on several recruiting missions. The kid's slight build and friendly face helped to set at ease the minds of any suspicious citizens Jonas wished to speak with.

The sound of conversation, of chirping insects, and the squawk of birds high in the trees brought the forest to life all around them.

It wasn't so bad here. At least, *he* didn't think so.

Cleo scratched her arm where she'd been bitten by a mosquito, seeming more annoyed than fearful now that this indignity had been heaped upon her. Too bad. It wasn't the finest golden palace, or even a reasonably decent inn, but it would have to do.

Brion approached. "Need any help here?" he asked, flicking a look at Jonas.

"No," Jonas replied. "Everything's fine. Go find your girlfriend and keep her out of my way. I don't need any more trouble tonight."

"You mean the girlfriend who, depending on the day, hates my guts almost as much as she hates yours?"

"That's the one."

Brion moved away past the fire, slapping a boy named Phineas on his back. They laughed about something while glancing back in Cleo's direction.

"That's Brion," Jonas said. "He's a close friend of mine. Strong, loyal, brave."

"Good for him." Cleo narrowed her eyes. "You're their leader, aren't you?"

Jonas shrugged. "I do my best."

"And on your orders they'll kill me—even your close friend Brion. Or would you prefer to do it yourself?" When he didn't answer right away she turned to look directly at him. "Well?"

He drew closer and curled his fingers around her upper arm.

The girl spoke too loudly and much too freely. She was worse than Lysandra. "You'd probably be smart not to make such suggestions out loud, your highness. You might give some of my rebels ideas. Not everyone agrees with my decision to bring you here."

She tried to pull away but he held firm.

"Unhand me," she snapped.

"This is politics only, princess. What I've done today—what I'll do in the days ahead—is for my people. Only them." Jonas's gaze shifted to the left and he swore under his breath when he saw who now swiftly approached.

Lysandra's hair was loose from her braid, a long, wild tangle of dark curls. Her brown eyes fixed on Cleo. "So this is her, is it? Her *royal highness*?"

"It is," Jonas said, already weary. Dealing with the stubborn and opinionated Lysandra was exhausting even on the best of days. "Lysandra Barbas, please meet Princess Cleiona Bellos."

Cleo remained silent, wary, as the girl looked her up and down.

"She's still breathing," Lysandra observed.

"Yes, she is," Jonas confirmed.

Lysandra walked a slow circle around Cleo, eyeing her gown, her jewelry, the pointy tips of her gold sandals peeking out from beneath her skirts. "Should we send the king one of her royal fingers as proof that we have her?"

"Lysandra," Jonas hissed, his anger rising. "Shut up."

"Is that a yes?"

"Let me guess," Cleo said, her expression pinched. "This is one of your rebels who did not approve of your plan to kidnap me."

"Lysandra has her own ideas on what decisions I should be making these days."

The rebel girl swept her disapproving gaze over Cleo again. "I don't fully understand the worth in kidnapping useless girls who serve no purpose other than looking pretty."

"You don't even know me," Cleo snapped. "And yet you've decided you hate me. That would be as fair as my hating you, sight unseen."

Lysandra rolled her eyes. "Let's just say that I hate all royals equally. And you're a royal. Therefore, I hate you. Nothing personal."

"Which makes absolutely no sense. Nothing personal? Hate is something I take quite personally. If I've earned it, that's one thing. If I haven't . . . it's a foolish decision for you to serve out such a strong emotion without thought."

Lysandra's brows drew together. "King Gaius burned my village to the ground and enslaved my people. He killed my mother and father. And my brother, Gregor—I don't know where he is. I might never see him again." She spoke even more furiously. "You, though—you don't know pain. You don't know struggle and sacrifice. You were born with a golden spoon in your mouth and a gilded roof over your head. You're betrothed to a prince!"

Again, Jonas opened his mouth to speak. This was leading them nowhere and had gained the attention of a dozen more rebels, who were now listening intently to the girls.

But the princess spoke first. Cleo's eyes flashed. "You don't think I've known pain? Perhaps it's different from the horrors you've experienced, but I assure you, I have. I lost my beloved sister to a disease no healer could name. I found her body myself, cold in her bed only hours before King Gaius invaded my home. My father was murdered trying to defend his kingdom from his enemy. He fought side by side with his men rather than hide himself away where he might have been safe. My mother died in childbirth with me and I never met her—but I knew my sister hated me for years because of this. I lost a trusted guard, a . . . a boy I'd given my heart to, when he defended me against the very prince I'm now betrothed to against my will. I have lost almost everyone in this world I love in such a short time that I can barely remain standing and contain my grief." She drew in a ragged breath. "Think of me what you will. But I swear to the goddess I will have my throne back—and King Gaius will pay for his crimes."

Lysandra stared at her for another moment, her eyes now brimming with tears. "You're damn right he will." Without another word, she stormed away from them and disappeared into the dark forest, followed after a moment by Brion.

Had Cleo won the girl over or had her speech fallen on deaf ears? Jonas didn't know. And he still wasn't sure how much of Lysandra's bravado was real and how much was generated to make her look tough in front of the others. But the pain in her eyes whenever she spoke of her village, of her parents and her lost brother . . . that was real. He understood her pain, just as he understood Cleo's. For two very different girls, they had a lot in common.

He realized the princess was glaring at him.

"Yes?" he asked.

Cleo raised her chin. "If you decide to kill me when King Gaius refuses your demands, know I will fight for my life until my very last breath."

"I don't doubt it for a solitary moment." Jonas cocked his head. "Though I think there's some sort of misunderstanding here. I don't plan to kill you—now or later. But am I going to use you against the Damoras as much as I possibly can? You bet I am."

Her brows drew together. "How?"

"He holds you as a symbol of hope and unity to the Auranian people. The rebels shall do the same. If he refuses to meet my demands to ensure your safe return, you will stay here with us as a rebel. If the golden princess chooses to stand with us in the face of the king's lies, that is a very strong statement."

Her mouth dropped open, and she was about to protest, but he held up his hand.

"I do believe he values you alive. But, of course, I'm not an idiot. He assumes that we'll choose the violent path if he doesn't comply, and this would also serve him well. Any footing the rebels have gained in the view of those people would be lost if you're harmed. But it's not my plan to hurt you in any way. You are worth more to me—and to the king—alive than dead. So I suggest you settle in, get comfortable, and wait it out. We'll feed you, give you a place to sleep. This forest has a fierce reputation, so rarely does anyone sane venture in here."

Cleo swept her eyes over the length of him. "Obviously."

He offered her the edge of a grin. "I know my means of getting you here were far from gentle. But I swear no one will abuse you now that you're here. You're safe. And know this: I personally plan to shove my blade through the king's heart and free my people from his tyranny. When I have that chance, you might just get your throne back. But Auranos is not my concern; Paelsia is."

He let his words settle in.

Cleo nodded. "And the future of Auranos and its citizens is mine."

"Another thing we have in common—a love of our individual lands. That's good. So, tell me, princess, will you continue to fight me on everything I do? Or will you be nice and cooperate?"

Cleo didn't speak for a long, silent moment. But then she met his gaze full-on, and it was every bit as fierce as his was. "Fine. I'll cooperate. But I might not be nice about it."

He couldn't help but laugh. "I can live with that."

CHAPTER 15

CLEO

THE WILDLANDS

It had been seven days surrounded by a swarm of rebels. With the fine clothes she'd arrived there wearing, she stuck out in the camp like a sore thumb. After a day, she'd asked for a change of clothing and received some ragged garments to wear. Jonas gave her an extra tunic and a loose pair of trousers held up only by the power of a drawstring cinched tightly around her waist.

Among the rebels, Cleo had drawn closer to those who didn't look at her as if they despised her simply for being royalty. Among these rare few was Brion, Jonas's second in command, and a young, skinny boy named Tarus, who sported a shock of red hair that immediately reminded her of Nic.

Nic.

Worry ate at her with each hour, each day that passed since she'd been taken from the dress shop. Was he all right? What would the king do to him? And Mira . . . she must think Cleo dead by now. If only Cleo could get a message to her.

She'd asked Jonas if she could send one. He'd replied simply with a "no." And then he'd walked away from her, ignoring her outrage.

Presently, she sat with Brion, Tarus, and one of the very few female rebels, Onoria, around the campfire. Auranian days were warm and temperate and filled with light, but at night here in the Wildlands, the breeze seemed every bit as cold as she imagined Limeros to be.

"Every hawk you see is a Watcher watching us," Tarus said. "My pa told me that."

"*Every* hawk?" Brion scoffed. "Not every single one. Most are just birds, nothing more magical than that."

"Do you believe in magic?" Cleo asked, curious.

Brion pushed a long stick into the crackling fire. "Depends on the day. Today, not so much. Tomorrow . . . maybe."

Cleo glanced up. "So what about *that* hawk? Is that a Watcher?"

A golden hawk had settled into one of the few trees that didn't have a sleeping shack built into its branches. It seemed quite content to sit there and look down on them.

Onoria looked up at it, pushing long strands of dark hair out of her eyes. "I've noticed her before. She never hunts, just watches us. Or, really, if you ask me—she watches Jonas."

"Really?" Cleo said, now intrigued.

"See? Definitely a Watcher if she's taken a special interest in our leader." Tarus stared up at the bird with admiration. "Their wings are made from pure gold, did you know that? That's what my ma told me."

Cleo remembered her hours of research as well as the legends she'd heard all her life. "I've heard they can also look like mortals if they choose to—with golden skin and beauty unlike anything seen in our world."

"I don't know about that. I've seen a few unreal beauties in my life." Brion grinned. "You're not so bad yourself, princess. And Onoria . . . you too, of course."

Onoria rolled her eyes. "Save your charm for someone who cares."

Now Cleo couldn't hold back her smile. "I assure you, I'm not a Watcher. If I was, I'd escape back to the safety of the Sanctuary as soon as I could."

"Gotta find a wheel for that," Tarus said.

Cleo looked at him. "What did you say?"

"A stone wheel." He shrugged. "Don't know if it's true, it's just what I heard from my grandma."

The boy's family seemed filled to overflowing with storytellers.

"What do you mean, a stone wheel?" asked Onoria. "Never heard of that before."

"It's how they get back and forth between the mortal world and the Sanctuary in hawk form. They have these magical, carved stone wheels hidden here and there. Might look like nothing but a ruin to us, but without the wheels, they're trapped here."

"Don't let Jonas hear you talking like that," Brion said. "He won't listen to any nonsense about magic or Watchers. He thinks it makes Paelsians weak to hold on to legends rather than look at cold, hard facts."

Magical stone wheels. It was certainly a charming story. Silly, but charming.

How much of such legends passed down from generation to generation could potentially be true, though? Jonas was naive to dismiss such talk without any consideration at all. Cleo had met an exiled Watcher without knowing it. She'd held magic in the palm of her hand. Sometimes it was far closer than anyone would ever believe.

How she wished she had her ring; it had been a horrible mistake to hide it away. It was far too precious to be out of her sight.

Cleo was about to ask Tarus if he knew anything about such an object, or if his family had told him any stories about the Kindred, when she felt an almost physical burning on the side of her face. She glanced over to see that Lysandra was glaring at her from the other side of camp.

"She still hates me, doesn't she?" It was a discouraging thought. After their initial exchange, she'd hoped she might have won the girl over—at least a little. They'd both experienced loss, experienced pain. That bonded them, even if Lysandra didn't want to acknowledge it.

If Cleo was perfectly honest, she envied the girl her current freedom. To be among all these rebels and seem so liberated and so utterly unafraid . . . it was kind of amazing.

"I think Lys hates everybody," Brion said, gnawing on an already very bare bone of what remained of his meal. Onoria laughed at this comment under her breath. "Even me, if you can believe it. Although I think I'm slowly winning her over. Watch, soon she'll be madly in love with me. But . . . don't take it personally, princess."

She'd try her best. She took a deep breath and asked what was really on her mind. "Any news about the road? Has the king stopped construction on it? What do we know about the slaves?"

Brion looked away, toward the fire. "Beautiful night, isn't it?"

"Will Jonas send another letter?"

"The stars, the moon. Stunning, really."

"It is nice," Tarus agreed. "Only lousy thing here are the insects wanting to take a chunk of your flesh." To punctuate this, he slapped his arm to kill a bloodthirsty mosquito.

Cleo went cold. "Nothing's happened, has it?"

Onoria remained silent and averted her gaze.

Brion shoved the stick back into the fire, moving the burning wood around. "Nope. And, honestly? I doubt it will."

She stared at him speechlessly for a moment. "I *told* Jonas it was pointless. The king doesn't want me back alive—at least, not enough to meet the demands of a rebel. The wedding is inconsequential to him—as am I."

"Oh, don't worry, you're not," Tarus said, which earned him a sharp look from both Brion and Onoria. "What? Doesn't she have the right to know?"

Cleo's chest tightened. "Know what?"

Brion shrugged, his expression grim. "Jonas doesn't want me to say anything to you."

She grabbed the sleeve of his tunic until he finally looked at her. "All the more reason why you must tell me."

He hesitated only another moment. "King Gaius has sent out search parties for you. They've been scouring Auranos and Paelsia from coast to coast."

"And?"

"And he's leaving a trail of bodies behind, butchered, of anyone who gets in his way or refuses to answer questions. All of them dead as a lesson to others that he's serious—that he wants you found as soon as possible. So does he seem to want you back so you can marry his son right on schedule ten days from now? Yes. Is he willing to free the slaves on his Blood Road to do it? Afraid not." Brion's voice grew quieter, and he began to put out the fire, standing up to kick dirt on it. "I guess you'll be joining us permanently, princess. Welcome to your new home."

She went colder with every word he spoke. "No, you're wrong. Jonas is wrong. I can't stay here."

"The more harm the king does out there, the more Auranians will see he isn't as benevolent and generous as he claims to be in his speeches. They will finally see that he's their enemy, not a true king to be obeyed and respected."

Her thoughts raced. "Perhaps. But the king is going to tear apart this entire kingdom and kill anyone who stands in his way until he finds me. He wants everyone to see that I'm valuable to him—that he cherishes the princess of Auranos. Even though he couldn't care less about my life if it didn't help him fool the people into behaving themselves and not giving him any problems. Am I wrong?"

Brion's expression had lost every bit of its previous humor. Onoria and Tarus looked on grimly. "Unfortunately, I don't think you're wrong at all."

With the bonfire out and the camp now in darkness, Cleo looked up to see a glimmer of stars and a bright full moon beyond the ceiling of leaves. Across the camp, through the shadows, her gaze moved to Jonas, who was speaking to Lysandra, the muscles in his back tense.

"Jonas!" she called out to him.

He turned to look at her, moonlight highlighting his handsome face—just as an arrow pierced through the air and sliced into his shoulder.

He grasped the arrow and tore it out, his pained gaze frantic as he sought hers again. "Run, Cleo. Run now!"

Dozens of red-uniformed guards spilled into the camp. Cleo scanned her immediate surroundings for a weapon—a knife, an ax, anything that could give her some protection and the chance to help fight back against their attackers. But there was nothing.

A guard in a red uniform was headed directly toward her, his sword drawn.

With a frantic look over her shoulder to see her new rebel

friends scatter in every direction, she began to run, ducking past trees and bushes in an attempt to escape the guard. Her impractical palace shoes, a stark contrast with the rest of her simpler clothes, sank into the soft dirt with every step.

But the guard was too fast to outrun. He easily caught up to her and grabbed hold of her, turned her around, and slammed her into a tree trunk so hard that she lost her breath and her vision swam. "Tell me, little girl, where is Princess Cleiona?"

When she couldn't find the air to speak, to respond to his harsh demands, he peered closer at her, his sword biting into the skin at her neck. For a moment she was terrified he would slice her throat wide open and leave her there to bleed to death before she could claim her identity.

But then there was a flicker of recognition in his cruel, narrowed eyes. Even with her hair wrapped tightly into a bun, her face dirty, her clothes that of a Paelsian rebel, did he still recognize her as the princess he'd been sent out to find?

An arrow whizzed so close to her face that she felt the wind from it as it caught the guard in the side of his neck. He stumbled back from her, clawing at his throat as blood gushed from him with each beat of his heart. He dropped to the ground, thrashing in the moss and leaves for a moment longer and then went still. Before Cleo could think, could take a breath, Jonas was there. Her heart leapt at the sight of him.

He grabbed hold of her arm. "We need to move."

"The camp . . ."

Whatever expression he wore was lost in the shadows, but his tone was tight. "It's lost. We have a secondary location in case of ambushes. We'll meet the others there tomorrow." He grabbed her and they began running.

"Why didn't you tell me there were search parties out looking for me, murdering everyone they come across?"

"Why would I?" His shirt was soaked with blood, but the wound in his shoulder didn't seem to slow him down at all.

"Because I have a right to know!"

"You have a right to know," he muttered, his tone coated with mockery. "Why? Could you have done anything to stop it?"

"I could have gone back to the palace."

"That's not part of my plan."

"I don't really care! I can't let more innocent people die."

Jonas stopped, his grip on her arm tight enough to be painful. He looked so frustrated that for a moment she thought he might shake her, but then his expression eased.

"Many people will die, no matter what happens next—innocent or not. King Gaius may have already stolen your kingdom, but the war continues. And it will continue for as long as he sits his royal arse on that throne. Do you understand this?"

Cleo's jaw tensed as she looked up at him, angry now. "I'm not an idiot. I understand."

His glare burned. "Good. Now shut up so I can get you to safety."

Jonas's viselike grip loosened only slightly as they hurried through the forest.

"We can hide here. I found this grotto only yesterday."

Cleo was caught off guard when Jonas pulled her sharply to the right, through a curtain of moss and vines, and through the hollow of a massive oak tree. It led, very unexpectedly, directly into a cave six paces in diameter. It was formed from the thickness of branches and leaves arching over their heads and shielding them from both the guards and any moonlight peeking through the lush green canopy above.

Cleo opened her mouth to speak, but Jonas pressed her back against the wall of this natural barrier.

"Shh," Jonas cautioned.

Cleo concentrated on trying not to tremble from the cold and her swelling fear.

She could see the guards from where they stood and she held her breath—even the sound of breathing might give away their location. The opening to the grotto was clearly visible through the hollow of the large tree by the torches the guards held. Red uniforms moved past the entrance and guards poked at bushes and shrubs with their swords. Their horses snorted and pawed at the ground.

They were going to be discovered any moment. Jonas's grip tightened on her, betraying his own trepidation.

The sharp tip of a sword pushed back the vines only inches from Cleo's face, and she stifled a scream with the back of her hand.

"This way," one guard shouted at the others, and the sword withdrew. "Make haste, they're getting away!"

She let out a shuddery sigh of relief as the sound of their pursuers faded into the distance.

Moments later, she jumped as a flame caught her attention. Jonas had struck a piece of flint from his pocket and lit a candle he drew out of a cloth bag hidden in the cave.

"Let me see your neck." He brought the candle close to her, rubbing his thumb over her skin where the guard had pressed his blade. "Good. It's only a scratch."

"Put that out," she warned. "They'll see."

"They won't see. They're gone."

"Fine. Then give it to me." She held out her hand. "I should look at your shoulder."

Jonas winced as if he'd forgotten he'd caught an arrow.

"I'll have to stop the bleeding." He handed her the candle, then shrugged the shoulder of his shirt down to bare half his chest and his upper arm. Cleo brought the flame closer to see the wound and grimaced at the sight of all the blood.

"That bad?" he asked, glancing at her reaction.

"Not bad enough to kill you, obviously."

Jonas quickly worked his shirt off all the way. His one shoulder was coated in blood around the wound. Otherwise, the flickering light showed his skin to be tanned and flawless and every bit as muscled as, if she admitted it to herself, she'd expected.

Cleo immediately snapped her gaze back to his face.

"Hold the flame still, your highness," Jonas said. "I have a hole in my shoulder I need to fix or I'm going to keep bleeding."

Her eyes widened as he pulled the dagger at his belt—polished silver inlaid with gold, a wavy, tapered blade, and a jeweled hilt. She recognized it immediately as the same dagger once owned by Aron, the one he'd used to kill Jonas's brother. "What are you going to do with that?"

"Only what I have to."

"Why have you kept that horrible thing all this time?"

"I have plans for it." He held it over the flame, heating the blade.

"You still want to kill Aron."

Jonas didn't answer her, but a little of the hardness in his gaze faded. "My brother taught me to do this, you know. Tomas taught me so much—how to hunt, how to fight, how to fix a broken bone or patch up a wound. You don't know how much I miss him."

The pain in his dark eyes pulled at her own. It didn't really matter who someone was, princess, peasant, rebel, or just a boy or a girl. Everyone mourned when their loved ones died.

The past was far too painful and summoned memories of those she too had lost. Cleo wanted to change the subject. "What does that do, to heat the blade?"

"I need to burn the wound to seal it. Crude, but effective. I've taught my rebels to do the same when necessary."

Jonas pulled the jeweled knife away from the flame. After hesitating only a moment, he pressed the red-hot metal against his shoulder.

The horrible sizzling sound and the acrid scent of burning flesh turned her stomach and nearly made her drop the candle. She scrambled to keep a tight hold of it.

Sweat now coated Jonas's brow, but he hadn't made a single sound. He pulled the dagger away. "It's done."

"That's barbaric!"

He gave her a considering look. "You haven't experienced much adversity in your life, have you?"

She immediately opened her mouth to protest but found that if she were honest, she couldn't. "Truthfully, no. Until recently my life was a dream. The worries I once thought I had now seem incredibly petty. I never gave a single thought to those who had it worse than I did. I knew they existed, but it didn't affect me."

"And now?"

Now she saw with more clarity than she ever had in her life. She couldn't stand by and watch those in pain without wanting to do something to help. "At the end, my father told me when I become queen that I'm to do a better job than he did." The image of her father dying in her arms came back to her with agonizing clarity. "All these years, and Paelsia so close to us . . . we could have eased your suffering. But we didn't."

Jonas watched her quietly, silently, his face catching the small light of the flickering candle. "Chief Basilius wouldn't have accepted help from King Corvin. I saw with my own eyes that the chief lived as high as any king did while letting his people suffer."

Cleo looked away. "It's not right."

"No, you're damn right it's not." He raised an eyebrow. "But you think you're going to change things, do you?"

She didn't hesitate in her answer for a moment. "I know I am."

"You're so young—and more than a little naive. Maybe too naive to be queen."

Her eyes narrowed. "Insults, rebel?"

He laughed at this. "When we first met you called me a savage. Now I've earned the slightly more respectable title of rebel."

One moment he mocked her, the next he seemed so sincere and real. "When I first met you, you *were* a savage."

"That's entirely debatable."

"That you've held on to this weapon for so long makes me wonder how much has really changed."

"Looks like we'll have to agree to disagree." He shrugged the sleeve of his shirt back on but didn't fasten the ties across his bare chest.

"I guess we will."

"We'll have to stay here for the night." Jonas glanced past the camouflage covering the entrance to the cave, his jaw tight. "I hope my friends managed to get away."

"I hope so too." Cleo didn't want any of them to die—not even the unfriendly Lysandra. The girl only acted as she did out of pain. She'd lost so much. They all had.

Jonas turned from her. "You need your beauty sleep, princess. I'll keep watch."

"Jonas, wait."

When he glanced back at her she pulled the tie from her long hair and let it cascade over her shoulders. His dark eyes followed the fall of her golden hair down to her waist as if mesmerized. "I need to go back."

Jonas's gaze snapped back to her eyes. "Back where? To camp? Can't do that, your highness. It'll be watched by soldiers for days to come. We'll go to the other location at daybreak."

"No . . . that's not what I meant. I need to go back to the palace."

He gave her an incredulous look. "You can't be serious."

"I am."

"Then let me make it very clear to you, princess. You're *not* going back to the palace. Not a chance. Got it?"

Cleo began pacing back and forth in the cramped space, her heart pounding. "The king will not agree to any rebel demands to have me released—but he still wants me back for the wedding to his son. The road will continue on and your keeping me here will have no effect at all. The longer you hold me hostage, the more people will die!"

"I thought I already explained to you, princess, that in war people die. It's the way it is."

"But your plan isn't working. Don't you see? Keeping me in your camp does nothing except give King Gaius full permission to kill. My absence has not solved any problems for me or for you; it's only created more of them. I must find the search party and . . ." She tried to picture it, what she could possibly do to end this without more blood spilled. "And I'll tell them I escaped during their attack. That's why I took my hair down; they'll recognize me immediately, even in these clothes. They'll take me back."

"And then what?" His tone grew sharper. "Nothing has changed."

"Nothing *will* change if we continue along this path."

Jonas stared at her as if he honestly couldn't understand why she insisted on arguing this point. "Is forest living too hard for you? Too scary to make your home deep in the Wildlands with the rest of us? Need to return to your luxurious life? To your beloved betrothed, Prince Magnus?"

Her cheeks flushed. "I despise him every bit as much as his father."

"Words, princess. How am I to believe them? Perhaps you're so committed to the prince and your upcoming royal wedding that you're having second thoughts about the defeat of King Gaius if it means joining me and living away from such luxuries. After all, your road to become queen is split into two paths, isn't it? One is alone as heir to the throne of Auranos, the other is on the arm of the Prince of Blood when he takes his father's place."

This boy seemed to live and breathe to argue with her. "Don't you remember, Jonas? You yourself told me that would never happen. That they'd kill me before I ever become queen, no matter what. You think that's suddenly changed?"

He faltered. "I don't know."

"Exactly. You don't know. Apart from those who are being slaughtered by the king's men, I have friends at the castle who are in danger without me there. And—and I have something else of great value I can't turn my back on."

"What?"

"I can't say." The ring was a secret that she refused to share with anyone. She desperately wished she had it with her right now.

Jonas glared at her. "Princess, you are such a—"

But then he froze, grabbed the candle to snuff out its flame, and pushed her against the wall.

Then she heard what he had—voices outside the safety of the cave. The guards had returned to give the area another sweep. Her heart pounded so loud she was certain it would give away their location. It felt like hours that they stayed like that, as quiet and still as marble statues. Pressed up against him, Cleo smelled his scent again, pine needles and open air.

"I think they're gone," he said at last.

"Perhaps I should have called out to them. They could have rescued me from you."

Jonas snorted softly. "I'm good, but I'm not sure I could take on a dozen guards to save not only my neck but yours as well."

He was so unbelievably frustrating! "Sometimes I really hate you."

Finally Jonas eased back from her a fraction. "The feeling is entirely mutual, your highness."

He was still too close to her, his breath hot against her cheek. She couldn't put her thoughts in proper order. "Jonas, please, would you just consider—"

But before she could speak another word, he crushed his mouth against hers.

It was so unexpected that she hadn't the chance to even think of pushing him away. His body pressed her firmly against the rough cave wall. His hands slid down to her waist to pull her closer to him.

And just like that, with his proximity, with his kiss, he managed to fill her every sense. He was smoke from the campfire, he was leaves and moss and the night itself.

There was nothing gentle in the rebel's kiss, nothing sweet or kind. It was like nothing she'd ever experienced before, and so very dangerous—every bit as deadly as the kiss of an arrow.

Finally, he pulled back just a little, his dark eyes glazed as if half drunk.

"Princess . . ." He cupped her face between his hands, his breath ragged.

Her lips felt bruised. "I suppose that's how Paelsians show their anger and frustration?"

He laughed, an uneasy sound. "Not usually. Nor is it typically the answer to someone who tells you they hate you."

"I . . . I don't hate you."

His dark-eyed gaze held hers. "I don't hate you either."

She could easily get lost in those eyes, but she couldn't let herself. Not now. Not with so much at risk. "I *need* to go back, Jonas. And you need to find your friends and make sure they're all right."

"So he wins?" he growled. "The king spills more blood and gets exactly what he wants?"

"This time, yes." She absently rubbed her hand, wishing she could feel her ring. It might give her the strength she needed to face what was ahead.

"And you'll marry the prince so the King of Blood can distract the masses with a shiny ceremony. I don't like that at all."

Distraction. Shiny ceremony.

Cleo gripped his arm and looked up at him, his words sparking another plan in her mind like flint to a stone. "The wedding."

"What about it?"

"The Temple of Cleiona—that's where it will be. Father took me there as a child and let me explore to my heart's content. I used to look up at the statue of the goddess, stunned that I was named for such an incredible, magical being. My sister and I—we played hide-and-seek there, just as we did at the palace. But there are even more places to hide at the temple. This could be the perfect opportunity for the rebel cause—a chance to get close to the king. Closer than anyone is able to get on a normal day. He means to use my wedding as a distraction—but he too will be distracted that day!"

Jonas didn't speak for a long moment. "What you're suggesting, princess . . . it could work."

"It'll be dangerous."

The edge of a grin appeared on his lips. "I wouldn't have it any other way."

"Wait—no. No!" What a horrible suggestion she'd just made! What was she thinking? "There will be too many guards—it's far too risky. It's not worth it."

"You can't take back your words that easily. This—it's an *incredible* idea. I should have thought of it myself. Of course, the wedding! The Temple of Cleiona . . . the crowds will all be outside distracting the guards. Inside . . . it's the perfect opportunity to assassinate the king and the prince. We remove the king and his heir. We take control. Paelsia is freed from oppression. And you could have your throne back by nightfall."

She could barely breathe.

Assassinate the king and the prince.

Well, of course, Magnus would have to die as well. He was next in line to his father's throne. "You really think this could work?"

His grin widened. "Yes, I do."

"You're mad."

"Hey, you're the one who suggested it, your highness. Perhaps we're both mad." His gaze swept the length of her. "Such ruthlessness in such a petite package. Who would have guessed it?"

This was truly insane. But what other choice did they have?

Sometimes, to regain sanity, one had to acknowledge and embrace the madness.

"I'll do whatever it takes to get my throne back," she said.

At that moment, she meant every single word.

"Then we're in agreement. It's time for my rebels to make a de-cisive stand, even one that comes with great risk. I will be at your wedding, invitation or not. And the king and the prince will both fall beneath my blade." He raised an eyebrow. "The only question is, can I trust you to say nothing of this plan?"

Her heart raced like a wild thing. "I swear on my father's and sister's souls I will say nothing."

He nodded. "Then I suppose it's time for you to go back to the palace."

Silently, they left the cave and made their way through the dark forest until they came upon the guards' camp. They had a large fire lit—the sight and scent of it noticeable even at a dis-tance. No reason to hide from predators when these men were the worst and most dangerous this forest currently had to offer.

From the corner of her eye, she saw a hawk—was it the same one from earlier?—take perch in a nearby tree.

Jonas drew Cleo to a halt. "I still don't like this."

"I don't like it much, either. But I need to go."

When his gaze locked with hers she remembered their kiss all too clearly. Her lips still tingled from it. They stood for a moment, not speaking.

"Be ready on your wedding day," he said. "Ten days from now everything changes forever. You understand?"

She nodded. "I understand."

Jonas squeezed her hand and finally let her go. With a last look, she turned from him and walked confidently into the guards' camp.

CHAPTER 16

QUEEN ALTHEA

AURANOS

Just before dawn, Queen Althea left the safety of the palace to emerge into the warm night air. She wore a commoner's cloak to hide her identity, just as she'd done a handful of times before. No one would ever guess who she really was.

The witch was also cloaked and waiting in the usual spot. Althea approached her, heart pounding.

A necessary evil. I'm only doing what I must.

Witches were said to be descendants of exiled Watchers. When these immortals entered the mortal world, they too became mortal. They were able to breed with other mortals and have offspring, some of whom could channel small amounts of magic—or so the legend went.

This witch, placed in the Limeros dungeon by a word from

Sabina, the king's former mistress, was capable of more than that. Sabina had allegedly seen her as a threat since her own magic had faded over the years.

Even before her family had left to mount the siege upon the Auranian palace, Althea worked swiftly and secretly to free this witch from her prison. She found a sickly, bone-thin woman who could barely speak. She had her hidden away at the castle, fed, bathed, and clothed, then offered her freedom—for a price.

She was to help the queen learn more about Lucia's *elementia*.

The witch agreed, and Althea learned the true prophecy about Lucia that Gaius had never shared with her. She learned stories about the Watchers, about the Kindred, about Eva, the original sorceress. About Cleiona and Valoria, who envied their sister Eva's power so much that their greed drove them to steal the Kindred for themselves—an act that resulted in their total corruption by a power so vast they had no chance to control it. In the end, neither won. They destroyed each other.

As a devout worshipper of the Goddess Valoria, Althea had been stunned and sickened by all this. She wanted to deny the truth of it but found the more she learned, the more she could not. The witch was an Oldling, one who kept these stories, passed down from generation to generation; one who worshipped the elements themselves as if they too were gods and goddesses.

If this witch was to regain her weakened power, blood magic was the only option, and she would need more than a sacrificed animal.

And the queen needed her magic.

No common mortal was good enough, the witch said. It had to be someone with strong blood, a pure heart, a bright future. Althea found a boy named Michol, one of Lucia's suitors. He had come by the castle one day looking for the princess shortly before she departed with Gaius and Magnus for Auranos. He was so young, so alive. The queen enticed him into her chambers with the promise of a betrothal to her beautiful daughter.

There, the witch was waiting with her dagger. The boy's blood ran red and true.

Instead of inciting pity, however, Michol's dying screams only fueled the queen and gave her much-needed strength. The boy had to be sacrificed so Lucia could be saved from the darkness of her magic. And saved Lucia must be—even if it eventually meant the girl's own death.

Any good mother would have done the same.

Althea remembered that night only too clearly.

The magic had shimmered in the air, making the queen catch her breath as the fine hair on her arms stood up.

Michol dropped to the ground, dead, his cheeks wet with tears. The witch's hands were coated in his blood and she pressed them to her face. Her eyes glowed so bright—like the sun itself.

"Is it working?" the queen asked, shielding her eyes. "Do you need another? I can find a servant."

"I can see," the witch said, a smile of joy stretching her lips wide. "I can see everything."

"Then tell me what I need to know about my daughter."

The room sparkled as if stars had fallen from the night sky to hang in midair around the witch and the fallen boy.

"She's not your daughter," the witch whispered. "No, not of birth."

"In my heart she is my daughter."

"She is very dangerous. Many will die because of her magic."

The queen already knew that Gaius was set on Lucia being a part of his war—that this was his whole purpose for bringing her into the castle sixteen years ago. He wished to use her *elementia* for his own gain.

"Tell me more," Althea urged.

"The sorceress will die," the witch said. "After many others have fallen before her. But this is very important: her blood cannot be spilled in death— if it is, great pain will rise from the earth itself. Pain unlike anything this world can endure. Her bloodless death is the only way to stop this."

A chill went down the queen's spine. "When will she die?"

"I can only touch the future right now, not see it clearly. But she will die young."

"She'll be corrupted by her magic." The words hurt the queen's throat. "And there's nothing that can be done to save her." The truth was far harsher than she expected. But instead of fear, Althea's heart ached for the girl she'd claimed as her daughter for sixteen years.

"The sorceress Eva was rumored to wear a ring that controlled the battle of power within her. Otherwise it's like a tearing, dark against light, a balance that cannot be contained forever. One will always try to dominate. Darkness will always try to extinguish the light. The light will always try to repress the darkness. There is no true hope to control this without the balancing magic of the ring."

Finally, a glimmer of optimism took seed in the queen's heart that this did not have to end with more death. "Where can I find this ring?"

"It was lost at the same time as the Kindred." The witch shook her head. "I don't know where to find it, but I know it still exists."

"How do you know?"

"I didn't before, but . . ." Her eyes glowed bright. "I know now. I can see it, but I know not where it is. Alas, there isn't much time to find it before the girl will lose herself to her power."

Althea wrung her hands. "If we can't find the ring in time, how can Lucia control her magic?"

"She must be kept from using her elementia. The more she uses it, the more she will be consumed by it."

"How can I stop her?"

The witch had suggested the sleeping potion, each batch of which required the blood magic gained from three sacrifices. It put a mortal into a deep sleep, the witch promised, one that couldn't be explained. One that couldn't be detected, not even by another witch.

Once the potion was made, Althea and the witch had left for Auranos by ship, arriving only to learn that Lucia had been injured in the explosion. The queen rushed to her bedside to find Lucia surrounded by three medics. They'd covered the girl's pale arms with leeches meant to drain any poison from her blood.

Lucia was so weakened and dazed that she couldn't speak, and the healers said she'd been conscious for only moments.

Althea had arrived just in time. The queen shooed away the medics, marking each of their faces so she would remember who had witnessed this. They would each have to die.

Without delay, she put the potion into a glass of water and held it to Lucia's lips. The girl drank. And then she fell deeply asleep.

Every day since, the queen had visited her daughter's bedside to check on her, looking for the signs that she would soon awaken. She secretly met with the witch under the protection of darkness every seven days to receive another dose of the potion—knowing full well that three more had to give their lives to buy another week.

Althea had lied to Magnus and to Lucia. The girl had not wakened again since the very beginning. But when she'd found him with Lucia, she knew it was important to plant a seed in her son's mind. Magnus hadn't taken the news that his sister had fallen unconscious once again well, but he couldn't claim to be surprised it happened.

The grief etched into her son's features alarmed even the queen. The boy was normally so controlled, so restrained. Lucia's condition had stripped that away. Althea supposed she should feel guilt, but she didn't. All she felt was certainty that what she did was justified. Was essential. More important than anything else.

The queen had assigned the witch the task of finding the sorceress's ring, but the woman had had no luck in locating it.

If they didn't find it soon . . .

There would be no choice but to quietly end Lucia's life. This would effectively put a stop to Gaius's plans. It would stop a monster. And it would prove to Althea that she'd finally exerted true strength of will against a husband who believed she had none at all.

This added a drizzle of sweetness to an otherwise bitter decision.

The witch stood up from her seat on the bench in the public gardens, her gray cloak masking her identity perfectly. The shadows of the night wrapped themselves around her like a second skin. The queen scanned the area to see if there were any witnesses, any guards patrolling the area.

There were none. She breathed a slow sigh of relief.

"The potion's hold is weakening," Althea said, her voice hushed. "I'll need it more often. But she's asleep again, and for now, that's all that matters."

The witch reached into the folds of her cloak.

The queen drew closer. "You will be well rewarded, I promise. I'm very grateful for all you've done so far. You should know I've come to consider you a valued friend."

To her right she glimpsed the outline of a body on the ground.

Her gaze snapped back to the cloaked figure before her.

"Who are—?" she began, but got no further.

The sharp tip of a dagger sank into her chest. She gasped out in pain as her assailant twisted the knife. A cry died in her throat and she fell to the ground.

The taste of failure and of death. Both so very bitter. Without the love of a mother, Lucia's destiny was now set.

"I'm sorry, my daughter," she whispered with her last breath.

Above her, the cloaked figure turned away and swiftly moved back in the direction of the palace.

CHAPTER 17

MAGNUS

AURANOS

Magnus tossed and turned all night. His dreams were plagued with images of Lucia crying and begging for him to save her from shadows that moved toward her like clawed hands. He finally reached her and pulled her into his arms.

"I love you," he whispered. "And I will never let anything hurt you."

He slid his fingers through long silky hair, which unexpectedly changed from ebony to pale gold.

He woke, lurching himself up to a sitting position, coated in sweat. It was dawn.

"Enough," he mumbled. Enough of nightmares. They arrived so regularly of late that he should be used to them by now. Each horrible dream seemed to revolve around the loss of Lucia. His continued obsession with his adopted sister was driving him insane.

He needed to leave the palace, to clear his head. It had become a prison for him these last few weeks. He rose and dressed hurriedly in riding clothes before making his way to the stables. There, he saddled a black stallion the stablehand warned him had a fierce and untamed reputation. But he wanted a horse that would give him a challenge—anything to take his mind off his troubles. He set out on horseback alone.

Magnus rode hard for hours, far out into the green country-side of Auranos. By midday he had reached an isolated stretch of hills known as Lesturne Valley. He continued west until he arrived at the coastline just south of Hawk's Brow and dismounted so he could stand at the edge of the shore and look out at the Silver Sea. The ocean was calm and blue, its waves lapping gently at his feet. It was the same body of water, but here it was so different than the gray, rough waters the castle in Limeros overlooked from on top of its cliff.

How long would he be forced to remain in this land? If Cleo was dead . . . that would certainly end the betrothal and then he could perhaps return to Limeros. Even still, he could summon no joy from the thought of the princess's death. She hadn't asked for this fate any more than Amia or Mira had.

Irrelevant. Why did he even waste thought on such things he had no control over?

And standing here, staring out at the water, was a pointless waste of time. Plus, his boots were getting wet.

Without further delay, Magnus climbed back on the horse and headed back in the direction of the castle.

By mid-afternoon, he was still a few hours southwest of the City of Gold when he came upon a village and realized he was hungry—starving, actually. After only a moment's hesitation, he entered the village. He'd chosen to wear a simple black cloak that didn't easily give away his royal identity. He kept the cowl up over his head, effectively shielding his face. And it seemed to work. From under his cloak he glanced at the villagers milling about the busy little town; no one seemed to recognize him. Very few even glanced in his direction.

It did not surprise him. Only a handful from this kingdom had ever seen the prince up close or away from the side of his more infamous father.

He could work with that.

Magnus tied his horse to a pole outside a busy tavern and entered the dark interior, wasting no time before he approached the barkeep. He ordered cider and a plate of meat and cheese, sliding three pieces of silver across the counter in payment. The barkeep, a man with a thick beard and bushy eyebrows, set to filling his order. While Magnus waited, he looked around. There were two dozen others in the tavern, eating and drinking, laughing, and making conversation.

He tried to remember the last time he'd been among commoners without being recognized. It had been . . . never.

This was new.

When his plate of food arrived, he began to eat. The food was not unpalatable, and, if he were being honest, it was better than that he was used to back home in Limeros.

Or perhaps he was simply hungry today.

When he was halfway finished, a sound cut through the buzz of conversation in the tavern. It was a woman quietly sobbing. He stopped eating and glanced over his shoulder. At a nearby table, a man faced a woman, holding her arms and talking quietly to her, as if comforting her.

One word of their emotional discussion cut through to him apart from all the rest.

"... witch ..."

He froze, then turned back around to face forward. The barkeep moved past and Magnus reached out to grab the man's arm. "Who is that woman at the table behind me?"

The barkeep glanced over to where Magnus indicated. "Oh, her? That's Basha."

"Why does she cry? Do you know?"

"I do. I probably shouldn't, but I do."

Magnus now slid a piece of gold across the counter. "Is she a witch?"

The man's jaw tensed, but his focus was on the piece of gold. "It's not my business. Nor is it yours."

The gold was joined by a friend. Two pieces of gold now sat upon the counter next to Magnus's half-eaten plate of food. "Make it your business."

The barkeep was silent only for another moment, but then he swept the coins off the counter with one smooth motion. "Basha's daughter was taken to King Gaius's dungeon only days ago, accused of witchcraft."

Magnus fought to keep his face expressionless, but the news that his father had begun arresting witches here in Auranos . . . he'd had no idea. "She's accused. But is she able to access *elementia*?"

"That's not for me to say. You should talk to Basha yourself if you're so interested." He produced an open bottle of pale Paelsian wine. "Trust me, this will ease your introduction. It's the least I can do for my wealthy new friend."

"Much gratitude for your assistance."

Perhaps this day wasn't a complete waste of time after all. A skilled witch might be able to help Lucia more than any healer ever could. Magnus took the wine and moved toward the old woman seated next a fireplace that blazed despite the heat of the day. Her companion had his arm around her now. The woman was in tears, her eyes red from both sorrow and drink.

Magnus placed the bottle of wine in front of her. "Much sympathy, Basha. The barkeep told me of the recent troubles with your daughter."

Her gray eyes flicked to him with suspicion for a split second before she pulled the bottle closer, tipped it into her empty glass to fill it, and drank deeply. She wiped her tears with the back of her hand. "A gentleman amongst us. How welcome. Please join us. This is Nestor, my brother."

Nestor was also clearly drunk, and he offered Magnus a crooked grin as the prince sat on a rickety wooden stool. "Basha wants to seek audience with the king himself to ask for Domitia's release. It's an excellent idea."

"Oh?" said Magnus, unable to hide his surprise. "You really think so?"

"Damora is a harsh king only because he has to be. But I heard his speech. I liked what he said about the road he builds for us all. He is a man who can be reasoned with. One who wants the best for all of us, no matter what part of Mytica we call our home."

His father would be so pleased.

"Is she a skilled witch or was she falsely accused?" Magnus asked.

Basha narrowed her eyes at him for a moment before she replied. "Domitia is blessed by the goddess with gifts beyond this mortal world. But she is harmless. She is good and sweet. There's no reason for her to be seen as a danger."

"Are you also blessed by the goddess in this way?" Magnus asked, with hope. He could arrange to have Basha's daughter released from the dungeon if she might prove useful, but to have two witches to help Lucia would be even better.

"No, not me. I have nothing of the sort at my disposal."

Disappointment thudded through him. "If you are aware that witches are real, do you know much about the legend of the Kindred?"

"Only that it's a bedtime story I told my daughter when she was a child." Basha took another deep drink of the wine, then frowned at him. "Why do you wish to know so much about magic and witches? Who are you?"

Magnus was spared from answering by a commotion at the door. A pair of men entered the tavern, laughing and boisterous. "Wine for everyone," one of them announced as they moved toward the barkeep. "I've been appointed the official florist for the royal wedding and wish to celebrate my good fortune!"

An excited cheer resonated through the tavern, and the man was slapped on his back and offered words of congratulations—except for one gray-haired man at the bar.

"Bah," he said. Wrinkles splayed out from the corners of his eyes and down his hollow cheeks. "You're all fools to buy in to such romantic drivel. The prince of Limeros and the princess of Auranos are a match made in the darklands by the darkest demon himself."

Magnus hid his raised eyebrows in a deep swallow of cider.

"I disagree," the florist said, his enthusiasm undeterred. "I think King Gaius is right—such a union will aid relations between our kingdoms and help push forward into a bright and prosperous future for us all."

"Yes, relations between kingdoms. Kingdoms that he now controls with little resistance, apart from a few scattered rebel groups who don't know their arses from holes in the ground by what little they've done to rise up against the King of Blood."

The florist paled. "I caution you against speaking so freely in public."

The old man snorted. "But if we are ruled by such a wondrous king as you believe, I should be able to speak my mind wherever and whenever I like. No? But perhaps I've seen more years and more troubles than the rest of you young people. I know lies when I hear them, and that king speaks them whenever his lips are moving. In a dozen years, he reduced the citizens of Limeros to a shivering mass afraid to speak out against him or break any of his rules for fear of death. You think he's changed in a matter of months?" He drained his glass angrily. "No, he sees our vast numbers when compared to his legion of guards. He sees that we are a force to be reckoned with if we ever were to stand up against him united. So he must keep us happy and quiet. Ignorance is a trait shared by many Auranians—always has been. It sickens me to my very soul."

The florist's smile had tightened. "I'm sorry you can't share in the joy the rest of us feel. I for one am greatly anticipating Prince Magnus and Princess Cleiona's wedding—and their upcoming tour across the kingdom. And I know the majority of Auranians feel the same."

"The princess is currently held captive by rebels. You really think there will be a wedding?"

The florist's eyes grew glossy and a hush fell upon the tavern. "I have hope she will be rescued unharmed."

The old man snorted. "Hope. Hope is for fools. One day you will see that I am right and you are wrong. When your golden days tarnish and the King of Blood shows his true face behind the mask he wears to appease the soft, ignorant masses in this once great land."

The mood in the tavern had grown more somber the longer this man spoke. Magnus looked away from the argument to realize that Basha was staring at him, her brows drawn tightly together.

"That's who you remind me of, young man. You look a great deal like Prince Magnus, the son of the king."

She'd said it loud enough to gain the attention of other nearby tables. A dozen pairs of eyes now fixed upon him.

"I've been told that before, but I assure you I am not." He rose from his seat at the table. "Much gratitude for the information you've given me, Basha." Although, nothing worthwhile. Only more disappointment. "I wish you a good day."

He departed the tavern, looking neither left nor right, pulling his cowl closer around his face.

Magnus's head ached by the time he returned to the palace. It was late in the day and the sun was setting. On his way from the stables, his path crossed with that of Aron Lagaris.

"Prince Magnus," Aron said. His voice sounded different, stronger. Perhaps the boy was taking his new station seriously and had refrained from drinking a bucket of wine already today. "Where have you been?"

Magnus leveled his gaze with Aron's. "My father seems oddly fond of you as his newest kingsliege, but has he suddenly assigned you to become my keeper?"

"No."

"My personal bodyguard?"

"Uh . . . no."

"Then where I have been is none of your concern."

"Of course not." Aron cleared his throat. "However, I should let you know that your father wants to see you immediately upon your return from . . . wherever it is you've been."

"Does he now? Then far be it for me to keep the king waiting another moment."

Aron did an awkward half bow, which Magnus ignored as he swept past him. A day that started with nightmares and disappointment did not seem to be improving.

The king stood outside his throne room, his favorite hound next to him. He spoke quietly with Cronus. As soon as he spotted Magnus, he sent the guard away with a flick of his wrist.

"What is it?" Magnus asked, frowning.

The king acknowledged his son with a nod. "You should know that Princess Cleiona has returned to us."

It was the last thing he expected to hear. "She has? How is this possible?"

"She escaped from the rebels after an attack on their camp last night. She ran into the forest, hid from her captors, and made her way into the custody of my team of guards. She's shaken but unharmed."

This news came as a strange relief. "A miracle."

"Is it?" The king pressed his lips together. "I'm not sure about that."

"I was certain they'd kill her."

"As was I. And yet, they didn't. It leaves me with certain suspicions. A girl of sixteen without any survival skills finds herself in the hands of violent rebels who are currently making their home in the thick of the Wildlands. Yet she easily escapes? Without a bruise or a scratch? Now that I know the leader's name in this particular group of heathens, this leaves me with many questions."

"Who is the leader?"

"Jonas Agallon."

It took Magnus a moment to place the name. "The wine seller's son from Paelsia. The one with the murdered brother. He was a scout for Chief Basilius."

"That's right."

"Who told you this? The princess?"

"No—in fact, she claims to have been kept secluded during her captivity and did not see any of the rebels' faces. My guards were unable to find the princess specifically, but in their travels they did uncover some information about the rebels. This was one piece of information."

Magnus considered all of this. "Are you saying that you believe her to now be aligned with the rebels?"

"Let's just say that I plan to keep a very close eye on her in the days ahead, and you should do the same. Especially with the wedding so close now."

A muscle in Magnus's cheek twitched. "Of course. The wedding."

"Is there a problem with that?"

"None at all." He turned to study the Limerian coat of arms that now adorned the wall, which included the image of a cobra and a pair of crossed swords. "That she has returned in time for the wedding makes me believe she is in no way aligned with these rebels. I would think she would have liked to avoid such a ceremony if she could, even if it meant remaining among their kind."

"Perhaps you're right. But she is back. And you should also know that we're expecting a very important guest for the wedding. The message reached me only this morning that Prince Ashur Cortas of the Kraeshian Empire will be attending."

The name was well known to Magnus. "What a great honor."

"Indeed. I was very surprised and very pleased the prince accepted our invitation on behalf of his father." The king said this tightly, as if he did not mean it. The Kraeshian Empire lay across the Silver Sea and was ten times the size of Mytica. Prince Ashur's father, the emperor, was the most powerful man in the world.

Not that Magnus would ever say such a thing out loud in front of King Gaius.

His father was silent for a moment. "There's another grave matter I must discuss with you. Please come inside." The king turned to the throne room and entered through the large wooden doors, his hound's claws scratching against the marble floor as the dog stayed at his master's side.

Please. It was a word so rarely used by his father that it sounded like one from a foreign tongue. Slowly, he followed the king into the room.

"What's wrong? Is it Lucia?" Magnus asked, his voice strained.

"No. This unfortunate matter doesn't concern her."

The fear that had tightened like a fist in his chest unclenched. "If not Lucia, then what do you need to tell me?"

The king looked off to his left and Magnus followed the direction of his gaze. Upon a marble slab lay the queen, her arms folded across her stomach. She was very still, very silent.

Magnus frowned. Why would she be sleeping in the throne room?

It took him a moment to understand.

"Mother . . ." he began, his breath coming quicker as he approached her.

"It's the work of rebels," the king said, his voice low and even. "They were upset that we refused to meet their demands about ceasing construction on the Imperial Road. This is my punishment."

The queen's face was pale, and Magnus could have sworn she was only sleeping. He reached out a hand toward her but clenched his fist and brought it back to his side. There was blood on her pale gray dress. So much. His own blood turned to ice at the sight of it.

"Rebels," Magnus said, the words hollow in his throat. "How do you know?"

"This was the weapon used. The murderer left it behind." The king held up a dagger, one with jewels embedded in its hilt, the silver blade wavy. "Such evidence has helped us pinpoint his identity."

Magnus's gaze moved from the ornamental weapon to his father's face. "Who is he?"

"This very dagger once belonged to Lord Aron. It was what he used to kill the wine seller's son in the Paelsian market—Jonas Agallon's brother. That was the last time Lord Aron saw this weapon."

"You're saying Jonas Agallon is responsible for this."

"Yes, I believe so. And I also believe that by leaving the dagger behind, he wanted us to know it was him."

Magnus fought to keep his voice from trembling. "I will kill him."

"There's no doubt that the boy will pay dearly for this crime." The king hissed out a breath. "I've underestimated the rebels. To be so bold as to assassinate the queen . . . it's a crime that Jonas Agallon will pay for very dearly. He will beg for his death long before I'll give it to him."

This woman who'd given birth to Magnus eighteen years ago, the one who read him stories and danced with him as a child. The one who dried his tears . . . the one who'd shown her long-buried affection to him that day in the temple . . .

She was gone forever.

"Strange, though," the king said into the heavy silence. "Another body was found close by, also stabbed. It was an accused witch we'd had in the dungeons in Limeros, one I had long since forgotten about."

With an aching heart, Magnus studied the gray strands in his mother's hair, which contrasted so greatly with the ebony darkness of the rest of it. She hadn't liked that. She hadn't liked looking older, especially when compared to the king's mistress, who'd magically retained her beauty. "I don't understand. Did the witch have something to do with the rebels?"

"It's a mystery, I'm afraid."

"I must start looking for Agallon." Magnus forced the words out. Speaking was the last thing he felt like doing right now. "Immediately."

"You can join the hunt upon your return from the wedding tour."

He turned on his father, his eyes blazing. "My mother has been murdered by a rebel and you want me to make a tour across the kingdom with a girl who hates me."

"Yes, actually. That's *exactly* what I want. And you will do it." The king regarded Magnus with patience in his dark eyes. "I know you loved your mother. Her loss will be felt for a very long time— all of Mytica shall grieve her. But this wedding is important to me. It will seal my control over the people in this kingdom with no more opposition than necessary as I move ever closer to having the Kindred in my grasp. Do you understand?"

Magnus let out a shaky breath. "I understand."

"Then go. And keep the information about the witch to yourself. We don't want any rumors started that the queen associated with such lowly women."

Magnus frowned at the ludicrous notion. He'd assumed the rebels were acquainted with the witch, not his mother. "Do you think she did?"

"Honestly, I don't know what to think right now or what would possess Althea to leave the palace in the wee hours of the morning." The king glanced down at the face of the wife he'd had for twenty years. "All I know is my queen is dead."

Magnus left the throne room where his mother lay, his steps faltering when he got around the next corner and into an empty alcove—no guards, no servants. Suddenly, he couldn't breathe. He couldn't think. He staggered over to the wall and braced his hand against it. A sob rose in his throat, but he fought with all his strength to swallow it back down.

Moments later, a cool, familiar voice intruded into his grief. "Prince Magnus, I suppose you'll be very glad to know of my safe return. I hope you didn't miss me too much."

He didn't reply. All he wanted was some privacy.

Princess Cleo regarded him, her arms crossed over her chest. Her pale hair was loose, wavy past her shoulders to her waist.

"I'm kidnapped by rebels, held as their prisoner for an entire week, escaped with only my wits to aid me, and you don't even have a greeting for me upon my return?"

"I will warn you, princess, that I'm not in the mood for foolishness right now."

"Neither am I, so I suppose we have something in common. And I thought there was nothing we shared." Her gaze held not an edge of friendliness, but a tight smile lifted the corners of her mouth.

"Smiling?" he managed. "Whatever have I done to deserve this? Or perhaps you've already heard the news to help brighten your day."

"News?"

He felt impossibly weary. "The news of the queen's death."

A frown creased her brow. "What?"

"She was murdered by rebels." He took in her unconcealed look of shock. "So there you go. Something for you to celebrate."

Magnus turned away from her, ready to find solace in his chambers, but the princess grabbed his arm to stop him. He sent a dark look at her over his shoulder.

"I would never celebrate death, no matter whose it is," she said, her gaze filled with anger and something else. Something that looked vaguely like sympathy.

"Come now, I'm sure you wouldn't mourn any Damora."

"I know very well what it's like to lose a parent in a tragic way."

"Oh, yes, we have so much in common. Maybe we should get married."

She released him, her expression souring. "I was trying to be kind."

"Don't try, princess. It doesn't suit you. Besides, I don't need or want your kindness or your sympathy. Both feel alarmingly false coming from you."

Something hot and wet slipped down his cheek. He swiped at the unbidden tear and turned his face away, appalled that she'd seen it.

"I never would have believed you'd care so deeply for anyone," she said softly.

"Leave me alone."

"Gladly." But now she sounded uncertain, as if the sight of him crying over his dead mother had deeply confused her. "But, wait, before you go . . . I'm sorry to disturb you, I just don't know who else to ask. I need to talk to my friend. To Mira. I can't find her anywhere. I'm told she's no longer Princess Lucia's attendant. Do you know where she's been reassigned?"

He took five steps down the hall before she called out to him. "Prince Magnus, please!"

He turned. At that moment, there was nothing in Cleo's expression except the need for him to help her in some small way. She believed he could do that much.

"Apologies, princess," he said, holding her gaze, "but while you were gone my father took the life of your friend Mira for over-hearing a private conversation. I do regret that he made that decision, but I can assure you her death was quick and painless."

Horror crossed her face. *"What?"*

"She was taken away, her body burned, the bones buried in the servants' graveyard. Again, I am sorry for your loss. There's nothing to be done to fix this."

The sound of Cleo's grief-filled wail followed him all the way back to his chambers.

CHAPTER 18

JONAS

THE WILDLANDS

That same hawk was back again, perched in the trees. She kept Jonas in sight for most hours of the day. Perhaps he was being paranoid, especially since he didn't believe in legends . . . but, still.

If she was a Watcher, then Jonas hoped she would approve of the plan he'd just laid out before his rebels, explaining how they would assassinate King Gaius and Prince Magnus at the princess's wedding.

"Let me get this straight." Lysandra was the first to speak up when he was finished. "You won't attack the Blood Road like I want, but you think you can march into the royal wedding at the Temple of Cleiona and kill both the king and the prince where they stand."

"That is what I said, isn't it?"

"I thought maybe I'd heard you wrong."

"Do you have a problem with my plan?"

"Several problems, actually." The girl looked stunned, as if he'd managed to take her by surprise. She stood next to Brion, who regarded him with bemusement.

"Anyone else with problems?" Jonas turned in a circle to survey the rest of the group. The rebels spoke quietly to each other, eyeing him with varying expressions—from interest to awe to wariness. "Or is Lysandra the only one who always wants to oppose me on every decision I make?"

"We were all nearly slaughtered by the king once already. You want him to have another chance at it?" a boy named Ivan said. Originally, Jonas had thought him someone with leadership qualities, but Ivan rarely took an order without debate and complaint. Everything was a fight with him. And the bravery he showed by his size and muscles didn't seem to go much further than the surface.

Ivan had a point, but it wasn't a very good one. Not one rebel had fallen beneath the Limerian guards' blades the night they'd invaded the camp, which was both a miracle and a relief. The plan to scatter and regroup at their secondary location had been a sound one. Jonas took this as a sign that they were meant to fight another day.

Yes. Cleo's wedding day.

"This will work," Jonas said, his voice loud enough for all fifty of his rebels gathered around to hear. "King Gaius will fall."

"Show him," Lysandra said.

Jonas frowned. "Show me what?"

Brion stepped forward. He had a piece of parchment in his hand, which he unrolled and held up for Jonas to see.

On it was a sketch of a dark-haired boy and a proclamation.

JONAS AGALLON

WANTED FOR KIDNAPPING AND MURDER

LEADER OF THE PAELSIAN REBELS

WHO OPPOSE THE GREAT AND NOBLE KING GAIUS'S

RIGHTFUL REIGN OVER ALL OF MYTICA

10,000 CENTIMOS REWARD

DEAD OR ALIVE

His mouth went dry. He handed it back casually. "Doesn't look anything like me."

Lysandra made a disgusted grunting sound. "You see what we're dealing with here? You're famous."

"This means nothing. It stops nothing. Besides, I might be guilty of kidnapping, but I haven't murdered anyone." Not yet, anyway.

"Do you think lies will stop the king? He means to end you, and he's offered the greedy Auranians a reward to help pinpoint your location."

"For ten thousand centimos, I'm tempted to turn you in myself," Brion said.

Jonas snorted uneasily. "For ten thousand centimos, I'm tempted to turn *myself* in."

"This isn't funny." Lysandra gave both of them a dirty look.

He had to agree; it wasn't. But he wasn't surprised that the king would do something like this. In fact, it was a good sign that the king had begun to consider the rebels a serious threat. If Jonas had to be the face—albeit a poorly sketched one—of the rebel resistance, then he would take on that mantle with pride.

"I thought you wanted me to make a move like this, Lys," Jonas said, trying to ease the anger he saw rising in her expression. "You've wanted us to attack the road camps ever since you joined us."

"And I saw for myself how unprepared for an attack of that magnitude we are. I know now that we can't go in as a random assault, not with so few of us. We would be slaughtered if we don't go in with a plan. So I'm working on just such a plan. I'm figuring out what point of the road is the weakest, where we could make the most difference."

"You can't say that it's a bad move to take the king out, can you? If he's dead, his road will cease construction. Agreed?"

She glared at him. "I can agree on that much."

"Then there's no problem."

"Wrong. There is. He needs to die, I agree. But this is to be your first act of true rebellion, beyond destroying frescos of his face? Suddenly, you've become a stealthy assassin, able to sneak into a heavily guarded temple and get close enough to sink a blade into both the king and the prince without anyone stopping you. Even with the offer of a reward for your capture plastered all across Auranos?"

"Concerned for my safety." He forced a grin that was far from genuine. "That's so sweet of you."

"I know why you're doing this." Lysandra raised her voice for all to hear. "Our leader wants us all to saunter into a heavily guarded wedding so he can save his beloved damsel in distress."

"That's not it." The words hissed out from between Jonas's clenched teeth. "This is to rid Paelsia of the King of Blood's tyranny. To free our people. I thought that was what you wanted, just as the rest of us do, but now you're trying to say anything to deter me?"

"I'm not saying it wouldn't be the greatest gift in the entire universe to watch the king die so he can pay for his atrocities. His death would be the answer to every problem we have."

"Then what are you saying?"

"I'm saying I think you will fail," she said flatly. "That unfortunately today your reach exceeds your grasp. And that you can't see this for yourself because you've been blinded by golden hair and blue-green eyes."

Jonas had told not one person of the kiss in the cave with the princess—not even Brion. He still wasn't sure what the kiss had meant, if anything. All he knew was that watching Cleo walk away into the guards' camp was one of the most difficult things he'd ever had to do.

The other rebels muttered to each other. Jonas couldn't hear what they were saying, but it didn't sound favorable to him. Lysandra was like the edge of a blade that could slice these rebels apart just when he needed them to stick together.

"Enough squabbling, you two," Brion growled. "It's not helping anything. It never does." He rolled up the reward parchment and tossed it into the campfire.

"This has nothing to do with the princess," Jonas snarled, but he knew it was at least partly a lie. After all, it had been Cleo's idea—and he still believed it was a damn good one. "And I'm not going in blind. Nerissa's information has been very useful. She has it on the authority of at least two of the king's guards that the majority of security at the wedding will be outside for crowd control. Inside, there will be guests, temple attendants, the priest. A handful of guards at the most. I can get us in there to do what we have to do."

Lysandra crossed her arms over her chest. "How did Nerissa get such information? Oh, wait, let me guess. Did she seduce the guards? Does that girl have any other skill?"

Seduction was Nerissa's specialty. And now that she could never set foot in Hawk's Brow again, after assisting Jonas with Cleo's kidnapping, she was very eager to prove herself as an aid to the rebels. In fact, Nerissa had expressed a great interest in seducing Jonas himself. While he had declined her attentions, he'd been more than happy to put her expertise to use elsewhere.

"Brion," Jonas said under his breath. "A little help here?"

"Nerissa hasn't seduced me," Brion said. "Well, not yet. I think she's getting around to it eventually. I'm guessing she has a list."

"*Brion.*"

His friend let out a long sigh. "Look, Jonas, I know you want to do this. That after so long of not taking a bold action like this, you're itching to jump on any opportunity. But—I don't know. I think Lys might be right on this one. It's too risky right now. You have to see that, right?"

Jonas stared at his friend as if seeing him for the first time. "Of course it's risky. But if it works, it will mean everything."

"If it doesn't, then . . . it means nothing. And you'll be dead."

"You're taking her side."

The patience was fading from Brion's gaze. "It's not a matter of taking sides. It's an attempt to see the situation clearly."

"You used to be the first one to jump into a fight. What happened?" His temper and frustration had risen and with it his tactlessness. "Oh, wait. I know what happened. Lysandra happened."

Any remaining friendliness disappeared from Brion's face. "That's a low blow."

"You're not thinking with your head when it comes to her. Sorry to break it to you, but taking her side isn't going to make her fall in love with you. So you should stop following her around like a lost puppy."

He finally looked directly at his friend, just as Brion's fist slammed right into his face. Jonas staggered back from him.

"If I want your opinion," Brion said in a growl, "I'll beat it out of you."

Jonas swiped his hand beneath his nose. "Hit me again and

we're going to have a problem."

This time, Brion shoved Jonas so hard that he slammed into a tree trunk.

Now the rebels were much more vocal than before.

"Come on, Jonas! Don't let him do that."

"Knock him out, Brion!"

"Kick his arse! Let's see some more blood!"

Paelsians always did enjoy a good fight.

"Stop it," Jonas growled as Brion drew closer, his fists clenched at his sides.

"Or what?"

"Or I'll stop you."

Brion had a tendency to brawl at any given moment, but he'd never once fought with Jonas. Despite the warning, Brion approached again, but Jonas was ready this time. He punched Brion in the stomach, then in his chin, knocking his friend backward and to the ground. Lysandra ran to the boy's side, glaring at Jonas.

"This doesn't change the fact that I think she's right and you're wrong," Brion managed to groan. "Feel free to go after the king at that wedding, but it'll be at your own peril."

Jonas turned to the other rebels, furious now that his best friend, someone he considered a brother, refused to stand with him on this decision. "You know my plan. With or without help I will be at the royal wedding in four days. I will assassinate King Gaius myself. I welcome any volunteers who want to join me. After this, we won't be put on reward signs; we will be held up as heroes. Think about it."

Then he turned his back on the lot of them and walked into the darkness of the thick forest to clear his head.

CHAPTER 19

LUCIA

AURANOS

Darkness became her world, and Lucia was left with two horrible thoughts that echoed, bouncing against each other over and over again.

My mother thinks I'm evil.

My mother wants me dead.

Finally, after far too long waiting in the smothering emptiness, there was a dawning, and she found herself once again in the familiar lush, green meadow with its jeweled grass and crystalline trees.

The Sanctuary.

Or, rather, a dream version of the Sanctuary. But it felt so very real—from the warm breeze to the emerald grass beneath her bare feet, to the sight of the glittering city in the distance beneath the seemingly endless clear blue skies. So real it was difficult to tell the difference.

She sensed Alexius's presence behind her but didn't turn.

"You left me for far too long," she said quietly.

"Apologies, princess."

Before this, they'd had four shared dreams. Dreams in which they walked through this meadow, as far as the diamond-encrusted stone wheels, talking about everything. About Lucia's childhood, about her relationship with Magnus and all its recent complications, about her mother, about her father, about her magic. Perhaps she'd shared too much, but with Alexius, she felt . . . comfortable. Which was surprising, considering who and what he was. An immortal Watcher two thousand years old.

She had never felt like this before. About anyone.

He asked her questions about herself, so many questions. And she answered them. However, he was skilled in evading the questions she asked of him in return. She still didn't know why he brought her here, and her mind was in a fog whenever she was in this meadow. Despite her best intentions, the gravity of what had transpired in her waking life seemed to fade away when she was here.

Death. Destruction. Prophecies. Magic.

She needed answers. Perhaps he had been purposefully evading her since the last dream—letting her stay adrift in sleep all this time.

This, then, was her chance to find out more, and she would not let herself become distracted by this golden creature who made any other thoughts drop from her mind. Lucia turned to face him directly. "What do you want from me?"

The beautiful boy smiled at her as if he couldn't stop the expression from appearing on his face. "It's good to see you too, princess."

Such a smile. Her gaze moved to his lips before snapping back to his silver eyes. "My mother wants to kill me because of my *elementia*."

His smile fell away. "I assure you, she will do nothing of the sort."

Lucia looked down at her hand and willed fire into it. It flickered to life immediately. "Will this power I have corrupt me? Will it make me evil?"

"*Elementia* is neither good nor evil. It simply is. The world was created from the elements. *I* was created from the elements."

"And you're not evil." Despite the flames, she shivered as he drew closer.

Another smile. "Evil is a choice one makes, not a natural state of being."

"Always?"

His brows drew together. "This troubles you."

"Of course it does." She wrung her hands, dousing the fire. "How do I get rid of it?"

"Get rid of—?"

"My magic. What if I don't want it? What if I want to be normal?"

Alexius studied her as if he didn't understand. "You can't change what you are. The *elementia* is a part of you."

"How can you say that when I didn't have it for sixteen years? My life was—well, it was uneventful and sometimes dreary, but it wasn't like this. I couldn't kill someone with a thought by setting them on fire. I wasn't looked at with fear and hate. I didn't have to worry about mastering something dark and unpleasant that seeps through my very skin like a poison."

"You must not think of your magic like that, princess. It's not a curse, it's a gift. One many would give everything they have to possess—including many of my kind."

She shook her head. "Watchers are made from magic."

"Made from it, yes. But we can't wield it as easily as you can."

Lucia paced to the edge of the meadow, her arms crossed tightly over her chest. "What do you need my magic for, Alexius?"

She had to know this. She could think of no other reason for this boy to continue to visit her if not to use her in some way.

Not a boy, she reminded herself. *Not even close.*

"There's not enough time left to explain." He scrubbed his hand through his bronze-colored hair and glanced back in the direction of the city.

"Not enough time before what?"

"Don't you feel it? You're on the very brink of waking. And this time, you'll stay awake. I feel it because it is taking a great deal of my energy to stay in this dream with you."

Her heart skipped a beat. She was waking? Finally?

It was all that she'd wanted. But now . . . there was too much more that needed to be said. She wasn't ready to say farewell to Alexius. Not yet. The thought of it made her heart ache.

"How will I see you again? Will you visit my regular dreams?"

"Yes." Alexius stepped closer to her and took her hands in his, his expression tense. "There is so much I want to tell you. That I . . . *need* to tell you, even if I've been sworn to secrecy."

So real—he felt so real. Warm skin, strong hands. He smelled of spices—exotic and entirely unforgettable.

"So speak now, quickly—tell me what you need to say. Don't keep me waiting."

"Do you trust me, princess?"

"I can't think of a single reason why I should," she whispered, locking gazes with him.

He raised an eyebrow. "Not a single reason?"

She almost smiled. "These secrets. They're secrets about me. Am I right?"

He nodded once.

"I need to know what the prophecy really said about my magic. All I know is that it said I was to become a sorceress, one able to channel all four parts of *elementia*."

"Yes, it did say that. And you can."

Frustration welled within her. "But for what purpose? I *can* work some magic, but I don't *want* to."

His grip on her hands tightened. "There's more to Eva's prophecy—a part that is most important. Most guarded."

"Tell me."

"That you will be the one to free us from this prison and reunite us with the Kindred." He glanced toward the crystal city, a wary look on his handsome face. "That you will save us all from destruction."

She searched his eyes. "What do you mean by destruction?"

He shook his head. "Without the Kindred in our possession, the magic that existed here a thousand years ago has been fading away little by little. When it's gone, *elementia* is gone. Not just in the Sanctuary, but in all the world. All life is created from the magic of the elements. And without that magic, there is nothing left. So you see, princess? You are the key to our future—to everyone's future."

She shook her head. "That's impossible. I don't know how to do that. You think I can help save the world?"

His expression grew troubled. "I wasn't supposed to tell you this. Not yet. She'll be angry with me, but—but you have a right to know."

"Who are you speaking about? Your friend Phaedra? The one who interrupted us before?"

He shook his head. "No. Someone else. Tell no one of what I've said to you, princess. And trust no one—*no one*—not even those you feel are worthy of your trust.

"Alexius . . ." His expression was so full of anguish, so full of passion . . . and all of it seemed to be directed at her.

"I wasn't supposed to feel anything for you," he whispered, drawing her closer. She couldn't look away from him. "When I watched you from afar, I had that distance. That objectivity. I lack that now."

Lucia could barely breathe as she watched him, her skin heating where he touched her.

"You have become very important to me," he continued haltingly, "more important than I dare admit even to myself. I never understood how an immortal could fall in love with a mortal. It wasn't logical. I thought them fools to give up eternity for a handful of years in the mortal world with the one who held their heart captive. I don't think that anymore. There are some mortals who are worth sacrificing eternity for."

The fire in her cheeks went forgotten. She found she was stepping closer, so close, to him.

"I should never visit your dreams again," he said, pain crossing his face. "There are dangers ahead that you cannot fathom. But, no . . . there *must* be other ways to get what is needed. And if there are, I will find them. I swear this to you."

She had no idea what he was talking about now, only that he had admitted that he was falling in love with her. Hadn't he? "Yes, you *should* visit my dreams. You can't leave me now. You're important to me too, Alexius. I—I need you in my life."

That anguish remained in his dark silver eyes. So incredibly intense. So filled with the answers she needed to questions that she hadn't even asked. And then he cupped her face in his hands and bent to brush his lips against hers.

Perhaps he'd meant it as a chaste kiss, but it quickly became anything but. His hands slid down to her waist and he crushed her against him, deepening the kiss. She touched his face, his chin, and slid her fingers into his hair. He tasted like nectar, spiced honey . . . sweet and addictive. She wanted more. Her hands moved to the ties of his shirt, pulling them free to bare his chest. He had a mark, a glowing swirl of gold, over his heart. "What is this?"

"A sign of what I am."

So beautiful. He was so beautiful that she never wanted to wake up. She wanted to be with him forever.

"I love you, Alexius," she whispered against his lips. He tensed at her words, and she very nearly regretted letting them escape, but then his mouth was on hers again, hard and demanding, stealing both her breath and her heart. . . .

And then darkness spread across the meadow, obliterating it from view and sweeping Alexius away from her.

A cry caught in her throat.

Lucia slowly opened her eyes to find herself in a large, canopied bed, under soft, white silk sheets. Her gaze was fixed upon a flickering candle on her bedside table.

A strange and unfamiliar ache gripped her heart.

Alexius.

A young girl wearing a plain gray dress dozed in a nearby chair. After a moment, her eyes popped open and then widened. "Your highness . . . you're awake!"

"Water," Lucia managed to say.

The girl scurried to get water. "I must inform the king immediately."

"Not yet. Please, give me a moment before you do anything of the sort."

Of course, the girl obeyed. She brought water, which Lucia drank only after a short hesitation. Then the girl fetched fruit, cheese, and bread.

"Two months," Lucia whispered with dismay when she asked how long she'd been asleep. "How have I survived so long?"

"You've been able to accept a specially prepared drink that has sustained you," the girl explained. "The healers said it was a small miracle."

Yes, a miracle. One that enabled her mother to administer the potion that kept her asleep. A tremor of anger coursed through her and the drinking glass she held shattered.

"Princess!" the servant girl cried out, clearly horrified that she'd injured herself, as she began picking up the sharp pieces of glass.

Lucia looked down at her bleeding hand, cocking her head as she considered the stinging wound. The King of Blood was her father. Did that make her the Princess of Blood? Her blood was so bright red it very nearly glowed.

Drops of crimson fell to the crisp white sheets. The girl quickly bound her hand with a cloth.

Lucia pushed her away. "It's nothing."

"I'll get some fresh sheets."

Lucia regarded her. "Don't look so scared. Like I said, it's nothing."

She unwound the bandage and concentrated on her cut flesh. Her hand began to glow with a beautiful, warm golden light. A moment later, her wound was completely healed.

Her mother had been wrong about her. She wasn't evil. *This* wasn't evil. Using her *elementia*, especially after such a long absence, felt right. It felt *good*.

"I have heard rumors," the girl whispered, awed, "about what you can do."

The girl was much more of a nuisance than a plain little mouse should ever be. "Rumors that I'd strongly suggest you put out of your mind lest they grow sharp teeth to devour you with."

The girl paled. "Yes, your grace."

"Go fetch my brother for me. *Only* my brother."

As the little mouse scurried away, Lucia found herself shocked by the rudeness of her words. She usually treated servants with much more kindness than this. What was happening to her?

Lucia turned her head toward the balcony window in this unfamiliar room. She looked out at the blue sky dotted with fluffy white clouds and the rolling green landscape beyond. Undeniably beautiful, but not home. Not perfect, white, frost-covered Limeros.

A golden hawk touched down on the railing of the balcony and at the sight of it Lucia sat straight up, the effort making her dizzy. The hawk studied her for several moments, his head cocking to the side.

"Alexius?" she whispered. "Is that you?"

The bedroom's heavy wooden doors swung open, crashing against the wall, and the bird took flight from its perch. Lucia turned with a scowl toward the door to see Magnus standing there.

"Lucia . . ." He swiftly came to her side. "I swear to the goddess, if you fall asleep again, I'll be furious with you!"

Despite her flash of annoyance at disturbing the hawk, it was so good to see him again. His dark hair had grown long enough that it nearly hid his brown eyes. She hadn't noticed this on her previous brief awakening. "I won't fall asleep again because I won't let it happen again. Magnus, Mother has been putting a potion in my water. She's the one who's kept me asleep all this time."

He stared at her. "Why would she do such a thing?"

"Because she thinks I'm evil. She told me herself she wanted to kill me." She reached out to clutch his hand. "I never want to see that woman again or I can't be held responsible for what I might do to her to protect myself. She's always hated me, Magnus. Now I feel exactly the same way toward her."

Every candle's flame in the room suddenly rose a half foot, blazing as hot as Lucia's temper. Magnus eyed them warily before returning his gaze to hers.

"Lucia . . . Mother is dead. She was murdered by rebels a week and a half ago."

"Dead?" Lucia's mouth went dry. The next moment, the flames she'd summoned with barely a thought extinguished completely.

She waited to feel some sort of reaction—some kind of grief or sadness or . . . anything at all. But there was nothing.

"I will find her killer. I swear I will. And I will make him pay for what he's done." Magnus's voice caught and he pulled from her grip to pace the room, keeping his face in shadows.

"I'm sorry for your loss," she whispered.

"A loss to us all."

He mourned their mother—deeply. But Lucia found that she did not.

Magnus strode across the room, absently stroking the scar on his cheek. He always did so when he was thinking deeply, whether he realized it or not. "Mother's body was found with a witch—also murdered. Likely, this witch was supplying her with the sleeping potion. I just don't understand why she'd do such a thing. What was she thinking?"

So her mother consulted with witches, did she? To fight fire with fire—magic with magic. "We'll never know for sure," she said instead. She reached out to Magnus and he came back to her side, grasping her hand in his again. "Help me up. I need to get out of this bed."

He did as she asked, supporting her. But as soon as her weight was on both legs, she found she did not have the strength to stand on her own.

"Not yet, I'm afraid," he said, helping her back into bed. "You must rest."

"I've been resting for two months!"

A weary smile curled up the side of his mouth, though his dark eyes were still filled with grief. "Another couple of days will have to be added. You're not going anywhere today. Too bad, really. On any other day, I could sit here till nightfall and fill you in on everything else you've missed. For example, how I feel about being trapped in Auranos. Always bright and shiny and delightfully green—and I truly could not hate it more. All I wish to do is join the hunt for the rebel who killed our mother. But that will have to wait."

"Wait for what?"

Magnus stood up from the side of the bed and leaned his arm against the poster near the base. "Until I return."

"Where are you going?"

His brow furrowed. It was as if he didn't wish to speak his thoughts aloud.

"Magnus, tell me. What's wrong?"

"Today's an important day, Lucia. I find it quite ironic that today, of all days, is when you've finally returned to us. To *me*."

"What's today?"

"It's my wedding day."

She gaped at him and struggled to sit up amongst the many

cushions and pillows surrounding her. "What? Who are you marrying?"

His jaw tightened. "Princess Cleiona Bellos."

Lucia could not believe her ears. "This has been arranged."

Magnus gave her a look. "Oh, not at all. Since helping to take her father's kingdom and destroy her life, I couldn't help but fall madly in love with her. Yes, obviously it was arranged."

Her brother, betrothed to Princess Cleiona—the golden princess of Auranos! "And you're not pleased."

Magnus rubbed his forehead as if the very thought of this pained him. "Pleased that I'm to be wed to a girl who hates me? That I feel nothing for her in return? All to help serve Father's political agenda? I would say 'not pleased' is putting it rather mildly."

She understood why such a strange union would make sense, despite her initial surprise. But this felt deeply wrong. "He may be the king and your father, but he's not your lord and master and you're not his slave. Refuse to marry her."

He studied her for a long moment. "Do you want me to refuse?"

"It has nothing to do with me, Magnus. This is your life, your future."

From his suddenly pained expression she knew this was not the reply he'd hoped for.

She inwardly cringed at the memory of Magnus admitting the depth of his desire for her, of forcing a kiss upon her she didn't want, nor that she returned.

"Nothing has changed between us, Magnus," she whispered. "Please understand that."

"I do understand."

"Are you sure about that?"

"Yes." The word was a hiss.

They might not share blood, but to her, he *was* her brother in every way that counted. To feel anything else for him was impossible. When he'd kissed her, she'd felt only disgust.

But when Alexius had kissed her . . .

"Don't cry," Magnus said, reaching forward to gently stroke the tears from her cheeks, tears she was surprised to find herself shedding. "I must wed the princess. There's no other choice."

"Then I wish you all good things, brother."

She couldn't help but notice her choice of words made him wince. She'd disappointed him, but there was nothing she could do about it. She didn't love Magnus the way he wanted her to. And she never would.

Lucia pushed his hands away and turned toward the balcony again, searching for any sign of the golden hawk that had been there before, desperately wishing that Alexius would soon visit her again so he could guide her. So he could be with her.

Somehow, some way.

CHAPTER 20

CLEO

AURANOS

It was the morning of Cleo's wedding.

And it would be the day that King Gaius would die.

For you, Mira. Today he will pay for his crimes in blood.

Fire burned within her. Today, she would have her vengeance.

Currently, however, her two Limerian attendants tugged so painfully at her hair that she wanted to cry like a little girl, not a future queen. "I don't know why I can't just wear it down," she growled.

"The king commanded that it be plaited like this," Dora haughtily explained. "And it will only take longer if you keep squirming about."

Cleo had to admit that the king's interfering attention to detail had paid off. Her hair did look beautiful in this style, a crisscrossing of tiny braids, woven together in an intricate pattern. Still, she hated it. She hated everything to do with this wedding—doubly so as the servants helped her into the beautiful but heavy gown

Lorenzo had finished for her. He'd personally come to the palace to take her measurements the day after she'd returned from the Wildlands, full of endless, groveling apologies that his seamstress, unbeknownst to him, had been working for rebels. The girl had disappeared, but Lorenzo swore that if he learned anything new about her location, he would inform the king.

In Cleo's mind, the seamstress was less an aid to the rebels and more a simple-minded girl who would do anything a handsome and exciting boy like Jonas Agallon asked of her.

Jonas . . .

The gown sparkled even in the dim light of Cleo's chambers with the sheer number of crystals sewn onto it. And it weighed nearly as much as she did. Helena and Dora laced her up mercilessly, cutting off her breath.

She tried not to worry that she'd received no message from Jonas confirming the rebels' plans to attack in the week and a half since she'd returned to the palace.

Did she really trust him?

Currently, she had no other choice.

Jonas would do this for Paelsia—to save his people. Despite the kiss they'd shared, she knew he wasn't doing this for her.

How you'd laugh at me, Mira. A kiss from a Paelsian rebel a week ago and I remember it as clearly as if it happened just now. I'd give anything to have you here to talk with about it.

She watched herself in the mirror as the girls worked on her hair. The glint of the purple stone in her ring caught her eye. Knowing she wore it, hidden in plain sight, made her heart race. But there was no way to know how this day would turn out, and it was her most precious and important possession.

In the reflection, she caught sight of Nic, who'd appeared at her doorway, his expression grim. She hadn't seen him smile once since she'd broken the news to him about Mira. The pain on his face had shattered her heart. He felt that he had failed to protect his sister when she needed him the most. But he swore he would never fail Cleo.

Now he stood at the doorway to her chambers, waiting to accompany her to the carriage that would take her to the site of her wedding.

To the site of her destiny.

This day would go down in history. The Auranian people would speak of today for centuries to come. They would write books, compose songs, and pass tales down through generations of the day that Princess Cleiona joined forces with the rebels to defeat her enemy and free the entire kingdom from a king's tyranny—even if that kingdom had never fully realized the extent of the evil the King of Blood could unleash.

And peace would reign across all of Mytica for another millennium.

The crowd of thousands cheered upon seeing her step out of the carriage when she reached the Temple of Cleiona. Guards were everywhere outside controlling the masses, holding them back.

She coaxed a smile to her lips and waved at the crowd.

This was good to see. The rebels could use such a large gathering as camouflage, even with the many guards patrolling on foot and on horseback.

Gaius's Imperial Road began here at the temple. It stretched out into the distance, a perfectly formed ribbon of gray rock against the green landscape.

Jonas had said that there were people enslaved and abused on the road sites in Paelsia, where most of the long miles of construction were taking place. But here, and along the path they'd taken in the carriage where they'd passed workers, she didn't witness such atrocities. Those who toiled appeared clean and well rested, working hard, but not to any extremes.

But of course not. This wasn't a barren and isolated location in Paelsia where the king could hide such treatment. For one who wished to be embraced by his new subjects here in Auranos, to show them such clear evidence of his cruelty might push more to oppose him and join the ranks of the rebels. This was only more proof of his lies. And it was just one more reason the king needed to be stopped.

Several of her father's former council members and their wives—important nobles, one and all—drew closer to her as they emerged from their carriages. They purred compliments and admired her dress. They squeezed her hands as they bowed and curtseyed before her. Each and every one wished her all the best on this, the most important day of her life.

Cleo's cheeks began to ache as her false smile quickly grew difficult to maintain. Still, she lingered outside near the crowd for as long as she could.

"It's time, your highness," a tall, imposing man with dark hair and green eyes said. It was Cronus, the captain of King Gaius's palace guard. A man Cleo distrusted every bit as much as the king himself, since he followed every order without hesitation no matter what that order might be. If the king commanded Cronus to kill Cleo with his bare hands, she had no doubt he would crush her without delay. He frightened her, but she refused to let that fear show on her face.

Cleo cast a final glance over her shoulder, scanning the area for any sign of Jonas. Then her gaze locked with Nic's. He nodded, his expression tense. Finally, she took Nic's arm and he led her up the stairs to the temple, with Cronus right behind them.

A second massive statue of the goddess Cleiona blocked Cleo's view of the main hall until she moved past it to see the tall and thick white marble pillars lining the long aisle. It was a huge, cavernous space, three times as large as the palace's great room. On either side of the aisle were hundreds of guests.

There were very few red-uniformed guards in here. Most were outside controlling the crowd.

Good.

"I wish I could save you from this, Cleo," Nic whispered.

She couldn't reply to him past the lump of fear and dread in her throat.

With a last squeeze of her arm, Nic let go of her and moved to take his position near the wall at the front of the temple, his attention not leaving her for a moment.

By the altar, forty paces away, Prince Magnus waited. He was dressed all in black, including a stiff, formal black overcoat edged in gold and red, which had to be stiflingly hot today. The king was by his side, along with a Limerian priest in red robes who would perform the ceremony. Standing nearby were his temple attendants, also in red robes. Red and white flowers were everywhere, along with literally thousands of lit candles.

Every face turned toward her.

"Walk," Cronus commanded.

Cleo tensed.

She had to give the rebels a chance to make their move. Because they would. They had to.

And yet, for a moment she wasn't sure her feet would carry

her. Her legs had turned to jelly. But there was nothing else she could be right now except strong. Anything she had to do to help Auranos, she'd do.

And at the moment, it was to walk and to meet her fate at the altar of this temple.

So, thinking of her father, of Emilia, of Mira and Theon, she walked.

She'd been to weddings before, and this was really no different, apart from the scale and grandeur. On her way up the aisle she saw many smiling and approving faces she recognized, marking them in her mind as friends of her father's who now welcomed his enemy with open arms. Cowards, one and all. Anyone loyal to her father, loyal to Auranos, would not be smiling at the sight of her being forced to marry her enemy's son.

There were also many, though, who looked stricken at the sight of her, their faces drawn and filled with sympathy. She tried very hard not to look these people in the eyes for fear they'd see her own pain.

She once had imagined marrying Theon, she remembered. In her fantasy, the temple had been filled with joy and happiness, and it was her father standing next to Theon at the front of the temple. Not the King of Blood.

Cleo didn't spare a look at the king. She didn't even glance at the prince, although she felt his dark eyes on her. She concentrated on the aisle only, and anyone in her peripheral vision.

Aron sat near the front, his expression difficult to read. He looked annoyed, mostly. And, as usual, drunk.

Next to Aron sat a man Cleo knew to be Prince Ashur Cortas from the Kraeshian Empire. She'd heard of his arrival for the wedding, as representative of his father, the emperor. Many whispers had traveled through the palace in the last few days about this very important guest, most from the servant girls, who were excited to be anywhere close to the famously handsome, incredibly powerful bachelor from across the sea. Perhaps he'd come here also to find a bride, some guessed. Some hoped.

So few guards in here, but so many guests—many of whose faces Cleo didn't recognize. Friends of the king.

Enemies of Auranos.

Jonas, this is your chance. Please don't let me down.

Finally, she was at the front standing next to the prince. His expression was dour, his gaze flat.

"And here we are," he said to her.

She pressed her lips together, saying nothing in reply. If everything went right today, Prince Magnus would die alongside his father. He deserved to die for what he'd done to Theon.

Still, she felt a tiny pang of guilt that he would pay so dearly for his father's more lengthy list of crimes.

He's evil, she reminded herself. *Just like his father. A single tear spilled over his mother's death means nothing. It changes nothing!*

"Let us begin," the priest said. His dark red sash represented the blood of the goddess Valoria and was attached to his bright red robes with two gold pins of entwined serpents. "This joining of two young people in the eternal bonds of marriage is also a symbol of the joining of Mytica as one strong and prosperous kingdom under the rule of our great and noble king, Gaius Damora. Valoria, our glorious and beloved goddess of earth and water, who generously gives us all strength, faith, and wisdom every day of our lives, also gives her blessings today on this fortuitous union."

"Try to withhold your enthusiasm, princess," Magnus muttered, "at least, until the end of the ceremony."

With each word the priest spoke she'd swiftly lost her ability to keep hold of anything but a tense expression. Her hard-won strength had already begun to falter, giving way to clawing panic and legs that threatened to crumple beneath her.

"I'll try my best," she bit out.

The king simply watched all this, his expression unreadable.

"Don't tell me you're not pleased to be here," said the prince under his breath.

"Likely every bit as pleased as you are."

"Join hands," the priest instructed.

She eyed Magnus's hand with dismay.

"Oh, come now," he said to her. "You're breaking my heart."

Cleo's jaw tightened. "Such damage would require you to be in possession of one."

He took hold of her hand. His was dry and warm, just as she remembered it from the day they were betrothed on the balcony. He held her hand as if it was distasteful for him to touch her. It took everything inside her not to pull away from him.

"Repeat the vows after me," the priest said. "I, Magnus Lukas Damora, do pledge to take Cleiona Aurora Bellos as my wife and future queen. A bond that will begin this day and go forth unto eternity."

Panic gripped her. It was much too soon for the ceremony to come to an end! Was this it?

There was a pause and a tightening of the prince's grip on her hand. "I, Magnus Lukas Damora, do pledge to take"—he let out a breath as if fighting to continue speaking—"Cleiona Aurora Bellos as my wife and future queen. A bond that will begin this day and go forth unto eternity."

Cleo began to tremble. *Eternity. Oh goddess, please help me.*

The priest nodded, dipping his hand into a bowl of fragrant oil he held before him. He dabbed a little of the liquid on Magnus's forehead.

The priest turned to her. "Repeat after me. I, Cleiona Aurora Bellos, do pledge to take Magnus Lukas Damora as my husband and future king. A bond that will begin this day and go forth unto eternity."

She had no voice, no words. Her mouth was too dry, her lips parched. This could not happen.

"Repeat the words," the king said, his voice low, but his gaze was as sharp as the edge of a dagger.

"I—I Cleiona Aurora B-Bellos . . ." she stuttered, "do pledge to take—"

The sound of metal striking metal caught her attention from the rear of the temple. The next moment, four of the temple attendants in red cloaks threw back their hoods to reveal their faces.

Cleo's heart leapt into her throat to see that one of them was the rebel leader himself. Jonas's gaze flicked to hers for the briefest of moments before he surged forward, drawing a sword from beneath his stolen robes. Cleo's head whipped toward the back where she saw the scattering of red-uniformed guards quickly fall under the blades of rebels who'd been in disguise. Some frightened and confused cries sounded out from the gathered witnesses.

"Nic!" she cried out. If the rebels confronted Nic in his Limerian uniform they wouldn't know who he was—what he meant to her. He was in danger.

Why hadn't she considered this before? Despite the promise to say nothing about Jonas's plan, she could have warned him!

Jonas grabbed Magnus just as the prince reached for his own weapon. Jonas held his sword to the prince's throat, flicking a glance at the king.

It had all happened in a flash—barely time to think.

Jonas smiled thinly, his eyes narrowed. "Seems you have some celebrating to do, your majesty. So do we."

King Gaius glanced over the group of rebels, at least twenty dangerous-looking boys who'd now taken hold of the temple. They stood before the fallen guards and blocked the entrances, sharp weapons in hand.

"You're Jonas Agallon." The king's expression was calm despite the fact that his son was currently frozen in place with the edge of a sword digging into his throat. "We met before when you accompanied Chief Basilius to our meeting with King Corvin. Seems like a very long time ago."

If anything, Jonas's gaze grew more steely. "Here's how this is going to go. First I'm going to kill your son. And then I'm going to kill you."

King Gaius spread his hands. "It does seem you have us at a great disadvantage, doesn't it?"

Cleo's heart began to pound even harder, if that were possible. She craned her neck to send a frantic, sweeping glance through the temple. Twenty rebels had quickly disarmed and overtaken the dozen Limerian guards stationed inside the temple, all of whom were now dead or unconscious.

But where was Nic?

"Surprised how lax your security is in here. Outside was much trickier to navigate—and, I'll admit, it's going to be a difficult escape, but we're up to the task, I think." Jonas looked smug and satisfied, like a hungry cat who'd cornered a tasty pigeon. "Frankly, I think you'd have been smarter to use a smaller, less public venue for such an important event—somewhere you kept secret. Too bad you didn't."

"I'm sure you would have discovered that location," the king said. "You're that good. I'm thoroughly impressed by your skills: I'm sure your people follow your every order precisely and with great admiration."

For a king facing assassination, he was so calm it was eerie.

"Father," Magnus gritted out. A trickle of blood slid down his skin from the edge of Jonas's blade.

"What do you want?" King Gaius asked Jonas again, not sparing a glance at his son's face.

"What do I want?" Jonas asked disbelievingly. "Exactly what I just said. I want to see you pay for the crimes you've committed against my people. I've seen your road with my own eyes, your majesty." The title was used mockingly. "I've seen what you've authorized your guards to do. I asked for it to be stopped, but you ignored my demands. Your error. Today, it will stop with your death."

"I can offer you great riches."

"I want nothing but your blood."

King Gaius smiled thinly. "Then you should have been much swifter about making it flow. That was *your* error, rebel."

An arrow sliced through the air, catching the rebel standing next to Jonas in the chest. The boy fell to the ground, twitching violently before his body went still.

Cleo watched with horror as half the wedding guests stood up from their seats and charged the rebels.

The lack of guards inside the temple was only an illusion. They'd been pretending to be witnesses to the wedding—they were the faces she didn't recognize. And they attacked the now-outnumbered rebels with full strength.

Taking advantage of the distraction, Magnus knocked the sword from Jonas's grip. Then Magnus grabbed the front of Jonas's cloak and threw him up against a marble pillar hard enough that the back of Jonas's head cracked against the hard surface.

Cleo was shoved forward as a rebel and a guard fight came too close. She scrambled out of their way, fighting to move against the heavy, binding skirts of her gown, which made it feel as if she was moving through mud. She missed the swipe of a dagger by mere inches.

"You killed my mother, you son of a bitch," Magnus snarled at Jonas. "I'm going to tear out your heart and shove it down your throat."

Jonas blocked the prince's clenched fist. A nearby rebel took a sword to his chest and he staggered back, slamming into Magnus, knocking the prince's grip free from Jonas.

The blood of the fallen pooled on the marble floors—so red against the white. Cleo stared at it, unable to process how quickly everything had fallen to chaos.

At that second the temple began to shake, trembling at first and then more and more violently. The floor cracked open with an enormous splintering sound, and several guards fell screaming into the jagged, gaping chasm. The massive statue of Cleiona toppled over and crashed to the ground, crushing three people. Everyone standing was knocked off their feet. Cleo, still crouched on the floor, threw her arms defensively over her head.

King Gaius shakily rose to his feet though the ground was still shaking horribly, his furious gaze searching the temple until it landed on Cleo.

He didn't notice what was right behind him.

A marble pillar had dislodged from the broken roof and was falling. The king was directly in its path.

But before he was crushed, Magnus launched himself toward the king and knocked him out of the way. The heavy pillar crashed, shattering into hundreds of pieces on the still shaking ground.

Prince Ashur rose to his feet, his voice booming. "Everyone, out of the temple. Now."

The hundreds of wedding guests tried desperately to flee the violent and bloody battleground, running for the exits as fast as they could. Several were crushed by more pillars falling in their path.

The world was ending right before Cleo's eyes.

An arm came around her waist, pulling her back behind the altar as the violent quake finally eased and the world stopped shaking.

"Do you know you almost got killed?" Nic snapped.

"Nic!" She grabbed him into a tight hug. "Thank the goddess you're all right!"

"All right? I'd say we're as far from all right as we can get."

Cleo crawled to the side of the stone altar to look at the destruction before her. Jonas lay dead on the floor of the temple.

No, please no. It cannot be!

No, wait. Two guards rushed past his still body. When they had moved out of view, though, Jonas began to stir. Cleo watched him come back to consciousness and push himself up to a sitting, then a standing, position, a hand clamped over his wounded side where he had been injured by a blade. His face, too, was bloody. His gaze went from unfocused to grim and moved through the temple, over his fallen rebels, until he finally locked eyes with Cleo.

He held his hand out to her, as if beckoning her to join him. To flee with him while there was still time to escape unseen with the rest of the guests.

She shook her head.

They couldn't both escape this, not with him injured and her in this weighted gown. She had to stay—for Nic. For Auranos.

But he could still save himself. And if he wanted half a chance at that, he had to leave now while he was out of sight of the guards. *Go!* she mouthed. *Go now!*

He hesitated only another moment before he shed his red robes, turned, and fled the temple, joining the cluster of the escaping guests as they emerged into full daylight.

"Cleo," Nic whispered, clenching her hand so tightly it hurt. "This is bad. So bad."

Truer words had never been spoken.

The rebels had lost. And, oh, how they'd lost.

Every one of them apart from Jonas now lay dead on the broken, crumbling floor of the temple. The guards, who'd been dressed in regular clothes to blend in with the rest of the guests, were beginning to stalk around to make sure the dead rebels *were* dead, thrusting sword or spear through the still bodies to make sure they'd never move again. There was so much blood spread throughout the temple.

So many had died in so little time.

Nic offered her a hand and helped her to her feet. A gory splash of blood now defiled her beautiful gown. Nic looked at it with alarm before he began checking her.

"It's not mine," she said, her voice brittle.

"Thank the goddess!"

"My fault, Nic. This is . . . it's all my fault."

"What are you talking about? No, it's not." He grasped her arms. "You had nothing to do with this."

He hadn't known of the plan because she hadn't told him. The one person she trusted more than anyone—and she hadn't told him a thing. If he'd died today as well, she could never have forgiven herself.

Scattered bodies lay in crimson puddles across the pale marble floor. Glazed eyes stared off in every direction, some directly at Cleo as if blaming her for their deaths.

Magnus leaned against a pillar and gingerly touched the shallow wound at his throat. He looked exhausted, but his gaze sparked with outrage. His attention finally fell on her. She looked away before she was forced to meet his eyes.

The king approached. There was a gash on his forehead. Blood dripped into his eyes and he wiped it away with the back of his hand.

He'd almost died—she'd seen it herself. He'd nearly been crushed by a pillar, but his son had saved him. And now all he had to show for his brush with death was a bit of blood.

"Did you know this would happen?" Magnus asked.

Cleo's stomach clenched and her fingers dug into Nic's arm as if to borrow some of her friend's strength. As she opened her mouth to deny any prior knowledge of the rebel attack, the king answered instead.

"I thought there was a strong chance of it, but I wasn't sure."

"But you took precautions."

"Of course I did. I'm no fool."

"And yet you said nothing to me." The words were edged in poison. "This is not the first time you didn't tell me anything of your plans, Father."

"I didn't want to spoil the day any more than it needed to be." The king's gaze slid to Cleo's. "It's very distressing." He gestured at the death and carnage before them. She couldn't look away from the steady drip of blood down the king's forehead. "You are, after all, only a sixteen-year-old girl, accustomed to a much more privileged and protected life. This must all be quite a shock."

"It is," she whispered. "The attack. The—the earthquake. I believe it's a sign from the goddess. The wedding will have to be postponed. It's really such a shame."

When the back of his hand struck her cheek, she reacted more from shock than from the stinging pain. Her hand flew to her face and she stared at him with wide eyes.

"You think I'm going to make it that easy for you, you deceitful brat?" He grabbed hold of the front of her dress and yanked her closer. He flicked a look at Nic, who'd lurched forward to protect Cleo. "I warn you, boy, do not look at me that way if you want to keep your eyes. I will gore them from your head and serve them to Princess Cleiona as part of her wedding feast."

"But—but how can we continue?" Cleo stammered. "All this blood! All these bodies! The temple is in shambles, the roof will collapse at any moment. We must leave! The wedding can't—"

He slapped her again, harder this time, and she bit her lip in pain. "They underestimated me, those rebels. They have no idea how much I consider every move I make. They thought they could walk in here so easily and kill me. No one can kill me." Still, he eyed the fallen pillar uneasily before turning a furious glare on Cleo. He grasped her throat so tightly with one hand that she began to choke. She clawed at his arm but he just tightened his grip until she stopped fighting. Spots swam in her vision.

"Father, stop it," Magnus said.

"Be quiet, boy. I need to make the princess aware of a couple of important things." His cold gaze sank into her like death itself, drawing her deeper into darkness. "If you ever underestimate my desire to hold on to this throne, my dear, you will deeply regret it. Consider today only a small demonstration of this."

She tried to speak, but his strangling grip only tightened like a vise.

Cronus had drawn closer, his sword drawn and pointed toward Nic to keep him back.

Magnus paced angrily in a circle. "Father, this isn't necessary. You're killing her."

"I told you to be quiet. Don't make me say it again." A sinister smile then curled up the side of the king's mouth as he gazed down at her. "Do you know what everyone will say about today? They'll say that a beautiful wedding was disrupted by heartless rebels. That they wanted to keep you from exchanging your vows with my son. That they failed and we succeeded. That true love conquers all, no matter what the opposition might bring—even the shaking of the world itself. The people will find comfort in such stories in the difficult months and years ahead. Do you think I would marry off my son to an admitted slut like you for any other reason? They'll devour such a story and ask for more. They will come out in droves to see you on your journey across my kingdom. They will worship you and Magnus like a god and a goddess because they are stupid and naive. And this is exactly what I want. For the more they focus on you, the less they'll focus on what I'm doing and why I'm doing it."

He finally released her and she gasped for breath, hands flying to her bruised throat. Nic stood nearby, his fists clenched at his sides, his body shaking. Had he made a threatening move toward the king, Cleo knew he would have died. Just as Jonas's friends and rebels had died today.

There was no hope in death, only an end.

The king shoved Cleo closer to Magnus.

"Continue," he snapped.

The priest was there, a streak of blood on his cheek to match his red robes.

"Hands—" His voice shook. "Take her hand."

Magnus grabbed hold of Cleo's hand. She looked up at him, but he didn't meet her gaze. His eyes were straight forward, his jaw tense.

"Repeat after me," the priest said after a moment. "I, Cleiona Aurora Bellos, do pledge to take Magnus Lukas Damora as my husband and future king. A bond that will begin this day and go forth unto eternity."

Her throat felt crushed, her face stung, her cheeks were wet with tears. Everywhere she looked she saw blood and death and despair.

"Say it." The king's voice was low and dangerous. "Or you will watch me cut your friend into small pieces. First, I'll remove his toes, then his feet. Then his fingers and hands. I will feed him piece by piece to my dogs while he screams for a mercy that will never come. My dogs do so love fresh meat." His eyes flashed with fury. *"Say it."*

"I, Cleiona Aurora Bellos," she choked out, "do pledge to take Magnus Lukas Damora as my husband and future king. A bond that will begin this day and go forth unto eternity."

The priest anointed her forehead with the fragrant oil. Even though he was from Limeros, she was certain she now saw pity in his eyes. "And so it is, and so it shall be, from this day forward until death and beyond. You are wed. You are husband and wife. It is done."

It is done.

CHAPTER 21

ALEXIUS

THE SANCTUARY

Melenia looked up as Alexius entered her chambers in the crystal palace. It was a room filled with light and flowers. A floor-to-ceiling crystal window looked out to the expansive city far below, where other immortals made their home.

The window bore a jagged crack down the center. The massive tremor in the mortal world had been clearly felt here as well. Many immortals, in fact, had panicked, believing this to be the end.

But Alexius knew differently.

He'd already been on his way to see Melenia when it happened. His steps were focused, his mind clear. There were matters that needed to be discussed, and they couldn't wait another day.

As she stood from the seating area, her diaphanous robes swished around her curves. Her eyes were blue—a vivid sapphire shade that no one could ever mistake as mortal.

"I'm glad you're here," she said before he had uttered a single word. He was struck by her beauty, as he always was. She held her hands out to him as he drew closer. "You can celebrate with me another sign of our success. We're close now. So close I can taste it."

"And what does it taste like?"

"Like sweet victory. At long last." Her smile fell as she saw he did not look pleased by this. She reached up to press her cool hands against his warm cheeks. This woman seemed so small and fragile before him, but he knew she was anything but. He'd never known anyone stronger in his entire existence. For so long, he had admired that strength. "What is wrong? You look so troubled."

"I am troubled. The princess awoke from her deep slumber earlier."

"I see. And now it will be more difficult for you to access her dreams."

"That's not it."

She watched him carefully. "Then what is it? Unburden yourself to me, Alexius. You know you can trust me. We share all of our secrets, don't we?"

So many secrets, he'd lost count of them all. "Two disasters in the mortal world. The tornado and the earthquake. It's unfolding exactly as you said it would."

"Yes."

Melenia was a very special immortal, different from the others. More powerful in so many ways. She could see many things the others couldn't—that which happened here in the Sanctuary and beyond into the mortal world. Her sight was clear and focused and always had been.

"And you continue to visit the king's dreams?" he asked.

There was a pause this time before she spoke. "Not recently. He already knows what I need him to do."

It was another of Melenia's many secrets. Elders did not possess the ability to enter the dreams of mortals. Such a task was never easy and was always draining of one's magic and physical strength. But for an elder, it was impossible.

Except for Melenia.

"It won't be long before my road is finished," she said. There was joy in her voice.

Yes, her road. A road that had to be swiftly built by mortal hands. A road that needed to pass certain locations along its twisting path.

And, of course, since it wasn't *only* a road, one mustn't forget that there needed to be a great deal of blood spilled on it.

Blood—everything depended on blood. It was elemental. It was magic. Even when it flowed from the veins of mortals.

And when the road was finally completed . . .

"I need to know if there's another way," Alexius said, the words thick in his throat.

Melenia's brows drew together. "Another way?"

He raised his gaze to meet hers, trying to shield the ache in his chest beneath his golden, swirling mark. Other immortals didn't know of Melenia's plans, but he did. He'd agreed to them when originally enlisted to her cause. He'd been certain he could stay the course.

Now he doubted himself.

Understanding entered her blue eyes. "I wanted you to make contact with her. To speak with her. To establish whether or not she was truly the sorceress prophesied by Eva so many years ago. You did as I asked of you perfectly."

"She's an innocent, Melenia."

"No mortal who lives and breathes more than a day is innocent."

"Help me understand. How are you so certain that your plan is the only one there is to find the Kindred? To release us from this prison? How are you so sure of it?"

Her jaw tensed as she swept past him toward the edge of her chambers, indicating the walls with a wave of her hand. Etched into the silver and crystal were the symbols of the elements—earth, fire, air, and water. It was her shrine to the Kindred, one many immortals had in their living quarters. They prayed to the symbols, hoping for answers, for guidance in the long days, years, centuries that had passed with no change and no escape.

"Because they speak to me," Melenia said very simply, running her fingers lightly over the triangular symbol for fire. "They tell me what to do. How to find them. And your princess is the key. When my road is complete, her blood will be spilled. All of it."

A shudder went through Alexius.

Once, he was prepared to sacrifice Lucia for the sake of saving his world before the magic faded completely from it. He'd been committed to the cause, as had a select few immortals chosen specially by Melenia to join her small army.

Melenia turned from her shrine to study Alexius and she tilted her head. "I wanted her to fall in love with you, to make her more willing, more pliable. But you've fallen for her as well, haven't you?"

"No." He bit out the bitter word, feeling the falseness of it leave his mouth.

"You can't lie to me. I know the truth when I see it." She sighed. "This complicates matters."

"I need to go to her."

"Yes, I'm sure you think you do." Her hand remained upon the symbol for fire as she gave him a quizzical look. "You're not the only one currently infatuated with a mortal. Phaedra has allegedly been watching one closely as well. A rebel."

His gaze snapped to hers. "A rebel?"

"I don't trust her. She sees too much. She knows too much, just as Stephanos did. I worry that your friend is becoming a liability to my plans."

She said it lightly, but a gnawing concern began to build within Alexius's gut. If Phaedra proved herself a problem for Melenia, then he worried deeply for her. Phaedra did not guard her thoughts or her words. She spoke her mind too plainly and she acted spontaneously and without thorough consideration of any risks. Such behavior could earn her enemies. Powerful ones.

Perhaps it already had.

"Why must your plans remain secret?" He asked the question that had been plaguing him for months. "To find the Kindred, to break the chains keeping us trapped within the Sanctuary: it benefits all of us. Why not tell Timotheus or Danaus of the princess? Of the road?" He hesitated. "Is there something more you seek that they would not approve of?"

"Don't worry about such things. And don't worry about your princess."

"I need to go to her," he said again. "Now. It cannot wait."

"No, you don't need to go anywhere. Not yet. Not until I'm ready for the final piece of this puzzle to snap into place."

"The final piece of your puzzle means her death."

"You agreed to this, Alexius. You agreed to what would save your kind, save the world. Do you really want to change your mind now?"

"What I want is to find another solution."

"There are no other solutions." She came toward him and took his hands in hers, squeezing them tightly. "I understand, I do. I understand what it's like to love someone forbidden to me. To pine away for him. To ache for his touch and know that a future together is impossible. I know to what lengths someone is willing to go to help the one they love more than anyone else."

His eyes met hers, hope flooding his heart.

She fixed him with a cool smile. "And I know how dangerous it is to have thoughts like these."

"Melenia . . ."

"Say nothing more. I need you to regain your objectivity and your devotion to me and my cause. The princess's life will be sacrificed for the sake of the Kindred. Their magic is all that matters."

"I need to talk to her." The words stuck in his throat.

"No, you don't." Her grip on him tightened and he couldn't pull away. He felt a draining sensation spreading through him. She was draining his magic, his ability to shift form, to enter the dreams of mortals. To do anything but breathe and exist.

It would be all it took to keep him away from Lucia.

There was a reason why Melenia was the most powerful immortal of them all. She could do *this*.

"Not all love is eternal," she whispered to him as he weakened and fell to his knees before her. "Not all love has the power to change worlds. What you feel for the princess is a passing fancy, that is all. Trust me, Alexius. I'm only doing this to help you."

He'd promised Lucia he would come to her in her dreams. He'd come here to try to find a way to save her life.

On both tasks he'd failed.

Yet he knew that Melenia spoke the truth, that he was thinking irrationally and was in danger of becoming a liability to her plans. The life of one sixteen-year-old sorceress was not worth the destruction of everything and everyone.

Lucia would have to die. And one day very soon, he would be the one to take her life.

There was no turning back.

CHAPTER 22

LUCIA

AURANOS

"Is my magic evil?"

It was the first thing Lucia asked when her father had come to visit her bedside before he left for the wedding. She needed to know the truth, and her father was well known for his candor. Magnus would easily lie to protect her feelings. Perhaps he already had. And Alexius—did she really believe anything he'd told her? Had he even been real? Now that she was awake, she'd begun to doubt what she'd seen. What she'd felt. The thought that he might only have been a dream was now a heavy weight that lay on her chest.

"No, it's not evil," the king replied, kneeling beside her bed and grasping her hands tightly in his. He smiled brighter than she'd seen in ages. "It's incredible. It's wonderful. You are a sorceress, Lucia. A beautiful and powerful sorceress. You've been blessed by the goddess with a great gift."

His words were so sincere they brought tears to her eyes. "No, it's a curse. Mother believed so."

"She was wrong. Your mother was wrong about many things. If anything, your *elementia* will be a challenge to you, but one you shall easily master. I have a new tutor at the ready. She and I have been waiting for you to wake up. She will visit you later today to begin your lessons." He stood so he could lean over and kiss her forehead. "Know this: I am so lucky to be able to call you daughter. I would not feel this way if I had any doubts about you, Lucia. I have none at all."

Tears burned in her eyes at his beautiful words.

"To wield this power is your destiny. One cannot avoid their destiny. One shouldn't even try, since it will only bring pain. Embracing it is the only sound answer—the only answer that will give you peace."

There were times when she'd had misgivings about her father, especially his tendency toward cruelty. She'd seen how he'd treated the citizens of Limeros, servants, and even Magnus himself over the years. She was well aware of his wider reputation.

But to her recollection, he'd never been cruel to her. Only kind. Only encouraging.

"Thank you, Father." She sat up, ignoring the dizziness that came from such a sudden movement, and embraced him. He was the strength she needed today.

"Of course, my child." He patted her cheek. "Now, I must make the journey to the temple. I only wish you could be there today, but it's best that you rest."

The temple. The wedding. "Father . . . Magnus doesn't want to marry the princess."

"But he will. Despite any initial protests, Magnus always does exactly what I tell him to do." He studied her face. "In part, I did this for you, you know."

She frowned. "For me?"

"I know how Magnus feels about you."

Shame swelled inside her and her cheeks warmed. "I don't know what to say."

"You needn't say anything. It's not your fault. It's his. It's a shameful weakness on his part that he can't seem to control—and I can't allow it to continue."

"And you think forcing him into a marriage with Princess Cleiona will make him feel differently?"

"If nothing else, it'll be a distraction. And they'll be leaving at first light for their wedding tour, which will give you the time to fully focus on your magic and not worry about your brother's unrequited love." He raised an eyebrow. "You don't share Magnus's feelings, do you? While I don't approve of the desire he harbors for you, if you felt the same for him—that would change everything."

Her face heated even more. "No, I don't. And I never will. The way he looks at me . . . I wish I knew what to say to him—to make him forget such unwelcome thoughts."

The king turned his head slightly. "You know how I feel about eavesdroppers, my son."

Lucia was confused by his words until she looked past the king to see that Magnus stood in the doorway to the room. Her heart sank. How much had he heard?

"Apologies, Father. I only came to say farewell to my sister." Magnus's flat gaze moved to her.

"Magnus . . ." she began, but he turned and left without another word.

The king's attention returned to Lucia as she settled back down upon her pillows, her stomach now a hard, twisted knot. She'd hurt Magnus with her unthinking words.

She seemed to always be hurting him.

"It's for the best," the king said. "Everything turns out the way it was meant to in the end."

"Of course," she whispered.

When he left for the wedding, Lucia was all alone with her thoughts and regrets until the *elementia* tutor arrived much later.

Her name was Domitia, a witch who lived in a village a few hours from the City of Gold. She had a bright smile, long, straw-colored hair, and fine lines around her green eyes. She coaxed Lucia out of the bed slowly, and soon the dizziness faded and strength returned. The sleeping potion had finally left her system, the weariness dissipated, and Lucia felt ready to learn more about her magic from a knowledgeable tutor.

"I'm so pleased to be able to assist you!" Domitia said—no, gushed. "The king was very wise in choosing me."

If the king did not find a specific use for a woman accused of witchcraft—be it in Limeros, or now here in Auranos—she faced a death sentence. Domitia quickly explained that she'd been captured in a recent sweep by guards, based on local rumors about her talents. Luckily for her, the king was searching for a suitable *elementia* tutor for his daughter and had freed her from the dungeons.

No wonder the woman's demeanor was so cloyingly chipper.

"Let's start with something simple, shall we?" Domitia said. "I'd like you to concentrate on these candles and light them one by one. I've been told you have a strong hold on fire magic."

The witch had lined up ten candles of differing heights and thicknesses on a nearby table.

"You could say that."

The witch had no idea Lucia was a prophesied sorceress. For

all she knew, the king's daughter was just another common witch saved from the dungeons only by her royal status.

"I can do fire magic myself. Allow me to demonstrate." The witch's forehead wrinkled as she studied the bare wicks of the candles. It was an amusing sight as she strained, her face scrunching with effort as if she was seated upon a chamber pot.

Lucia kept watching. One of the wicks began to glow. The witch's breath came quicker and a thin layer of perspiration appeared on her forehead. Finally, a small flame danced upon the first candle.

Domitia exhaled shakily. "See? It can be done."

"Very impressive," Lucia said, even though a prickly impatience had now taken seed beneath her skin.

The witch nodded to acknowledge the magnitude of what she'd done. "It's your turn, princess."

Lucia's gaze lingered on the unlit candles. "Do you know anything about prophecies, Domitia?"

"Prophecies, your grace?"

"Those pertaining to *elementia*."

Domitia pursed her lips as her expression grew thoughtful. "Of course, there are many rumors of such things. It's difficult to piece together what is real from what is false."

Lucia had to determine if this woman was of any true worth to her. Alexius was gone, and while she hoped he would soon visit her dreams as he'd promised, she had to look for other answers. She required a skilled guide with knowledge of what she was and what she could do.

"Would you say you're more accomplished than the average witch?"

Domitia brightened at the question. "Oh, yes, your grace! I have the ability to access not only fire magic, but some water as well. These elements are complete opposites that often cancel each other out. They rarely appear within the same witch. I am very blessed to have this ability."

"Show me your water magic," Lucia said.

The witch wiped the sweat from her brow and moved across the room to get a goblet, which she filled with water from a nearby pitcher. She brought it back and placed it down on the table next to the lit candle.

"Watch," she said, again scrunching her face as she studied the water.

Lucia observed over the witch's shoulder to see, after a time, the water slowly begin to swirl. She waited, but the witch gave her a triumphant glance.

"Disappointing."

The witch looked at her with shock. "Disappointing? My magic has taken me years to master to this level."

"Your mastery is questionable." Lucia sighed. "I'm afraid, from what I've seen here, you don't know nearly enough to be able to help me. But I do appreciate your visit."

Alarm lit in the woman's gaze much quicker than she could light a candle. "Apologies, your grace, that I've disappointed you. I want to help you as much as I can. It's all I care about."

"Of course it is," Lucia murmured. "You must know my father's penchant for ending the lives of accused witches who serve no purpose to him."

"And yet his own daughter is one." Domitia's cheeks then began to flame. "Oh—apologies again. I don't mean any offense. Please forgive me!"

Was this the sort of power her father favored so much? The

ability to incite fear in someone by uttering a few simple words? Lucia was disturbed to realize it was a curiously pleasant sensation.

"You don't need to be afraid of me," Lucia said more gently.

Domitia wrung her hands. "I—I'm not. Of course, I've heard troubling stories about the king, and the prince as well, but I've been assured that you are kind and gracious. A true princess in every sense of the word."

"I certainly have tried to be in the past." Lucia trailed her fingers over the table the practice candles were set upon. "But lately, I must admit, I've become increasingly worried."

"Worried, your grace?"

Oh—how was she to put into words how she felt? It was difficult to wrap her mind around it fully, but she couldn't ignore the truth of it. "I have something within me that . . . *hungers*. I can only explain it as a caged beast. I didn't feel it when I was asleep, but now that I'm awake I find it impossible to ignore."

"I don't understand, princess. A beast within you? What does this mean?"

"They tell me it's not evil. It doesn't feel evil, really. But there is a darkness taking hold," Lucia said, and as she spoke she realized just how true her words were, "as if the night itself wraps me in an embrace that grows tighter every moment."

Domitia's gaze filled with understanding. She nodded. "What you're feeling is perfectly normal for one able to harness any part of *elementia*. But don't worry. Without blood sacrifice, our powers can't be any more destructive than what I've shown you here today." She leaned over to blow out the candle she'd lit earlier. "Now it's your turn. Try to light this candle and we'll take it from there. All right?"

The dark beast within her rolled over at Domitia's dismissal of her previous words of warning. For that was what they were—a warning.

"Certainly," Lucia said.

All ten wicks caught fire at once, the flames rising high into the air to lick the ceiling. The witch gasped and staggered back, drawing a shaking hand to her mouth.

"But—but, princess. I've never seen anything like this!"

Lucia couldn't help but smile at the terrified confusion on the woman's face. "No, I don't suppose you have."

Domitia's wide eyes reflected the flickering fire. "And you do this with no effort at all. . . . Incredible . . ."

"Oh, there's effort, I assure you. It's a muscle inside me that begs to be flexed. Answer me this question. It's a question I've posed to several people so far, yet my dead mother's opinion still lingers as if her ghost now haunts me. Is this magic I wield evil?"

"Evil?" Domitia repeated, her voice shaking. "I don't know."

"Wrong answer." Lucia thrust her hands out toward the witch, summoning air magic. It wrapped itself around the woman and slammed her up and back against the wall, pinning her there like a butterfly on a board.

Domitia gasped. "What are you doing?"

It was an excellent question. What was Lucia doing?

Whatever it was . . . it felt good.

The fire blazed behind her—so hot that sweat dripped down her back. Too hot. She needed something cold to balance it. Fire and water were opposites. The witch herself had said they often canceled each other out.

Lucia wanted to know if this was true. She glanced at the goblet of water the witch had used. A focused thought drew the water from its container, and it traveled through the air until level with where Lucia stood.

She studied it, cocking her head, and she thought of home. Of Limeros.

The water froze in the air, forming itself into the shape of a spear.

The witch yelped as the sharp piece of ice moved closer to her, close enough to touch her throat. The dark beast within Lucia approved of this. It had a great thirst for fresh blood now that it had finally awoken.

"I will have to tell my father when he returns from my brother's wedding how disappointed I am in his poor choice of tutor."

"Princess, please!" Domitia shrieked. "I will do anything you ask of me! Please don't hurt me!"

The words were hollow in Lucia's ears. Instead, she focused on the spear of ice, pressing it close enough to break the witch's skin. A bright line of red blood spilled down her throat. The sight of it fascinated Lucia. How much blood could be spilled before the woman perished? And would this blood sacrifice help increase Lucia's power even more?

A rumble sounded loud all around her and the floor began to shake. Lucia lost her footing and fell hard to the ground, bruising her shoulder. The spear of ice fell and shattered.

"What is this?" Lucia managed. "What's happening?"

The candles fell off the table, their flames extinguishing before they landed on the floor. Lucia's gaze whipped toward the witch, who held her hand to her injured throat and stared at the princess with fear as the earthquake finally came to a stop.

Lucia's heart leapt into her throat as the beast within her withdrew into its dark cave.

Goddess, what had she been thinking? She'd nearly killed this poor woman!

Domitia's voice trembled. "What are you?"

Lucia forced herself to look the witch directly in her eyes. "You will say nothing of what happened here if you value your life."

"Princess—"

"Leave me!"

She didn't have to say it again. Domitia fled the room without further argument.

Lucia's heart pounded loud as thunder in her ears.

This is what my mother meant. She was right and everyone else was wrong.

She felt the truth in the thought. And what scared her more than anything else that had happened today was that a small part of her didn't care.

A glimpse of golden feathers caught her eye as a hawk took flight from her balcony.

"Alexius! Come back!" She raced to the marble railing to see the hawk soar high into the blue sky until it disappeared from sight.

The sliver of hope that had briefly caught fire in her chest turned to bitter ash.

CHAPTER 23

CLEO

AURANOS

"It's remarkable, really," the king said loud enough for all to hear. He stood before the guests at the evening wedding banquet he'd insisted go on as scheduled at the palace, despite the carnage they'd left behind at the temple. "This young girl next to me had enough courage to say she wanted to continue with the ceremony and marry my son, not only in the face of a violent and horrific attack by insurgents, but after the world itself had been rocked beneath her feet. Tonight we shall mourn those we lost, but also celebrate together, victorious."

Cleo wore a blood-free gown. Her hair had been neatened, her face washed. She sat stiffly between Magnus and his father on the dais and twisted her amethyst ring until it would surely leave a groove in her finger. The guests, she noted when she looked up from her golden plate that bore food she couldn't stomach, looked every bit as stunned by the day's events as Cleo did. Five of their fellow wedding guests had been killed by the collapsing temple before the rest had escaped outside.

These people didn't want to be here any more than she did.

"I welcome this beautiful princess into my family. And I so look forward to introducing her to Princess Lucia when my daughter is finally well enough to leave her chambers. Despite its difficulties, today has been an incredible day of miracles and blessings."

Miracles and blessings. It was all she could do not to leap from her seat and run screaming from this hall.

"Let us toast to the happy couple." The king raised his glass, as did everyone seated at the long wooden tables, mountains of food and drink heaped before them. "To Magnus and Cleo. May their days together be as happy as mine were with my beloved, departed Althea."

"To Magnus and Cleo," the guests echoed immediately.

Cleo's knuckles were white on her goblet and she raised it to her lips, only to find her hand was shaking. The taste of the sweet wine offered small comfort. Such a familiar taste now—this Paelsian wine. It teased her with the chance for escape. Perhaps she would drink enough wine tonight to drown herself in.

Nic caught her eye from the back of the hall, where he was standing guard at the far entrance. No guests were allowed to leave until the king decided the banquet was finished.

A sob rose in her throat, but she swallowed it down with another gulp of wine. A servant was at the ready to fill her glass when it was empty and she had another. Then another. Instead of the world brightening, though, it only seemed to grow darker, with shadows slithering across the floor, clutching at her ankles and legs.

As the banquet wore on, Cleo couldn't stop thinking of Jonas. What must he think of her now? At her suggestion, so many rebels had been killed.

Magnus was a constant presence, so close that she could feel the heat emanating from his body. He smelled of the leather from his overcoat and a deep, warm sandalwood. He hadn't spoken a single word to her since they'd left the temple. They'd ridden in the same carriage, but he kept his gaze on the view outside, on the landscape passing by on the return journey. He was sullen, cold. As he always was.

"Ridiculous," she mumbled. "All of it."

"I couldn't agree more," Magnus replied.

Her cheeks heated. She hadn't meant to say this out loud. She'd had too much wine, downing glass after glass as it had been presented to her. Magnus had been drinking nothing but spiced cider. She realized she now did an excellent impression of Aron—who sat in the front table and cast occasional drunken, miserable glances in her general direction.

"I need air," Cleo whispered after a time. "May I have a moment?"

Would Magnus expect his wife to always ask permission for her every move? Would he be cruel to her and controlling on this, their first night of marriage?

First night.

Her heart began to race at the thought. She wanted to remain in public for as long as possible. What came later she couldn't deal with. Not with him. *Never* with him.

"By all means," he said, not bothering to look directly at her. "Go get your air."

She left the dais without delay. Her walk was more of a stagger as the amount of wine she'd consumed during the banquet became more apparent. Too much. And yet, not nearly enough. She moved as calmly as possible toward the archway leading to the hall . . . to escape.

Or as much of an escape as she could manage with a limitless number of guards keeping watch over her every move.

Cleo pressed her hand against the wall to steady herself. Once she found an exit to a balcony, she grasped hold of the railing and tried to calm herself.

"Quite the ceremony," a voice greeted her from the shadows, and she jarringly realized she wasn't alone. Prince Ashur was already taking air on the balcony.

She attempted to compose herself. "It certainly was."

The prince wore a dark blue overcoat, trimmed in gold. It fit his impressive form perfectly. His shoulder-length black hair was tied back from his face, but one long lock fell over his left eye. "I can't honestly say I've ever been to a wedding like that before. If I were a superstitious man, I might be more wary of returning to the palace tonight. It was very brave of you to want to continue on despite such unpleasantness."

Cleo let out a half laugh that sounded more like a hysterical hiccup. "Yes, so brave of me."

"You must be very much in love with Prince Magnus."

She pressed her lips together to keep herself from blurting out the truth. She did not know this man, only that his father had gained his expansive empire by conquering other lands, crushing each one easily. Cleo's father had once told her about the Emperor Cortas and how his empire compared to that of Mytica . . . like a watermelon next to a grape. At the time, she'd found such a comparison amusing.

Why would a watermelon care about a wedding taking place on a grape? To her, it seemed a waste of the prince's time.

"Why are you here, Prince Ashur?" she asked, then cursed herself for being so blunt. The wine had succeeded both in clouding her judgment and loosening her tongue.

Luckily, he did not seem offended by her question. Instead, he smiled—a devastatingly charming smile that proved why most every woman who crossed this exotic prince's path swooned at the sight of him.

"I have something for you, princess," he said. "A wedding gift, just for you. Of course, I have also given a larger gift from my kingdom to both you and Prince Magnus in the form of a villa in Kraeshia's capital, but this . . . this is a small token of friendship. It is something given in my land to a bride on her wedding night."

He pulled a small, bound package from beneath his coat and handed it to her.

"Tuck it away. Open it when you're alone. Not now."

She looked into his eyes, confused. But she nodded and slid the small object into the folds of her gown.

"Much gratitude to you, Prince Ashur."

"Think nothing of it." He leaned against the balcony railing, gazing out at the rolling vista visible beyond the city walls. In the moonlight, his eyes appeared to be silver, but she wasn't sure what color they really were. "Tell me of the magic here, princess."

The question took her by surprise. "The magic?"

"It's quite a history Mytica has for such a small group of kingdoms. Such mythology, what with the Watchers . . . the Kindred. Fascinating, really."

"Just silly stories told to children." She clasped her hands together to cover up her ring. There was something in the prince's voice . . . something that told her he wasn't asking this only out of random curiosity.

"I don't think you really believe that." He gave her a sidelong glance. "No, you strike me as the kind of girl who, despite her youth, has very specific beliefs."

"Then that just proves how little you know about me. Ask any-one. I'm not interested in history or mythology. I don't think very deeply about anything at all, especially not fantastical things like magic."

Prince Ashur looked at her steadily. "Does the Kindred exist?"

Her heart began to pound harder. "Why do you care if it does or not?"

"That you ask that proves how little you know about me," he said, echoing her previous words. "It's all right, princess. We don't need to discuss this right now. But perhaps one day soon you'll wish to talk more about this with me. I plan to stay here for a while and explore. There are answers I seek and I won't be leaving until I have them."

"I wish you the very best of luck in finding your answers," she said evenly.

"Good night, princess. And my sincere congratulations on your marriage." He bowed his head and left the balcony.

Cleo waited until she was quite sure he had left before she put her hands on the balcony railing and leaned her full, drooping weight on her wrists. The Kraeshian prince was here not only to attend the wedding but also to find out about the Kindred.

Which could mean only one thing: he wanted it for himself.

He couldn't have it. No one could. If the Kindred did indeed exist, it belonged to Cleo. She had the ring that would enable her to use it—and use it she would, to reclaim her kingdom.

She rubbed her ring, then forced herself to return to the ban-quet. The king eyed her with displeasure as she approached the dais. His forehead was bandaged, some blood from his wound soaking through the gauze. "It's time for you to go upstairs and prepare yourself for your wedding night."

Her mouth went dry. "But, the feast—"

"The feast is over for you." A hateful smile snaked across his face. He raised his voice so everyone could hear him. "I would like you all to bid good night to the bride and groom. We would not want to keep them from where we all know they'd rather be."

Some laughter rose from the gathered crowd, many of whom by now had had enough Paelsian wine to help forget the troubles of the day.

"Go with Cronus," the king said to Cleo, grabbing her arm so he could draw her close enough to hear his lowered voice. "You'll be prepared as if you were any other blushing bride. No one will ever know your chastity is long gone. Consider yourself very lucky that I still consider you of value despite this rather large flaw in your character."

Magnus did not even spare her a glance.

Cronus stepped forward. "Follow me, princess."

There was no room for argument in the guard's harsh tone.

Cleo cast a glance at the gathered guests, who offered her tense smiles as she trailed after Cronus. Nic's attention was also on her, his body rigid, an apology in his tortured gaze that he was unable to save her from what was to come.

The chambers Cronus guided her to had been prepared specially for the bride and groom. It included a room that had once been reserved for very important guests of her father. A massive four-poster bed sat against the far wall. A fire blazed in an enormous fireplace, and the room was otherwise lit by hundreds of flickering candles. Rose petals of all colors had been artfully strewn across the floor in looping patterns, leading toward the bed.

Her attendants were there and worked feverishly to loosen her braided hair, to change her into yet another gown, this one gauzy and flowing, its thin fabric leaving little modesty for her to cling to. They rubbed her wrists and her throat with scented oils that had the same cloyingly sweet perfume as the rose petals.

"You're so very lucky, princess," Helena said. "I would give my younger sister's life to spend even one night with Prince Magnus. And now you get to spend all of your nights with him."

"And I'd give my *older* sister's life," Dora said pointedly, with a sharp look in Helena's direction.

"I only hope that the rumors aren't true." Helena's gaze snapped to Cleo's, and she gave the princess an unpleasant smile. "For your sake."

Cleo frowned. "What rumors?"

"Helena," Dora said from between clenched teeth. "Be careful what you say."

Helena laughed lightly. "Don't you think the princess has the right to know that her new husband is said to have forbidden feelings for Princess Lucia, and she for him? Such love between siblings . . . quite the scandal if many learned of this."

"Pardon my sister," Dora said, her cheeks reddening. "She has been drinking tonight in celebration of your wedding. She doesn't know what she's saying."

Cleo narrowed her eyes. "I'll remember you attempted to save her from spreading such unsavory lies." She would never admit that this information was very interesting to her, whether true or not.

Without another word, the girls moved away from her and were gone from the room like wisps of smoke. Cronus pulled the door shut behind them. Cleo ran to it and tried the handle, only to find it locked from the outside.

She was trapped.

Before, when she'd been able to walk around freely, she could almost fool herself into believing she still had some power. That was such a lie. She had no power here at all.

Magnus would dominate her. He would abuse her as his father had today. As the attendants prepared her for her wedding night, the mirror had reflected the faint bruise on her cheekbone where the king had struck her and on her throat where he'd come close to strangling her.

But Cleo had chosen this. She could have escaped with Jonas, but she'd chosen to stay here. There had to be a reason for that . . . a higher goal than fleeing with the rebel.

She ran over to her discarded banquet dress. Her amethyst ring glinted in the candlelight as she pulled out the gift Prince Ashur had given her. She slowly unwrapped it, only to see an unexpected edge of gold.

It was a golden dagger. A beautiful one, with an artfully carved hilt and a curved blade. She remembered the prince's words: *"It is something given in my land to a bride on her wedding night."* With a chill she recognized its purpose: something that could be used by an unhappy bride to take her own life if she felt she had no other choice.

Or . . . the life of her new husband.

The sound of the door unlocking and opening had her scrambling to hide the weapon behind her back. A moment later, Magnus entered. His black gaze moved through the large room, pausing on the candles, the rose petals, and then finally coming to rest on her.

Again, she regretted having drunk so much wine. She desperately needed her thoughts to be sharp, not muddy.

"So it seems we're finally alone," he said.

Cleo was certain he could hear how loud her heart now beat.

Magnus leaned over and picked up a red rose petal, squeezing it between his fingers. "Did they really think this all was necessary?"

She moistened her dry lips with the tip of her tongue. "You don't find it . . . romantic?"

He released the petal and it fluttered slowly down to the floor, where it landed like a splash of blood. "As if I care about such drivel."

"Many men would on their wedding night."

"About roses and candles? No, princess. Most men couldn't care less about such things. There's only one thing men are interested in on their wedding night and I think you're already very aware what that is."

Her heart doubled its pace.

Whatever stricken expression she now wore coaxed a low chuckle from his throat. "That look . . . such contempt. Am I really that ugly to you?"

The question took her by surprise. Ugly? Despite the scar, he was far from ugly—at least, physically.

"Far worse," she said honestly.

He trailed his fingers over the length of his scar as he studied her for a moment.

She clutched the dagger. If he came any closer she would use it.

"Believe me, princess, I have no illusions of any of this. I know you hate me and that will never change."

"Should it?" Her words came out hoarse. "Actually, I can't think of a single reason why I should feel *anything* toward you."

"No, it's well within your rights to feel nothing toward me at all—as it is in many arranged marriages. But hate is *something*. The problem with hate, however, is it leaves you at a disadvantage. It clouds your mind every bit as much as five goblets of wine can."

Magnus moved toward the bed, his gaze focused on the thick mahogany posters. He traced his index finger along the carving on one of them. He was now closer to her. Too close. She didn't step away. She didn't want to give him the satisfaction of seeing her fear, especially now that there was no one around to intervene.

"This reminds me of my grandfather." Magnus's tone turned wistful. "He had a book about sea creatures and he told me stories about them when I was a child. He snuck past my father so he could do so, after my nursemaid put me to bed. My father never cared much for amusing stories—or amusing *anything*, really. If I couldn't learn something tangible from a book it was banned from the palace. Or burned. But when my grandfather was king it was different."

Cleo hadn't noticed the carving on the bedpost until now. Fish and shells and maidens of the sea with tails instead of legs, all carved intricately into the dark wood. It was beautiful and crafted by a renowned artist from Hawk's Brow whom her father had com-missioned to carve many other fine pieces around the castle.

"I've heard a little about King Davidus," she said when silence fell. "He was different than your father."

Magnus snorted softly. "He was indeed. Makes me wonder sometimes if my grandmother had taken a demon lover that helped create my father. My grandfather was firm in his rule, of course. He was no pushover. But he was kind and his people loved him. He didn't need to govern his kingdom with an iron fist and the threat of blood." His gaze met hers, and something slid behind his eyes that looked like grief. "He died when I was six years old. He drank something that didn't agree with him."

"Someone poisoned him?"

There was still that strange and unexpected pain in his eyes, but his mouth pressed into a hard line. "Not 'someone.' I saw him put the poison in the goblet, emptying it from a hollow ring. I watched him hand it to my grandfather. Watched my grandfather drink it."

Cleo was silent, listening.

"And when my father saw that I'd seen what he did, he smiled as if I should approve. I didn't understand at the time, but I do now. My father will do whatever it takes to rid himself of someone standing in his way. Nothing has changed. Nothing will ever change. Understand that, princess, and your life will be much easier."

What was this? A warning? Was Magnus actually trying to help her?

"You don't think *me* a threat, do you?" she asked carefully.

He drew closer to her—much too close. She clutched the knife behind her so tightly the handle dug painfully into her palm.

"It doesn't matter what I think," Magnus said. "There's no magic behind a thought, unless you're a witch."

"So you do whatever he says, whenever he says it."

"That's right. And I'll continue to do so."

"He means to kill me, doesn't he?" The very thought caused more fear to slither out from its hiding places—but it was joined by a boiling rage.

A small frown creased his brow. "Paranoid, are we? Not the usual attitude of a brand new bride."

Cleo glared at him. "Don't patronize me. I know what you're planning."

"Do you?" He cocked his head. "I find that utterly impossible to believe. After all, the one who could have spied for you is gone. You cleverly positioned Mira in a way that could have netted you some valuable information."

Pain wrenched in her chest at the mention of her dead friend.

She hadn't suggested Mira be Lucia's attendant so the girl could spy, only that it might help her survive.

"And now she's dead because of you!" It took every ounce of control she had not to pull the knife out from behind her back and thrust it into his chest.

His expression darkened at the accusation. "No, I defended her. Or I tried to. My father acts before he thinks, especially when it comes to nosy servants. I would have spared her life."

"You're a liar!"

"I'm not lying. Not about this. Your friend Mira was treading in very dark places just by being in the same room with a Damora, and she paid a high price. As did your guard in Paelsia."

Tears sprang unbidden to her eyes at the mention of Theon. "Never speak of him again."

"I will never ask for your forgiveness for what I did." Magnus looked away. "But I know I acted out of panic and cowardice that day. For that, and only that, I am ashamed of my actions."

A hot tear slipped down her cheek. "My family is dead. My kingdom has been stolen from me. My friends are dying at your and your family's hands."

"And you still breathe only at our mercy."

"Merciful isn't a word I'd ever use to describe any of you. And I don't believe a word you say about your grandfather. If he was of your blood then he was a tyrant and a bully too. Limerians are as cold as the kingdom they rule. No wonder your heart is forged of ice."

This earned the edge of a very unpleasant grin. "Before, you said I had no heart. This is definite progress, princess." He studied her. "Now, enough about history. What are we to do about the problem you present to me this fateful evening?"

"What—?" Cleo didn't get out more than this before Magnus grabbed her arms and roughly turned her around. She shrieked as he snatched the dagger from her grip, then shoved her so that she staggered back and landed hard on the bed. She stared at him with horror as he inspected the golden blade.

Magnus flicked an icy glance at her. "Did you mean to use this little dagger on me, princess? And here I've been nothing but cordial to you this evening."

She couldn't take her eyes off the weapon. Images of him using it on her as punishment blinded her to anything else.

He paced slowly, watching her, like a predator who'd cornered his prey. "Who gave this to you?"

She bit her tongue to keep from saying a word.

He glanced at the knife again. "This is an ornamental bridal dagger from Kraeshia. What a generous gift from Prince Ashur. I hope you thanked him for this." When she didn't speak, he continued. "No words, princess? And here you always have something cutting to say. Perhaps now that I've removed your sharp weapon, there will be no more cutting tonight."

He tucked the blade into his coat and took a step closer to her.

Cleo scrambled off the bed and put some distance between her and Magnus, succeeding only in backing herself into a corner. "Stay away from me!"

He watched her with amusement. "What is this? A frightened rabbit trying to find shelter from the wolf? Apologies if I find such a facade of innocence difficult to swallow."

"You will not touch me tonight." She forced herself to sound strong. "Or ever."

Magnus was in front of her in an instant, grabbing hold of her arms to push her up against the hard stone wall. He lowered his face to hers so they were eye to eye. His body pressed against hers, locking her in place so she couldn't break away.

"Oh, look. I'm touching you." His gaze brushed against her face, stopping briefly on the faint bruise on her cheek. His brows drew together as his eyes again locked with hers. "Do not presume to tell me what I can and cannot do, princess. Any power you imagine yourself to have here is only what I allow. Please remember that."

"Let go of me."

"Not yet."

He wasn't hurting her, but she couldn't move, could barely catch her breath.

Magnus spoke very slowly and very clearly. "Do you see? You're at my mercy." He leaned even closer so he could whisper. "Whatever I want to do to you, be it to inflict pain or pleasure, I will do whenever and however I like. Understand that."

Suddenly, Cleo couldn't breathe at all.

His grip on her tightened, his words hot against her ear. "My father wanted this union, not me. But this is what I must do to keep my position as his heir. One day everything my father has will be mine—his kingdom, his army, his power. I'm not risking that for anything or anyone. But let this much be crystal clear between us: I would sooner share flesh with a beast from the Wildlands than you. I believe its claws would be much less sharp."

Magnus let go of her and stepped back. Her breath returned in a rush as she stared at him with shock.

"I could have you executed for this." He touched the dagger beneath his coat. "You know that, don't you?"

Cleo just nodded, keeping her gaze locked on his. Looking away now would only show her at her weakest.

"If you value your life and that of your good friend, your only friend, Nic, you will behave as a doting and besotted bride on our trip across this goddess-forsaken realm that begins tomorrow. You'll put on a good show for the brainless masses who choose to believe my father's lies about us. Do you understand me?"

She nodded with a jerk of her head. "Yes."

Magnus turned to leave. Before he closed and locked the door behind him, he paused long enough to say one last thing. "And should anyone ask, this night surpassed every one of your wildest fantasies about me."

CHAPTER 24

LYSANDRA

THE WILDLANDS

At dawn, Jonas and a score of enthusiastic volunteers had departed in search of glory at the royal wedding while the other half of their numbers remained behind at camp. Lysandra waited for news, busying herself with hunting and making arrows. Several scouts had been sent out—including Nerissa—in search of more information about the road. Lysandra was still determined to find a weakness there. Something to exploit. Something to help her find and free her brother. Something to give her an edge if, by chance, Jonas failed in his quest to end the king's life today.

Many hours later, there was an earthquake that knocked everyone off his or her feet. Brion immediately dove for Lysandra just as he'd done during the tornado in Paelsia, wrapping her in his strong arms as if he could protect her from any harm. When the violent shaking finally ceased she squirmed away from him.

"I . . . I need to go hunting again," she said.

"Lys . . ."

"No, just . . ." She glanced around at the other boys, who were now whispering to each other and laughing, despite their unease about the strange tremor. Brion's crush on her was well known to everyone in camp by now, thanks to Jonas. "Just give me some space, all right?"

His expression fell. "I'm sorry. Of course."

Lysandra grabbed her bow and headed deeper into the forest. Why should she feel annoyed toward the one boy in camp who'd been more welcoming than any of the others combined? The one who defended her to his own best friend when no one else did?

All she knew was that she didn't feel anything other than friendship for Brion—and even that was frequently challenged.

She had no time for thoughts of friendship . . . or of romance. Not now. And definitely not here.

"Stupid," she mumbled after wandering aimlessly through the forest not too far from camp. Leaves and fallen branches crunched beneath her feet with each step she took. She wasn't sure who or what she referred to, but just saying the word aloud seemed to help.

After the tremor, most of her potential prey had found shelter in well-concealed hiding spots. It took until near dusk before she spotted a deer in the distance. She stilled herself, holding her breath. Slowly, she aimed her arrow toward the animal.

You'll make a good meal tonight, my little friend. Hold still.

The sound of something heavy crashing through the forest startled the deer and it took off before Lysandra could release her arrow. She swore under her breath. Someone must have followed her from camp.

"It better not be you, Brion," she muttered, and turned in the direction of the noise.

A familiar form burst from the thick foliage beyond the trees she stood behind. He stumbled and fell, before scrambling to regain his footing.

She frowned. "Jonas?"

Behind him was a Limerian guard on horseback, who leapt off his mount and grabbed Jonas by his hair. "Didn't think I'd catch you, rebel?"

Jonas didn't say anything, but his knees buckled again. His face was covered in blood and his eyes were glazed.

The guard drew his sword and held it to Jonas's throat. "I know who you are—Jonas Agallon, Queen Althea's murderer. If I took your head back to the king, I'd get myself a fine reward. Got anything to say about that?"

"He doesn't," Lysandra whispered, then raised her voice. "But I do."

As the guard glanced over his shoulder at the sound of her voice, she let her arrow go, hitting her target perfectly in his left eye socket. He was dead before he hit the ground. Lysandra swiftly closed the distance between her and Jonas, nudging the guard's body aside.

"What happened?" she demanded, grabbing hold of his shirt. "Are there more guards after you?"

His breath came quickly, but he didn't reply. As she inspected him, she saw he'd been injured. There was a deep wound on his side and the back of his skull bore an alarmingly bloody wound.

Her heart sank. "I told you not to go today, you fool. When are you going to start listening to me?"

She staggered from his weight as he crumpled against her. Checking over her shoulder to see if there were any more guards in pursuit, she dragged Jonas further away from the dead soldier and laid him down on the ground near the roots of a large oak tree, being very gentle with his head. She quickly ripped the fabric of his shirt open to get a better look at the wound on his side.

She grimaced at the sight of the torn flesh. "What am I going to do with you?"

She tore a long strip of fabric off her own shirt, which was cleaner than his, in order to press it against his wound and try to stop the bleeding. He could cauterize it himself later.

If he lived.

No, you'll live, Jonas, she thought. *You're much too stubborn to die today.*

A hawk had taken perch above them in the oak tree, and it looked down at them as if curious about what they were doing.

"Unless you're going to help," Lysandra said to it, "mind your own business." Lysandra had noted its markings from last time. Just another female who'd found herself infatuated with the handsome rebel leader. She reached for a rock and hurled it at the bird. It flapped its wings and flew away.

"Your infamous charm seems to bypass species, Agallon," she mumbled.

Jonas groaned as she used another torn piece of her shirt to wipe at the blood on his face. Her hands froze at the sound. His lips moved. He was trying to say something, but she couldn't make it out.

She leaned closer. "What?"

"So bad . . . I'm so sorry . . . failed you . . ."

His eyes opened to lock with hers. His were a shade of brown that reminded her of cinnamon, her favorite spice, and they had gold flecks just around the black irises—so black, just like his thick lashes. It wasn't the first time she'd noticed this.

"You need to get up," she said, her voice suddenly hoarse. "Come on. We need to move."

"You . . ." he managed.

"Yes, it's—"

He pulled her closer. Close enough to brush his lips against hers.

Lysandra stared down at him with shock. "Jonas . . ."

"Cleo . . ." he whispered.

She reared back from him completely, confusion disappearing only to be replaced by a fresh burst of annoyance. Then she hauled back and whacked him hard on the side of his face.

"Snap out of it, idiot. If you think I'm the princess then you're in worse shape than I thought."

Jonas jolted up to a seated position, holding his hand against his face. His brows were drawn tightly together.

"The guard," he said.

"I killed him." Lysandra could see in his eyes that he didn't remember what just happened. Perhaps for him it had only been a dream.

"Good." He pushed himself up to a standing position, then grimaced as he touched his injured arm.

"What happened? Where are the others?"

He gave her the bleakest look she'd ever seen, one that made her blood run cold before he even spoke another word. "Dead."

"*All* of them?"

"Yes."

She couldn't speak for a moment. "Damn you, Jonas. I shouldn't have bothered saving your arse just now. You don't deserve it."

"You're right, I don't." He swallowed hard, his jaw tight. "But now I need to get back to camp."

There was nothing more to say.

Twenty rebel boys had offered to go with Jonas to the temple in hopes of a glorious victory against King Gaius. Thirty had remained behind at camp, continuing to practice and plan.

Only Jonas had returned.

"Our friends . . . they fought bravely, but we were outmatched," Jonas finished grimly. He and Lysandra were back at the camp and he related the story of the massacre to the others. "I'm so sorry. It was a mistake to go and I take full responsibility."

Silence fell as sharp as an executioner's ax.

No one made a sound, except for one or two quiet sobs. The younger rebels didn't have control over their emotions yet—not when it came to their grief. The older ones stood rigid, their attention fixed on the ground before them. The sound of crickets and the crackle of the fire were all that could be heard in the gathering darkness.

"This is your fault," Ivan said. "Your idea. Your big plan that couldn't fail."

Brion stood at the opposite side of the fire from Jonas. "He didn't know this would happen."

"Didn't know. Right. But he told that princess, didn't he? She probably blurted everything to the king."

"She wouldn't do that," Jonas said, his head in his hands.

"Why wouldn't she? What's she got to lose with the blood of rebels spilled on her wedding day?"

"What's she got to lose?" Jonas growled. "Everything. It would have been her victory too if we'd won today. We didn't. She's still forced to be with the enemy and her rightful throne still belongs to the King of Blood."

"And you're the only one who lived. Maybe *you're* the one who tipped off the king to gain favor and get your face off those reward signs."

Jonas's expression darkened. "I would sooner offer my throat to the king than tell him anything of our plans. And you bloody well know it."

Ivan approached Jonas, taller than him by a half a foot. "Remind me again why you call yourself our leader?"

Jonas stood. Despite his injuries, he held the boy's gaze steadily. "Remind me again why you call yourself a rebel. You haven't stepped up in weeks, Ivan."

Ivan slammed his fist into Jonas's jaw. Jonas staggered backward and fell hard to the ground.

"You think you're so great," Ivan snarled. "Well, this is proof that you're nothing. You're worthless, and because of your foolhardy plan, twenty of us are dead. You think we'll keep following you after this?"

"Yes, actually," Lysandra spoke up, "we will."

Ivan turned a furious glare on her. "What did you say?"

Out of the corner of her eye, she saw Jonas struggle to get back up to his feet.

"Did he make the wrong choice in going to that temple today? Yes, he did. But he made a choice. And if it had been successful the lot of you would be cheering his name at the top of your lungs. Twenty rebels died today—twenty who were willing to die to have a fleeting chance of stopping King Gaius and freeing our people from slavery and oppression. Was it worth it? I didn't think so before, but I'm starting to now. Maybe if more of us were brave enough and crazy enough, we would have gone too. Maybe if we'd all gone together, we would have won."

Ivan looked at her with disgust. "What do you know? You're just a girl. Your opinion's meaningless. You should be cooking our dinners, not fighting beside us."

This time she slammed her fist into Ivan's jaw. It didn't knock him on his arse, but it did get his attention. He made a move to hit her back—and she was ready for it—but Jonas was there, roughly nudging her out of the way. A moment later, Brion was at his side.

"Back off, Ivan," Jonas growled, his expression one of misery. "This isn't her fault, it's mine. I came up with the plan. I gave the order. And twenty boys followed me to their deaths. You want to hit anyone? Hit me. That goes for the rest of you, too."

"Today was a failure," Lysandra spoke into the silence that fell. "I'm sorry our friends had to give their lives. But it's going to happen again. We're not all going to live to see the end of this. That's what you agreed to when you signed up to be a part of this resistance. Every day we're getting stronger, more skilled, and smarter. And we will be making more bold moves against the king—moves that will hurt him next time and stop his Blood Road forever. We'll hurt him until we can kill him. It's our only reason for breathing now."

"I want nothing to do with this," Ivan growled, wiping the trickle of blood from the corner of his mouth.

"Then we want nothing to do with you," Brion said. "Get out. Go home to your mommy. If you don't want to be here, we don't want you here."

"Jonas will be the death of you," Ivan snapped.

Brion looked firm. "Bring it on."

Ivan finally turned his back, and with a last glare at Lysandra, he did exactly what they suggested and left camp.

"Anyone else want to quit?" Brion asked, raising his voice. "Or are we still in this till the end, no matter what?"

Slowly, one after one, the remaining rebels spoke up. Tarus spoke first, his voice tentative but strong. "I'm still in!"

"We're with you!"

"Till the end!"

Despite the reaffirmed loyalty, the gathering could never be called pleasant. There was grief. There were sadness and tears. But at least it wasn't an ending, Lysandra thought. It was a new beginning, a commitment to the cause, forged from blood and loss.

Jonas turned to Lysandra, his brows drawn together. "Never thought you'd stand up for me."

"I wasn't standing up for you." She threw a stick into the crackling fire and then shook out her aching hand and rubbed her knuckles. "I've just been wanting to punch Ivan in his ugly face for a while."

"That makes more sense, actually."

She took a deep breath and turned to face him. "But hear me on this, Jonas. You will take my plans seriously from now on. We must attack the Blood Road. We must shut it down. My fate lies on that road—my fate and the fate of our people."

He was silent, but then he nodded. "You're right. I'll listen to you."

"Don't make a mistake like this again, Agallon."

His jaw tightened. "I'll try."

"Try very hard or we're going to have a problem, you and me."

"Understood." He held her gaze intently a moment longer, as if searching for something deeper in her eyes. She was the first to look away.

Jonas then clasped Brion's shoulder for an unspoken moment. It had been awkward between the two for days ever since their argument. Brion hesitated not at all before gripping Jonas in a bear hug. Jonas's dark, pain-filled eyes lightened for the briefest of moments in relief before he moved off to tend his wounds.

"You two all right?" Lysandra asked.

Brion shrugged. "Maybe."

"You're like a brother to him."

"The feeling's mutual."

"I'm glad you were mad at him before today." She crossed her arms tightly and looked directly at Brion. "If everything had been good between you, you would have been by his side at the temple. And you could have died."

"Good point." There was something stiff about his expression that she didn't understand. It wasn't grief, it was . . . frustration. "I guess I understand things better now."

"What things?"

"The way you look at me." Brion shrugged. "It's not nearly the same as the way you look at Jonas. You're in love with him."

She gaped at him. "Twenty of us died today and this is your brilliant observation of the night? You need to pull your head from your arse and focus on what's important."

Lysandra walked away from him angrily, not knowing how to deal with such an asinine accusation. She did realize, however, that she had not tried to deny it.

CHAPTER 25

CLEO

AURANOS

Aron was present at dawn as Cleo prepared herself to leave for the dreaded wedding tour.

"May you have a safe journey, princess," he said, accompanying her through the halls toward the waiting carriages. "I will be leading the charge to find the murderer of the queen while you're gone. Prince Magnus will join me on the hunt the moment he returns if the rebel is still at large."

Leading the charge? *Aron?* "Obviously the king has great faith in your abilities as kingsliege."

"He does. More than you know." Aron leaned closer to speak confidentially. "I couldn't help but notice that the prince left your wedding chambers last night only minutes after entering. Is there a problem already in your joyous union?"

"None at all." She fixed a bland smile on her lips. "I shall miss you while I'm away, Lord Aron. You are so very amusing to me."

He frowned. "Cleo—"

"It's *Princess* Cleiona. Take care to remember my official title, especially now that I'm happily married to the king's son. Now, if you'll excuse me."

She brushed past him and continued to the carriage without further delay.

What a jackass. It did give her comfort to know that he was part of the hunt for Jonas; that Jonas had even been pinpointed as the queen's murderer was ridiculous. They were only looking for a reason to kill the rebel leader with full support of any citizens who might see him, and they'd found it. But with such ineptitude and with Aron "leading the charge," the rebel leader would surely remain free forever.

I will see you again, rebel, she thought. *Someday. Somewhere. Till then, please be safe.*

And so the wedding tour began. They were scheduled to wind through Auranos before moving on to Paelsia and Limeros. From town to town, the appearances varied only slightly. Cleo and Magnus emerged before a gathered crowd, usually an enthusiastic one, before listening graciously to mayors' speeches and bards' ballads. In a village on the southern coast of Auranos, a small group of children performed a skit for Cleo and Magnus's amusement. The children were adorable and so excited about this royal visit, and Cleo tried her very best to appear attentive and enthusiastic. Magnus, however, just looked bored with all of it and already impatient for the tour to be over so he could join Aron and the king's soldiers on the hunt for Jonas.

After the skit was over, there was a greeting line. Cleo performed her actions by habit until one woman clutched Cleo's hand and looked into her eyes with worry.

"Are you all right, princess?" she whispered so no one except Cleo could hear.

A lump immediately formed in Cleo's throat, but she tried to smile. "Yes, of course. I am perfectly well. Much gratitude for your village's warm welcome to me and my—and the *prince.*"

She couldn't call him *husband.*

All across her beloved Auranos, most citizens welcomed the royal couple with great fanfare, exactly as the king had predicted. But in every crowd there were a few disbelievers—those who clung to sidelines and shadows, signs of dread and suspicion in their eyes. They knew, Cleo saw, that this union was not as glorious or exciting as their neighbors believed. They knew that the king was not to be trusted—that his words were just that, and promises could be broken as easily as bones.

How she wished she could assure this small but noticeable percentage that one day she would change things for the better—for everyone. But no, she had to play the part of a young princess in love with her new husband in order to ensure her own survival.

There was a bright side. While away from the palace, she realized, she'd have another, better chance to gather information about local folklore and legends; she would learn more about the Kindred and how her ring could play a part in finding it—all under Magnus's nose.

The thought warmed her at night and helped keep her spirits high during the day. Still, for a journey surrounded by attendants and guards, not to mention the sullen, untalkative prince, she quickly became desperately lonely.

It was at King's Harbor, where they were about to board a ship to take them to Trader's Harbor in Paelsia, that she spotted Nic standing on the dock by the large black ship that rose from the water like a sea monster. He wore his red uniform like every other Limerian guard who'd accompanied Cleo and Magnus on this journey. His carrot-red hair stuck up in every direction. And he had a huge grin on his face.

Cleo's mouth fell open at the sight of her dearest friend, but she stopped herself from immediately running to him and throwing herself into his arms.

"Something wrong, princess?" Magnus asked.

"It's just . . . Nic." Her heart pounded. "He's here."

"Yes, he is."

"You're not surprised?"

"No. I requested it."

She turned to stare at him with shock and suspicion. "Why?"

He shrugged. "Your misery has been palpable for days, and it reflects poorly on me. For some reason, you value the presence of this fool. So here he is for the rest of the tour until I can finally get back to the castle and head out on a journey that really matters to me. He can handle our luggage and clean up after the horses. I'm sure I'll find many interesting uses for him."

Disbelief clouded her thoughts. "You summoned him here so I wouldn't be miserable."

Magnus's upper lip thinned. "I need you to keep up your end of the bargain as we continue to feed these stupid people my father's pretty lies. That's all."

"Thank you," she whispered, her throat tight at the thought that he'd do something so unexpectedly kind, despite his harsh words.

He offered her the barest edge of a glance. "Save your gratitude. I don't need it."

She sent a glare in his direction, but it was wasted. He'd already moved away to speak with a guard near the ship.

Cleo approached Nic as regally as possible but couldn't keep her grin from spreading. "You're here."

He smiled too, far too broadly to appear professional. "On royal orders."

"Well, I'm so glad you're being royally ordered around."

"In this instance, I'd have to agree."

With Nic in tow, the journey continued on to Paelsia, and they toured through several villages and vineyards—though never coming near the Imperial Road, Cleo noticed. The poor villagers gathered to watch silently. Cleo's presence did coax some children out of their homes, and they were fascinated by her beautiful and colorful dresses. The children's eyes were filled with the boundless hope their elders lacked. Noticing this broke Cleo's heart.

Paelsians were not fooled as Auranians were by anything the king said. These people had already seen his deception, his cruelty, with their own eyes. Such things could not be forgotten or forgiven.

By the time their entourage sailed up the coast to Limeros's Black Harbor, Cleo was dismayed that she'd learned nothing useful about her ring, which sat heavy on her finger as it had since she first left the City of Gold. Nor had she learned anything more than repeated stories about the Kindred. The time to find such information grew shorter with every day that passed, and her anxiety increased.

Now that their journey had reached Limeros, Cleo had to bundle up in a thick ermine-lined cloak to keep out the chill of the frigid, frozen landscape. Where Auranos had a palace that literally sparkled like a jewel under the bright sunshine, the Limerian castle seemed to absorb light, killing it on contact. It was large and black and ominous, its spires rising up into the cold sky like the claws of a demon. Its windows were the only things that reflected light, much like the eyes of some ravenous beast.

Magnus's true home suited him perfectly.

"Is that all of them?" Magnus asked, eyeing the trunks that Nic had unloaded from the carriages.

"It is, your grace." To his credit, Nic managed to say this without sounding sarcastic. Sweat coated Nic's brow after he'd single-handedly dragged all their luggage chests into the castle.

"Good. Now go see to the horses. I must check if there are any messages waiting for me here from my father." He turned on the heels of his black leather boots and stalked off down the hall without another word.

"I hate him," Nic snarled.

"So do I," Cleo replied.

"Could have fooled me by how much you've been snuggling up to him on this trip."

She grabbed his arm as he was about to walk away, digging her fingers in until he looked at her again. "Anything you think you see between us is for show only. Remember that."

Nic's shoulders slumped. "Apologies, Cleo. Of course I know that. This all must be so hard for you."

"Thank the goddess you're here with me."

He raised his eyebrows. "Oh?"

She grinned, his hurtful words already forgotten. "I mean, who else would carry my chests of gowns so well?"

He laughed as she pulled him into a tight hug, never wanting to let him go. "I'm here for you, Cleo. Whenever you need me."

She nodded, pressing her face against the rough fabric of his uniform. "I know."

"You're so brave—spending time with that monster. Forced to share his bed." A look of hatred crossed his face as he leaned back from her. "Every night I imagine killing him for you."

Cleo grabbed hold of Nic's hands, squeezing them tightly in

hers. "Don't worry about me. I can handle the prince." She wanted to tell him that Magnus did not share her bed and that she spent every night alone, but she held her tongue. No one, not even Nic, could know such things. "Please rest up so you can be by my side tomorrow. I need all the support I can get."

"I'll rest up. As soon as I take care of the horses for *his majesty*."

"See you tomorrow." She went up on her tiptoes to kiss Nic's cheek. At the last moment he turned his face so she kissed his lips instead.

This earned her a newly brightened ear-to-ear grin. "Till tomorrow, princess."

After a sleepless night, she'd been woken early by Dora and Helena, who were just as disrespectful to her here as they were at the Auranian castle. They helped her dress and look presentable. She wore a new fur-lined cloak draped over one of her finest new gowns. This, as well as the cloak, was red, to pay tribute to the official color of Limeros. The color of blood. Likely, not a coincidence at all. On the sleeves of the gown, golden snakes were embroidered, the kingdom's sigil. Also appropriate for a kingdom filled to overflowing with serpents.

Outside the castle, following in Magnus's footsteps, she turned a distracted glance toward the gathered nobles who'd joined them today for an official presentation of a wedding gift by Lord Gareth, a close friend of the king's. To their left was a pathway that wound through the ice gardens and into an intricate labyrinth of frost-covered hedges. To the right was a large clearing with a long, rectangular frozen pond, which led toward the castle itself. Beautiful but stark and pristine. Not an ounce of warmth existed in any direction.

"This is said to have belonged to the Watchers themselves."

Her gaze immediately snapped back to Lord Gareth. She finally noticed the object they had halted near, the gift from Lord Gareth. It was a carved stone wheel taller than Cleo's shoulder that protruded from the frozen ground at the entrance to the gardens.

"What about the Watchers?" she asked, struggling to keep her voice steady.

"Oh yes," Magnus said. "Please tell us. It's all so fascinating."

It was rare that the prince said anything that didn't mock whomever he spoke with. It was equally rare, she'd found, that anyone caught on to this as easily as she did.

Cleo remembered the rebel boy, Tarus, mentioning stone wheels that were associated with the Watchers and the Sanctuary. This couldn't possibly be the same thing. Could it?

The balding but distinguished-looking lord clasped his hands in front of him, rocking on his heels, seemingly pleased he now had the royal couple's full attention. "The Watchers watch us in the form of hawks."

"A child's tale I've heard a thousand times," Magnus said, dismissively.

"Is it? Or is it true?" The lord appeared to welcome the chance to debate this. "Magic is very real, your highness."

Magnus watched him, his gaze steady. "What makes you believe that?"

"I've seen many things that can't be explained. I've met witches who can reach into themselves and use small pieces of *elementia* to create magic in the mortal world."

Every piece of Cleo's attention was now focused entirely on this man. This was it. This man could be the one to tell her what she needed to know most. "Is the Kindred real? I've heard stories about the elemental crystals, but they could just be legend."

He glanced at her. "I believe it's true. There is a whispered prophecy that says when the sorceress is reborn, she will be the one who leads the way to the Kindred."

Cleo listened intently. A sorceress would lead the way? There was one thing she believed most of all—that the ring she now wore had once belonged to the sorceress Eva.

What did this mean?

The skies were gray today and snowflakes began to fall, speckling Cleo's red cloak and the clothes of the nearby dignitaries with dots of white.

"Tell us more about this wheel, Lord Gareth," Magnus said.

Heart pounding, she twisted her hands together, feeling the cool surface of her amethyst ring beneath her touch. She glanced toward Nic, who stood stiffly next to the other guards, as still as statues. His disdainful gaze was fixed entirely on Magnus.

The man moved toward the wheel and slid his hand over the curve of it. "Wheels identical to this are scattered across Mytica. For centuries no one has understood what they are and where they come from. Only that they're very old and somehow connected to the Watchers."

"How many wheels are there?" Cleo asked.

"A dozen have been found and documented. Each exactly the same but in different stages of disrepair."

"How do you know they have something to do with the Watchers?" she asked, ignoring Magnus's curious look at her.

The lord kept his hand on the wheel as he admired the carved surface of it. "There was an old man who lived in northern Limeros. Near the end of his days, he swore to all who'd listen that he was an exiled Watcher who had left the Sanctuary never to return. Once here, he became mortal, he aged, he became senile. His children, grandchildren, great-grandchildren listened patiently to his ramblings, but didn't think much of it. He spoke of the wheels being here for a reason. He asked to be taken to one so he could touch immortality once again."

The stone wheel seemed so innocuous to her, something no one would ever look twice at. "And did he?"

"No. He died before that could happen."

"Likely, just an old man who didn't know what he was saying." Magnus's expression was completely unreadable. "Much gratitude for this rare and generous gift, Lord Gareth. The wheel will be the highlight of this garden, I'm sure."

"It's my pleasure, Prince Magnus, Princess Cleo. May you have many happy years together." He bowed and moved back to join the others.

"Prince Magnus!" a woman with gray hair and a wrinkled face called out to him. "Might I have a word? My son is still not betrothed and I was thinking about your sister . . . well, could we speak?"

"This tour cannot come to an end soon enough," he muttered before moving off to join the enthusiastic woman.

Now alone, Cleo touched the smooth, cold surface of the large wheel. A skilled hand had created this once, many years ago.

"*It's how they get back and forth between the mortal world and the Sanctuary in hawk form,*" Tarus had told her. "*They have these magical, carved stone wheels hidden here and there. Might look like nothing but a ruin to us, but without the wheels, they're trapped here.*"

But this stone had been moved from its original location. Would it still work?

After a moment, the stone, which had been cold as ice beneath her touch, began to warm.

Her heart quickened to see her ring begin to glow—and something deep within the purple stone, something that looked like sparkling, molten gold, started to swirl.

The wheel quickly grew as hot as fire beneath her touch and a tremor of energy shot up her arm. Fear got the better of her, and she yanked her hand back. The stone in her ring stopped glowing, but she was captivated by that small speck of gold still visible down deep—so deep she felt as if she might fall into it and lose herself.

A wave of dizziness swept through her and she swayed on her feet before her legs gave out completely.

But she didn't fall. Someone was there, reaching an arm around her waist to steady her. She looked up expecting to see Nic, but it was Magnus.

His dark brows were drawn tightly together. "Problem, princess?"

A quick glance at the gathered crowd showed that no one watched her with anything more than concern over her current state of well-being. No one guessed what she'd just seen.

The noblewoman Magnus had been speaking to gawked at her. "She's so pale. Is she well?"

"Well enough," Magnus replied, his words clipped. "Much gratitude for your concern, Lady Sophia. I think I'll take a short walk with my . . . with the princess before my speech so she can clear her head. Perhaps all this excitement is too much for her. Is that what it is?"

"Yes, of course. I—I need to clear my head." Cleo swallowed hard and glanced at her ring. The swirling had stopped and the strange speck of molten gold was no longer visible within the stone.

Nic gave her a strained and concerned look as Magnus led her away and toward the labyrinth.

What would have happened if she'd been brave enough to keep her hand pressed against the wheel? Would she—a mere mortal—be able to journey to the Sanctuary? Would it offer her some glimpse as to where to find the Kindred?

If she didn't find the answers, she would allow Auranos to continue to be held under the iron fist of King Gaius. And she'd be letting her father down. How she wished he was still alive to guide her now. Sometimes when she least expected it—like now—the bottomless emptiness of all she'd lost mercilessly pulled her downward.

"Is there something wrong?" Magnus asked. "You're upset."

Cleo wiped away a tear and didn't bother looking directly at him. "Do you care?"

"I care that a sobbing princess doesn't present a very good picture of a happy marriage."

"I'm not sobbing." She gave him a hard look. "Perhaps you'd prefer it if I were."

"Such belligerence, princess. Whatever have I done to deserve this today?"

"You're breathing." The words were out before she could restrain them, and she bit into her lower lip. She decided to change the subject. "What is this place?"

"The Limerian palace grounds, of course."

"No, I mean *this* place. This maze. Why's it here?"

He glanced around. "Afraid of getting lost?"

"Can't you just answer a simple question without being difficult?" Again, she bit her lip and studied the ground, fighting her constant frustration when it came to dealing with the prince.

Magnus let out a soft snort. "I don't think you're capable of asking simple questions. But all right. I'll play along. This was a present for my sister six years ago. Lord Psellos wanted to garner favor for his son and an eventual betrothal, so he had this constructed as a birthday present." His lips curved at the memory, the smile helping to soften his sharp features. "Lucia loved this maze. She'd challenge others to race through it. Often, she'd have to go back in to retrieve someone who'd become hopelessly lost. Usually it was me."

The swift change in Magnus's mood as he spoke of Lucia was surprising. Cleo recalled the sordid gossip Dora and Helena had shared with her about Magnus and Lucia. "You love your sister."

His jaw tightened and he didn't reply for a moment. "You think me incapable of such an emotion?"

"Again, that's not really an answer, is it?"

"Perhaps it's a question that doesn't deserve one."

She glared at him. "For a moment I thought . . ."

"What, princess?" He eyed her. "That you'd found more evidence of that heart you continue to question?"

As if such a discovery were even possible. "I would never make that mistake. After all, you are your father's son."

"Yes. And you must never forget it." His jaw tensed. "It's nearly time for my speech. There are certain expectations of being the son of King Gaius. Making speeches is one of them. If nothing else, it brings this tour to an end. I've been receiving updates and understand that Lord Aron has thus far failed to capture the rebel leader. I will join the search the moment I return to Auranos."

That Jonas was still free was a great relief. Cleo crossed her arms, trying to block out the chill by pulling her fox fur cloak tighter against her throat. For a moment, she grappled for what to say next. She didn't wish to discuss Jonas or the rebels. Such dangerous topics could lead her onto treacherous ground. It was best to focus on today. On Magnus's upcoming duties as heir to the king's stolen crown. "Your father excels at speechmaking."

"He does indeed."

Cleo frowned at him as she realized something very important. "Wait. You're stalling, aren't you?"

"Stalling?"

"You brought me for this tour of the maze not to help clear my head, but to delay your speech. It's officially your first one, isn't it? You're nervous about it."

Magnus stared at her. "Don't be ridiculous."

He said one thing yet acted another way. But she could suddenly see him clearly—clearer than ever before. "King Gaius adores the sound of his own voice. But you . . . you're different." And here she'd believed father and son were alike in every way.

"I don't need to listen to this nonsense."

His steps picked up speed as he continued through the maze. Cleo was now completely lost. She had to keep pace with him or he might leave her behind to freeze to death. She pulled at her crimson skirts to keep them from dragging on the ground and getting damp from the frost.

"Public speaking should come naturally to you, given your heritage."

He gave her a dark look over his shoulder. "Spare your breath, princess. I don't need any words of encouragement from you."

Annoyance flared within her, chasing away her bemusement. "Good. Because I don't really care. I hope you make a fool of yourself. I hope they laugh at you. It would serve you right."

The wounded look this statement received surprised her.

Cleo found it difficult to believe this horrible boy could possibly lack confidence at something so expected of royalty. Magnus effortlessly managed to intimidate everyone who crossed his path—his very presence, his height, his strength, his position and title, the harsh tone of his voice; they all ensured that anyone with less power cowered before him.

Had she managed to find a weakness?

There was an opening in the snow-encrusted hedge up ahead. They'd reached the end of the maze. Cleo let out a sigh of relief as she ran her thumb over the surface of her ring. As if to mirror her nervous gesture, Magnus ran his fingers over his scar. She'd noticed it was something he did regularly, if unconsciously.

"That happened when your family visited my father ten years ago. I remember." Her curiosity got the better of her. She had to ask. "I assume it was an assault by a stranger, not an accident."

The look he turned on her held nothing pleasant in it. "Neither an assault by a stranger or an accident. It was a punishment, handed forth from my father himself to forever remind me of my crime."

Her eyes widened. His own father cut him so horribly? "What crime did you commit as a child to warrant such a punishment?"

His hand dropped to his side, his expression equal parts hard-edged and wistful. "For once in my life, I wanted to possess something beautiful, even if it meant I had to steal it. Clearly, I learned my lesson."

Stunned, Cleo watched him rejoin the gathered crowd. Many lords and other important men waited to clasp his hand in friendship. His confusing words repeated in Cleo's mind as their wives gathered around her, welcoming her to Limeros and congratulating her on her marriage to the prince.

They were then led back toward the castle, with the swelling crowd gathered in the palace square awaiting Magnus's speech, cheering the very sight of the two royals. A cloaked figure parted from the crowd and began to swiftly move toward Cleo and Magnus's entourage. He was so subtle that no one paid him any attention until he was only ten paces away, at which point he pulled a dagger from beneath his cloak and lurched forward.

Magnus lunged and thrust his arm out, catching Cleo across her chest as he shoved her back. She fell hard to the ground. The man arched the dagger toward Magnus, catching him in the arm before the prince deflected the blow and slammed his fist into the man's stomach.

The rest of the guards restrained the man, quickly disarming him. Nic was at Cleo's side then, helping her back to her feet. She stared at Magnus, now holding his injured arm, a look of rage on his face as he glared at his attacker.

"Who are you?" Magnus snarled.

The guards yanked back his hood. For a crazy, heart-stopping moment, Cleo was certain it would be Jonas.

But it wasn't. It was a boy not much older than Magnus whom she'd never seen before today.

"Who am I?" he snapped. "I'm someone whose village you destroyed. Whose people you enslaved to work your precious road. Someone who sees through your father's lies and wants to watch you both bleed and die."

"Is that so?" Magnus stepped forward to inspect the boy with withering distaste. "It seems you've failed in your quest."

"She didn't want me to try to kill you." The boy struggled against those who held him firmly in place. "I disagreed."

"She? Who are you talking about?"

The would-be assassin raised his chin, his eyes cold and full of challenge. "The Watcher who speaks to me in dreams. Who guides me. Who gives me hope that not all is lost. Who tells me that that which *is* lost should never be found."

Magnus's gaze narrowed. "And this . . . *Watcher* . . . didn't want you to try to kill me."

"On that much we disagreed."

"Obviously."

Twisting her ring nervously, Cleo watched Magnus closely for his reaction. The prince claimed not to believe in magic and all but mocked Lord Gareth for his choice of wedding gift. Yet a mention of Watchers now seemed to give him pause.

An assassination attempt—especially one as bold and as public as this—should earn an immediate command of execution.

Silence fell as all waited for Magnus's decision.

"Take him to the dungeon," he said, finally. "But not the one here. Take him to Auranos where he'll be questioned further. I'll send message to my father today."

"Your highness, are you certain that's what you want?" a guard asked.

Magnus sent a cutting look in the man's direction. "Don't question me. Just do it."

"Yes, your highness."

Cleo watched tensely as the boy was dragged away, a hundred questions swirling in her mind. Was what he claimed real? Or was the boy simply mad?

Why did Magnus want him returned to Auranos for questioning? Did the prince believe what he'd said?

"Your highness," another guard said, approaching Magnus. "My deepest apologies that he was able to get so close to you."

Magnus's jaw tensed. "See that it doesn't happen again or you'll be joining him."

"Yes, your highness. Your arm . . ."

"It's nothing. Lead the way to the balcony."

"That son of a bitch shoved you," Nic whispered to Cleo. "Are you all right?"

"I'm fine." But confusion still clouded her thoughts and not only about the boy's claims. Magnus had acted instinctively at the sight of the dagger. He hadn't shoved her to be cruel. He'd done it to . . . protect her.

Cleo was breathless as they were led to the black balcony overlooking the gathered crowd in the square below. Snow still fell in soft flakes, coating the ground with a layer of pristine white. The sky was the color of slate. The moment she and the prince came out into view, the crowd began to cheer at the top of their voices. Such a welcome would have been close to pleasant before, but after the drama that had just occurred . . .

It was an important reminder that this was all lies. A thin layer of snow that would soon melt to reveal the ugliness that lay beneath its beauty.

The prince moved to the railing, holding up his hands to silence the crowd. And then he began to speak—confident, proud, and with command . . . or so it seemed.

His mask was perfectly in place. He was Prince Magnus, heir to the throne. And he held his own, even a short time after an assassination attempt.

Even Cleo had to admit that it was impressive. That *he* was impressive.

"And here we are," Magnus said, his voice loud and clear, his breath freezing in the cold air, "after much struggle and conflict. It has not been an easy path, but to achieve great change it takes great strength and fortitude. My father's road, which will end at the Temple of Valoria, represents this change, this uniting of three lands. Beside me is another symbol of such a change to this kingdom. Princess Cleiona is the bravest girl I've ever known—one who has faced so many hardships in such a short time and weathered them all with incredible strength and grace. I'm honored to now stand by her side."

He flicked her a glance, his gaze hard and unreadable. She returned it with one of her own. Such beautiful words, she could almost fool herself into believing he spoke from his heart.

"I am certain that for every day of happiness the princess and I will share together, this kingdom will benefit in kind."

Oh, he was droll. And he knew it, too. There was now just the edge of humor in his gaze that he might ever refer to their forced union as a path to romantic bliss.

An uproariously loud cheer accompanied the end of his speech. His shoulders relaxed a fraction—barely noticeable if she hadn't been looking. Her gaze moved to the tear in his shirt and the wound beneath that still bled, dripping down his arm to fall to the floor.

Red. The color of Limeros.

The crowd had started to chant something, but for a moment she couldn't understand.

"What are they saying?" she asked.

Magnus's jaw tensed.

"A kiss," said Lord Gareth, who stood farther back in the shadows. As one of the king's closest friends, he had been invited to join them on the balcony for the speech along with several guards, including Nic. "The crowd wishes for the royal couple to show their love with a kiss."

Magnus turned his head away from the cheering crowd. "I'm not interested in such irrelevant public displays."

"Perhaps not. But they would like it anyway."

"A KISS! A KISS!" the crowd chanted.

"I mean," their advisor continued wryly, "it would not be the first, would it? What difference would such a small request matter to please this hungry crowd?"

"I don't know," Cleo began, sickened by the thought of it. How far was she willing to go to appear agreeable? "Quite honestly, it seems like a bad—"

Magnus took a tight hold of her arm and turned her around. Before she could say another word, he put his hand behind her neck, drew her closer to him, and kissed her.

Every muscle in her body stiffened. It was the sensation of being a bird caught in a hunter's trap. Her wings screamed out for her to fly away as fast and as far as possible. But he held her firmly in place, his mouth against hers, soft but demanding a response.

She gripped the front of his shirt. It was all too much—she wasn't sure if she was pushing him away or pulling him closer. Much like diving into deep water, she had no idea which way would find her air to breathe or which way would drag her down deeper into the depths where she would surely drown.

And for a moment, just a moment, she found it didn't seem to matter.

The warmth of his body against hers on such a cold day, his now-familiar scent of sandalwood, the heat of his mouth against hers . . . it all made her head spin, and logic fell away.

When he pulled back, her lips felt as if they'd been set ablaze, a fire that continued to burn as bright as the flames now spreading across her cheeks.

Magnus leaned closer so he could whisper in her ear, his breath hot against her already flushed skin.

"Don't worry, princess. It was the first and last."

"Good." Cleo let go of him and moved off the balcony, past Nic, so fast she stumbled on the hem of her red gown. The sound of the crowd's cheers quickly became a distant echo in her ears.

CHAPTER 26

KING GAIUS

THE SANCTUARY

The dream finally came after far too many weeks of waiting.

"You said I was immortal," the king snarled when he sensed Melenia's presence. He didn't wait for her reply; he turned and stormed toward her, grasping her shoulders and shaking her. "Why did you lie to me?"

"I didn't lie."

He slapped her hard across her face, the sting of it more satisfying that he'd expected. Inflicting pain upon this beautiful golden creature gave him great pleasure.

She pressed her hand to her cheek, but her eyes did not fill with tears as so many others' would. No weakness crossed her gaze as she steadily held his.

"I did not lie," she repeated, enunciating every word. "And you will strike me again at your own peril, my king."

There was an edge of caution in the statement, one only the most foolish would ignore.

He forced himself to calm down. "I was nearly crushed in the Temple of Cleiona during the quake. I tasted the bitterness of my own mortality."

"But you're not dead, are you?"

He hadn't left the palace since that day. With the potential of rebel assassins lurking in every shadow, the threat of natural disas- ters striking at any given moment, he had become increasingly paranoid. He was far too close to achieving all he'd ever wanted to take any unnecessary risks.

After what had happened at the temple, his confidence had been shaken. He didn't trust Melenia anymore. There had been a fleeting time when he considered her both an intellectual equal as well as an object of desire. When he believed she would become his next queen, to rule by his side for all eternity. A woman he might be capable of worshipping. A woman he might even be capable of loving.

No more.

Now all he wanted from her were answers.

"When," he growled. "When do I get my hands on the treasure you've promised me for these many months?"

"When the road is complete."

It was far too long to wait for any tangible proof of what she'd told him. His patience stretched thin and brittle. "How is Lucia integral to finding the Kindred? Will she sense its location with her magic? Does more blood need to be spilled to help her?"

"I already told you, my king. Blood will be spilled. Much of it. Blood is essential to our plan."

"Tell me more. Tell me everything."

The hint of a smile dared to curl up the corner of her mouth. "Oh, my king, you are not nearly ready to hear *everything*."

"I am!" he insisted.

"Not yet. There are . . . sacrifices that must be made. Sacrifices I'm not convinced you're prepared for."

"What sacrifices?" He would risk anything, sacrifice anything to get what he wanted. "Tell me!"

She raised an eyebrow. "Sometimes I really don't know why I bother with you. Perhaps it's because you amuse me."

He would be an amusement to no one. "You prophesied that I would rule the universe with the power of an immortal god."

"I did, didn't I? Strange thing about prophesies, my king. They aren't always set in stone. Such a prophecy requires me to assist you in what must be accomplished in the mortal world, as I already have in so many countless ways. Don't make me regret my decision."

He wanted to kill her. To crush her between his hands. To watch the life fade from her beautiful blue eyes. To have her beg for mercy with her last breath.

Did an immortal bleed red? This too he'd like to discover.

Instead of admitting to his darkening thoughts, he lowered his head in deference. "Deepest apologies, my queen. You see how stressed I've become of late. How anxious I am for progress. It has been a difficult time for us all, especially with my deep concern for my daughter's well-being. But she's awake now and out of harm's way. And her magic is stronger than ever."

"I'm very glad to hear it." She walked a slow circle around him. For the first moment in his life, he felt as if a predator was eyeing him for weaknesses.

He'd never felt like prey before.

"I need to journey to the road camp in the Forbidden Mountains to see Xanthus," he said. "I need to speak with him, for him to show me what he's doing, to assure me that all is progressing with the road as it should. Messages sent by raven are not enough to reassure me."

"No, you must not go. You must remain here."

"Why?"

Her brows drew together, her exquisite face growing very serious. "I do not wish to worry you, but . . . if you leave the confines of your palace, your prophecy is forfeit. There are countless dangers and many currently wish you dead. I promised you immortality, my king, but only if you stay secure while our plans solidify."

He stared at her, shocked, for a long, silent moment. This was precisely what he'd feared. "So I'm to stay here, locked up, like a child that must be protected from potential dangers?"

Something unpleasant flashed through her eyes. "Imprisonment is a state I am very familiar with, my king. Believe me, your confinement will be much briefer than mine has been. If you must learn more of the road, and if you won't take my word for such things, you can send someone you trust in your place to speak with Xanthus."

But Gaius trusted no one.

No one—except for his children. Except for his son.

"I will send Magnus," he said firmly. He hated that he couldn't leave, but he didn't doubt her warning. His mortal life was fragile, as everyone's was. He was too close to what he wanted to risk his neck to a rebel's blade. "When he returns from the wedding tour and joins the hunt for the rebel leader, I will have him inspect the road camp in the mountains and speak with Xanthus. He will be my official representative."

"Very good. I hope the prince proves his worth to you on this quest," Melenia purred. "I know you've had some difficulties with him."

"I'm hard on him because I know he needs a firm hand. He's at a difficult time in his life. But, despite some resistance, he has proven himself to me again and again. He will not let me down."

"Yes, send your son to find the answers to reassure you. We are closer than you think."

He clasped her face between his hands, a gentle touch now when before he was rough. She didn't pull away as he drew her closer to kiss her. Her mouth was as sweet and warm as it would be in the waking world.

When this was all over, when he had the Kindred in his possession and was an immortal god free to journey wherever he pleased, he looked forward to discovering how pleasurable it would be to kill the woman he now embraced.

By then, he would have no use for a queen.

CHAPTER 27

MAGNUS

LIMEROS

Magnus had come to regret summoning Nicolo Cassian to ease the princess's suffering on the wedding tour. The boy despised him, blamed him for his sister's death, and would gleefully shove a sharp blade into him the moment his back was turned.

Nic's palpable animosity had shot up even more during the last days of the tour after the unplanned kiss on the balcony. It was jealousy, pure and simple. Clearly, the boy imagined himself in love with the princess.

This, if nothing else, could prove an amusement.

"Beautiful, isn't she?" Magnus said casually to Nic the morning they were set to begin the journey back to Auranos. Cleo climbed aboard one of the carriages, assisted by a guard.

"She is," Nic hissed.

He had to wonder if Cleo had shared any details of their unconsummated union with her friend. That would be deeply unwise of her. "With every day that passes I realize how lucky I am to have such a creature to share my life with. So cool and innocent on the surface, yet so passionate in our private moments. Insatiable, really." Magnus smiled at the guard. "Apologies, Nic. I shouldn't discuss such things with a mere servant, should I?"

Nic's face reddened to nearly the color of both his hair and his uniform. For a moment, Magnus was certain the top of his head would erupt like a volcano.

Very amusing, indeed.

Then Nic spoke loud enough for only Magnus to hear.

"Know this much, your highness. She'll hate you forever for what you did to Theon."

Magnus's amusement fell away and he turned a glare of warning on Nic, but the guard had already stalked toward the carriages.

The late spring thaw had quickly set in, one that swept away some of the snow and ice for a precious couple of months here in western Limeros before everything froze over again. As Magnus stepped aboard the carriage, he noticed that he'd crushed a small purple wildflower that had managed to struggle through the remaining frost. He stared at the decimated spot of color with dismay before a guard closed the door, shutting off his view of it.

"You look ill. Is there something wrong with you?" Cleo asked. It was the first thing she'd said directly to him since the kiss he'd forced upon her yesterday.

She'd hated it. And she hated him.

So much is wrong with me, princess. Where do I even begin?

"Nothing is wrong." Magnus turned to look out the window as the carriage pulled away. He had no idea when he'd next return here to his true home—a place of ice and snow and small crushed pieces of beauty. "Nothing at all."

• • •

Magnus met with his father the moment he returned from the tour. His prisoner had been delivered to the dungeons, and Magnus explained what had happened. He knew it was possible he'd overreacted by bringing the boy back to Auranos after hearing the mention of dreams and Watchers. But the king seemed pleased by his decision. The boy would be questioned further to see if he spoke truth or nonsense.

The king informed him that not only would Magnus be joining Aron on the hunt for Jonas Agallon, but they would also be journeying to the Paelsian road camp located in the Forbidden Mountains, where Magnus was to meet with a man stationed there named Xanthus.

Xanthus was an exiled Watcher assigned as the road's engineer by the king's mysterious dream advisor, Melenia. Xanthus was her representative in the mortal world. He did as she commanded. And Melenia commanded that the road be built and infused with Xanthus's earth magic in order—the king was certain—to coax the hidden location of the Kindred out of the very elements themselves, which were now connected by the twisting ribbon of road.

To Magnus, it was all as hard to swallow as an entire roasted goat. Especially the fact that the king was now certain, thanks to his dream advisor, that if he took a step beyond the palace walls, he would be slain.

Even still, Magnus had seen enough magic in past months to agree readily to any chance to gain more information that would put the Kindred in his family's hands, no matter how far-fetched such possibilities were.

Magnus did not argue. He did not debate. He did not laugh or roll his eyes.

All he did was nod. "As you wish, Father."

By the rare and genuine smile he received from the king, this was the correct answer. "Good boy. Now, go and visit your sister. She has greatly anticipated your return."

Considering how uncaring she'd sounded when Magnus overheard her discussing him with their father on the day of the fateful wedding, Magnus was surprised when Lucia greeted him back at the Auranian palace with a warm embrace and a kiss on both of his cheeks.

She was every bit as beautiful as she ever had been—even more so than the last time he'd seen her, since the color she'd lost during her slumber had returned to her cheeks. Today, however, there was a thick layer of apathy on top of his appreciation for his adopted sister, much like storm clouds hiding the sun's true brightness. This apathy had grown substantially in the time they'd been apart. The conversation he'd just had with his father had done nothing to improve his mood.

"I've missed you so much," she said, smiling. "I've already heard wonderful things about your speech in Limeros. I only wish I could have been there to hear it."

Magnus regarded her coolly. "It's too bad you weren't."

"It must have been quite a hardship to have spent so much time with Princess Cleiona," she said with sympathy. "From what I've heard of the spoiled girl, I dread our eventual meeting."

"She's not like that at all. Spending time with my new bride has been both an honor and a delight. Despite our many differences, she makes me happier than I ever could have anticipated."

Lucia's eyes widened as if she didn't hear the sarcasm behind his words. She'd always been the only one able to see beyond his masks in the past—she'd known him better than anyone else. But perhaps they'd spent too much time apart lately and she'd lost her talent to read him.

"If you'll excuse me, sister." He swallowed his disappointment. By now, it was a familiar taste. "I must leave once again. I only hope my beautiful new bride does not miss me too much while I'm gone from her side."

Even though he knew meeting with the exiled Watcher could give him more clues about how to find the Kindred, all Magnus currently cared about was vengeance. Finding the rebel who'd killed his mother helped sharpen his focus like a killing blade.

The rebels, however, were much harder to track down than he'd thought. Privately, he'd ridiculed Aron's failure to gain any clues to Jonas Agallon's whereabouts. Now, after a full week of searching with no success, he too felt the staggering weight of failure.

At dusk, the prince's entourage arrived at a camp set up by a unit of guards in eastern Auranos, barely an arm's reach from the edge of the thick tangle of Wildlands, following rumors of the rebels' shifting travels. Next, Magnus was pained to admit, they would have to put the search for Jonas on hold to journey into Paelsia itself and head directly to the road camp currently located in the shadow of the Forbidden Mountains.

Magnus's large tent was readied for him to take dinner and rest for the night. The sun had mostly set, but there was still enough light to see. A campfire crackled nearby. The days in this particular region were warm and temperate, but at night, and so close to the Paelsian border, it cooled down considerably. The cool air held the scent of the smoky fire and roasting venison and the sound of hidden insects buzzing and chirping in the thick forest only thirty paces from camp.

"I think we make an excellent team," Aron said, jarring Magnus from his thoughts.

Lord Aron Lagaris might now have the official designation of kingsliege, but he was a complete waste of space, Magnus reflected sourly—nor did he have any clue of the real reason they were next headed to the road camp other than for a general inspection. The silver flask Aron continually drank from was an annoyance— almost as much as the boy himself. Magnus had no respect for anyone who relied on artificial means to maintain their courage.

Magnus removed his black leather gloves and warmed his hands over the fire as he gave Aron a sidelong glance. "Do you, now."

Aron took yet another swig from his flask. "I know things have been a bit tense between us, what with the Cleo issue . . ."

"'Cleo issue'?"

The boy nodded. "It's best in the end that a princess marry a prince. I suppose."

"Ah. I suppose." Oh, this was deeply unpleasant. Being trapped into meaningless small talk with an idiot had never intrigued him, even on a good day. Which this wasn't.

"I only hope for your sake that she's forgotten the night of passion we shared."

Magnus gave him a hard look. "You are deeply unwise to broach this subject right now."

Aron immediately blanched. "I mean no disrespect."

A hot rise of anger fought to push past his simple annoyance. "Of course you do. All that ever comes out of your mouth is disrespect, Lagaris."

Aron raked a hand through his hair and paced back and forth, taking another quick swig from his flask. "It's just that to wed a girl who could not keep herself pure for her future husband—"

"Close your mouth before you insult my bride's honor with another word." Magnus drew out his dagger to absently run it under his fingernails. Aron followed the blade's movements with fearful eyes. "She belongs to me now, not you. Never forget that."

Not that he really cared, he reminded himself sternly. He had not touched Cleo apart from the kiss in Limeros. And that had been under duress.

Still, Magnus had to admit the girl was an excellent actress. With his lips pressed to hers, he could have sworn he tasted warm honey rather than cold venom in her response. And he also had to admit, if only to himself, that such unexpected sweetness had coaxed a much longer kiss than he'd originally planned.

The princess was dangerous yet could appear so very innocent to one who didn't know the truth—much like a spider and her shimmering web. Perhaps Magnus would do best to look at Aron as a hapless fly who'd once found his way into that trap through no fault of his own.

At that moment, a group of guards approached with a prisoner, his hands bound behind his back. The boy was no more than eighteen, his brown hair dark and unruly, his skin tanned from the sun, his eyes flashing with anger.

"Who is this?" Magnus asked, his gaze sweeping the fierce-looking boy.

The lead guard shoved the prisoner forward. "Part of a group of rebels attempting to steal weapons from us."

"A *group* of rebels? And yet you captured only one."

"Apologies, your highness. But, yes."

"How many were there?" Aron asked.

The guard had begun to sweat. "Three, my liege."

"How many did you kill?"

A muscle in the guard's cheek twitched. "The rebels are vicious, Lord Aron. They're like wild animals, and—"

"Perhaps you did not hear my question correctly," Aron snapped. "How many rebels did you kill of the three?"

The guard blinked. "I'm afraid none today, my liege."

Aron glared at him with disgust. "Step back. Now."

The guard retreated.

What a complete jackass Aron was, spouting threat and intimidation as if he had the strength of will to back it up.

"Yes, your grace?" Aron asked evenly, noticing he'd gained the prince's full attention.

"May I question the prisoner, or would you like to have the honor?" It was an honest question, if offered on a slightly menacing level.

Aron gestured with his hand. "No, please. You go right ahead."

How shocking. It was the correct answer. "Much gratitude, Lord Aron."

Magnus indicated that the guards should bring the prisoner further into camp by the fire. There the rebel stood with his hands bound, but his shoulders were squared as he met Magnus's gaze directly, without flinching.

"Welcome." Magnus began with a smile, one that would mirror his father's ease, if not the king's famous charm. "I am Magnus Lukas Damora, crown prince and heir to the throne of Mytica."

"I know who you are," the boy said with distaste.

"Good. That will make things much simpler. Whom do I have the pleasure of addressing?"

The boy's lips thinned, his eyes stony.

Magnus nodded to a guard, who backhanded the rebel. Blood trickled from the corner of his mouth, but his gaze only grew more defiant.

"Whom do I have the pleasure of addressing?" Magnus asked

again. "This can go easy or it can go hard. The choice is yours. Answer my questions and I am capable of benevolence."

The boy laughed at this, spitting out the blood that filled his mouth. "Prince Magnus benevolent? This I find hard to believe."

Magnus's smile thinned. "Your name?"

"Brion Radenos."

"Very good, Brion." Magnus leveled his gaze at the boy's. "Now tell me, where is the rebel leader, Jonas Agallon?"

Brion cocked his head. "Jonas Agallon? Never heard of him before."

This boy tried his patience. "You lie. Tell me where he is."

Brion laughed at this. "Why would I?"

Magnus regarded him with distaste. "Jonas Agallon crept onto palace grounds and stole the life of Queen Althea. There is proof of this. He will pay for this with his own life."

Brion's brows drew together. "I've seen the posted reward for his capture; I've heard the rumors. But you're wrong. I don't care what proof you think you have, he had nothing to do with that murder."

The anger swiftly rising inside Magnus literally made him tremble. The nearby guards glanced at each other uneasily. "For a moment, I thought you were intelligent. But you're just a fool whose mouth is bigger than his brain."

This observation received a cold glare. "Jonas didn't kill the queen."

More rage lit beneath Magnus's skin. He reached out and grasped the boy's throat. "I'll ask one more time. Your helpful response will net you a reward and freedom rather than pain. Where is Jonas?"

"Kiss my arse." The boy's gaze flashed. "You think you're so strong, so powerful. You're not. You're weakened by your blindness— just like your father. His greed will be his undoing. The people in Auranos will not be fooled forever by him. And they will rise up in great numbers along with Paelsians to crush the both of you. Maybe we can even convince the Limerians to join in as one great army against all who wish to oppress us."

Magnus tightened his grip, causing the boy's face to turn red. Brion spat, and the saliva caught Magnus in the eye. He released the boy and wiped it away with disgust.

"I see." His heart drummed fast and loud in his chest. "You've chosen the hard way. Fine. I'll get my answers whether it's now or whether it's back in the dungeon on the rack. Perhaps it will give me the chance to capture Jonas if he attempts to save you."

"He damn well better not even try."

"Time will tell." Magnus turned away, trying very hard to maintain his mask and not show how much his mounting frustrations weakened him.

"This piece of rebel scum will tell you nothing here or anywhere else," Aron growled. He stood only a couple paces away, watching their exchange with a tight look on his pale face. "We don't have time to take him back to the dungeon. We move on to the road tomorrow and we can't spare any guards."

"This is more important, Lord Aron."

"I disagree, your highness. Rebels are best made an example of, not coddled and questioned."

"Did it sound like I was coddling him?" Magnus gritted his teeth and glanced away.

"This is not how King Gaius would deal with this situation."

The boy was so very annoying, Magnus could barely form words to respond. "Oh, no? And, pray tell, Lord Aron, how would the king deal with this situation?"

"Like this." Aron had drawn out his sword and was holding it with both hands.

Magnus's chest tightened in sudden alarm. "Aron, don't—"

But he paid Magnus no attention. Without another word or another threat, and with his eyes glittering with excitement, Aron drove his sword through Brion's heart.

Brion's eyes went wide and he gasped, a sickly, bubbling sound. Blood spilled over his bottom lip as he collapsed to the ground and let out a last hiss of breath.

Magnus stared down at the dead boy with shock.

"The king personally executed a troublemaker at the Temple of Cleiona during the opening ceremonies of the Imperial Road. You must remember that as well as I do." Aron wiped the bloody blade on a handkerchief he pulled from his pocket. "I know he wouldn't want this one to be handled any differently by his kingsliege. I will tell your father that you were instrumental in this rebel's immediate execution. I promise not to take full credit for it."

Magnus grabbed Aron by the front of his shirt and shoved him backward into the fire. The boy let out a wheezing shriek and scrambled to get up, batting at the embers that had begun to set his clothes ablaze.

Magnus was incensed. "He was my chance to find Jonas, you drunken imbecile!"

Aron sputtered, his cheeks now flushed. "He would have told you nothing more than his name! Sparing his life only made you look weak in front of the other men. You should be thanking me!"

Magnus leaned closer so he could snarl into Aron's ear. "Pray to your goddess that we find the rebel leader very soon, or my disappointment will be leveled upon you and you alone. Do you understand me, you little shit?"

Aron's eyes narrowed into slits as Magnus released him—both fear and hate now playing within. "I understand, your highness."

CHAPTER 28

JONAS

AURANOS

Brion crumpled to the ground.

Jonas couldn't breathe, couldn't speak, as he watched from the tree line, stunned. It was only a dream. It had to be. This was a nightmare he would wake from at any moment.

Then his vision turned red with hate, red with rage. He surged forward, ready to kill Aron with his bare hands—to tear him apart until he was a pile of bloody meat.

But before he could clear the protection of the thick trees, Lysandra threw her arms around him to stop him. Tears streamed down her cheeks as she grabbed hold of his face to force him to look at her rather than the sight of his fallen best friend.

"Jonas, no! It's too late," she whispered harshly to him. "Brion's dead! If you go out there they'll kill you too!"

It had been only moments. The boy he'd known since both nursed at their mothers' breasts lay on the ground thirty paces away. Blood seeped from his chest wound to soak into the earth.

Brion stared off toward the forest as if his unseeing eyes searched for Jonas.

It was like Tomas's death all over again—someone he loved dearly had been ripped away from him without warning by Aron Lagaris.

"Let me go!" A raw cry of grief rose in his throat and again he tried to move away from Lysandra. A stinging slap drew his attention and he stared into her furious gaze.

"They will kill you if you go out there," she growled.

"This is my fault. *Again*. It's my fault. It was my decision for us to try to steal the guards' weapons. When they saw us—" His voice broke and he threw his arms over his face as though by blocking out the forest they could block out what had happened. "Brion was protecting me so I could get away."

"He was protecting both of us." Tears poured down her face. "This is not your fault. We needed the weapons. We could never have predicted. . . ."

"I need to kill Aron Lagaris. I need to have vengeance." He drew in a shaky breath, keeping his attention on Lysandra's tear-streaked face. She hadn't let go of him yet. She was an anchor for him— a weight. If she wasn't here, he'd already be out there fighting. Bleeding. Dying. He'd expected hatred and fire from this girl for this. Instead, she pulled him into a tight embrace as they shared their grief.

"You will have vengeance," she assured him. "As will I. But not here. Not now."

Jonas thought he might retch. He kept seeing Brion crumpling to the ground. Lysandra was still talking. He clung to her words like a lifeline.

"We knew the prince would be coming in this direction—it was

Brion's idea to track their progress, Jonas. You can't blame yourself!
Look at me." She grabbed his face again, forcing him to meet her
tear-filled eyes. "Thanks to Nerissa we know where they're going
next—and why. Now is the time to act, once and for all. This is it,
you must realize that. Don't you?"

He tried to think. He tried to see past his rage and his grief.

A plan began to formulate—blurry at first, but steadily growing clearer and stronger.

This is it, Lysandra had said.

She was right.

Brion's death would not be in vain—Jonas would not let it be.
It would mark the moment Jonas could finally see with the clear-
est vision of his entire life.

The Blood Road was the key to the king's downfall.

And it was time for the rebels to end this.

By the time they returned to their band's current campsite, night
had closed in all around them, and the Wildlands were dark and
filled with eerie noises that hinted at hungry things waiting to
reach out and devour anyone who crossed their paths.

Jonas now felt like one of those beasts, like he could kill anything or anyone that got in his way.

"Now what do we do?" Tarus asked from the shadows, surrounded by the others. Lysandra had told them of Brion's death.
Tarus's voice trembled. "They're killing us off one by one."

"All this time," Jonas began, finding what strength he had left
to speak loud enough for all to hear, "I've been searching for a way
to cripple the king. To take back the power stolen from Paelsia from
the moment the chief was murdered. I admit that at times I feared
this task couldn't be completed. After the disaster and defeat at the

Temple of Cleiona I doubted. Doubted myself, doubted everything. For a moment, I allowed the King of Blood to defeat me.

"He has the numbers. He has the guards and soldiers. He has the weapons. And he has fooled the Auranians so much that the majority of them stand by like cattle foolishly waiting for slaughter. And now, from the reports I've received, the king has sequestered himself within the City of Gold, letting others fight his battles, untouchable and safe from any harm."

"Then what good does any of this do us? How can we hurt him?" another boy demanded.

"We've been searching for a weakness," Jonas said, "something that could hurt the king. Something we could use against him, to draw him out. Once, I believed that might be Princess Cleiona. That plan didn't work out quite the way I'd hoped. It proved one thing to me—we need someone who holds greater importance to the king."

"Who?" Tarus asked, his eyes wide.

"Tomorrow at dawn, Prince Magnus, Lord Aron, and a large group of guards are set to head for the Forbidden Mountains. We have information that they are to inspect the road camp there—a location we were not aware of until very recently."

"Who told you about this?" Phineas asked.

"A reliable source," Lysandra replied. She and Jonas shared a tense look. This was information they had received only days before, information that had led to them spying on the prince's camp in the first place. Former seamstress Nerissa had taken on the mantel of rebel spy with great enthusiasm. Palace guards positioned close to the king enjoyed unburdening their souls after a hard day at work in the arms of a pretty and *very* friendly girl. Lysandra had not approved of Nerissa's methods of obtaining information, but she couldn't very well argue with her success—not when it had finally given them the key to what would be their ultimate victory.

"So we are to kidnap Prince Magnus," a rebel guessed.

"Yes." Jonas's eyes narrowed. "But he's not our only target. There is someone else at the camp who, we believe, means as much to the greedy king as his own blood. A man named Xanthus, who holds such a high level of secrecy, according to my source, that it intrigues me. He is the head engineer for the entire road and I have been assured that he is essential to the operation. He has the plans, he makes the decisions. Not one piece of stone is laid without his approval. Any new instructions or changes are sent directly from him, with an official seal, to the other camps."

"How can one man have that much power?" Phineas asked.

"I don't know, and frankly, I don't care," Jonas replied. His words sounded heedless but his plan was anything but. "All I know is without Xanthus in place, the road will cease construction. And the king is invested in this road, both with gold and with time. He wants it. It matters greatly to him. Taking both Xanthus and Prince Magnus and holding them hostage will net us what we want—the king himself. It will draw him out of his safe little golden palace and right into our grasp."

"It's simple." Lysandra took over. "We will follow Prince Magnus and his group to the road. We will then wait until they rest, until they are lulled into a false sense of security, and we will attack just before dawn breaks. We will locate both Xanthus and the prince and take them both, killing anyone who gets in our way. This is it. This is our chance to finally make a difference and save our people from the king's tyranny."

"But we need every one of you to help us," Jonas said. "*Everyone.*"

"It'll still be a blood bath," another rebel standing next to Phineas spoke up, uncertain. "You think we're going to lay down our lives for this? Based on information from your 'reliable source'?"

"Yes!" Lysandra spun to trap the rebel in her fiery gaze. "We *will* lay down our lives if that's what it takes! I watched Brion die today and to the very end he was brave and strong. We owe it to him. I can only hope to be half as brave as he was. I'm willing to die if it means I can show the King of Blood that I am not now nor will I ever be one of his slaves!"

"We shall cut King Gaius where he's sure to bleed buckets," Jonas said firmly, "and we *will* have our victory. Come on. Who is with me? Who is with Lysandra?"

One by one, the gathered rebels stepped forward, voices growing ever louder in enthusiasm and strength.

"I am!"

"And I!"

"Yes! Enough weakness, we'll show the King of Blood our strength once and for all!"

"Once and for all!"

CHAPTER 29

LUCIA

AURANOS

Magic burned beneath Lucia's skin, begging to be released. It felt as trapped as she did in this strange palace with its brightly lit hallways and glittering, golden floors, different from the dark and cool Limerian castle in so many ways. She missed her real home more than she would ever have thought possible.

The bunny was not helping matters at all.

"You've grown so quickly, Hana." She held up the bundle of soft fur to look into the rabbit's sweet face. Its heart beat quickly against her touch and its nose twitched. This was one of the few things that could make her smile.

Finally, Lucia put Hana down into her small pen in the corner of her chambers and went to the balcony, her gaze moving out across the green fields and hills that surrounded the City of Gold beyond the glittering walls.

It was all so painfully beautiful. To punctuate this, a pink and purple butterfly flew by on a warm breeze.

"Ugh." Lucia turned away. She didn't care about butterflies. She cared about hawks and had searched the skies endlessly for a sighting of one, just one! But there was nothing.

It had been five long weeks since the last time she saw Alexius, when he promised he would see her again—when they'd kissed so passionately and she'd been torn from his arms by waking. If he was real, why hadn't he come to her again? It wasn't just a dream. It *wasn't*. She knew Alexius was out there somewhere.

She gripped the banister, and it warmed beneath her touch before beginning to crumble into dust from a surge of earth magic. She let go of it immediately and wiped off her hands, glancing around nervously to see if anyone had witnessed this, but of course there was no one. After learning of the fright she'd put into her *elementia* tutor, her father had strongly suggested she remain alone in her chambers until he sought the help of another.

And so she had. But after so many days trapped in such a small space, she needed to be free.

She was curious to know if the king had had Domitia executed since she had not fulfilled her purpose. It saddened Lucia that she didn't care what the woman's fate had been—life or death.

Once she would have cared.

The butterfly lit on the edge of a nearby flowerpot and she eyed it, fighting the sudden urge to squash its beauty in the palm of her hand.

"What's happening to me?" she whispered.

She'd been cooped up in this room for far too long. Answers were what she needed more than anything. Books had always given her knowledge in the past. Why would now be any different? She'd heard that the Auranian palace library was second to none. Perhaps there, unlike the Limerian library, which contained only books of hard knowledge, she might find more answers about *elementia*. About the sorceress and the Watchers.

Her decision made, Lucia left her chambers and moved through the hallways, looking neither left nor right, except to ask a guard for directions to her destination. The library was on the other side of the palace and the hallways were virtually deserted, apart from the occasional guard who stood as still as a statue. Magnus had always prided himself in his ability to move through the castle unseen—like a shadow. It was a true talent, one she'd only started to appreciate.

She missed Magnus, she realized. She missed the days when they had talked for an entire afternoon about bards or books or nothing, how they laughed about some silly private joke, like the way Lady Sophia always slipped pastries into the pockets of her dress at palace dinners and thought no one noticed. She missed the way she could coax a smile from him even on his darkest days.

Was that now stolen from her forever?

It's my fault. I should have been kinder to him in my thoughts and words.

He was angry with her now and hurt by her continual rejection of his love. Hopefully, when he returned at long last from the hunt, she could earn his forgiveness and make him see that though they could never be together, their filial relationship was more important than any other. She needed him and he needed her. There was no question that she had to put right between them what had gone so very wrong.

For now, Lucia forced these thoughts away and focused again on her goal. She wanted to take every book she could that might help her learn more about who she was and what she could expect from her magic. Take them and devour them, feeding herself with the knowledge like a feast laid out at a banquet.

When she reached her destination, her footsteps slowed at the sight of the enormous room beyond the archway. Her heart skipped a beat at the sight of books laid upon shelves that rose as high as small mountains. There had to be tens of thousands of books here, all shapes and sizes. All subjects. All offering knowledge beyond anything she'd ever dreamed of. Light from a multitude of stained glass windows shone down into this haven, casting a kaleidoscopic sparkle, as if the library itself were touched by magic.

"Well, Princess Lucia, you've strayed from your chambers. At long last, we get to meet."

The voice broke the spell she'd fallen under, and her gaze moved to the girl standing before her with two books tucked beneath her arm. Lucia recognized her immediately. Her fair face, her aquamarine eyes, her pale, golden hair that fell in waves all the way down to her waist. She was shorter than Lucia by several inches, but despite her small stature she held herself tall, her shoulders back, her chin tilted upward. A curious smile played at her rosy lips.

This was the distraction the king wanted so Magnus would no longer focus his unwanted attention upon Lucia. Princess Cleiona was just as beautiful as she'd heard. And Lucia found that she hated her immediately.

She, however, pushed a smile onto her own lips to mirror the other princess. "Princess Cleiona, it's a great honor."

"Please, feel free to call me Cleo. After all, we're sisters now, aren't we?"

Lucia tried not to cringe at the reminder. "Then you're most welcome to call me Lucia." She shook her head, still awed by her surroundings. "I can't tell you how incredible this library is. You've been so lucky to have this all your life."

Cleo's eyes did not hold quite as much amazement as Lucia's

did. "I must confess, I never came here as much as my sister did. She loved it. She always had a book to read. I wouldn't be surprised if she'd already worked her way through half of these by the time she . . ." Her words trailed off, and her cheeks were tight as she brought her pained gaze back to Lucia's.

Lucia's distaste faded somewhat in sympathy for this girl who'd lost so much. Her sister, her father, her kingdom. All taken by an enemy force, which included Lucia herself. And now, this library belonged more to her than it did to Cleo.

"Your sister sounds much like me, then," Lucia said gently. "I love to read."

"Then you'll fit in very well here."

"I'm glad to get the chance to talk to you." The other princess, despite her new status as Magnus's wife, was watched carefully and kept in a different wing of the castle. Her prison might be a gilded one, but it was no less secure. And yet, here she was today, roaming about unescorted, with no guard to be seen. Had this enemy to her father's throne managed to ease herself into King Gaius's good graces after the successful wedding tour?

"And I'm very glad that you're feeling better. Everyone was terribly worried about you, not understanding why you remained asleep for so long." Cleo looked at Lucia curiously, as if expecting a reason to freely be given.

"It was the strangest thing." Lucia shook her head, back on her guard. "And I'm afraid it may always remain a mystery."

"There was a rumor that you might have been cursed by a witch. That you were under a magic spell."

Lucia frowned deliberately, as if this sounded ludicrous to her. "Magic? Do you believe in such silly things?"

Cleo's smile stretched thinner. "Of course not. But servants like to talk, you know. Especially when it's about royalty. They love to make up all sorts of interesting tales."

"They certainly do. But no, I was under no magical spell, I assure you." The lie felt so natural it took no effort at all to deliver.

"I'm very glad to hear that." Cleo shifted her books in her arms.

"What are you reading?" Lucia asked, cocking her head so she could make out the gilded titles stamped onto the leather spines. "*A History of Elementia.* My goodness. That sounds like a strange choice of book for one who doesn't believe in magic."

"Yes, doesn't it?" Cleo's knuckles whitened on the edge of the large book. "It was one of my sister's favorites. Reading such things makes me feel that her spirit is close, guiding me."

This conversation was far more work than Lucia expected it to be. There was a time, back before the battle that had put this kingdom in her father's hands, that Lucia had imagined their meeting, hoping that they might become close friends. She'd begun to doubt that possibility now. She strained to read the title of the second, smaller book, which was covered in dust, as though Cleo had unearthed it from a long-forgotten stack, and her heart began to pound harder. "*Song of the Sorceress.* What is that about?"

Cleo glanced down at it. "Poetry about a powerful sorceress who lived at the time of the goddesses. Her name was—well, *your* middle name . . . Eva. Quite a coincidence, isn't it?"

Lucia's throat tightened. "Yes, quite."

This was a book she needed.

"I should probably leave you to your own book search. I'd say you have permission to borrow whatever you like, but I don't suppose you need it, do you?"

There was just a drop of acid contained within those words.

Lucia was pleased by it; pleased to know that the girl was not all she appeared—a polite and perfectly poised princess. She wore masks, the same kind that Lucia and Magnus did. Was it possible to be a member of a royal family and not have such a tool at the ready? Thinking this, Lucia felt her heart soften toward the other girl once again.

"I know this is all difficult for you," Lucia said, touching Cleo's arm as she moved past her. "I understand."

"Do you?" Cleo smiled, but her eyes were cold. "How nice to know of your empathy for my situation."

"If you need to talk, please know that I'm here for you."

"As I am for you."

Something caught Lucia's eye then and she looked down at Cleo's hand.

"Your ring." She frowned. "Is it . . . glowing?"

Cleo took a step back, her face growing pale. She glanced down at her ring, a delicate golden filigree with a large purple stone she wore on the index finger of her right hand. She adjusted the books so her hand was now shielded. "A trick of the light, I'm sure. Nothing more."

How strange. "Well, in any case, I hope to see much more of you from now on."

"Yes. I feel the same way. Since we're now *sisters*."

Was it only her imagination too that the word was delivered as sharp as a dagger?

"Do you know when Magnus will be back?" Lucia asked.

"Didn't he tell you?"

"No."

"I was under the impression that your brother shared everything with you."

Lucia pressed her lips together, choosing not to answer. There was a time when this would have been true. Lately, however . . .

The thought that she'd lost her brother's confidence suddenly pained her, an ache she felt deep in her heart.

"To answer your question," Cleo said, "I don't know when he will be back. I can only hope it will be soon."

"Do you miss him?"

Cleo's smile held. "Why wouldn't I?"

Lucia regarded the girl for a moment before she spoke again. "Who would have thought that two people so very different would find love in the midst of this landscape of conflict."

Cleo's gaze was continually moving, over Lucia, over their surroundings. She was alert, this princess. And Lucia sensed there was much more behind those innocent-looking eyes than anyone might believe.

"Who indeed? You're very lucky to have grown up with an older brother like Magnus."

"Yes. Just as you're lucky to get the chance to spend the rest of your life by his side."

"Indeed."

Lucia watched her carefully, searching for any sign of deception. Was this true? Was Cleo actually happily in love with Magnus and he with her?

Impossible.

"He can be difficult," Lucia warned. "Moody. Temperamental. Argumentative."

"Who isn't, at times?"

"He's very forgiving, though." Lucia arched a brow. "After all, he forgave you your unfortunate and shameful loss of chastity to Lord Aron Lagaris, didn't he?"

Cleo blinked, the only sign that her words had come as an unexpected slap. Lucia took a measure of joy from that but knew it was petty.

During Magnus's wedding tour absence, the king had filled Lucia in on many interesting facts. Everything she missed while she'd been asleep.

The princess's lips thinned. "As you said, I'm very lucky."

"I'm sorry for stating this so bluntly, but as you know, servants talk." No reason to let Cleo know the king had said anything. Servants were always easiest to blame for everything.

"Yes." A fresh smile now snaked slowly across Cleo's face. "I've heard things too. About you."

"Oh? Such as?"

"I'm sure it's a lie. Unlike some people, I prefer to make my own judgments, not have my head so easily filled with the gossip of servants."

Lucia bristled at the sly insult. "What have you heard?"

Cleo moved closer as if ready to speak in quiet confidence. "I heard that you and Magnus had an unsavory relationship before coming here to Auranos. That you're in love with your own brother."

Lucia's mouth fell open. "That's not true!"

"Of course not. As I said, I make my own judgments. But, despite the distasteful and unnatural leanings of such an attraction on your part, I would understand it. Magnus is very handsome. Don't you think?" A mocking smile curved the edge of the girl's mouth, as if she knew she was getting under Lucia's skin and pushing the boundaries of her patience.

And she was. Lucia's magic growled and paced in its cage. She wasn't in love with Magnus and she despised such an accusation.

How would Cleo like to know that it was actually Magnus who felt the unnatural and disgusting love for *her*?

But had that changed? Had this girl seduced Magnus and taken him away from Lucia forever? He was ready to be hers—now and always. She didn't want him romantically, but she didn't want to lose him to this meaningless princess.

Irrational—I'm being irrational.

At that moment, she didn't really care.

Fire magic was the closest to the surface, and her mind reached for it even without her conscious permission. The unlit torches set into the walls of the library caught fire and began to blaze hot and bright. A crack began to slither down a large stained glass window before it shattered, shards of glass raining down on the smooth floor.

Cleo's head whipped in the direction of the broken window and the torches, her eyes widening with alarm.

"What's happening? Is it another quake?" Her gaze snapped back to Lucia, who now had her fists clenched at her sides, trying with all her might to calm herself before something truly horrible happened.

Before she lit her brother's bride on fire and listened to her dying screams.

Sudden clarity reached Lucia with the force of a fist slamming into her stomach and she gasped out loud. This wasn't right. This wasn't her. Something was making her act irrationally and violently. It was her *elementia*. It had closed its hand on the back of her neck like a master with a favored pet, controlling her, commanding her.

The torches returned to a normal height, still lit but now flickering harmlessly as they added more light to the already bright room.

"It's nothing." Lucia echoed Cleo's previous words as she brushed past the wide-eyed princess to go farther into the library. She had research to do. She wouldn't let this stupid girl continue to distract her. The broken glass crunched under the leather soles of her shoes. "A trick of the light, I'm sure. Nothing more."

CHAPTER 30

NIC

AURANOS

There was no time to wait. He had to speak with Cleo *now*. Nic searched the castle until he finally found her outside in the sunny courtyard seated upon a bench, surrounded by trees heavy with fruit and fragrant blossoms. She was so intent on her reading that she didn't hear him approach. He glanced over her shoulder to see that she was immersed in a book so old its pages were yellow and brittle. She slid her index finger over an illustration of a ring with a large stone and a band like winding ivy.

"That looks like your ring," he said with surprise.

She slammed the book closed and turned to face him, her eyes wide. Then she exhaled shakily. "Oh, Nic. It's just you."

He'd rarely seen her as nervous as this. Nic looked toward the four other guards who kept watch over this area. They each stood against the stone walls as still as statues, far enough away that Nic and Cleo didn't risk being overheard by them.

Cleo's knuckles had tightened on the book she now clutched to her chest. Nic tilted his head to read the title: *Song of the Sorceress*.

He couldn't allow himself to be distracted. He had something to say and he needed to speak before they were interrupted. Privacy for a member of the palace guard—even a reluctant one like him—was fleeting.

"We need to escape this place," Nic whispered. "We must go while we can, while there's a chance to leave here undetected. We need to leave tonight."

"No, Nic." Cleo's eyes locked with his. "This is my palace, my throne. I can't leave. Not yet."

"I've been thinking about it every day, and I've reached a breaking point, Cleo. When the prince returns . . . I can't protect you from him every hour of the day and night. I won't let him kill you like he did Mira."

"Nic." Pain flashed through her eyes at the mention of her lost friend. "I mourn Mira as deeply as you do, but it was the king who killed your sister." She placed the book down beside her and grasped his hands. "Magnus spared your life—and he protected me in Limeros during the assassination attempt."

He stared at her incredulously. "Are you really attempting to defend the same boy who murdered Theon? Who stood next to his father as they conquered this kingdom? You're not . . . you're not falling in love with him, are you?"

Cleo flinched as if he'd slapped her. "I'm doing nothing of the sort. I despise Magnus and I always will."

He swallowed hard, ignoring the flash of guilt that he'd accuse her of something so unfathomable. "I don't know why you wouldn't want to leave this place and never look back."

"Because it holds my childhood and sixteen years of happiness.

It holds memories of Emilia and my father—and of your sister as well. This is my kingdom—*our* kingdom."

"It's different now."

"You're right. It is." Cleo glanced down at the book, placing her hand on its cover. She paused for a few long moments, and then he saw her take a deep breath. "All right. You saw the drawing in here. You saw the ring and how much it looks like the one I now wear."

He frowned. What was she getting at? "I did."

She met his eyes. "That's because they are one and the same. My father gave this ring to me in his dying moments." Her voice caught. "There's very little tangible information about it, but some believe it is a key to locating the Kindred and harnessing its power. It is the very same ring that the sorceress Eva possessed, which allowed her to touch the crystals without being corrupted by their power. I need to find those crystals, Nic. I need their magic. With it, I will defeat King Gaius and take back my kingdom."

His head spun. "Your words . . . they're mad."

"No, this is real. I know it is."

Nic tried to process everything she was saying, but one thing stood out, something he couldn't get past. "Why didn't you tell me any of this before now?"

She faltered. "I didn't want to endanger you—and I wasn't sure what to do, what to believe. Not completely. But I do now. This book confirms what I already knew to be true. My ring can help me destroy King Gaius."

His gut churned, but despite such revelations, one thing stayed true from the moment he walked out here. His goal had not changed. "If anyone else learns that you possess this ring . . ." He took her hand in his, the purple stone cold against his skin. "We'll leave tonight and we'll find it together."

Her gaze turned bleak. "Nic. Please understand that I can't leave."

There had to be a reason why she resisted this plan, which solved so many problems. And he could think of only one. It was one that tortured him. "When you kissed him in Limeros, it looked so real—it looked like you *wanted* to kiss him."

Cleo groaned with frustration and pulled her hands from him. "I already told you that whatever you saw between us was for show only."

He had believed that at the time. But the image of Magnus drawing the princess to him and kissing her before the cheering crowd had worked like a slow-moving poison injected beneath his skin. He had to get this out. He had to speak from his heart or he knew it would be too late.

Nic took her hands in his again and knelt before her. "I love you, Cleo. More than anything in this world. I beg you to run away with me—away from all this."

The other guards had finally taken notice of the two and drawn closer.

"Is everything all right, your highness?" one called out to her.

"Yes, of course. My friend is just being silly." She smiled sweetly in their direction before casting a sterner look at Nic. "You're going to get yourself thrown in the dungeon for such foolish behavior."

Pain blossomed in his chest as if he'd been struck by a blade. He was silent for a moment, his disappointment crushing him. He pushed back up to his feet. His heart was a heavy weight. "I need to go. I need to think."

"Nic!"

He left the courtyard without looking back.

• • •

"Another." Nic signaled for the server. He'd lost count of how many drinks this would make. And he planned on many more before he'd pass out later on his hard cot in the servants' quarters.

"She doesn't love me," he slurred, tossing back the glass of fiery liquid. "So be it. May both our unavoidable deaths be swift and painless here in the heart of our enemy's lair."

The tavern was called the Beast, because it looked like a great black creature crawling up out of the dirt. Also, because it was well known to give its patrons a beast of a headache the following morning. At the current moment, Nic really didn't care.

"You look like you've had a rather bad day." The voice was lightly edged with an exotic accent. "Does the drink help?"

Through his haze of alcohol Nic was surprised to see Prince Ashur of Kraeshia take a seat next to him. He knew the prince had chosen to remain in Auranos after the wedding, temporarily residing in the west wing of the castle. All palace guards had been ordered to keep a close watch on the handsome bachelor—orders that came from the king himself. Some of the guards whispered that the king saw the prince as a threat to his power. After all, Ashur's father had conquered half the known world as easily as taking candy from a baby.

For a moment, Nic couldn't find his voice.

"It's a wine made from fermented rice, imported overseas from Terrea," he finally replied. "And, no, it doesn't help. Not yet, anyway. But give me time."

"Server," Prince Ashur called out. "Another fermented rice wine for my friend Nic, and for me."

Nic eyed him curiously as the server delivered the two glasses moments later. "You know my name."

"I do indeed."

"How?"

"I've asked about you." The prince tossed back the drink, his dark brows drawing together with a grimace. "Now that is *deeply* unpleasant."

"What have you asked about me, might I . . . uh, ask?"

A lock of ebony hair had come loose from the tie at the nape of his neck and fallen across the prince's forehead. He pushed it back. "I know you're good friends with the princess. I saw you speaking with her earlier today in the courtyard—and it did not strike me as a conversation between a princess and a guard. Despite your guard's uniform, I believe you to be one with both influence and knowledge in the palace."

"Then you'd be wrong." He glanced at the prince from the corner of his eye. Perhaps the king was right to worry about this prince. Nic wondered with an edge of worry what the prince might have overheard today. "Where are your bodyguards?"

Ashur shrugged. "Around, I suppose. I'm not an advocate of being swarmed."

"You should know that the City of Gold is not without its dangers."

The prince eyed him with amusement. "Duly noted."

Nic's gaze moved to the twin daggers the prince had sheathed to either side of his leather belt. Perhaps the prince could protect himself just fine without comment or concern.

Five . . . six . . . ten drinks, and Nic found he had few filters attached to his tongue that might keep him from speaking disrespectfully. "What do you want from me, your grace?"

The amused expression remained on the prince's handsome face. "To talk."

"About what?"

Ashur swirled the next drink in his glass. "About Princess Cleo's amethyst ring."

Nic went very still. Until today he'd never given a thought to Cleo's ring. "The princess has a lot of jewelry. I don't keep track of it."

"I think you know the one I'm talking about. After all, you're her closest confidant." He raised an eyebrow. "Although, perhaps not as close as you'd like to be."

The prince looked at Nic as if he knew more than he possibly could. It was unsettling. Again, he wondered how much of the conversation with Cleo this man could have heard, unseen by either of them. Or was he only guessing?

Nic shifted uncomfortably on his seat. "The princess is not a subject I wish to discuss."

Ashur smiled gently. "Unrequited love is a painful thing, isn't it?"

Something in Nic's chest twisted. He didn't like how this prince seemed to know him so well, seemed to look inside his soul so deeply. "The worst."

"Tell me what you know about the Kindred." Ashur leaned his chin on his fist as he studied Nic. "I believe it's real. Do you?"

"It's just a silly legend." It came out in a whisper as his heart began to race.

Why was the prince asking these things?

"My father has conquered many lands filled with great riches. He doesn't believe Mytica is large enough to hold anything to be interested in. But he's wrong. I believe Mytica is the most important realm that has ever existed. I believe Mytica is the gateway to great magic that lies dormant across all parts of this world, including Kraeshia. Therefore, I'm here to find out if the 'silly' legends are true. And one of those legends happens to concern a rather special ring."

Nic downed his latest drink in one quick gulp. "Apologies, your grace, but if you're here in Auranos chasing after legends and magic, then you'll be sorely disappointed. Cleo wears a ring her father gave her before he died, that's all. It has no further significance than that."

"King Gaius must know about the Kindred," Prince Ashur continued, undeterred. "And I would imagine he wants it very badly. Without powerful magic to strengthen his hold upon this kingdom, he could be so easily crushed. Do you think he realizes this? But what does his Imperial Road have to do with anything? I believe he has ulterior motives for building it—motives that tie directly to the search for the Kindred. So many of his army patrol the road, spread thin across the three kingdoms of Mytica, leaving his castles in both Limeros and Auranos vulnerable to attack from overseas. Sounds like the move of an obsessed king with a very specific goal to me. What do you think?"

Despite the drinks, Nic's mouth had gone bone dry. "I have no idea how to respond to such statements."

"Are you sure about that? I think you have far more to offer someone like me than even you realize." Ashur leaned forward, locking his gaze with Nic's. The prince's eyes stood out from his dark skin, a pale grayish blue, like the surface of the Silver Sea itself.

Nic's heart pounded so loud and fast he couldn't hear the buzz of conversation in the tavern anymore. "I wish you a very pleasant evening. Good night, Prince Ashur."

He left the tavern and began walking through the maze of buildings and cobblestone streets to find his way back to the palace. However, soon he found himself hopelessly lost. Ten . . . eleven . . . fifteen drinks. How many had he had?

"Oh, Nic," he mumbled. "Not good. Not good at all."

Especially not when he realized someone now followed him.

He continued to walk swiftly while long, shadowy fingers seemed to reach out toward him. He kept a hand at his belt, prepared to draw his sword on any attackers. The city had its share of thieves and pickpockets ready to kill if they thought they might get caught. King Gaius was famous for his ill treatment of prisoners, and no one wanted to find themselves in his already overly crowded dungeons.

Nic turned the next corner and stumbled to a halt when he found himself in a blind alleyway.

"Lost?" It was Prince Ashur's voice that rose up behind him.

Tensing, he turned slowly. "Maybe a little."

The prince's gaze swept the length of him. "Perhaps I can help."

Still no bodyguards. This prince walked the streets of a potentially lethal city with no protection.

Had he been able to tell that Nic had lied? What was he willing to do to get the truth about the Kindred and Cleo's ring? And how fiercely could Nic defend that truth?

"I'll tell you nothing," Nic said, his voice hoarse. "I don't care what you do to me."

Ashur laughed at this. "You sound rather paranoid. Is that how wine from Terrea affects you? I'd suggest sticking with the Paelsian vintages from now on."

The lightness of the reply didn't set Nic's mind at ease in the slightest. His survival instincts, while currently dulled by drink, paced back and forth with growing alarm. The twin daggers the prince carried drew his attention again.

"You want answers I can't give you," Nic said, disturbed by how slurred his words came out. "Answers to questions I don't even know."

Ashur drew closer. "You're afraid of me."

Nic staggered back a foot. "Why have you pursued me out into the streets? I can't help you. Leave me alone."

"Can't do that. Not yet. First, I really must know something of great importance."

The prince moved closer still. Before Nic could fumble for his sword to protect himself from attack, Ashur took his face between his hands and kissed him.

Nic stood there, frozen in place.

This was *not* what he'd expected. At all.

The prince twisted his grip into Nic's shirt, pulling him closer and deepening the kiss until Nic finally surprised himself by responding. The moment he did, the prince pulled back from him.

Nic stared at him, stunned.

"See?" Ashur said, smiling. "Proof for you that there's more to life than drinking yourself into oblivion over a princess who thinks of you only as a friend. And there's more to this great big world than this tiny, troubled kingdom and its greedy little king, even if it is every bit as valuable as I believe it to be."

"Your grace—" Nic began.

"We'll talk again very soon, I promise," Ashur said, leaning in to give him another brief kiss that Nic didn't try to stop. "And you will help me find the answers I need. I know you will."

CHAPTER 31

MAGNUS

PAELSIA

Aron Lagaris had executed the rebel without hesitation. If not for this tangible proof of his ruthlessness, Magnus might have thought him merely a harmless peacock.

But Aron had a curious taste for blood. No wonder the king had appointed him kingsliege. He had seen in the boy what Magnus had not. Furious, Magnus slept not a wink all night, trying to make sense of everything. It still pained him that they needed to abandon the search for Jonas for now, but he reminded himself that meeting with Xanthus, learning more about the road, could bring him answers that would lead him ever closer to the Kindred.

The moon was high when they finally arrived at the road camp, dirty and weary from their three days' journey across the dusty Paelsian landscape. The Forbidden Mountains dominated the skyline, jagged and ominous black and gray forms with sharp, snow-covered tips reaching up into the night itself. This, of all the camps along the winding path of the road, was the most desolate of all, far from any inhabited villages.

The ground here was dry, cracked, and what little vegetation it bore was brown and withering. The air was not as cold as in Limeros, where one's breath would freeze into clouds as they spoke, but there was a dry chill here that nonetheless worked its way into Magnus's very bones.

It made him miss the more temperate climes of Auranos. So sunny and golden, and filled with light and life.

No, wait. What was he thinking? He *didn't* miss such things. He *didn't* care for Auranos. He looked forward to the day he'd return to Limeros and never look back. He much preferred frozen ponds to flower gardens.

"Your highness . . ." Aron said, his words strained as if he'd had to repeat himself several times to be heard. "Your highness!"

Magnus gripped the reins of his horse so tightly that they bit through the leather of his gloves. "What?"

"Not very hospitable a landscape, is it?"

On this much, they agreed. "No, it certainly isn't."

Small talk. Not his favorite pastime.

If they were to travel west, toward the Silver Sea, Paelsia would eventually become greener. That was where the locals planted their vineyards, the ones that grew such perfect grapes that they were sought after by every kingdom in the world for their wine. Every kingdom apart from Limeros, that was, which had forbidden intoxicating substances on orders of the king. The king had chosen not to create such laws in Auranos yet. To do so might very well tip Auranos to rebellion.

At the city of tents, they were greeted by a man with a bald head and a broad, greasy smile.

"This is such a great honor." The man grasped Magnus's gloved hand and kissed it. "Such a true honor to welcome you here, your highness." He nodded. "And Lord Aron. I've been greatly anticipating your visit."

"You are Xanthus?" Magnus asked.

The man's eyes widened and he began to laugh. "Oh, no. I am merely Franco Rossalas, assistant engineer on this site."

"*Assistant?* Where is Xanthus?"

"In his private tent, where he spends most of his time, your highness. Since you arrived later than we expected, he would prefer to speak with you there at first light, as he's already retired for the evening."

Impatience ignited within Magnus to hear such irrelevant drivel. "I was told he would be meeting me upon my arrival and now I find that he'd prefer sleep over civility? What greeting is this for the son of the king to meet only with the *assistant* engineer after my long and arduous journey here?"

Franco swallowed hard. "I will be sure to inform Xanthus personally of your displeasure. In the meantime, if you please, your highness, allow me to take you to see our progress here on his behalf."

For a moment, Magnus considered demanding that the sleeping fool be woken, but he held his tongue. Truth be told, he too was very tired. Perhaps their meeting could wait until tomorrow.

Franco led them to the road itself, explaining details as they walked and gesturing broadly with a flabby arm. Large swathes of mostly lifeless forest had been cut down to make way for the road. Trees with wide, brittle trunks lay throughout the camp like fallen giants. To the left the view was thick with sweaty, weary-looking men who toiled even in the darkness.

"Over here, we have men working constantly on the stone-work," he said, "which is a layer of the road, making it flat and easy for travel by wheeled vehicle."

"Honestly, Franco," Aron said with a sneer. "Such unnecessary explanations. Do you think Prince Magnus is a village idiot who doesn't understand road construction?"

Franco blanched. "Of course not, my liege. I just wanted to ex-plain it in a way that . . . that . . ."

"That even a village idiot could understand." Aron took out one of his cigarillos, lighting it off a nearby torch.

"I meant no disrespect of course. I beg for your forgiveness."

Magnus ignored the two and glanced off toward the clearing. The area was peppered with guards on foot and on horseback. A group of Paelsian slaves moved past where they stood, laden with heavy stones, their faces dirty, their clothes ripped. Those who didn't glance toward their superiors with fear instead cast bold glares of hatred.

It was a very different sight than the road crew based in Auranos.

Magnus watched until they disappeared behind the farthest tent. "When do the slaves rest?"

"Rest?" Franco repeated. "When they drop."

A young boy trudged past them with a stone that had to weigh half of what he did, his face a mask of pain and misery.

"How many have died?"

"Too many," Franco said with annoyance. "Paelsians are supposed to be hearty people, but quite honestly, I'm less than impressed by what I've seen here. They're lazy, selfish, and more often than not, only the whip will keep them focused."

While unquestionably effective, Magnus had never been fond of the whip as a form of punishment. "I wonder how you'd fare with the same amount of work. Would you be hearty enough to handle the stresses of such a job without the threat of a whipping?"

Franco's bushy brows moved upward, his face reddening. "Your grace, if it weren't for such discipline there would be little chance that the road would be finished in the timeline Xanthus demands from us, especially this section into the mountains."

"And is there any progress on the search?"

"Search?" The man frowned. "Search for what?"

"Never mind."

It would appear that the assistant engineer did not know the true purpose for this road, other than its being . . . a road. Such dangerous secrets would best remain hidden.

Aron's gaze slid past Franco's sweaty, pudgy face as they made their way back to the engineer's tent. A pretty girl was moving toward the tent, her arms heavily laden with firewood. She had light brown hair that fell down her back. Her figure, beneath the simple dress she wore, was thin but shapely. She was daring enough to look directly at Magnus with curiosity in her eyes as she passed without a word.

"And who is that beautiful creature?" Aron asked.

Franco glanced toward the girl. "That is my daughter, Eugeneia."

"Tell her to come here. I wish to be introduced to her."

Franco hesitated, glancing briefly at Magnus.

Magnus nodded to give permission for more introductions and Franco called out to the girl. She put down her heavy load, brushed off her hands on the front of her dress, and came to join them as they entered Franco's tent, shutting out some of the noise from outside.

"Yes, Father?"

"Eugeneia, I'd like you to meet our very important guests. This is Prince Magnus Damora and Lord Aron Lagaris."

Surprise lit her gaze and she immediately curtseyed deeply. "A true honor."

"Tell me, Eugeneia," Aron said, his eyes lighting up at the sight of her beauty up close, "how do you like spending so much time at this camp with your father?"

She flicked a glance toward Franco, then back at Aron. "May I be honest, Lord Aron?"

"Certainly."

"I don't care for it at all."

Franco clucked with disapproval and reached for the girl as if to pull her backward. Aron held up his hand to stop him.

"What don't you like?" he asked.

She studied the ground for a moment before raising her gaze to meet his. "My father is a brilliant engineer in his own right. It bothers me that he can make no decisions without approval from Xanthus, even if his decisions would improve things. It doesn't make sense to have one cruel, brutish man in charge of everything with absolutely no one able to disagree with him!"

Franco drew her to his side, tightening his arm around her shoulders. "Hush, girl. Your opinions are not necessary or appreciated. Do you want to insult our guests?"

A flush spread across her cheeks. "Please forgive me. I forgot my manners for a moment there."

"I appreciate your passion," Aron said. "It's so rare for someone to speak their mind so freely. It's refreshing, I think."

She bowed her head. "Thank you, my lord."

"Franco, I have a request," Aron said, his gaze still fixed on the girl.

"Yes?"

"I wish for your daughter to join me for a late meal in my tent."

Magnus rolled his eyes and turned away.

"Tonight?"

"When else?"

Franco cleared his throat, looking flustered by the request. "I suppose that is all right then."

"Father . . ." Eugeneia began, her tone doubtful.

"You will go with him." Franco's double chins lifted as he nodded. "Lord Aron is kind enough to take notice of you. The least you can do is share a meal with him in gratitude for such an honor."

The girl lowered her head. "Yes, of course."

The night stretched long and endless ahead of Magnus once he retired to his private tent. Thoughts of magic, of unsuccessful quests, of a dead mother, a slain rebel, a disrespectful exiled Watcher, and of a golden-haired, defiant princess filled his mind. He tossed and turned on his pallet. After a while, he decided that fresh air might help clear his head and rose.

He began to walk through the camp, past the long lines of tents of all sizes. He wondered which one belonged to the mysterious "cruel and brutish" Xanthus. Bonfires dotted the large clearing, sending sparks up into the darkening sky. Night-watch guards were set up to patrol while others slept, and they lined the area, their red uniforms easy to make out in the torch-lit surroundings.

Something hadn't sat right with him about Aron's request to dine with Eugeneia. He didn't trust the boy, not with a pretty girl like that. Not unchaperoned.

"It's none of your concern," he told himself.

This fact seemed to make little difference. He found himself at what he realized had been his destination all along.

Aron's tent was almost as big as Magnus's. Both were easily the size of a Paelsian cottage, with a seating area, a comfortable bed, a table to take meals at. Nothing like being at the Auranian palace, of course, but Magnus was accustomed to these sorts of austere accommodations.

He drew closer to the flap, glancing inside past the modest opening to see that Eugeneia had arrived and was seated at the table. Empty plates and platters lay discarded across the table. Their meal was over. Her hair was swept up off her shoulders into a braided coil and she'd changed her dress to one a bit finer than before.

"You must feel so honored right now," Aron was saying. "To be here with me."

He perched on the table next to where she sat. He ate a peach, slicing it with a fancy silver blade. The juice trickled down his chin before he wiped it away with the sleeve of his shirt.

She sat in a chair an arm's reach away from him. "Very honored," she said after a pause.

"The moment King Gaius met me, he knew I was destined for greatness. It's unheard of to be appointed to kingsliege at my age—especially not by a conquering king." He looked at her expectantly, waiting for her reaction.

"You must be very special, my lord."

"Do you want anything else to eat, my pet?"

"No—no, my lord. Much gratitude to you, but I really should go back. It's late." She glanced toward the flap and Magnus eased back into the shadows to keep from being seen.

"I don't want you to go."

"It'll be an early day tomorrow, and—"

Aron was on her in an instant, pulling her up out of the chair and pressing his mouth to hers.

She gasped against his lips as she wrenched away from him. "Lord Aron . . . I barely know you!"

"You know me well enough. You'll stay the night with me."

Her cheeks turned bright red and she wrapped her arms around her chest. "I don't think that's a good idea. My father—"

"Your father would give permission if I asked him. You think he wouldn't?" Aron gave her a wide, toothy smile. "He knows how important I am to the king. I do very special assignments for King Gaius—things not everyone would do. I take care of his problems under the cloak of night."

"Problems?"

"Stupid, ignorant people that stand in the way of what he wants. I've proven myself so fully to King Gaius that he would allow me anything I desire." His gaze swept the length of her with appreciation. "And right now I desire you."

"I must go." Eugeneia turned toward the flap.

Aron caught her arm. "I like a girl who plays hard to get, but my patience wears thin."

"I'm not the kind of girl who stays with a man she only just met, even if he is an important lord."

"Actually," his grip increased, "you are exactly the kind of girl I tell you to be."

"No, Lord Aron. I'm—"

Aron let go of her only to strike her hard across her right cheek.

Magnus tensed but stayed silent, watching. Waiting for the right moment.

Eugeneia pressed her palm against her face, now backing away from Aron toward the table. Her wide eyes glistened with tears. "Please don't hurt me."

Aron loomed over her. "Perhaps I didn't make myself entirely clear. I chose you above any of the Paelsian whores out there who'd jump at the chance to warm my bed tonight. Don't make me regret my decision."

He grabbed her tightly and drew her to his chest. His hands slid down her sides as he began to pull at her skirts.

But then he staggered back from her, looking down to see the tip of a knife imbedded in his thigh. It was the dagger he had used to cut the peach—Eugeneia must have lifted it. Magnus was impressed. He hadn't even seen her do it.

Aron glared down at her with pain and fury as he yanked it out, letting it clatter to the tabletop. He clutched the girl by her throat and slammed her down against the table.

Magnus's gaze moved to the dagger for an instant before he closed the distance in four paces and curved his hand firmly around Aron's upper arm.

"Not a good idea," he said.

Aron cast a look back at him. "This ignorant bitch cut me."

"Yes, she did. Let go of her." The best way to deal with this drunken fool was not to be overtly stern or forceful. Instead, he gave Aron a smile. "She's meaningless."

His eyes blazed. "I wanted her. And I get what I want."

"I can find you many girls, much more beautiful than this one. One, two, three at a time. Your choice. This one has proven she's not worth any more of your energy." Magnus eyed Eugeneia. "Isn't that right?"

She trembled with fear, but there was something harder in her eyes. Hatred for both of them in equal measure. "Yes, your highness. I'm not good enough for Lord Aron."

"Then I suggest that you leave."

She pushed herself up off the table and ran from the tent. Aron watched her flee with a dark look.

"How much have you had to drink tonight?" Magnus asked. From Aron's unfocused gaze and the stench of his breath, the boy was as drunk as Magnus had ever seen him.

"Enough."

"Really? That's too bad. I was going to join you in another round." Magnus tore a strip from the silk table covering. "Here, let me help you with that wound. Doesn't seem to be too bad."

Aron let him pad his wound, his face pained. "You know, I *could* use another drink."

"Thought you might agree." When he finished with the bandage, Magnus grabbed a flacon of wine. He poured two glasses and handed one to Aron.

Aron downed it in one audible gulp. "I'm ashamed that you witnessed that, your highness."

Magnus waved a hand as he took a sip of the wine. He'd not often indulged before; it was forbidden in Limeros. The wine was sweet, smooth, and not unpleasant. "Don't be. It only goes to show that women are volatile."

"Stupid, too." Aron downed his second glass after Magnus poured it for him. "Much gratitude, your grace."

"The more you drink, the less your wound will hurt."

"I hope you're right." Aron grimaced, touching the bandage gingerly. "I would have thought you angry with me for attempting to bed the girl."

Bed? Looked more like attempted rape to Magnus. "Not at all." Magnus forced his smile to stay firm. "She was an attractive little thing. Just not for you."

"Women are deceptive creatures of darkness whose beauty

lures us close enough so they can carve their claws into our flesh." A glint of humor lit Aron's gaze as he took another deep gulp of the wine. "Which is why they must be declawed as soon as possible, as you've done with Cleo."

"Sharp claws indeed." The mention of the princess, who had been on his mind far more than he liked while on this journey, had Magnus tipping his glass back and draining it before he realized what he was doing. "I'm curious about something, Lord Aron."

"What's that?"

"I confess, I don't know much about what you've done as kings-liege to prove yourself to my father. What you said earlier to Eugeneia—have you killed in the king's name? Apart from the rebel the other day?"

Aron nodded grimly. "I have."

Magnus leaned closer and offered the edge of a smile to set the boy's mind at ease. "I think we've managed to put aside our many differences and become close friends during this journey."

Aron's brows rose. "You think so?"

"Yes, of course. I would like to be friends with you. Friends share secrets. They lean on each other for support in times of need."

"It's been a long time since I had a friend like that," Aron said wistfully, swirling his wine.

"Me too." Not since Lucia, when she could look at him without revulsion tainting her opinion of him. The reminder of her was a dull pain in the center of his chest.

Even still, the world had taken on a shimmering edge that brought with it a sliver of light-headedness. Paelsian wine was very strong—it could inebriate a man with only one glass.

Cleo liked wine. He'd watched her drink a great deal of it on the night of their wedding, and also during the tour. Perhaps it was all that had helped her tolerate the pain of being near someone she hated so completely.

"My first assignment for the king weighs heaviest on me." Aron looked up at Magnus.

"Tell me more."

Aron turned away, his grip tightening on his glass. "The king swore me to secrecy."

"May I guess what he asked you to do? If I'm correct, I promise to forgive you."

That hopefulness again lit in Aron's eyes. "Really?"

"Really. After all, I took the princess away from you. I suppose that means I owe you a favor."

Aron considered this. "Very well. You can guess, but I doubt you'll be correct."

Magnus nodded, then he leaned over and snatched up the dagger Aron had dropped to the ground. He placed it between them on the wooden surface of the table. The jewels embedded in the hilt sparkled in the candlelight. The wavy blade was still coated in blood and sticky peach juice from before.

Aron stared at it as if seeing it for the first time.

"This is your dagger?" Magnus asked softly.

There was a noticeable hesitation before he spoke. "It is."

"It is identical to the dagger used to kill the queen; the evidence my father the king felt pointed entirely to the rebel leader. I had believed it was one-of-a-kind, but it appears you have its twin still in your possession. Just how many of these daggers exist, Lord Aron?"

Aron's brows were tightly drawn together. "There is a reason for this, I assure you."

"That's not an answer to my question. How many of these jeweled daggers exist? Two? One the rebel used to kill my mother and another in your personal collection? Or are there *three* daggers, Aron? If I found Jonas Agallon, would I see that he still had the dagger you left in his brother's throat?"

A chill had spread through the tent, but perhaps it was only Magnus's blood cooling with each word he spoke.

Lord Aron might have the appointment of kingsliege, but he was not a skilled knight. He was not a capable fighter. He had no great capacity to lie about something so important. He was only a boy who had aspirations of greatness and a taste for blood when it served him.

When the sweat that now beaded on Aron's forehead told more than words ever could, Magnus continued. "Ever since you executed the rebel I've had my suspicions. But they were only whispers in the back of my mind. You didn't want Brion Radenos to keep talking, to convince me that Jonas had nothing to do with my mother's murder. Because he didn't, did he? You were the one who killed her. You killed her at my father's command."

The accusation left a bitter taste in his mouth, but he felt the truth of it.

Such painful truth.

Aron eyed the dagger rather than meet Magnus's gaze. "She was a deceptive woman, one working hard to hold the king back from achieving his full glory. Cold and incapable of love, he told me, even toward her own children. She could have destroyed him. Destroyed everything."

"So you agreed to be her assassin."

"Yes. One does not argue with the king."

"No, not if one values his life." Magnus blew out a long sigh and attempted to steady himself, to shake off the mild inebriation caused by the wine. He placed the dagger down upon the table. "Believe it or not, I do understand. My father makes people do things they might not agree with. He manipulates them for his own gain and he's been very successful at it."

Even his own son.

"You said you'd forgive me," Aron said, his voice strained.

"I did say that, didn't I? But how can I forgive anyone for something like this? You murdered my mother." Magnus unsheathed his sword and pointed it at the boy.

Aron snatched the dagger off the table and held it out in front of him. "I will defend myself!"

"As you absolutely should."

"The king will give me protection again you. Against anyone who means me harm. He has seen how valuable I am."

"Is it something in the blood of *all* Auranians that they're so quick to believe my father's lies?"

Tears now spilled from Aron's eyes, the sight of which sickened Magnus. "Pull yourself together, you pathetic fool. This is no way for a kingsliege to behave."

"Forgive me, your highness. I am so, so sorry for what I did."

The fire within Magnus at the knowledge that this vapid peacock had been the murderer of his mother, that he'd helped the king frame another and kept the truth of any of it from Magnus, receded slightly. Killing Aron in wine-fueled vengeance would give him as little satisfaction as squashing a cockroach.

"We will take this matter up with my father when we return to the palace."

His father had much to answer for. He lowered his sword to his side and turned away toward the flap of the tent.

In the reflection of a silver goblet, he saw Aron lunge at his back, the dagger still clutched in his raised hand.

Magnus turned. He deflected the blade with his left forearm and with his right hand thrust his sword through Aron's chest.

The boy hung there, impaled, his eyes wide, and he stared at Magnus as if surprised. Such an expression on one who had fully meant to kill him only angered Magnus further. He twisted the blade and Aron let out a tormented cry, the sound of a dying animal, before the life finally left his eyes. With a sharp yank, Magnus pulled out the blade and the lord dropped bonelessly to the ground.

Magnus stood there for a few silent moments, staring down at his mother's killer while Aron's blood began to pool by his left boot. His glassy eyes stared up at the ceiling of the tent.

Just as Magnus had expected, there was no true victory in this death. Only emptiness.

But he now knew the truth. He'd never felt such hate before in his entire life. Hate for a man he'd always looked up to, even if he didn't agree with every one of his decisions; a man who wasn't weak, who did what he needed to do, who achieved power and glory with violence, intimidation, intelligence, and brute strength.

Once Magnus had aspired to be exactly like his father.

No more.

CHAPTER 32

JONAS

PAELSIA

The rebels made camp a mile from the line of tents by the Blood Road, not daring to light a fire. They watched and waited, staying huddled as a group for warmth, until the sun began to breach the gigantic mountains. Even the golden hawk that seemed to follow Jonas everywhere perched in the forest of brittle, leafless trees, waiting along with them.

"What is she?" he whispered to himself, looking up at her. "What does she want with us? With me?"

The hawk gave no answers. Instead, she flew away moments before they were ready to put their plan into action.

Jonas gave the order to move, and as silently as shadows, the forty-seven rebels spread out and entered the camp in their search for Magnus and Xanthus. Since there was no way for so many to stick together during the attack, the plan was to meet at a designated spot three hours' journey from here at nightfall.

They had their targets. They knew their task. Nothing would

distract them. And anyone who got in their way would die.

If all went perfectly, no one would even know they'd been there.

Then again, Jonas never expected this to go perfectly. He was prepared for obstacles. And so were his rebels.

Only minutes after their entry into the camp, a warning sounded out.

And then it was madness.

Guards began to spill from their tents and stations, swords in hand. Lysandra nocked arrow after arrow into her bow, letting them go like a predator lying in the shadows, silent death catching her marks precisely in the throat or chest.

"Go now while you can," she commanded Jonas as he fought off a guard, "and if you find Lord Aron before I do, kill him—and make it hurt."

The promise of blood—of the vengeance he'd craved for so long—fueled him like nothing else. He slammed the guard in the throat with his forearm and the guard dropped to the ground, unconscious. "Good luck, Lys. If this goes badly, I'll see you and Brion in the everafter."

"You really think that's where any of us are headed?" She actually gave him a grin, baring straight white teeth, her face lit by the golden glow of the dawn. It jarred him to realize that Brion had been right—this girl was absolutely gorgeous. "I'll see you in the darklands, Agallon. Save a demon or two for me."

She held his gaze for only a moment longer before slipping away from him without another word.

And Jonas went hunting for his prey amidst the confusion and turmoil. His main targets were Magnus and the road engineer, but he hoped to find Aron as well. Now Aron had Brion's as well as Tomas's death to answer for in blood.

He glanced into each tent he passed, roughly fighting off any-one he came across. And almost *too* easily the guards went down. They were so used to lording over weaponless and weakened slaves in this private, secluded location that they hadn't been prepared for an attack of this magnitude at the crack of dawn—nearly fifty rebels ready to do whatever it took to gain an advantage against the king who would enslave their brothers and sisters, mothers and fathers.

Jonas wiped a spray of blood from his face and continued on. He pushed open the next tent flap, and his gaze fell on someone he recognized immediately.

Aron Lagaris lay sleeping on the ground. Rage lit within him at the memory of this bastard killing his friend. Killing his brother.

"That drunk last night, were you?" Jonas snarled. "Wake up. I want you to know that I'm the one who ends your life."

He took another step, entering fully into the tent, now frown-ing. Aron's eyes were open and staring. The front of his shirt was stained with blood—blood that soaked into the dirt floor.

The realization hit him hard. Aron was already dead.

Someone grabbed him from behind, a strong arm crushing his throat.

"You think Paelsian scum like you can attack us so easily, that we won't be able to kill every last one of you?" It was a guard, a large one with bad breath. "Think again, rebel."

Jonas arched his blade upward, but the guard caught his wrist, wrenching it to the side to break the bone with a sharp crack. Jonas roared in pain and lost his concentration for a split second.

That was all it took.

The guard brought his own blade down, sinking it straight into Jonas's heart.

Then he yanked out the blade and shoved Jonas forward. Jonas stumbled to the ground hard, only a few feet from Aron. He looked up, gasping, his vision swirling. The guard was a hulking black silhouette surrounded by morning light.

He wiped the blood off his hands. "You honestly thought you could stop us with your little group of savages? Gonna go kill me a few more before breakfast." He was laughing as he left the tent.

Jonas's chest bloomed with agonizing, searing pain. His life bled out onto the tent floor, oozing bright red, sliding across the ground to mingle with that of Aron's.

"Brion..." Jonas's throat was thick, his eyes burning. A memory—his and Brion's childhood, running through the vineyard, stealing sweet, plump grapes, and being chased by Jonas's angry father, who'd—so unlike his son—accepted his destiny without a fight, who'd always followed the rules set forth by Chief Basilius, even when these same rules left his family's bellies empty.

Catching up to the always rebellious Tomas, who laughed at their antics—Tomas, who never followed a single rule in his life unless he made it himself. And Felicia, his bossy sister, who just stood with her hands on her hips, shaking her head and warning Jonas that he'd get in trouble one day for not toeing the line. Felicia was strong—strong enough to survive without him. Strong like their mother had been before the wasting disease had taken her. Jonas had heard rumors that Cleo's sister had died of a similar ailment.

I never told her that. I should have told her.

Images of the princess with golden hair slid through his mind. He was in the cave again, kissing her as if he had no choice, confused by such overwhelming feelings toward a girl he'd previously despised and wanted dead. But even the coldest hate can shift into something warmer if given enough time, just as an ugly caterpillar can turn into a beautiful butterfly.

Images of Lysandra, smiling, her unexpected beauty this morning like a blow to his gut. The flashing of her brown eyes when she was angry, arguing, always giving him a hard time. But he was glad he'd accepted her as one of his rebels because she was so skilled, so determined, so damn passionate she lit a fire inside of him with only a few words.

And now he would die staring into the glazed eyes of Aron Lagaris. For months, Jonas had wanted vengeance toward him so much, more than anything else. And now the boy he'd hated more than anyone else in the world was nothing more than a shell—an empty shell.

Death solved nothing. It was only an end.

And now his own end had come.

A small surge of light caught the corner of his fading vision. Someone had entered the tent. His last gasps of breath were so slight he would already look dead to anyone but the most skilled healer.

A figure sank to her knees next to him. A warm hand pressed to his forehead, another to his mouth to open it. He couldn't resist, couldn't speak. He couldn't even blink.

Something was pushed into his mouth. Small pebbles.

The pebbles heated on his tongue until they felt like burning coals. They melted like lava, burning him, spreading out over his entire tongue, his mouth, and down his throat.

He arched up off the ground as the fire slid to his belly and expanded from there—torture. In his last moments of life, someone was torturing him.

A firm hand pressed against his chest to keep him from lurching upward as his body convulsed.

Like a sun setting behind the horizon, slowly, slowly the pain receded until it was only a glow in the center of his body. His breath came quicker now. His heart pounded.

His heart? But how was this possible?

It had been sliced through, but now it sounded strong. He felt its beat—fast and hard, but steady. His vision cleared just as slowly, brightening and coming into focus until he could see who it was who'd been tormenting him.

The girl's hair shimmered like platinum—paler even than Cleo's. Her skin shone with sunlit gold and her eyes were light, a silvery color a few shades darker than her hair. She was wrapped in a tapestry, one pulled from the wall of this very tent. Otherwise, she was naked.

"I'm very angry at you," she said. "You went and got yourself killed."

His mouth was so dry. "I'm dead. This is my entry to the darklands."

She let out a sigh, one that sounded annoyed. "Not the darklands, although I'm sure you're headed there one day soon. Another few moments and these grape seeds wouldn't have been able to do anything for you."

Jonas studied her face, the long line of her pale throat.

"Who are you?" he whispered.

She regarded him steadily. "My name is Phaedra."

"Phaedra," he repeated, licking his parched lips. "Did you say grape seeds? What are you talking about?"

"Earth magic has pulled you back from the precipice of death. Earth magic can either heal or kill, depending on who wields it. You're lucky I like you."

He looked down at himself, pulling his ruined shirt to the side and wiping at the blood. So much blood, but there was no longer a wound beneath. His skin had healed. His body was whole again, including the wrist the guard had broken.

Had she said *earth magic*?

But magic . . . it didn't exist. He'd never believed.

This was impossible. And yet . . .

His gaze snapped to hers. "You saved my life."

"I did. I tried to resist, to continue to watch from afar. I still don't know if you'll be any good to me—to *us*. Getting captured is one thing. At least there's still hope for escape. But dying . . ." She groaned and placed her hands on her hips. "I couldn't help myself. I had to shift from my hawk form, and now—well, now I'm stuck here. You're lucky I always keep a few healing seeds hidden in my feathers for emergencies!"

This girl was mad. Completely mad. "Hawk form?"

"Yes, that is what Watchers can do."

His eyes bugged. *Watchers?*

"Here," she said. "Since I can no longer shift form, I'll show you proof of what I am another way. Or . . . what I was until now."

She pulled at the tapestry she'd used to cover herself. The cloth slipped from her chest and he gawked at it. Not for the reasons he would ever have gawked at a girl's breasts—although Phaedra's were the loveliest he'd ever seen in his life.

There was a mark over her heart—a swirl the size of his palm—like molten gold dancing on her flesh.

"It'll turn darker in the years to come," she said wistfully. "As my magic begins to fade."

He couldn't find his voice to speak, could barely find the air to breathe. Could this be true?

The hawk—the one who perched near camp every day. The one

who'd followed him here into Paelsia. The one he'd tried to ignore. Had it been Phaedra?

Magic was real? Watchers were real?

It flew in the face of everything he'd believed. But seeing it, seeing *her*, with his own eyes—

Jonas jumped as he felt the sharp tip of a sword press against his throat. He condemned himself for losing focus, for being utterly distracted by Phaedra's strange swirling mark and the proof of magic that caused his thoughts to become a jumbled, confused tangle.

His newly healed heart sank as he flicked his gaze toward Prince Magnus, who had silently and stealthily entered the tent.

"Apologies," the prince said. "I certainly wouldn't want to interrupt *this*."

Jonas winced. "What a coincidence. I've been looking for you."

"The feeling's entirely mutual, rebel."

Rebel. How were his rebels faring outside this tent? Concern tore through him. Lysandra would have to lead them on her own for now. He hoped she was having great success in finding Xanthus.

"I just saved his life and now you threaten it?" Phaedra pulled her tapestry back up to cover herself. "That's very rude."

The prince's face was shadowed. "You have no idea just how rude I can be. Shall I show you?"

"Take that sword away from his throat right now!"

The sword pressed harder against Jonas's windpipe. The barest of movements would sever it. Jonas was still so weak from blood loss, and the violent, magical healing had sapped his strength even more. He could barely move enough to protect himself, let alone Phaedra.

Magnus's gaze dropped to the edge of Phaedra's tapestry. "Is what you said to the rebel true? Are you a Watcher?"

"I am. And you're the son of the King of Blood, who searches

for the Kindred. Does he even know what he'll find if he's successful in locating it? Do *you*?"

Jonas let out an unwilling gasp as Magnus's sword nicked his
skin and a warm ooze of blood trickled down his throat.

"Much gratitude for the confirmation the treasure exists."
Magnus's gaze narrowed. "I must admit, I've had my doubts. How
exactly do I find it?"

She raised an eyebrow. "Your sister's magic is just like Eva's
was, isn't it? She's the key to all of this."

Magnus's expression darkened. "How can she locate it? And
when? Must the road be finished first?"

"Questions—so many questions." She cocked her head, studying him. "All I can tell you is she's in danger. Her magic puts her at
great risk. If it overwhelms her, all will be lost before anything can
be found—and I know you don't want that. I believe Lucia means
more to you than any treasure. And I know how to help her. Shall
I tell you?"

His eyes narrowed. "Speak."

"There is a ring that was forged in the Sanctuary from the pur-
est magic to help the original sorceress control the Kindred and
her own *elementia*. This ring is closer than you might expect."

"Tell me more." His words were sharp and eager now. "Where
can I find it?"

"If I tell you, you will release Jonas and you will have your father
cease construction of this road."

"And if you don't tell me, I'll slit his throat right now."

The part of her mark visible above the edge of the tapestry
swirled and brightened.

The sword's hilt began to glow orange. Magnus released it with
a gasp of pain.

"Wrong answer," Phaedra said. "Perhaps you're not ready for my help yet. Pity. Mark my words, one day you'll wish you'd been more amenable to my advice. Jonas, we must go."

She turned to the flap of the tent, but escape was blocked by someone new standing in their way.

He was tall, with bronze hair that swept his shoulders. His eyes were the color of copper. He was easily twice Jonas's age.

Phaedra eyes widened at the sight of him. "Xanthus."

He smiled at her. "It has been a very long time, Phaedra."

"Too long."

"You knew I was here, didn't you?"

She nodded slowly. "Yes."

"But you told no one else."

"The others think you're dead. And you've done a very good job of keeping yourself hidden all these years."

"But not from you."

"No, not from me."

"I have missed you, sister. So much."

"And I've missed you. Even though I hated you for leaving. For doing what *she* told you to do."

Pain entered his copper-colored eyes. "I never meant to hurt you."

"I know." She jumped into his arms, hugging him tight. "You can make it up to me. Leave this place. You can help me . . . help us. We need safe passage out of this camp."

Jonas tried to follow along, but he was lost. This man—Xanthus. He was the road engineer the rebels had targeted. But he was a Watcher too? Phaedra's brother? How was any of this possible?

"I was told you would come here," Xanthus said, still in Phaedra's embrace.

"Who told you?" She pulled back and looked up into his face, touching his cheek. But then her face paled. "She's evil, Xanthus. Why can't anyone see that as clearly as I do?"

"Melenia does what she must to save us all," Xanthus said. "And it's now, Phaedra. We're so close." He clasped her face between his hands. "And I'm so sorry. I wish you could be here when it happens. What we've waited so long for."

"Where else will I be? I've sacrificed my immortality, just as you did. We can be together again. The past is the past. Let's leave it there."

Xanthus's eyes narrowed. "I'm afraid not, my sister. You know far too much. I've been given very specific instructions from Melenia. And I am at her command—I always have been. I always will be."

His hands began to glow with golden light and Phaedra drew in another gasp that sounded pained this time.

"What are you doing to her?" Jonas demanded. "Unhand her!"

Magnus watched all this silently, with his arms crossed over his chest, a deep frown creasing his brow.

"Nothing can stop this," Xanthus said. "It is for the best. Try to remember that, my sweet sister. I did this because it's the right thing to do."

The glow covered Phaedra's entire form as Jonas and Magnus looked on, stunned by the display of magic.

But what kind of magic was this?

Jonas surged forward, grabbing hold of Xanthus's arm to pry it away from Phaedra. Xanthus grabbed Jonas by his bloody shirt and launched him backward. He flew across the room and hit the wooden table hard, breaking it.

Phaedra fell to her knees on the floor of the tent, her eyes glazed as they met Jonas's from where he now crouched ten paces away.

"I'm sorry," she whispered. "I failed. I wish I could have . . ."

She breathed out one last breath and the life left her eyes. A moment later the swirling of her mark spread to cover her entire body, and she disappeared in a flash of shimmering light.

Xanthus has vanished from the tent as well.

Jonas stared in shock at the place the Watcher had been only moments before. Then he flinched as the cold, sharp tip of Magnus's sword touched his throat.

"On your feet, Agallon."

Jonas forced himself up, and he eyed the prince with unbridled fury—the sour taste of it rising in his throat. "You act as if you have not just witnessed a miracle . . . and a tragedy."

"I'll admit, it was an unexpected sight before the sun has fully risen." Behind the prince's droll tone, Jonas heard a quaking. The sight of the Watcher's death—is that what it had been? Was Phaedra dead?—had shaken Magnus too. "But I'm recovering quickly. Time for a little trip to my father's dungeon along with your rebel friends. He'll be very pleased I've finally captured you."

How could he stand there and pretend that none of this mattered? That the world would never be the same? Watchers were not simply legend. Magic was real. Jonas was reeling. "I didn't murder your mother."

"I know. Aron Lagaris did."

Jonas shot a look toward Aron's body, and his gaze snapped back to Magnus's. "He killed my brother and my best friend."

"And now he's dead. He received the same end I originally planned for you. Although, I must admit, I planned on making you suffer quite a bit longer."

"It was supposed to be my blade that took his life!"

Magnus offered him a thin, humorless smile. "Get over it."

Suddenly, there was a scream from outside the tent. Many screams and terrified cries that no longer sounded like the familiar sounds of battle. It only took a moment to discover the reason why.

"Fire!" someone yelled.

A line of flames began to snake around the circumference of the tent, as if the earth itself had been set ablaze.

Magnus pulled his sword away from Jonas's throat and moved swiftly to the flap of the tent, pushing it aside.

The camp had ignited. Orange and yellow flames lit up the area, drowning out the glow of dawn over the mountains, torching the dry, fallen trees, the piles of wood, the tents. Guards and slaves alike ran screaming. Some were on fire—flames that turned gold and silver and a bright and unnatural blue. They screamed in agony as the fire scorched their flesh before the violent and overwhelming fire transformed their bodies to crystal that exploded into a million shards of broken glass.

Jonas stared at the sight of the deaths with disbelief.

This was no normal fire ignited during a battle.

This—this was a horrible, destructive, deadly magic. Fire magic.

"What is this?" Magnus said, his voice rising in fear.

Blood spilled on the Blood Road. Three times. Three disasters.

A tornado, an earthquake, a wildfire.

Jonas's newly healed heart pounded faster. He came up next to the prince. "Do you believe in fate, Prince Magnus? I never did before, but . . . do you?"

"Why do you ask?"

"Just curious." Jonas slammed his forehead against the prince's face. He'd been so still, so weakened since his resurrection. It had taken time to get his full strength back.

But it was finally back.

He grasped Magnus's sword, then brought his elbow up into the prince's face and hit his nose hard. Blood gushed and Magnus roared in pain. Jonas snatched the sword completely away from Magnus and swung it around to slice the other boy's throat. But Magnus was also fast, and he blocked the strike with his forearm.

By now, the tent was engulfed in flames. The fire licked at them both, so hot it burned.

Jonas spun the sword around and drove the hilt into Magnus's gut, earning a satisfying grunt of pain. But before he could manage another blow, Magnus grabbed for a handful of Jonas's hair, tearing it out by its roots and kneeing him in the chest. He then managed to yank the sword completely from Jonas's grip.

"We need get out of here or we'll die," Magnus growled.

"I came here prepared to die today. In fact, I already did."

Jonas tackled Magnus and lurched both of them backward. As they fell, Jonas angled himself so that it was Magnus's head that slammed against the side of the burning table. It was hard enough to stun the prince, and he knelt on the ground, gasping for breath, sword in hand.

Still, Magnus grasped hold of Jonas before he was able to slip away.

"I have a dungeon just for you, rebel," he promised.

Five guards approached the burning tent, shouting Magnus's name.

"Here!" he called out to them. "I have a prisoner!"

"Wrong," Jonas snarled, using every last piece of his strength to wrench away from Magnus's grip, yanking the sword away from the prince again. He brought the blade down, but Magnus rolled out of the way just in time.

Jonas swore, eyeing the approaching guards who loomed at the tent's burning entry.

"Seize him!" Magnus yelled.

"Perhaps another time, your highness." He'd come here to take Magnus as a prisoner, but if he tarried another moment, it would be the other way around.

Without wasting another moment, he cut through the side of the tent and burst out into the chaos outside, ducking and hiding to avoid being seen by any guards through the magical wildfire that raged all around them.

To his right, he saw an older, bald man and a young girl huddled close, away from the carnage, looking around with fear and confusion. The tents were all on fire now. The road camp was an inferno.

Strewn everywhere on the ground were burning bodies—guard or rebel, their blood spilled across the road as if it was a violent and fiery canvas. Some had turned to the strange crystal form after being touched by the fire—broken and scattered across the dusty ground.

Where is Lysandra?

It was his first coherent thought.

He strained his eyes to find her, to find any rebels, but he saw no one apart from those that lay dead on the ground. He couldn't count. He wasn't sure how many had fallen.

The body of a dead girl with long, dark hair lay across his path, an arrow pierced through her heart. He stopped breathing completely at the sight of her.

"No. Please, no." He crouched down, pushing her hair off her face.

But it was not Lysandra. It was Onoria.

A loss . . . a horrible loss to them all. Onoria was an incredibly brave and clever rebel.

After closing her eyes, he got up quickly and ducked behind a tent. He couldn't stay here. If he did, he would be killed, either by the fire that continued to rage or by a guard.

"Lys," he whispered. "Where are you? Damn it. Where?"

She had to be alive. Lysandra Barbas was not meant to die tonight.

No, he decided firmly. She *was* alive.

And if she was, he *would* find her.

CHAPTER 33

LYSANDRA

AURANOS

Lysandra stumbled as a guard shoved her into a dark and crowded cell, and she fell hard to the dirt floor. The stone walls were damp and smelled of mildew and death. At the top of the tall wall, there was a small window no bigger than her hand, just large enough to let in a ray of sunshine, taunting her with the freedom that had finally been stolen from her.

Only five of them had made it to their destination alive. Phineas had spoken up during the trip to the Auranian dungeon, mouthed off to a guard, and had his throat cut immediately, his body tossed off the side of a bridge.

The rest remained silent after this. Lysandra held tightly on to Tarus's sweaty hand most of the way. The young boy was terrified, but he tried to be brave. For her. She didn't know what had become of Jonas, but she refused to believe he was dead.

Why? So many of them had fallen.

But maybe Jonas was one of those who'd gotten away. Maybe

he was, even now, mounting a rescue attempt.

No. She wouldn't let herself think of such things that could only lead to disappointment.

If she was going to get out of here, she'd have to do it herself. Somehow.

She looked up at the tiny window bleakly. It was hopeless and she knew it. A tear slid down her cheek.

"Little Lys, don't cry." The familiar voice reached out from the darkness.

Her head snapped to the boy sitting in the corner.

"Gregor?" She couldn't believe her own eyes. She ran to her brother's side, dropping down next to him. She grabbed his dirty hands in hers to prove this was real. "You're here. You're alive!"

"Barely." He tried to smile. "It's so good to see you, sister."

"I thought you were dead! I searched for you in the road camps, but I couldn't find you anywhere!"

"I escaped and made my way to Limeros but was captured a couple weeks ago. They carted me all the way here on orders from the prince himself. Been in here ever since. Not much longer, though. I think they're finally finished asking me questions. They never seem satisfied with my answers. Only my death will please them now."

"Don't talk like that. This is what I needed, Gregor." Her heart grew lighter than it had in days. In weeks! "This is the sign I needed that everything's going to be all right. We're alive, we're together again, and we're going to get out of this."

His gaze grew distant. "That's what she told me, too. She always told me to have hope. I wish I could see her again, but she hasn't visited me for weeks."

Lysandra glanced around the small, stinking cell, her gaze

moving over the other prisoners, some of whom were sleeping. "See who?"

"The girl made of gold and silver."

"What?"

"She told me her name is Phaedra. She's visited me in my dreams, told me to be patient. That I will find new hope. I figure she must have been talking about you. They put you in my cell, Lys. *Mine*. In a place as big as this—that has to mean something, right?"

"Who is she? What do you mean she visited you in your dreams?"

He looked past her, his expression wistful. "She's a Watcher, little Lys. She told me not to despair. That I could still make a difference . . . and that there were others like me who could help. I thought she was mad."

"A Watcher visited you in your dreams," Lysandra said with disbelief. "Perhaps she's not the one who's mad."

He laughed, the sound dry and brittle. "You could be right."

"What else did this Watcher tell you?"

Gregor's brows drew together and he squeezed Lysandra's hands. "She said when the sorceress's blood is spilled and the sacrifice is made, they will finally be free." Her brother's haunted eyes met hers. "And the world will burn. That's what she said, little Lys. *The world will burn*."

CHAPTER 34

CLEO

AURANOS

"My son has returned to the palace." The king's words wrapped around Cleo's throat like an icy glove, stopping her in her tracks as she moved through the halls. "I'm sure you've greatly anticipated his return."

She turned slowly to see King Gaius standing in the shadows, accompanied by Cronus and his dreadful hunting dogs.

"With bated breath, your majesty."

"He captured a group of rebels who attacked one of my road camps. Those that did not fall under his blade have accompanied him back here for public execution."

Jonas. Her heart skipped a beat with both dread and anticipation.

"I feel safer already." She forced a smile to her lips.

"I'm sure you do." The king studied her with those cold, serpentine eyes. "I'm watching you, princess."

"As I am watching you," she replied sweetly.

"Remember one very important thing. You have no power here and you never will again. You continue to live at my whim, but I can take that courtesy away at any time without warning—just as I did with your little friend. What was her name again? Mira?"

Her blood turned to ice. "Good day, your majesty."

She continued down the hall smoothly until she turned the next corner. There she pressed up against the wall and commanded herself to stop trembling.

"He will not defeat me," she whispered, angrily wiping her tears away. "He thinks he has power, but it's sand falling through his fingers. He will lose it all and have nothing left."

But she knew her days were numbered. The wedding tour was over. The shine of the false "romance" between Magnus and herself had begun to fade. Her allies had dwindled to two boys—one who couldn't bear to look her in the eye after her rejection of him, and another who might be dead or bound for execution.

Cleo rubbed her ring, staring down at it and praying—though not to the Goddess Cleiona, not after what she'd learned of the thieving, power-hungry Watcher—for a way through the darkness that stretched out before her. "Please. Father, please help me. I don't know what to do. Am I a fool to believe that I have any chance against someone like King Gaius?"

The book *Song of the Sorceress* had told her more about Eva—that she could work magic with all four elements as easy as breathing. And at the end of the book there were two lines that had stayed with Cleo.

A thousand years after her death, the sorceress shall be reborn as a mortal beyond the Sanctuary's veil. Once awakened, her magic will reveal the hidden treasure sought by both mortals and immortals alike.

Eva had been killed by her greedy sisters, Cleiona and Valoria, who'd stolen the Kindred and used its power to become goddesses.

That was a thousand years ago.

A sorceress reborn—one who could harness all four parts of *elementia* with ease.

"There's something strange about that girl." Her attendant Helena had been speaking with her sister only two days after Cleo's return from the wedding tour, not realizing Cleo could hear them. *"The princess was tutored by a witch."*

"A witch?"

"The king chose the witch himself for the task, but now I think she's dead. I saw her before they took her away. Her face was filled with fear. She whispered about fire and ice. She believed Princess Lucia to be evil."

Servants did gossip about the most fantastical things. Yet Lucia had set the library alight. . . .

"Magic," Cleo whispered. "Is that what you were doing that day, Lucia?"

Was the gossip of servants true this time?

Eva's ring—the sorceress's ring—had glowed when Cleo touched Lucia. It hadn't done that with anyone else. Only with the stone wheel, said to be connected to the Watchers.

There had to be more to this.

Cleo moved through the labyrinthine hallways toward Lucia's chambers. No one stopped her. No one even noticed her.

What are you even thinking, you fool? she chastised herself as her steps quickened. *You believe the King of Blood's daughter—Magnus's sister—could be the sorceress reborn?*

At the door to Lucia's chamber, Cleo came to a halt. Her heart pounded loud in her ears as she raised her clenched fist and knocked. Then she waited.

But there was no response. Perhaps Lucia wasn't here.

Just before Cleo turned away, she heard something from within the room.

Someone was crying.

Summoning her courage, Cleo grabbed the handle of the door and turned it, pushing forward on the heavy oak barrier to peer inside.

Princess Lucia stood facing the open balcony, her hair a raven-black spill down her back. Her shoulders shook with her sobs—heart-wrenching, pain-filled sobs.

Cleo's own heart ached at the sound of it.

Before she realized it, she had entered the room and moved closer to Lucia, reaching out to grasp the girl's shoulder.

Lucia spun around, her eyes flashing with surprise.

Cleo gasped and her breath froze in the air before her. It was so cold in the room—like the gardens of the Limerian palace.

"I killed her." Lucia's voice broke on the words.

Cleo's gaze dropped to what the princess held in her arms. It was a small brown rabbit, coated in frost and solid as a block of ice.

"What did you do?" she whispered.

"I didn't mean to. I picked Hana up. Holding her makes me happy, makes me think of home. And I thought of the ice sculptures during Winter Festival, of mermaids, dragons, chimeras . . . so cold, so perfect. And—and my thoughts . . . they were enough to do this. She's dead and it's my fault!"

Conjuring ice . . . it was water magic. Powerful water magic.

Tears splashed onto Lucia's cheeks. "Goddess help me, I can't control this."

"You can," Cleo said. She still grasped Lucia's shoulder and her ring had begun to glow just as it had the last time. Her heart raced. "You can control this. Your magic—it's incredible."

"That's what Father says." Lucia's voice trembled. "But now everyone will know about this."

"No, they won't. I swear I won't tell anyone." Cleo gently took the frozen animal from Lucia and placed it down on the ground. Then she grasped the princess's hands in her own. "I can help you."

Lucia swallowed hard, frowning. "I feel calmer now with you here. More in control."

Of course you do. I have the ring that helps controls your magic.

No wonder it hadn't worked for Cleo unless she touched something magical. She had no magic of her own that needed to be tamed.

Not yet.

"We didn't get off on the right foot before, Lucia. I am sorry for that. But I do want to be your friend. You need someone you can trust. So do I." She couldn't lose her strength or her bravery now when she needed it most. "I know what you are and what you can do. You're a sorceress."

Lucia's eyes widened. "You know?"

So it *was* true. This—*this* was what Cleo needed. This was the sign she'd been searching for, praying for. The missing piece of her puzzle. The ring was only half of it.

Princess Lucia was the other half.

"Yes, I know."

"And you're not afraid of me?"

Terrified beyond words.

"No, I'm not afraid of you." Cleo smiled and pulled this dangerous girl into a tight embrace. "You and me—we're sisters now. We can help each other . . . if you want to."

Lucia nodded, pressing her face into Cleo's shoulder. "I want to."

This princess was the most powerful creature who currently lived and breathed. And Lucia's magic—aided by this ring—was essential to getting Cleo's throne back.

The key to destroying the King of Blood was his very own daughter.

ACKNOWLEDGMENTS

Thank you to my wonderful editors on *Rebel Spring*, Laura Arnold, Gillian Levinson, and Liz Tingue, whose insights and encouragement I gobbled up with great gratitude. Thank you to Ben Schrank, who brilliantly masterminds all that is Razorbill; to the lovely Erin Dempsey, Elizabeth Zajac, Jessica Shoffel, and Anna Jarzab, for their incredible support and wicked organizational skills I deeply envy; thank you so much to Emily Osborne and Shane Rebenschied for the stunningly beautiful cover art this series has been blessed with; to my delightful Canadian publicists, Vimala Jeevanandam and Vikki VanSickle; to everyone on the teams at Penguin US, Penguin UK, and Penguin Canada, who are all about getting YA fiction (including the Falling Kingdoms series) into the hands of readers. You are all awesome. And, as always, thank you to my agent Jim McCarthy for being both smart and hilarious—very often at the same time.

Last, but not least, endless thanks to every reader who's enjoyed the characters, the magic, and the mayhem so far in Mytica. I promise there's much more to come!

In FALLING KINGDOMS,
Mytica succumbed
to King Gaius's wrath.

◆

In REBEL SPRING,
war, magic, and greed sowed
the seeds for revolution.

◆

But lust for power and revenge
still reign supreme . . .
and no one is safe from the
Kindred's allure.

*Turn the page for
an exclusive sneak peak of*

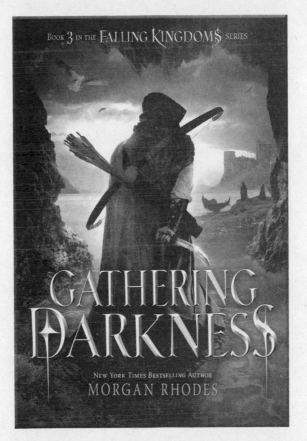

BOOK 3 IN THE FALLING KINGDOMS SERIES

GATHERING DARKNESS

New York Times Bestselling Author
MORGAN RHODES

**THE CAPTIVATING THIRD BOOK IN THE
FALLING KINGDOMS SERIES BY NEW YORK TIMES
BESTSELLING AUTHOR MORGAN RHODES.**

CHAPTER 1

JONAS

PAELSIA

"I've got a bad feeling about this."

Rufus's voice was as distracting as a persistent horsefly. Jonas sent his fellow rebel an impatient look through the darkness.

"Really. Which part?"

"All of it. We need to get out of here while we still can." Rufus craned his thick, sweaty neck to scan the line of trees surrounding them, guided only by the light of a single torch they'd shoved into the loose soil. "He said his friends would be here any moment."

He was referring to the Limerian guard they'd captured after discovering him straying too close to the edge of the forest. He was currently tied to a tree, unconscious.

But an unconscious guard wasn't any use to Jonas. He needed answers. Though, he had to agree with Rufus on one thing: They were swiftly running out of time, especially since they were so close to a village infested with the king's red-uniformed minions.

"Of course he said that," Jonas said. "It's called a bluff."

"Oh." Rufus raised his brows, as though this hadn't occurred to him. "You think?"

A week had passed since the rebel attack on the road camp in eastern Paelsia beneath the Forbidden Mountains. A week since Jonas's most recent plan to defeat King Gaius had gone horribly awry.

Forty-seven rebels had descended upon the sleepy campground at dawn in an attempt to seize the road engineer, Xanthus, and the Limerian heir, Prince Magnus, to hold as hostages against King Gaius.

They'd failed. A flash fire of strange blue flames had burned everything in its path, and Jonas had barely escaped with his life.

Rufus had been the only other rebel waiting at the meeting spot later that morning. Jonas had found him standing there with tears streaming down his dirty face, trembling with fear and rambling about fire magic and witches and sorcery.

Only two of forty-seven had been accounted for. It was a crushing defeat in far too many ways and if Jonas thought about it too much, he could barely see straight, could barely function beyond his guilt and grief.

His plan. His orders.

His fault.

Again.

Desperately trying to push aside his own pain, Jonas had immediately begun to gather information about other potential survivors—anyone who'd been captured alive and carted away.

The guard they'd found wore red. He was the enemy.

He had to have answers that could help Jonas. He *had* to.

Finally, the guard opened his eyes. He was older than most other guards, with graying hair at his temples. He also walked with a limp, which had made him easier to catch.

"You . . . I know you," the guard muttered, his eyes glittering in the meager torchlight. "You're Jonas Agallon, the murderer of Queen Althea."

He threw these words like weapons. Jonas flinched inwardly but showed no sign that the most heinous lie ever told about him caused him injury.

"I didn't kill the queen," he growled.

"Why would I believe you?"

Ignoring Rufus's squeamish expression, Jonas walked a slow circle around the restrained guard, trying to determine how difficult it would be to get him talking.

"You don't have to believe me." He leaned closer. "But you're going to answer some questions for me now."

· The guard's upper lip drew back from his yellow teeth in a snarl. "I'll tell you nothing."

He'd expected that, of course. Nothing was ever easy.

Jonas pulled the jeweled dagger from the sheath on his belt. Its wavy silver blade caught the moonlight, immediately drawing the guard's attention.

It was the very same weapon that had taken his older brother from this world. That vain and pompous Auranian lord had left it behind, embedded in Tomas's throat. This dagger had become a symbol to Jonas, representing the line he'd drawn in the sand between his past as the son of a poor wine seller who toiled every day in his father's vineyard, and his future as a rebel, certain he would die fighting for what he believed in most: freedom from tyranny for those he loved. And freedom from tyranny for those he'd never even met before.

A world without King Gaius's hands wringing the necks of the weak and powerless.

Jonas pressed the dagger to the guard's throat. "I suggest you answer my questions if you don't want your blood to be spilled tonight."

"I'll do more than bleed if the king learns I've done anything to help you."

He was right—the crime of assisting a rebel would undoubtedly lead to torture or execution. Likely both. Though the king enjoyed making pretty speeches about the united kingdoms of Mytica with a broad smile on his handsome face, he did not receive the nickname "the King of Blood" by being fair and kind.

"One week ago, there was a rebel attack on the road camp east of here. Do you know about it?"

The guard held his gaze unflinchingly. "I heard the rebels died screaming."

Jonas's heart twisted. He clenched his hand into a fist, aching to make this guard suffer. A tremor shook through him at the memory of last week, but he tried to focus on the task at hand. *Only* the task at hand.

Rufus raked his fingers through his messy hair and paced back and forth in nervous lines.

"I need to know if any rebels were captured alive," Jonas continued. "And I need to know where the king is holding them."

"I have no idea."

"I don't believe you. Start talking or I promise I'll cut your throat."

There was no fear in the guard's eyes, only a mocking edge. "I've heard so many fearsome rumors about the leader of the Paelsian rebels. But rumors aren't facts, aren't they? Perhaps you're nothing more than a Paelsian peasant boy—not nearly ruthless enough to kill someone in cold blood. Not even your enemy."

Jonas had killed before—enough that he'd lost count. In a foolish war that tricked Paelsians into allying with Limerians against Auranos. In the battle at the road camp. He'd only fought in order to strike down his enemies and bring justice to his friends, his family, and his fellow Paelsians. And to protect himself.

There had been meaning behind those deaths, even if that meaning had been jumbled and unclear. He fought for a purpose, believed in something.

He took no pleasure in taking lives, and he hoped he never would.

"Come on, Jonas. He's useless," Rufus said, his voice twisting with anxiety. "Let's go while we still can."

But Jonas didn't budge, and forced himself to focus on the task at hand. He hadn't come this far to give up now. "There was a girl who fought in the battle named Lysandra Barbas. I need to know if she's still alive."

The guard's lips twisted into a cruel grin. "Ah, so this is why you're so driven for answers. This girl belongs to you?"

It took Jonas a moment to understand his meaning. "She's like a sister to me."

"Jonas," Rufus whined. "Lysandra's gone. She's dead. Obsessing about her is only going to get us killed, too!"

Jonas cast a glare at Rufus that made the boy wince, but it was enough to make him shut his stupid mouth.

Lysandra wasn't dead. She couldn't be. She was an incredible fighter—skilled with a bow and arrow like no one Jonas had witnessed before.

Lysandra had also been opinionated, demanding, and incredibly annoying from the first moment he'd first met her. And if she still lived, Jonas would do anything to find her.

He needed her—both as a fellow rebel and as a friend.

"You must know *something*." Jonas pressed the dagger closer to the guard's throat. "And you're going to tell me right now."

No matter how high the stakes, Jonas would never give up. Not until his very last breath.

"This girl . . ." the guard said through clenched teeth, "is she worth your life?"

Jonas didn't have to think twice. "Yes."

"Then I've no doubt she's every bit as dead as you are." The guard smirked despite the trickle of blood now sliding down his throat. He raised his voice. "Over here!"

A crunch of dirt and a snap of branches were all that warned of the half dozen Limerian guards that now burst into the small forest clearing. Their swords were drawn, and two of them carried torches.

"Drop your weapons, rebel!"

Rufus swung his fist at an approaching guard, but missed by a mile. "Jonas, do something!"

Rather than drop the dagger, Jonas sheathed it, then drew the sword he'd stolen from Prince Magnus last week before Jonas had managed to escape. He hoisted it up in time to block a blow aimed directly for his chest. Rufus tried to fight back, punching and kicking, but it wasn't long before a guard grabbed hold of his hair, yanked him backward, and put a blade to his throat.

"I said," the guard hissed, "drop your weapon. Or your friend dies."

The world skidded to a stop as the memory of Tomas's murder once again crashed into Jonas. It had happened so quickly—no time to save him, no time to fight or even beg for his life. And then Jonas recalled another memory that would be seared into his soul forever: that of his best friend, Brion, slain by the same killer while Jonas watched, helpless.

With Jonas momentarily distracted, a guard took the opportunity to slam his fist into his face. As hot blood poured from his nose, another guard wrenched the blade from his grasp, nearly breaking his fingers. Another kicked the back of his knees and slammed him down to the ground.

The world spun and sparkled before his eyes as he fought to remain conscious.

He knew it would end now, that he'd been on borrowed time ever since his most recent brush with death. There was no magic here to save him this time. Death no longer scared him, but the timing was wrong. He had too much left to do. . . .

Just then, another figure entered the torch-lit clearing, causing the guards to spin around.

"Am I interrupting something?" said the young man. He looked a couple years older than Jonas, with dark hair and eyes. He wore a dark cloak, the hood back to show his skin was deeply tanned, and he gave an easy smile that showed straight, white teeth, as well as his apparent nonchalance at the fact that he'd just casually strolled into the middle of a battle. He scanned the area, starting on one side with Rufus, who was still being held in place, then making his way over to Jonas, who braced himself against the mossy ground with two swords pointed at his throat.

"Get out of here," a guard growled. "Unless you want trouble."

"You're Jonas Agallon," the boy said, nodding at him as if they were meeting in a tavern instead of the middle of the forest in the dead of night. "This is quite an honor."

Jonas never asked to be famous. But the Wanted posters clearly sketched with his face that had been tacked up throughout all three kingdoms had ensured otherwise. Despite having few victories and more false accusations than actual crimes, his name had quickly become legend.

And the high reward his capture offered sparked the interest of many.

The older guard had been cut free from his ropes and was now gingerly rubbing his wrists. "You've been following this rebel scum?" he asked. "Does that make you aspiring rebel scum? We'll save a spike back at the palace for your head as well. Seize him!"

The guards lunged for him, but he just laughed and dodged their grasp as easily as a slippery fish.

"Need my help?" the boy asked Jonas. "How about this—I help you, you help me. That's the deal."

He moved so well there was no way he was only a curious bystander. Jonas had no idea who he was, but right now he really didn't give a damn.

"Sounds good to me," Jonas managed.

"Then let's get started." The boy reached down and pulled out two thick blades the length of his forearms from beneath his cloak. He spun and sliced, moving faster than any of the guards could counter.

Jonas's head was still swimming, but he managed to elbow the guard behind him directly in his face. He felt and heard the crack as the guard yelped in pain.

He jumped to his feet and grabbed his sword, thrusting the hilt behind him to catch the guard in his soft gut.

The new boy took down the guard holding Rufus. Now free, the unskilled rebel just stood there in place, staring at the violent scene for a frozen moment, then he turned and ran out of the clearing without looking back.

A part of Jonas was disappointed in Rufus, but another part was glad the kid finally had a chance to escape a fight he hadn't been ready for since day one.

He might even stay alive if he played it smart and stayed out of trouble.

With the other guards now dead or scattered, unconscious, in the clearing, Jonas grabbed hold of his original prisoner and slammed him back against the tree.

The smugness in the guard's eyes finally turned to fear.

"Spare me," he gasped.

Jonas ignored him, turning instead to the boy who'd just saved his life. "What's your name?"

"Felix," he offered with a grin. "Felix Gaebras. Happy to meet you."

"Likewise. Thanks for the help."

"Anytime."

If Felix hadn't intervened, Jonas would be dead. No doubt about it. He'd given him a chance at another day, one in which he might make a difference. For that, Jonas was damn grateful.

Still, he'd be stupid not to be wary of any stranger who knew his identity.

"What's your price?" Jonas asked.

"Price?"

"You said if you help me, I help you."

"First things first." Felix approached, nudging Jonas out of the way and taking the guard by the throat. "I've been eavesdropping. Rude, I know. But I heard you say you didn't think Jonas was ruth-less enough to kill someone in cold blood. Well, what's your first impression of me?"

The guard drew in a shaky breath. "What do you want?"

"Answer the question. His friends—are any of them still alive?"

The guard trembled. "Yes. A handful were brought to the palace dungeon to await execution."

"How many's a handful?"

"I don't know exactly . . . three, four? I'm not sure. I wasn't there!"

Jonas winced. Three or four? There were so few survivors. . . .

"Names?" Felix pressed harder on the guard's throat.

He sputtered, his face reddening. "I don't know. I'd tell you if I did."

"How long till they're executed?" Jonas asked, trying to keep his voice steady. The thought of people he cared about trapped under the king's thumb turned his blood ice cold.

"It could be a few days or maybe a few months. Please, spare my life! I've told you all I know. Show mercy to me now, I beg of you."

Felix regarded him for a long, silent while. "How about I show you the same mercy you would have shown us?"

One swipe of Felix's blade, and the guard was silenced forever. His body slumped to the ground to join his fellow fallen guards in the flickering firelight, and Jonas found he couldn't look away.

"You know I had to do that, right?" Felix said, his voice as cold as stone.

"I know."

There was a hardness in Felix's eyes that was foreign to Jonas. They showed no flicker of remorse for what he'd done, nor did they show any joy.

It was true: The guard would not have shown them mercy. He would have executed them without a moment's hesitation.

"Much gratitude for saving my life," Jonas said as Felix wiped his blades on the mossy ground before sheathing them.

"You're welcome." Felix peered into the dark forest. "I think your friend ran away."

"He'll be safer staying far away from me." Jonas studied the bodies littering the area, then turned back to Felix warily. "You're an assassin."

With his fighting skills, his ease with a blade—it would have been obvious to anyone that he was a trained killer.

The coldness faded from Felix's eyes as he grinned. "Depends on the day, really. One does what one must with the talents they have."

That would be a confirmation. "So now what? I have far less gold than the wanted posters offer for my head."

"Somebody's a bit of a pessimist, aren't they? With the king's eyes everywhere lately, looking for anyone causing trouble, what I want is someone watching my back while I watch his. Why not partner up with the infamous Jonas Agallon, I say?" He glanced in the direction Rufus ran off. "I'm not seeing much competition. You need me. Simple as that."

"You want to be a rebel?"

"What I want is to cause trouble and create mayhem wherever I can." Felix's grin widened. "If that makes me a rebel, then so be it. How about I start by helping you save your friends?"

Jonas continued to eye Felix with wariness, his heart pounding as fast as it had during the fight. "The guard was only telling us what we wanted to hear. We've no way to know if my friends are really in the palace dungeon."

"There are no guarantees in this life, only strong possibilities. That's enough for me."

"Even if they are there, the dungeon would be impossible to breach."

Felix shrugged. "I kind of like impossible challenges. Don't you?"

Despite his best efforts to ignore it, hope had begun to well up in Jonas's chest. Hope often led to pain.

But hope could also lead to victory.

Jonas studied the tall, muscular boy who'd just taken out five guards single-handedly. "Impossible challenges, huh?"

Felix laughed. "The most enjoyable ones. So what do you say? Shall we be partners in anarchy?"

Felix was right about one thing: Jonas didn't have a long line of skilled rebels waiting to fight by his side.

He relented, grasping hold of the fluttering hope inside of him and smiling. "Sounds like a plan."

Felix grabbed Jonas's outstretched hand. "And I promise I won't run off into the forest with my tail between my legs like your friend back there."

"I'd appreciate that." Plans and schemes were already racing through Jonas's head. The future suddenly seemed infinitely brighter.

"Tomorrow we get started on freeing your friends," Felix said. "And sending as many of the king's guards to the darklands as we can."

As far as friendships went, Jonas thought, this was an excellent beginning.